SUMMONED

M.B. THURMAN

Summary: When Hadley Weston reunites with her estranged lover, Fitz MacGregor, she discovers that he is a witch. And she's one, too. As they work together to master her powers and recover a long-lost family artifact, they learn that the world as they know it may be in danger, and they may be the only ones who can save it.

www.thesummonedseries.com

ISBN 978-1-7361554-5-5

First Edition

Cover illustration and cover design by Jon Stubbington
Book design by Jamie Ryu

SUMMONED

M.B. THURMAN

This book is dedicated to you.
You are the real magic

*Many a strange occurrence has come to pass,
but none so strange as the discovery that you are
not at all who you thought yourself to be.*

PART ONE

CHAPTER ONE

Lake Crescent, Washington
Present Day

The note was tucked carefully under a stack of books on my old oak desk, and the paper's edges fluttered in the evening breeze filtering through the open window.

I froze as my eyes darted around the room.

I'd closed the window before popping down to the kitchen for a snack, and the unmade bed was littered with blankets from my rushed departure that morning. A cold cup of forgotten Earl Grey tea sat atop the desk, adjacent to the open laptop that lay nearby. Suitcases were scattered across the far side of the room.

Nothing else had been disturbed.

Only the open window and the mysterious note that lay just beneath it. I slowly crossed my bedroom to investigate.

I was accustomed to notes falling into my possession, but they were usually in unmarked envelopes that appeared in my mailbox or pushed just under my door. This was the first time I was certain someone had accessed my space. My fingers trembled as they tugged at the cream-colored paper.

Meet me Friday at 6 p.m.—the top of Notre Dame.
Don't tell anyone.
I'll adjust your travel arrangements.

Friday . . . only five days away.

I had job interviews lined up in London for the following week, and this would move my travel up, shortening my visit with my mom.

I glanced at the note again. I didn't need to pull Fitz's letters from my purse to know the penmanship matched perfectly.

After eight months of us being inseparable, we had been forced apart. Fitz and I had kept in touch through burner phones that showed up at my apartment and letters I mailed to various locations around Europe after the addresses came inexplicably into my possession.

I'd considered walking away countless times, but I knew Fitz held the answers I needed to finally understand myself—to understand the things I was able to do.

The snap of a branch pierced the still night air.

I approached the open window timidly, peering into the endless dark of the moonless night. My eyes strained to make sense of the fathomless depths, but to no avail—I could see nothing. The noise had come from a woodland animal, I reasoned.

Still, I pulled my window closed and double checked the latch before tugging the curtains together. I poured a glass of whisky and settled onto my bed with the note.

I unfolded the paper again, studying the words scribbled across it.

Lake Crescent, Washington
June 2021

I stared through the large window at the sheets of rain blowing across the lake, mesmerized by what I saw.

Although the PNW held a tiresome reputation as the rainiest portion of the U.S., it didn't often rain like this. I pushed open the cedar-framed window and was met by the cool summer breeze. I relaxed at the scent of evergreens. The patter of rain echoed through my bedroom. Gram had told me it would let up soon. I wasn't so sure, but Gram was always right about those sorts of things—and well, most things, come to think of it.

I hoped the rain would stick around so I'd get out of berry picking. It wasn't that I was opposed to helping Gram, but I'd had the strange feeling that I was being watched. I knew it was ridiculous. I had no evidence. And yet, I couldn't shake the unsettling feeling that had crept into the back of my mind.

I sat in silence as the rain stopped, and then bounded downstairs to perform my berry-picking duties. Pretending not to notice Gram's smirk, I grabbed the bowl from the counter and headed out the door to find the best berries for her jam.

The air held a thick, humid atmosphere that was more intense than usual, and I had a distinct feeling we weren't done with the rain just yet. Storm clouds rolled into the distance, fittingly in the direction of Mt. Storm King, and sunlight began filtering through the lingering haze. The majestic peak took the brunt of the weather in the area, and being the misty mountain that it was, Storm King attracted much of its own legend.

I completed my outing in record time. The sun cast its golden rays through the nearby trees. The light kissed the fresh raindrops, which caused the ground to shimmer all around me. Mesmerized, I stooped to get a better look at the ethereal scene when a splash in the stream startled me. Berries scattered through the blades of grass. I turned toward the stream but didn't find the source of the noise.

I froze and listened for anything odd but only found the usual trickle of water, the chirping of birds, and the crash of distant breaking waves. I reached for the bowl but was disturbed by a branch snapping in the direction of the stream. I mustered my courage and walked slowly toward the source of the commotion.

There was an infamous story of a beautiful waitress who was murdered and cast to the bottom of Lake Crescent. Her body had been preserved by the waters of our curious lake. I'd picked up a book in my teen years about the unfortunate young woman, and the image of her body still haunted me. The incident had occurred in the 1930's, with little criminal activity around the area since, but the feeling of being watched had truly rattled my mind.

I was nearing the edge of the stream when a woman's voice floated on the summer breeze. It was so beautiful; I swore it was a siren's call. I strained my ears, trying to make out the words.

The wee birdies sing and the wildflowers spring,
And in sunshine the waters are sleeping.

Barely breathing, I lowered myself along the stones on the cliff-side and stepped into the cool waters of the stream. It took mere seconds to find the source of the commotion, as one of the most beautiful women I'd ever seen stepped around the trunk of a massive spruce tree.

"Oh! Hello," she called excitedly.

She closed the short distance between us, her long, auburn hair hanging loosely down her back, complementing her tall figure. I would have been more in awe of her flawless, milky skin had her intense emerald eyes released me from their spell.

"I'm Izzy MacGregor," she said in a thick accent. Scottish, I thought. She extended her hand. "I'm sorry. Did I startle you?"

"A little." I laughed in response as I took her hand in mine. "I was just picking blueberries and heard some noise."

Her eyes dipped to my empty hands.

"I dropped the bowl. Berries *everywhere*."

Izzy giggled. "I'll help you pick them up. Lead the way."

"I didn't expect to see anyone else up here," I said as we climbed the bank.

"Oh, right. I'm visiting my parents. They just moved in next door, and I've been exploring the past couple of days. I was walking the stream out of curiosity."

"It's beautiful around here. Keep your eyes open though—a herd of elk have been congregating by the stream the past few days, and the moms can be aggressive with their new calves."

"Thank you. I'll be mindful of that," she said, grinning like there was some sort of inside joke I was missing.

"Have you seen them before? The elk."

She hesitated just long enough that I thought she wasn't going to answer my question. I turned the bowl right side up, and she finally met my gaze.

"They're fascinating creatures. I love wildlife." Izzy picked up a ripe blueberry and rolled it in between her finger and thumb, bringing it into the light. "Looks like the rain has been good to the crop. May I?"

I nodded, and she popped the berry onto her tongue, closing her eyes while she savored the taste. She was the kind of woman, I thought, who really *lived*. The kind of woman who stopped to feel the rain on her skin and whose laughter set a room alight, the kind of woman who lived intentionally. I couldn't place where the knowledge came from, but instantly, I *knew* her.

"They're sweeter this year than normal," I said, considering her. "You love nature, don't you?"

"Very much," she said. The sunlight touched her face, highlighting the freckles splayed across the bridge of her nose and cheeks.

Her gaze lingered on me, and she pursed her lips.

"What is it?" I questioned.

"My brother will be keen to meet you."

"Oh." I looked around like her brother might materialize at any moment. "He's visiting your parents too?"

"Aye. He's around here somewhere. Wanders the woods almost as much as me, that one."

"Why do you think he'll want to meet me?"

"It's just a feeling I have," Izzy said.

"Well, I look forward to meeting . . ."

"Fitz."

"Fitz," I echoed. A small jolt ran through my body at the feel of his name on my lips, and I took a deep breath, hoping to shake off the odd sensation.

I dropped another handful of berries into the bowl and dusted off my hands. I didn't know what else to say, but I didn't want our conversation to end. "Where is your accent from . . . if you don't mind me asking?"

"Scotland."

"I thought so. I'd love to visit Scotland."

"When you're ready, I'll tell you all the must-sees."

"Do you like Washington?" I asked.

"Very much. It's a bonnie place," she mused absentmindedly, dropping the last berry into the bowl.

"Iz—are you out here?" A man's voice broke the still afternoon air, and a thrill moved through me at the sound.

"Speaking of Fitz," she said conspiratorially to me. Then she called, "Aye, over here!"

Izzy eyed me pointedly before walking toward the nearby tree line. A man emerged from the verdant canopy. I studied his tall figure as he made his way to Izzy. He carried himself with ease and confidence. There was a prickle at the nape of my neck, though I couldn't understand the signal.

The two had a brief exchange before Izzy called across the clearing. "My dad needs me. It was lovely to meet you!"

She disappeared into the trees that separated our homes, and Fitz walked toward me.

As he came more clearly into focus, a small gasp disturbed the back of my throat. He was *beautiful*.

Fitz wore a thin crewneck sweater and jeans, and though there was something innately academic in his style, the way he carried himself was almost playful. As he neared me, I studied his structured jawline, which held the faint scruff of a few days without a razor, and I followed it to his strong cheekbones and his chestnut hair.

My heart beat wildly.

The world tilted beneath me as I met the emerald eyes of Fitz MacGregor. And there it was: the same feeling that coursed through me as with Izzy before. Fitz was complex, and I knew that instantly, the same way I knew he loved the sound of jazz and the taste of whisky on his tongue. Fitz was comforting, like the rain, a good cup of tea, the first few notes of my favorite album.

I *knew* this man.

His gaze was intense, somehow seeing straight through me, and my breath came short. His eyes lingered across my face, and at first, I thought I imagined it, but no—the rise and fall of his chest grew more exaggerated by the second.

We stared wordlessly long enough for my anxiety to flare. But he finally reached out his hand, and I placed mine into his expectant grasp.

An electric shock surged from my fingertips through my entire body, and I swallowed hard. My breathing grew more labored, and a jolt of panic coursed through me at my inability to understand the reaction.

"Glad to meet you." His attempt at civility couldn't mask the strain in his voice.

"I—I'm sorry, but I have no idea what's happening."

"You feel it too." It was more statement than question, but I nodded anyway.

"Should we . . ." I looked down at our linked hands.

"Oh, right. Sorry."

He released me, and it left me feeling utterly empty. Perspiration formed on my forehead, and my eyes flitted across Fitz's face searching for any signs of distress. He shoved his hands in his front pockets.

"The weather is mental. Maybe it was just static," he said.

"Static electricity? That's the best you've got?"

Fitz chuckled. It was a welcome sound. "Indeed, it is. Please, I'd love to hear a more plausible theory from you."

I raised my hands in mock surrender. "I don't have a theory yet."

"But you'll sort out a good one."

"I'll do my best." I smiled. Fitz's amusement was contagious.

The wind picked up, rustling his mess of chestnut hair, and a rumble of thunder pierced the quiet.

"Now, that's something you don't hear very often around here," he mused.

"We'd better get out of here before the bottom falls out, as my grandmother would say."

I wanted nothing more than to get to know Fitz. I wanted more time, and a wave of relief washed through me at his offer to walk me home.

We set off in the direction of my place and reached the porch just as the rain began to fall. I wasn't sure how to approach seeing him again without sounding overzealous.

"You're welcome to wait out the storm here, if you'd like," I finally said.

"Thank you. But I'm late for another commitment." I thought he seemed disappointed, but perhaps it was only my own hope. Still, he lingered, and his eyes studied me.

"I feel like I've met you before." The words tumbled out before I could stop them, and I groaned inwardly.

"I'd remember you if we had." Fitz smiled softly. "Perhaps in another life."

I wasn't so sure he was joking.

"I'd better be going," he continued. "But Izzy and I will drop by tomorrow if that's all right?"

"I'd like that."

"I'm glad to have met you, Hadley."

Fitz stepped into the rain. He paused, looking at me over his shoulder one last time as the rain streaked down his beautiful face. And with that, he disappeared into the trees that separated our homes.

I was so preoccupied I didn't realize until I walked into the house that I hadn't given Fitz my name.

CHAPTER TWO

Lake Crescent, Washington
Present Day

After Dad's untimely death eight months prior, my mother and I hadn't found the courage to organize his belongings. But I'd left my job as a public relations consultant in Boston two weeks ago and driven home to the glacial-fed waters of Lake Crescent in Washington State to spend time with my mother. I'd passed the better part of my trip home rifling through old chests in my father's study and sorting through his side of the closet with my mom.

When I'd first mentioned my upcoming trip to London to my mom, her face had fallen. Both of my parents had always encouraged me to see the world, and I knew my mom would never truly stand in the way of my growth. But life without Daddy was uncharted territory.

I settled into the oversized chair in the corner of my room and pulled my favorite blanket around me. The temperature had dropped earlier in the day, our first taste of fall, and it seemed a good time to conduct another search for job openings. I scanned one of the many career sites I'd been monitoring, and the hair on my neck bristled as my eyes swept over a newly posted opening: PR Manager, Edinburgh Castle. I followed the link to the "Careers" tab on the castle website and read the listing.

The position itself sounded like the right fit for my experience, and working somewhere like the castle would align with my love for history. And . . . Edinburgh was where I believed Fitz to be. I took a slow sip of tea as I debated my next move.

A knock at the door halted my decision making.

"Momma?"

My mom peeked her head around the door. "Ready to start dinner?" She'd lived in Washington State for over thirty years, but neither she nor my father had lost their Mississippi accents.

"I'll be right there."

She smiled brightly, and my stomach flipped. We'd cooked dinner together almost every night, but for the first time since my return, the experience wouldn't be pleasant.

My fingers flew over the keyboard. Within minutes, the application process was complete, and I was staring at a confirmation page.

There was no time like the present to inform my mom of my newly solidified plans.

"You're adding Paris *and* Edinburgh? Alone?"

"I've always wanted to see Paris. And I'm not positive about Edinburgh yet—I might not even receive an interview request."

My mom pursed her lips.

"This is something I need to do, Momma." I flipped the salmon

I was cooking for dinner, trying to keep the conversation casual and hide the annoyance in my voice.

"I just don't understand why you left your job in Boston. Or why you're looking for a new one in Europe, for that matter."

I let my eyes linger on the pan while I rolled through my thoughts.

I understood my motivations for the change perfectly, but the thought of talking about it with Momma seemed overwhelming; being honest about my grief seemed impossible.

"You know I've always wanted to go abroad, at least for a while," I said. "I think it'll do me some good."

My mom remained silent.

"And who knows. Maybe I won't even receive an offer from anyone. But this trip is about figuring all that out."

She narrowed her hazel eyes as she leaned against the counter. "Why can't Jordan go with you on the trip?"

Jordan had been my best friend since childhood, and we'd traveled to many a place together. But now she worked as an intelligence analyst for the FBI, and her team was always overtaxed.

"You know how difficult it is for Jordan to take time off," I said. "And after her promotion, she's swamped."

And if I was being honest, I needed to take this trip alone, even before Fitz's note had materialized in my room.

Silence.

"Can you pass me the salt?" I asked.

My mother sighed. She tucked the loose strands of her honey-colored hair behind her ear, taking her time.

"Do you really have to go right now? You could visit Gram for a couple weeks, and then maybe timing would work for Jordan to go with you. Or Tanner," she countered.

"Momma, if I do find a new job over there, I'll be living alone regardless. If I can't manage a solo trip, then I have no business moving halfway across the world."

"I don't know that you have any business doing that anyway."

I threw my arms up in protest. "You don't trust me?"

My mom paused, her eyes dropping to the floor for mere seconds. "Of course, I trust you, Hadley."

"Then what is it?"

"It's just your first time out of the country alone, and I can't help but worry."

"I'll be fine." I grabbed dishes from the cabinet to plate our dinner.

"I can't lose you too."

Her words stopped me in my tracks, and suddenly, I wasn't so concerned with dinner. I set the plates on the counter gently and met her gaze.

"Oh, Momma." My father's death had gutted her, but it was still unlike her to make such an honest confession.

She raised her hand. "I don't mean to sound dramatic. I just worry a little more these days. The world seems fragile lately."

"I'll be smart," I promised, my voice losing the last of its edge. "I'm not going anywhere for a very long time."

My words echoed through my thoughts—except in my dad's voice instead of my own. He materialized in my mind, his soft, gray eyes filled with pain. Even so, he wore a brave smile and reached for a hand I recognized well.

Is this Momma's memory?

My face was then reflected back at me: my concerned blue eyes, my favorite Mississippi State sweatshirt that I'd claimed from my father's closet the day prior, my hair which had inexplicably darkened to

14

an auburn during the course of a couple weeks right after his death.

"*She's so much like Matt.*"

My stomach lurched.

"*Oh, no,*" her voice sounded again.

The world tilted off-kilter as the realization sunk in. This wasn't like before.

I was reading my mom's mind.

"Hadley, are you okay?"

I couldn't speak.

"Hadley!"

I nodded.

"Are the panic attacks back?"

They'd never left, though she didn't need to know that.

"You're scaring me, honey. Can you breathe?"

I nodded. My mom had me sit in a nearby chair, and I focused until I was able to steady my irregular breath and my racing heart.

"Better?"

"Yes. I'm sorry."

"Don't apologize. But . . . what brought it on?"

"I don't know," I lied. "I think it's just the life changes catching up with me, you know?"

"If this is still happening often, I don't think you should travel alone," she said.

"It isn't. I promise you I'll be fine. I need you to trust me."

My mom hesitated, but she nodded reluctantly. "I thought it would be nice for you to come back here. Cathartic, maybe. But now I'm afraid I did the wrong thing."

"What?" I asked. "No, not even close. I wouldn't want to be any-where else right now."

My mom reached for my hand, and a pang of guilt filled my chest at the thought of leaving her alone again.

Lake Crescent, Washington
June 2021

I woke to an odd crackling noise. My eyes popped open and darted around nervously. I sat up and reached for the back of my head, feeling the damp strands in a state of utter confusion.

The night had settled in with the steady patter of rain, but at some point during the evening, the rain had moved out, and the moon's pale glow softly illuminated the forest. I was sitting on a fallen log, cocooned in a sea of deep green; verdant moss decorated many of the tree limbs, and lush ferns blanketed the earth. The leaves still dripped with the evening rain, and the earth was soft and quiet underfoot. I jumped from the downed log and navigated around several massive tree trunks attempting to orient myself.

Light glimmered from the opposite side of a towering spruce, and my eyes reeled to adjust to the sudden illumination. I crept to the tree and timidly peered around it. A tall figure draped with cascading auburn hair took shape in the glow.

Izzy.

She stood next to a large elk cow, and I almost yelled as Izzy reached toward its head. I had just warned her about this.

I'd seen countless elk over the years, but none that would allow you to even approach them. I was too late to warn her, and I froze as

I awaited the animal's reaction. Surely, it would attack her.

The elk, however, seemed perfectly content as Izzy ran her hand down the side of its neck. The animal looked squarely into her eyes before tilting its head. A small calf limped toward its mother with an injured hind leg.

Izzy proceeded toward the calf and took a seat on the cold ground. She touched her hand to its leg and whispered so lowly I couldn't make out the words. After a few minutes, she stood, and the calf walked over to its mother without issue. It was *healed*.

"Impossible," I muttered. I clasped my hands over my mouth immediately. My words had been barely a whisper, but they didn't escape Izzy's notice. I stepped from behind the tree.

"Oh!" Izzy gasped. "Hadley . . . What are you doing out here?"

"I was just wondering the same thing. I don't know how I got here."

"Don't you?" Izzy asked.

"No."

"What's the last thing you remember?"

"Falling asleep in my bed. I don't know how I got here. Why am I here?" My voice was filled with panic.

Izzy moved closer, and she seemed to glide above the ground as the ivory train of her dress floated behind her. Izzy's eyes were wilder than I'd ever seen.

I gasped when I realized a soft glow of light was pouring from her pale skin. The sight was ethereal, and it left me speechless, completely in awe. Every hair on my body stood on end.

"Is this a dream?" I asked.

"How should I know? If it were, I'd only be a figment of your imagination."

"I think you know."

Izzy opened her mouth to speak but was cut off by a distant buzz that vibrated through the forest. The sound grew in intensity like the hum of an airplane as it fired up on the runway.

"What is that?" I asked, to myself as much as to Izzy.

"I—I don't know." Izzy cocked her head toward the commotion, and her eyes widened. And when she spoke again, it was with urgency. "You need to go. *Now*."

"Why?"

"Someone's here. You aren't safe!"

"Izzy, what are you talking about? What's going on?"

"I don't know. I know it doesn't make sense. Please, Hadley. Please just get out of here."

"I don't see anyone. Are you sure someone's there?"

"This is dangerous. You must go."

A swirl of fog materialized in the distance. It was the softest shade of gray. It yielded a pair of eyes like pools of ink, and I could've lost myself in their depths. The sight was ominous—unnatural—and something in my gut told me that I should run, that I should be terrified, but I couldn't leave Izzy behind.

"Come on, Izzy! Let's go!"

Izzy shook her head, and in the face of danger, a calmness came over her. She placed her hand softly on my face.

"Go home," she whispered gravely.

A violent wind swirled through the treetops and formed a funnel cloud that plummeted to the earth.

Izzy stepped back. She pointed to the swirling cloud. "Run, Hadley!"

Taking a chance, I ran toward the cloud and was swept away. I screamed as the cloud engulfed me. I was robbed of my sight until I woke in my bed, gasping for air.

"A dream," I croaked out, still dragging in ragged breaths. "It was only a dream."

I fumbled my way to the bathroom sink and turned on the faucet, hoping a splash of cold water would do me some good. As I patted my face dry, something odd caught my eye in the soft illumination spilling in from my bedroom. I flipped on the overhead light and studied a patch of green caught in my strawberry blonde strands.

A jolt of panic shot through me as I pulled moss from my hair.

CHAPTER THREE

Lake Crescent, Washington
June 2021

The pebble bounced across the surface of the water before sinking to the lake's fathomless depths.

"You ever hear the native story about how this lake was formed?" Tanner asked, brushing his dusky strands away from his face.

Tanner and I had met during our undergraduate in a history class at the University of Washington and had bonded instantly. With his squared, chiseled jaw and athletic build, I'd seen him draw a lot of attention over the years, but it was his inward qualities that had endeared him to me. He'd been through the roughest chapter of my life with me, although he was there for many of the good moments, too. He'd grown up near Seattle after his parents relocated the family from Beijing when he was a baby. They'd bought a weekend home on Lake Crescent, only a few houses down the gravel road from my parents' cabin.

"Someone was talking about this at the lodge recently—warring tribes, right?"

"Yeah, the Quileute and Klallam tribes were fighting, and allegedly Mt. Storm King was tired of their battle and threw a chunk of itself into a river that was here at the time. They say it dammed the river and killed their warriors, but the lake was born. And so was peace."

"Seems like there's a lot of local legends about this lake."

"All that talk, but the lake still has her secrets," Tanner said.

A shiver ran through me. Tanner tossed another pebble toward the lake, and it skimmed the smooth surface before following its predecessor. It was one of the rare days where the lake looked like glass, and the temperature was cool for June. I'd thrown one of my dad's flannels over my favorite blue turtleneck, but I still found my layers weren't quite warm enough in the shade.

The sound of crunching gravel announced Jordan's return.

Her tall figure bounded down the hillside navigating the towering trees as she juggled three mason jars and a picnic basket. Tanner and I jogged up to meet her halfway, and a bright smile crossed her face.

"Compliments of Gram," she said.

"Oh, hell yeah!" Tanner reached for the basket, his eyes sparkling in anticipation. I swore they shifted with his mood. I'd seen them as dark as inky pools—onyx stones set against his golden skin. But other times, they appeared a softer shade of brown, bordering on russet.

Jordan passed off a mason jar to me, and I removed the silver, screw-top lid to enjoy some of Gram's famous sweet tea.

"Always makes me feel at home," Jordan said.

Jordan's family had relocated to Mississippi from D.C., and I'd spent all my childhood summers in the southern heat with my grandmother. Jordan and I met the summer her family moved to Starkville, and the two of us had become fast friends.

She had just graduated from Amherst in May, but her dream was to work as an intelligence analyst for the FBI. She was about to start the application process.

This summer, I had applied for an internship with the National Park Service to work at Olympic National Park, and luck was on my side. I was assigned to Lake Crescent Lodge, which allowed me to spend the season with my parents after my father's cancer diagnosis. Gram wanted to spend time with Dad as well, and with Jordan's break before her application process, we'd pivoted our summer tradition to Washington.

It had been a little over a week, and the three musketeers were already deep into the outdoors—we'd spent the morning kayaking.

We scattered ourselves along the old, wooden dock, and Jordan pulled a book from her backpack. She was an avid reader, and I'd rarely seen her without a book nearby.

"What's this one about?" I asked.

"Oh, it's so good. It's about a band of magical pirates who get marooned on an island surrounded by mermaids."

Tanner chuckled. He was often amused by Jordan's literary tastes.

"Shut it, Tanner."

The sunlight filtered through the nearby trees, casting dancing shadows across Jordan's deep brown skin. I'd always been fascinated by the way the light pulled flecks of amber from Jordan's dark eyes. Her tight curls were the color of a starless night sky, and she wore two space buns pinned at the top of her head, the rest of her hair spiraling to her elbows. Tanner had gifted her a Pearl Jam t-shirt, which she had promptly cropped and tossed on under a jean jacket. With her black ripped jeans and oversized sunglasses, she looked every bit the badass she was.

After sunning ourselves, Jordan decided we should take a walk, and we meandered along the gravel road that hugged the side of the mountains. The lake houses were below us, their driveways jutting straight down from the roadway.

"That's where Izzy lives." I pointed through the trees to the cedar cabin with its gabled roofline peeking up at us.

"It's beautiful," Jordan marveled.

"I'm ready to meet this family," Tanner said. "They sound . . . interesting."

The day after I met the MacGregor siblings, Izzy and I had ridden our bikes around the lake, but the following day the family seemingly disappeared, and I hadn't seen nor heard from them for several days. Even now, the house looked deserted. Something felt off about the situation, but I guessed the lake and I weren't the only ones with secrets.

Tanner wandered ahead of us.

"What if the MacGregors are in the witness protection program?" Jordan's eyes filled with wonder. "Oh! Or maybe in some branch of government ops?"

I laughed. "Of course, that's where your mind went."

Jordan shrugged.

"I like that theory more than your others, though."

Jordan cut her eyes in my direction as a knowing grin pulled at the corners of her lips.

"Hadley Weston," she said reproachfully.

"What?"

"How exactly would you know about those theories?"

I groaned. "I'm sorry."

"It's okay. Lord knows you can't help it."

Even though Jordan had grown accustomed to my oddities, I still felt horrible when I knew things she hadn't told me. She'd always understood me on some level—she knew about my ability, but never once made me feel like I was different from her.

On our return to my house, two figures materialized at the top of my driveway. One's long, auburn hair gave her away instantly, and the other made my heart stop.

Izzy skipped into my arms. "These must be your friends?"

"Jordan and Tanner, meet Izzy," I offered by way of introduction.

As Izzy, Jordan, and Tanner exchanged pleasantries, Fitz walked toward me.

"Hadley, it's good to see you again," Fitz said.

The sound of my name on his lips sent a thrill sparking through my body. The world began falling out of focus again, and I fought against my mind for control.

"Glad to meet you," Fitz said to Jordan and Tanner.

My eyes followed his movements warily. He shook hands with both Tanner and Jordan seemingly without incident. My fingers tingled as I recalled the shock between the two of us when we had touched. I took a deep breath and exhaled slowly, hoping it would help with my nerves. Fitz met my gaze curiously before offering a soft smile, and my nerves eased slightly.

"Mum was just about to put the kettle on when we left. Fancy a cup?" Izzy asked.

Jordan and Tanner looked to me for direction.

I nodded. "That sounds nice."

The MacGregor cabin was captivating. The high ceilings lent a roomy feel to the space, especially in conjunction with its open concept. The foyer opened into the kitchen and living room. Massive windows covered the wall facing south, allowing for a magnificent view of the lake and the short pier that jutted into the water. The tree line had been thinned in front of the house, but it ran wild on either side of the structure, maintaining the cocooned effect most of the homes around the lake boasted.

Izzy led Jordan and Tanner onto the back deck, but I meandered slowly through the space as I studied the details.

The interior of the home was mostly comprised of cedar boards, a real testament to the local logging community, and a stone fireplace promised a cozy winter spot. The furniture was a mix of creams and leather, and touches of tartan were spread across the space—the blanket on the couch, the dish towels in the kitchen, the runner in the foyer.

I turned to Fitz, who had stayed behind with me.

"The MacGregor tartan?" I asked, gesturing to the plaid pattern.

"You're a curious one, aren't you?"

"I apologize in advance."

Fitz chuckled. "I just completed my PhD, so curiosity isn't a crime as far as I'm concerned."

"Wow, congratulations. That's incredible. What was your area of study?"

"Scottish history with a focus in Divinity—medieval witchcraft and religion."

"Fascinating," I marveled. "Witchcraft has always been interesting to me."

"Oh aye?" he questioned, a gleam in his eye.

"I was *consumed* with the idea of witches as a child. My parents thought it was a phase, a passing fancy from Halloween. But then they realized my interest ran much deeper and that trying to sway me from the obsession was useless. It felt . . ."

"It felt what?"

I shook my head. "You'll think it's silly."

"Try me."

"It just felt so real. Like magic was all around me," I recalled sadly, remembering the child I had once been.

"No. That's not silly at all. I was fascinated by it myself."

"That's what led you to your focus in school?" I asked.

"Aye. I was so captivated by the subject, I traveled to the burghs in Scotland where accused witches were tried, and somewhere along the way I decided to study it seriously."

"What piqued your interest in that subject?"

"My family tree," Fitz said. "My father and I traced back to a grandmother who died in the witch trials in Forfar, Scotland in 1662."

"What was her name?"

"Esther MacGregor."

"I can't believe you were able to trace back to her. It must've been shocking to discover your ancestor was executed in a witch trial."

"I was horrified. It was a long time ago, but it felt personal. From there, I learned what I could about who she was and about the time period."

I nodded. "It changed your trajectory."

"I reckon you're right. I was debating on my degree program for university when we got our ancestry sorted, and this research settled my mind on Scottish history."

His eyes bore into mine. There was something unspoken in the air—I felt it—but whatever it might be, I couldn't quite grasp it.

He pushed his rolled sleeve a little further up his forearm, and a desire to touch him took hold. I wanted to know if he would shock me again. I balled my hands into fists, resisting the urge to reach out to him, when a noise startled me. I turned, losing my balance.

Fitz caught me just before I hit the ground and pulled me upright. A jarring shock pulsed through my arm from his touch, and we pulled away quickly.

"You good, Hads?" Tanner called, walking through the doorway.

"Yep, all good here," I assured. I turned to Fitz. "Sorry about that. I'm not usually clumsy."

"Nae bother," he said, his accent thickening.

"Have you ever had this happen before—the shock?" I whispered.

Fitz looked around, but the rest of our companions were lost in conversation on the far side of the room. He returned his focus to me. "Never."

"Me neither. I don't understand it."

"Neither do I."

A woman bounded down the staircase that hugged the east-facing wall. There was no question that she was Izzy's mother. Auburn hair hung just above her shoulders, framing an ivory face with a striking pair of eyes the same shade of green as her children's. A broad smile warmed her features as her eyes swept across us, and in that moment, I was certain that Ann MacGregor was every bit as charming, self-assured, and attractive as her young daughter.

"We're so pleased you're joining us for tea."

A round of thank-yous sounded before introductions were made, and I thought Ann's eyes lingered on me just a bit longer than with

Jordan and Tanner. Ann moved toward the kitchen to boil water, and Jordan's pointed look toward me confirmed my suspicion. Fitz pulled out a barstool for me. Izzy set plates of shortbread cookies and a cake topped with almonds on the table while Ann steeped the tea.

"This one's a favorite," Izzy shared. "Dundee Cake."

"I've never heard of that, but it looks delicious," Jordan said.

"Mum's specialty," Fitz chimed in. "It has spices, oranges, and raisins."

Ann beamed at her children's praise. "Hopefully, you like it."

"Love it." Tanner covered his face with a napkin, his praise barely coherent with his mouth full of cake. The group laughed.

A door opened to reveal an office. The man that stepped through the doorway was as tall as Fitz and shared his chestnut hair. His face held striking blue eyes the color of storm clouds, but the trait that stood out most was the presence he brought to the room. Though his family was happy he was joining us, something felt off about him to me. Ann kissed him lightly on the cheek and placed a steaming mug in his hand.

"Ian, meet Izzy and Fitz's new friends."

Introductions were made, and yet another set of eyes lingered on me. And this time, I felt even Tanner's observation. The pattern was impossible to ignore.

As the afternoon wore on, we settled into a rhythm of conversation. Jordan and I had countless questions about Scotland while the MacGregors had countless questions about us. And as the light grew golden, I realized we would be late for dinner with my parents. The rest of us were so consumed in our conversation that we'd lost Tanner and Ian.

Fitz and I rose in search of our missing companions.

The door to the study was cracked, and hushed voices floated from the other side. They were seated across from each other at an old wooden desk. The conversation looked serious.

"I've got it," Fitz whispered in my ear, sending a chill through my body.

He emerged with Tanner and Ian, and the latter two wore grim expressions. We exited the cozy home into the cool air of the June evening.

"What was that about?" I whispered to Tanner.

He shook his head in response. I was about to push him for more information when Fitz called my name. Jordan and Tanner walked to the top of the driveway, granting us privacy. Fitz leaned against the house, a smirk resting on his lips.

"May I see you tomorrow?" he asked.

"Gentleman." I smiled. "And the answer is yes."

"Late morning work for you?"

I nodded. "What'll we do?"

"You like plans, don't you?"

"I'm afraid so."

"Let's try skipping plans tomorrow. We'll let the day take us where it wills." He turned toward the door but paused, looking back over his shoulder. "Oh, but Hadley—wear something comfortable. We'll have ourselves a wee adventure."

CHAPTER FOUR

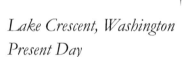

Lake Crescent, Washington
Present Day

As I followed the curves of Highway 101 around Lake Crescent bound for the airport, my mind was spinning. I'd promised my mom I'd be safe, and yet there I was, closing the distance between myself and a potentially dangerous situation. Truth be told, I had no idea what I was walking into, but I had to take that chance. I'd regret passing on the opportunity for the rest of my life.

I checked the time, debating whether I had enough of a travel buffer to stop at my favorite pullout along the lake.

Lake Crescent was a living, breathing entity—I knew it would sound odd to say it out loud, but it was. I'd never known another place so charged with magic. Even though I'd experienced so much hardship along its banks, I still found solace there. I didn't have time for a proper goodbye, but I decided I would stop for a few minutes and breathe its pure air once more before spending ten hours on a plane. I'd make it to Tanner's house in Seattle with a little less time to spare, but we had the airport haul down to a science.

I stepped from the car and walked toward the shoreline. The wind rustled the branches high above me, and the edges of my vision blurred with the deep green of lofty spruce, fir, and alder. The tree-topped mountains jutted straight into the smooth surface of the pristine lake from every side. I'd always felt shielded from the outside world here, like the lake was a world of its own. Its hues were dependent on the sun, and on that day, the light bathed the lake in aqua blue.

It was often said the lake didn't give up her secrets, and perhaps that was part of my kinship with her. The secrets I harbored were buried deep within me, just like the fathomless depths of the lake.

Lake Crescent, Washington
July 2021

I tugged at the rope as I took my final step onto the rocky surface of Mt. Storm King. Fitz and I had spent most of our days together over the past month, taking turns choosing our adventures. I'd decided to share one of my favorite hikes with him. There were countless trails with breathtaking mountainous views in Washington, but the perspective from high above my lake home was my favorite.

We walked cautiously along the center of the peak until reaching the best viewpoint on the mountain.

"Now, that's a braw view," Fitz marveled.

"That means good?"

"Oh aye. This is bonnie—you know that one by now?"

"Aye," I said, mimicking Fitz's tone.

He laughed, shaking his head.

I scanned the scene below us. Fitz was right: it was bonnie. The lake's sapphire surface was as smooth as glass below the plunging mountains surrounding it. The day had started out stormy, which wasn't common for July, but the clouds faded to soft gray, the wind died down, and the rain ceased its descent as we arrived at the trailhead, just as Gram had predicted. That woman was a marvel.

The storm had been enough to scare off the crowds that morning, which were usually thick in the summer months, and we shared the mountaintop with only a few others. We settled on to the edge of the rocky peak, and I stretched out appreciatively, happy to rest my feet for a bit.

"So, how's the job search going?" I asked.

"Slow. But that's by choice, so I can't complain."

"Same here," I said. "I'm stalling, but I can't stay here forever."

"I'm sure your parents are happy you're here."

"You're searching for a professorship?" I asked, steering the conversation away from my dad. He'd been feeling better the past couple of days, but the bad ones were still inevitable—and they were always in the back of my mind.

"What makes you think that?"

"Didn't you say you've always wanted to be a professor?"

Fitz's gaze jumped quickly to mine.

"What's wrong?" I asked.

"Nothing is wrong," Fitz said.

I narrowed my eyes.

"I never told you that—about wanting to be a professor." My heart dropped.

"This has happened a few times now—you've done this with Izzy too."

I remained silent.

"Don't be nervous. I just want to understand."

Silence.

"How do you know these things?"

"I don't know," I finally said.

"You're positive about that? That doesn't quite make sense."

I shook my head. My mind was racing.

Fitz grew pensive before swinging his legs around to face me. "Does this happen often?"

"No."

"Hadley . . ."

"What?" I asked.

"You're not being truthful."

"Excuse me?"

"I know that's a lie," Fitz said.

"And how would you know that?"

Fitz looked around, but none of our fellow hikers were in sight. "Because I know when people are lying to me. I feel it. I . . . see the lies."

My heart quickened. "See them?"

"Aye."

Why was he telling me this?

"What do you see when people lie?" I asked.

"The light around the person dims—it sort of wavers when they're not being truthful."

I paused before saying, "I—I know what you mean. Except that I see a transparent thread forming, and I feel it in the air. It makes the air feel heavy."

Fitz's eyes lit. "You have that ability too?"

I nodded, closing my eyes briefly.

"What happens with the thread?" Fitz asked.

"It depends. If it's a singular lie, it fades. I won't see the thread again unless we revisit the conversation. If they add on to the lie, another thread forms, and a knot ties them together."

Fitz smiled. "That's incredible."

"Is it?"

"I think so. It's certainly useful."

"I can't argue with that."

"Can you do anything else?" he asked.

I nodded my head.

"Like?"

I hesitated, not quite ready to share the rest.

"I'll go first?" he suggested.

"Please." My voice was shaky.

Fitz reached for my hand and gave it a quick squeeze. "I have a bit of a strange skill. It came on when I was a wee boy, and it's intensified as I've grown older. I'll show you, but it's a bit jarring."

"I'm ready."

He turned his head curiously, and suddenly, I could think of nothing but my conversation with Jordan and Tanner from the prior evening.

We were seated on the pier by Tanner's lake house, making plans for an upcoming hike. The memory was vivid. Waves licked the shoreline, and frogs croaked through the trees. I tried to push the scene from my mind, to focus on Fitz, but I couldn't escape it . . . until my mind went blank.

I looked at Fitz, but before I could speak, I spun into a June afternoon.

I was riding bikes with Izzy. We talked and laughed as we peddled our way around the lake.

The emotions that had plagued me that day came rushing back. I'd had the strange dream about Izzy wandering through the woods the night before, and I'd spent that afternoon in utter confusion, wondering whether it had truly been a dream. I gasped at the intensity, and my mind went blank.

"What the hell was that?" I asked, breathing hard.

"I'm sorry if that was intense. I wanted to find a couple recent memories that wouldn't be too taxing for you."

"You can read minds?" I asked.

"Not exactly. Not everyday thoughts as they run through people's minds, but I can latch on to memories. I can pull any of your memories to the surface."

"They felt so . . . vivid. It was like I was reliving them."

"Aye. It always happens like that."

"And I couldn't stop thinking about them. I couldn't get out of the memory."

Fitz nodded. "Not until I release you from it."

"Show me something else."

"Are you sure?"

"Yes," I responded, uncertain if I truly was.

Fitz searched my eyes, prying into the far reaches of my mind.

Slowly, his expression changed. The memory that rose to the surface took my breath away.

A large field with deep green ryegrass stretched across the distance toward the horizon, and a quaint, two-story farmhouse came into focus, the home where I'd spent so many summers. I studied every last detail. The white paint, large windows framed in maroon shutters, and a wrap-around porch were forever burned into my mind.

"All I need is a glass of Gram's sweet tea," I said.

"I don't think I can help you with that one."

It was disconcerting to hear Fitz's voice while I was so completely lost in my own mind. Gram's front porch was still the only thing I could see.

"Oh, don't even try. I'm pretty sure Gram could reach across the lake and slap you for messing with her tea."

Fitz laughed heartily.

I closed my eyes briefly, savoring the feeling of Gram's kingdom, and opened them again to Lake Crescent.

My body could no longer contain my emotions, and I laughed, though tears ran down my face.

"I'm so sorry. Maybe I shouldn't have done that," Fitz said.

"No, you don't understand."

Fitz's eyes flickered worriedly across my face.

"I'm happy," I said.

"Happy?"

"I've felt so strange my entire life, Fitz. I've never known anyone who can do strange things too. I've never known anyone who could understand me."

Relief washed over his face. "Thank god. I thought I had upset you."

"Quite the opposite."

"Well, fair is fair. Tell me about your other gift. Can you read minds? Is that how you know things we haven't told you?"

"Not exactly. I don't know what's wrong with me to be honest."

"Well, first of all," Fitz said, "there's not a damn thing wrong with you."

I remained silent. I couldn't agree with him.

"So, your ability . . ." he prompted.

"I don't know how I can do what I can do. I don't hear thoughts. Information just shows up."

"What do you mean exactly?"

"I just know things. I have no idea how I know them. I just do."

Fitz nodded thoughtfully. "So, you aren't asking for the inform-ation? You're not trying to gather information from anyone?"

"No. Never."

"Ah, and that's why you think we've told you those things. Is this new?"

"No, the information has been coming to me since childhood. I've done a pretty decent job over the years of discerning where the information came from—whether someone actually shared some-thing with me or not. But ever since I met you and Izzy . . ."

"What?"

"I'm having a lot more difficulty controlling it."

"I wonder if it has anything to do with me," Fitz said. "Maybe being around someone else like you has intensified your gift."

"How do you control yours?" I asked.

"Years of practice."

"Do you think you could help me?" I asked.

"I don't have your gift, but I think I can be useful. Let's give it a go, at least."

My heart swelled. "Thank you so much."

Fitz reached for my hand. After a moment, the shock faded to a dull roar that pulsed between us, but for the first time since I'd met Fitz, I counted that pain as a blessing.

CHAPTER FIVE

Seattle, Washington
Present Day

I pulled into Tanner's driveway, and his tall, muscular frame emerged from the front door before I could even put the car in park. He waved from the small porch before popping back into the house.

The cozy craftsman-style bungalow was painted a faded green and trimmed in white. Shrubs lined the porch, and a large spruce tree offered much-appreciated shade from the hot sun during the summer months.

Tanner reappeared and bounded down the front steps. I exited the car to greet him.

"Hads!" Tanner shouted lifting me from the ground. "God, it's good to finally see you!"

"It's good to see you too! Momma and I missed you last weekend."

"Some of us have to work for a living, Weston."

I scoffed, punching his shoulder lightly. "You know I'm heading to Mother England for interviews, right?"

"Nah, I'm glad you took some time off to help your mom. And I'm so proud of you for doing this. You excited?"

"Unbelievably excited. Momma? Less so."

He pulled a Mariners cap from his back pocket and pulled it over his dark hair. "Tell me all about it in the car."

Tanner was chattering in the driver's seat about a new training regimen he'd designed—he was one of the best personal trainers in Washington, and he'd built a successful business out of that.

"I was bummed to miss our annual Storm King hike, but it was the only day they could have me in for that interview. Even though my schedule is pretty stacked with clients, I think this gig could be a great decision, you know?"

"This is the one you mentioned the other night on the phone that you couldn't tell me about?"

"Yeah. I still can't tell you who it's with, but they're pretty major."

"Well, keep me posted—I mean, as much as you can."

My phone buzzed, pulling my attention to a new email.

Ms. Weston,

Thank you for your interest in our open PR Manager role here at Edinburgh Castle. The hiring manager for this position, Mr. Murray, would like to arrange an interview with you and has a strong preference for it to be in-person rather than via video conference. I see you've indicated you're traveling to the U.K. soon, and we would like to arrange the interview while you're in the area. If you'd like to move forward, please advise on your availability at your earliest convenience.

We look forward to hearing from you.

Sincerely,
Edna McLeod
Assistant to James Murray

"What is it?" Tanner asked.

"Nothing. It's just an interview request."

"That's awesome. Where?"

I hesitated.

"Spit it out, Weston."

I took a deep breath. "Edinburgh Castle."

"Scotland? I didn't know you were applying there."

"I wasn't . . . necessarily. This opening just came up while I was researching, and it looks like a great fit for me."

"I see." He paused. "Isn't that where Fitz lives?"

". . .I don't know for sure if he's still there."

Tanner cut his eyes to me. "You're playing with fire."

I gazed out of the passenger side window hoping Tanner would let the conversation drop. The skyscrapers of downtown Seattle flashed by. I'd always loved the drive down I-5 through the downtown corridor. An ache plucked at my heartstrings. I'd missed the PNW more than I wanted to admit, even to myself. Boston hadn't been easy, but Boston was over.

A new adventure was just what I needed.

Forks, Washington
September 2021

At first sight of the Cedar Creek Inn, a deep breath escaped my lungs, my mind momentarily devoid of trouble.

The three-story farmhouse oversaw a large field and the great trees covering the mountains to the south, white paint stark against deep green. Memories bubbled up—my dad walking me down the narrow lane along the inn as a child, in search of elk grazing the fields; my mother lounging on the front porch, a good book in hand.

I parked along the old wooden fence outlining the property, and Fitz emerged distractedly from the car. It had been his turn to pick our outing, and he'd chosen the inn without hesitation.

Tanner had given me a look of disapproval when I'd told him I was going to share my love for the inn with Fitz. I knew he was worried about my relationship with Fitz . . . whatever it may be. But as Fitz and I gazed at the inn, my happiness was palpable—it was one of the few places where I could always breathe easily.

"I see why you love this place," Fitz murmured under his breath.

A Scottish flag hung from the front porch, floating gently in the breeze alongside the American flag. Fitz turned to me, a question resting on his features.

"When guests visit from other countries, Ben and Sarah hang their flag alongside our stars and stripes," I explained. "They're welcoming you."

Fitz grinned broadly.

My eyes scanned the house and surrounding area, registering the subtle changes since my last visit—a fence repair, a fresh coat of paint on the porch, a new sign. But it was mostly just the same. The soft trickle of water from the creek was perceptible in the quiet afternoon. Cows dotted the field, their bodies basking in golden rays, strewn all around an old wooden barn. The structure was popular with tourists, likely one of the most photographed barns in the world. The wood had grayed, faded by the rain, and was contrasted with a blue roof, bright in the afternoon sun.

The front door swung open, revealing a familiar face. His eyes twinkled brightly in recognition behind silver-rimmed glasses, and a crimson Washington State University cap and gray Cedar Creek Inn polo proudly proclaimed his love of both.

"Hadley!" he exclaimed, his voice warm and inviting. "It sure is great to see you again."

"It's great to see you too, Ben."

A woman's voice floated on the afternoon breeze. "I thought I heard you, Hadley. Welcome home!"

Ben's wife, Sarah, stepped around the corner, her arms extended in my direction. She hadn't changed a bit. Her hair was the color of snow, framing blue eyes and a face defiantly untouched by time.

Ben and Sarah had been staples in my childhood. My parents and I had visited their inn for many years. They'd become like second parents to me, and occasionally, when college life became too noisy, I'd found my weekend escape in this very home. Introductions were made, which included a sly look from Sarah as Fitz shook Ben's hand.

I showed Fitz around the inn while Ben and Sarah pointed out their most recent updates to the rooms. Eventually, Fitz and I settled on to Adirondack chairs on the back porch. The promise of fall floated in the afternoon air, but the sun's warm rays kept us comfortable.

The back door swung open, and a young woman bounced across the threshold, her usual exuberance lighting up the space around her. Blonde curls tumbled to her shoulders, framing her storm-cloud eyes.

"Addy! I'm so glad to see you!" We embraced warmly. "I hated that I missed you last time."

"I was so bummed! But I'm glad I didn't miss this visit." Addy nodded toward Fitz.

"Oh, right. This is Fitz."

She grinned, eyeing me meaningfully before shaking his hand. "I did come out here on a mission. Sarah has fresh baked cookies. You want coffee or tea to go with them?"

We both requested tea, and Addy bounded back through the doorway.

"She's sweet," Fitz said, nodding toward the door.

"She's curious. The only guy I've ever brought here is Tanner." I rolled my eyes. "Why *did* you decide on coming here?"

"The way you've spoken of Ben and Sarah, the house, all of it . . . I wanted to see it."

I tilted my head. "But why?"

"Because it's important to you."

Addy flung the door open, a tray of cookies in hand. She was followed by Sarah, who held two steaming mugs and two plates.

"Cookies make any afternoon a good one," Sarah said as she handed off the mugs.

Fitz eyed the cookies appreciatively. "I couldn't agree more."

"Well, you know where we'll be if you need us."

Sarah and Addy headed for the door.

"You don't want to join us?" I asked.

"No," they answered in unison. They chuckled before closing the door behind them.

I groaned. "Sorry."

"For what?" Fitz asked innocently. He grabbed a cookie from the nearby tray and leaned back in his seat.

"You know for what."

He laughed. "Perhaps. Is their assumption incorrect?"

"That something is going on between us?"

"Aye."

"We spend a lot of time together. But we spend a lot of time with Jordan. Tanner. Izzy."

Fitz's gaze was unreadable. I babbled on. "Whatever they think is going on, I don't think that's your intention here."

"Oh aye?" Fitz cocked his head to the side and studied me long enough that my breath hitched. I hoped he didn't notice. "I don't think that's quite true."

"And what is?" I challenged.

Fitz's eyes flickered across my face, and humor faded from his features. "It's exactly what they think. I think you already knew that."

"I know . . . but you're confusing. You seem interested, but then you keep a distance from me." My eyes flickered to the space he'd left between us.

"I didn't want to make you uncomfortable. The shocking . . ."

I set my open hand on the arm of his chair. He hesitated before holding it in his own. Pain traveled through my body and goose-bumps rippled across my skin, but I was determined not to let go. And after a moment, the pain eased.

"Not so bad," I said.

"All right then." Fitz said, amused.

We sat silently for a moment before Fitz's expression grew pensive.

"What is it?" I asked.

"This isn't just friendship, and we both know it. You and I gravitate to each other."

We sat, hands linked, while we enjoyed our afternoon tea, and after helping Addy with the dishes, we decided to take a walk. We meandered the old lane near the inn in companionable silence, taking in the scenery. We passed the barn, and the lane narrowed. The green fields stretched toward the low mountains, and a chorus of frogs was all that disturbed the quiet. The evening was still, peaceful, and the chill of dusk crept into the air.

"I have so many memories from this place," I said absentmindedly.

"Would you share one of them with me?" Fitz asked. I leaned against the nearby fence.

"You mean . . . ?"

"Aye. But only if you want."

I nodded.

"Think of one you'd like to share, and I'll take it from there."

I rolled through a few options before laughing. "I've got it."

The scene unfolded like I was living the moment all over again. I was walking the lane with my parents about ten years ago, and our dog, Max, was with us. Max was a border collie, and we were forever trying to help him run off his energy. My mom held his leash loosely in her hand while she talked distractedly with my dad about our upcoming family vacation. I studied my father. It was years before his diagnosis, and it was a real gift to catch another glimpse of his healthy years.

Suddenly, Max turned his head, and his ears perked up. He jumped the fence, ripping the leash out of my mom's hand, and tore across the field before we could even process what he had done. I was horrified when I realized the object of his focus. A herd of roughly forty elk were congregated in the back field.

"Dad!" I yelled. "The elk!"

"Oh, no. Here, Rach," he muttered, tossing his phone to Momma.

He jumped the fence and ran as quickly as his feet would carry him over Max's path.

"Matt! Be careful!" My mom yelled.

I jumped the fence and followed my father's path, my mother's protests fading with my progress.

Max was determined to do what collies did: herd. Max was running around the elk, and my dad was running behind Max. One of the elk chased Max while he chased the rest of the herd, and my dad stumbled backward, realizing the danger.

"We're going to have to tackle him," I said.

"Yeah, we just have to wait until the right moment," he said, eyeing the massive creatures.

After a series of unsuccessful attempts, we finally found our opportunity. As Max zoomed past us, Dad risked it all and jumped with full force, landing unceremoniously on top of Max. Max yelped in surprise. My dad winced at his clumsy landing. I shrieked at the scene unfolding. But Max was caught.

By the time Dad and I returned to Momma, Ben and Sarah had joined her. They'd happened upon the scene during their evening walk. Luckily, no one was injured, and the whole episode ended in laughter.

As the memory faded, the group's laughter was replaced with mine and Fitz's. A few tears dropped down my cheek.

"Sorry," I stammered. "I forgot how funny my dad looked chasing that damn dog."

Fitz carefully wiped away my tears.

"It was nice to see Dad like that too—healthy. It felt real again."

"I'm glad," Fitz said softly.

As our laughter faded, we held each other's gaze, and though I felt the strangeness of the moment, I couldn't seem to look away.

"What's the matter?" Fitz asked.

"It's nothing really. Just sometimes when we lock eyes . . ." I trailed off.

"It's difficult to look away? It's the same for me," Fitz said.

But it was more than that. Sometimes the world felt like it was spinning out of control, but if I just kept my eyes on his, everything else faded out of focus. I think I would have found peace in it if I could just let the moment be.

Fitz reached timidly toward my cheek before letting his hand drop.

"Why, Fitz?" It was nearly a whisper, but I knew he'd heard me.

He shook his head and gripped my hand. The now familiar shock blew through me.

"I think we should give this a minute." He nodded to our linked hands, and I understood.

Once the pain eased, Fitz ran his fingers through my hair to the base of my neck. His eyes wandered from my eyes to my jaw, and his hand followed his gaze as his thumb skimmed the length of my face. It traveled slowly to my lips, and his eyes followed. His eyes darkened as he made his decision. He leaned forward and met me in a soft kiss. My entire body tingled with butterflies before a small tremor radiated through me. I gasped softly, and he pulled back.

"Are you good?"

"Yeah, I'm fine."

He paused.

"I don't know where our paths lead from here, Hadley. There's so much uncertainty." His voice grew husky, and his accent thickened. "Would you still want to risk this if I told you it might *no* end well for us? If I told you I cannae guarantee your happiness?"

"No one can promise happiness. That's like promising sunshine in this rainy little town. Neither of us can guarantee anything . . . But I think we're worth the risk."

"We shouldnae be doing this." His brows creased, and a frown spread across his features. "You deserve better than what I can give you."

Fitz was right about the uncertainty of our futures . . . our careers, my dad, the oddities between us . . . There was so much we couldn't explain. But I wouldn't allow uncertainty to decide my future.

I shook my head and pulled his face to mine until our lips almost touched. "You don't get to decide that for me. I'll decide that for myself."

CHAPTER SIX

Seattle, Washington
Present Day

Tanner pulled into the departures lane and hopped from the car to grab my suitcase. He rolled the luggage to the sidewalk before pausing.

"Come on, Hads. Out with it."

"What do you mean?"

"You were distracted the whole ride over even before you got that email. Something is bothering you. Talk to me."

I sighed, debating telling the truth. It was Tanner . . . I'd never been any good at lying to him.

"A letter showed up in my room this week. Fitz asked me to meet him in Paris."

"*What?*"

I nodded.

"Oh, shit."

I laughed. "Yeah. My sentiments exactly."

"You're going to do it?"

"I have to. I've been waiting for this moment for over a year."

His dark eyes narrowed. "Are you sure? I mean, you're sure the note was from Fitz?"

"Positive," I said.

"And you're sure you want to do this?"

"Tanner," I warned.

"Nah, no hate. I'm just asking. You're ready for this? For whatever this is?"

"There's only one way to find out."

"You remember those self-defense moves I taught you and Jordan, right?"

"*Tanner!*"

"What? Just in case it's not Fitz waiting for you over there," Tanner said.

"He'll be there. I'm certain of it," I said, more confidently than I felt.

"If you say so."

"I say so. Now, I really have to go. I'll text you later."

"Knock 'em dead, Weston."

"Love you, big guy."

"Yeah, love you too. Stay safe. Call me if you need me, okay?"

I hugged him and sprinted for the door.

I paused at the entrance and turned back to find Tanner standing right where I'd left him, with his brows knit tightly and his lips straightened into a grim line. I'd seen a similar expression the first evening we'd visited the MacGregors when Tanner sat across the desk from Ian. My heart sank at the thought of leaving him with worry, and I thought about turning back. Instead, I simply waved before rushing through the doors.

Lake Crescent, Washington
March 2022

Fitz's parents were hosting a going-away party for me before I left for Boston, where my first job out of graduate school awaited. Everyone was there: my parents, Fitz, Izzy, Jordan, Tanner, Ben, and Sarah. The party was in full swing, but the emotions swirling through my body were too much to bear, so I sought out a quiet corner in the adjoining room. I stood near the window, my eyes transfixed on the rough surface of the lake.

Footsteps disturbed my reverie, and I turned to find Fitz. Over the last six months, Fitz and I had grown closer, spending most of our days together. His family had joined mine and Tanner's tradition of celebrating the holidays with our families at the lake. Fitz had been helping me navigate the ups and downs of my father's illness. We worked on recognizing patterns with our touch and came to understand that strong emotions heightened the intensity of the shocks.

Life hadn't been easy, but it was better with Fitz.

But over the last week, I'd sensed something was wrong. Fitz had been so proud of me when I shared news of my job offer with him. I knew how difficult this would be for our relationship, but I believed we could work through it. So why was it that I'd seen the distance grow in his eyes and had felt his increasing despondency washing through me?

Fitz reached for my hand, and a shock moved through my body. A soft smile spread across his lips, but his nerves radiated throughout the room. My chest tightened.

"A bit much in there?" he asked, his Gaelic dialect thick on his tongue.

"You know me. I'm loads of fun at parties."

"Part of your charm."

"Since when is anxiety charming?"

His eyes turned mischievous. "Since I met you."

I laughed, shaking my head lightly.

"I have something for you."

He placed a small box in my waiting palm. I ran my fingers across the silky, sage paper and the large, ivory bow.

I opened the gift slowly, my hands shaky on the paper, and a sort of reverence fell across the room. It was our last day together before everything changed, after all, and there was something sacred about these few peaceful moments I had alone with Fitz. I finally unboxed the gift, and I couldn't conceal my gasp.

A slim, golden band was lightly hammered and held a pearly white moonstone in a round bezel at its center. It glowed like its namesake in the soft rays of the pale sun. The light pulled hints of blue to the surface of the otherwise crystal-colored stone.

"Fitz! This is too much."

"How did I know you'd say that? Always underestimating what you deserve."

I shook my head softly.

"Tell me something. Do you like it?" Fitz's teasing tone fell to softness in an instant.

"Of course, I do," I whispered.

"Then promise me you'll wear it. Nothing would make me happier."

"I promise." My response was barely a whisper, but the smile on his face let me know he heard me.

I slipped the ring onto my finger and paused briefly before enveloping him in a warm embrace. He stiffened at the shock as our bodies met, but he quickly composed himself and wrapped his arms around me.

"Hadley," he said hesitantly. I released my grip and found his brows knitted tightly as his lips fell into a hard line. "After you leave tomorrow, you and I won't be in contact for a while."

My mind spun so quickly, I was sure the ground itself was slipping away.

"Why?"

"I'm not supposed to tell you why. I'm supposed to tell you something . . . anything but the truth, but I can't do that. I can't lie to you."

"I don't understand—are you breaking things off?"

"No, of course not . . . I know this doesn't make sense. I don't want it to be like this, but it isn't my choice."

I reached for his hand, holding it in both of my own. The pain returned before falling into a dull ache, and I wondered if my touch was adding to his discomfort.

"Isn't your choice? Then whose is it?" I asked.

"I know you don't understand it right now, but I promise that I'll be able to explain everything one day."

"When?"

"I don't know exactly. It won't happen for a while, but it will happen. I swear," Fitz said.

"You know what?" I released my grasp, feeling like I was letting go of more than his hand. "Screw this."

"Hadley."

"No. Maybe we haven't talked about it lately, but you and I both know damn well what we have." My voice rose, attracting the attention of our friends and family in the next room.

Fitz took my arm and led me onto the back deck, away from their questioning glances.

Though the sun was still present, the wind had shifted overnight and brought with it the cold air of the west, which tore through my loose hair and sent strands of strawberry blonde floating all around me. I pushed my hair away from my face, the act further incensing me, as Fitz turned on his heel, rage burning through his green eyes.

"I didn't say a bloody thing about not knowing what we have," he growled.

"So, what? You tell me something like this and then it's just supposed to be okay?"

"I know it's not okay! I never said it was. I'm doing my best here."

"Not good enough."

Fitz's glare tore through me.

"This is ridiculous," I said.

"Look," he began, pausing briefly. "You have no idea what this is doing to me. I have no choice. Please just try to trust me."

"How am I supposed to trust you?"

His eyes widened, the anger fading with my freshly delivered blow before he turned toward the lake.

"Don't you dare turn away from me," I said.

"I know you're pissed. I would be too." He paused, turning to face me once again. "I've already said too much, and that's because I care about you."

"I need more."

"You're different, Hads. And so am I . . ."

"Come on. Don't give me this crap, Fitz."

"No, you need to listen. The things we can do—that's why we'll be apart for a while. When I can come to you again, I promise I won't waste a second."

"Wait, this is because of our abilities or because of this weird connection we have?"

"Both."

"Are you in trouble?"

"Yes and no," Fitz said.

"Real helpful."

"Damn it, Hadley," he muttered under his breath.

"What? Give me something."

"Aye, it's about our abilities, but our connection has something to do with it as well. This isn't exactly normal—it's special to you and me. That's all I can say about it. You have no idea how much trouble you're getting me into."

"Except that no one else knows about this conversation, right?"

Fitz's lips curved into a humorless smile.

"I love your curiosity, your love for learning. But it's going to make you mental and get us both into trouble."

"Fitz, you have to give me a little more context, and I think you know that."

He paused as his eyes narrowed. "Give me a moment."

I nodded, and he disappeared inside the house. When he returned, a large blanket was draped over his arm, the red-and-black checkered pattern looking at home against the wooden cabin. Fitz draped the blanket around my shoulders and led me toward the trees bordering the house. Gravel crunched underfoot, and I already knew where we were going: a lofty evergreen that had fallen years ago. I'd had many a conversation, with both Fitz and Izzy, sitting atop that magnificently large old spruce.

My feet met the firm end of a broken branch with a certainty that came with familiarity, and I hoisted myself onto the spot we'd worn smooth. I settled in comfortably while allowing myself to adjust to the energy of the space. I couldn't explain it, but the air always felt different around the fallen tree.

Fitz eased himself down next to me, the tinny sound of his jacket disturbing the quiet. His eyes were distant, transfixed on the waves breaking on to the shore a few feet from us. Finally, he faced me.

"We've talked about our oddities, you and I."

I nodded.

"The truth is there are people who know about the things I can do. And those people . . . Hadley, they work for the government."

"*What?*"

"You're safe, but I'm going to leave the States for a while."

"Wait a second . . . like, the U.S. government?" I asked.

"It's more complicated than that. But I do need to leave."

"I . . ." I cleared my throat. "I don't understand. You're in danger?"

"I know they want to talk to me. I spoke with my family, and we feel it's best for me to leave the States, at least for a while."

"Won't they be able to trace you?"

"Don't worry about that," Fitz said.

"What would happen if we kept seeing each other? What would they do?"

"I'm not sure."

A transparent thread wavered between us. It wasn't an outright lie, but it wasn't the plain truth either. And that wouldn't work for me.

"What would they do, Fitz?" My voice was even, but the warning was clear.

"They haven't communicated consequences yet. But based on the information my dad and I have gathered . . . it would be bad. Unless you want me to *really* disappear from your life, we need to do as they ask, at least for a bit."

I was stunned. "No. That can't happen."

"We'll sort this out," Fitz said. "I'll find a way to communicate with you. And eventually, we'll find a way around all this."

"How do you know things will be okay?"

He turned his head ever so slightly, his eyes piercing mine.

"You're not going to tell me."

Silence.

"So, you're going to leave here, lay low, and then what?"

"I'll figure that part out eventually." He shrugged. "Right now, I'm focused on making my first move while keeping you safe."

"You need to worry about keeping *yourself* safe. Don't worry about me."

Fitz turned to me, placing his hands on either side of my face. "That's impossible . . . for me to not worry about you. Surely you know that."

I rested my forehead against his. I closed my eyes, attempting to quiet my raging mind, before pulling back, my eyes searching his.

"Is it crazy that there's a part of me that wants to come with you?"

He ran his thumb softly across my cheek. "The most selfish part of me wants that more than you know."

"But you're not going to let that happen."

"You know me well." He sighed. "I want to keep you safe. I need some time to sort this out, but I *will* sort this out. I promise I'll find a way."

"I could help you," I said.

He shook his head. "Go to Boston. Start this new chapter of your life. Stay safe, Hadley."

I opened my mouth to protest, but he was faster.

"Think of your father."

A lump rose in my throat. I understood Fitz perfectly. It was hard enough to leave for Boston while my dad was still battling cancer.If I went with him, there would be no regular phone calls, no video calls . . . and I couldn't do that.

"I choose you or I choose my family?"

"No," Fitz whispered. "You're going to choose a life for yourself. One where you'll still talk to your family and support your father."

There was a flurry of emotions inside of me: anger, sadness, fear—they were all racing for control. I wanted to object. It wasn't in my nature to accept defeat. But I couldn't do this. I couldn't disappear on my family. I couldn't put my dad through that. And I wouldn't risk Fitz's safety.

"Hadley . . ." he whispered.

I knew what he sought. "I'm okay."

"I'm so sorry."

A tear spilled down my cheek. "You say we'll find a way to overcome this, so why is it I feel like I've just lost you? I'm missing you so much even while you're still here. I already feel your absence, Fitz, and it is *everywhere*."

I found the courage to face him after my confession. Though his expression was impassible, tears fell from his eyelashes, staining his perfect face with grief. The ache in my chest intensified. I cradled his face in my hands, sweeping my thumbs gently across his cheeks.

"You said I had no idea what this was doing to you," I began, sniffling, "but you're wrong . . . because I can *feel* what you feel too."

His pain filled every fiber of my being. We'd likely never understand why we felt each other's emotions as though they were our own, but I was okay with the pain. It was the loss of that connection I feared most.

"I wish I loved you less," he said. "I don't want to put you through this. But there's no helping it." He pulled me closer to him, and I gasped at the charge of electricity that sparked through me at his touch. It was amplified. He loosened his grip, but I tightened my own, shaking my head.

"I don't want to hurt you," he said.

"I don't want you to let go."

He nodded.

"Is this hurting you?" I raised our linked hands.

"It's bearable. It . . ." He trailed off.

"It what?"

He shook his head.

"Say it, Fitz."

His eyes glistened with tears, and my body filled with the butterflies of uncertainty. His free hand slid to cradle the base of my neck, and I felt his resolve crumble just as strongly as if it were my own.

"It hurts worse to let go," he admitted.

"Then don't."

"I have to, Hadley."

CHAPTER SEVEN

Paris, France
Present Day

Though a rooftop in Paris seemed an unlikely place for our reunion, I stood atop Notre Dame, waiting expectantly. I pulled the note from my pocket and ran a thumb across my name written in ink, as if the note would disappear if I let it out of my sight. The paper's edges had already softened from my constant handling.

I turned to Notre Dame's sweeping view, the full grandeur of the city on display. Block after block of historic architecture lay on either side of the Seine down to the Eiffel Tower and beyond toward the high-rise skyline—surely a mesmerizing scene under different circumstances.

A faint chill crawled the length of my spine, rattling my already growing nerves.

Not for the first time, I considered that the note wasn't from Fitz.

I reached for my right hand, needing to feel the smooth surface of the moonstone ring I couldn't remove. I closed my eyes, anticipating the deepened state of awareness brought on by the stone, my thoughts churning, my senses heightened.

My nerves prickled from the back of my neck to the base of my spine, and I couldn't deny the gnawing sign of being watched. I'd felt the unsettling sensation countless times over the last couple of years—since just prior to meeting Fitz. The observations had grown more frequent since he and I had parted at the lake, and the feeling more intense.

I glanced over each shoulder, answering the compulsion that bordered on habit. Eyes landed sporadically on mine as I scanned the bustling, historic attraction, but I found nothing suspicious.

A cool breeze nipped at my neck, a subtle reminder that the day was fading. I checked my watch. It was an hour past our intended meeting time.

I meandered around tourists that lingered in the waning daylight, excited by the prospect of golden hour photos and sunset views. A couple wrapped their arms around each other as they gazed at the scene, tender smiles spreading across their lips. I tried to push my disappointment from my mind, but my chest tightened.

Finally, I had to consider that Fitz wasn't coming.

The setting sun and my fading optimism tempted me to trade the stone gargoyles of Notre Dame for a quiet space. Recalling a cozy little café near my hotel, I swept the Parisian skyline one last time before turning to leave.

I wound my way toward the door when the sensation of being watched prickled up my spine again. But something was different . . .

and it stopped me in my tracks. A scene took hold of me, and I saw myself reflected from another point of view.

"Not again," I whispered, panic-stricken. I took in a deep, ragged breath before turning slowly.

A tall man stood near the stairwell, his head turning toward me. My eyes swept over him. From his brown oxfords and dark wash jeans to his gray sweater and the chestnut hair peeking from underneath the hood of his olive jacket, he was as perfectly put together as he'd always been.

He pulled the hood down, and the sun's golden rays illuminated a face forever etched into the fabric of my mind. As I neared, his expression grew easier to read. His eyes were hopeful, following my movements tenderly. His mouth was set tight, holding all his fear and doubt. I paused just before him, staring wordlessly into his emerald eyes. The breath caught in the back of my throat.

"Fitz."

He smiled.

And there he was. A perfectly familiar stranger. The ghost that had haunted me for over a year, the only person who held the power to break me over and over again. My heart ran wild, and I found some comfort in the fact that his must be doing the same. His fingers twitched, and I thought he might reach for me. Instead, he tightened his hands into soft fists. He closed his eyes briefly, an attempt to blink away the mist.

I took Fitz's hand in mine, and a burst of electricity coursed through me, taking my breath away. We broke away quickly, shaking our hands like it would help expel the pain.

"Oh, shite!" The intensity of his whisper made me smile. "We're off to a great start."

I shrugged. "It's pretty on-brand for us, to be honest."

He laughed softly, and between my nerves and the infectious sound of his laughter, I did the same.

"You've changed." He reached timidly for my hair, allowing my auburn locks to fall through his fingers.

"In some ways," I said softly.

His eyes were troubled as they swept across me, scanning for other changes, I guessed. A deep melancholy settled between us, and I was desperate to make it stop.

I extended my hand. "Let's try this again?"

"Aye, who needs their hands anyway?"

As our fingers met, a tremor radiated through my body, though softer than before, and I figured our calming nerves might have something to do with that.

"Now, that's better," Fitz said.

"Much better," I agreed.

A surge of emotion bubbled through me, and I had to be honest with myself about how badly I'd missed Fitz. My eyes welled with tears.

"Come here," Fitz said.

He tugged at my hand, pulling me into his embrace. A long-standing tightness eased from my chest, and I leaned into him, finally allowing myself to believe the whole scene was real. I hadn't dreamed it. He gave a tight squeeze and released me, the scent of whisky and spice dissipating with the warmth of his touch.

"I can't believe we're here," I said.

"Aye . . . surreal, isn't it?" he asked, his Gaelic dialect thick on his tongue. "I'm sorry I was late."

"Why *were* you late?"

"I was . . ." He trailed off, registering the people surrounding us, before dropping his voice. "I was followed."

"By?"

"No idea—not the usual folks."

My thoughts flooded with questions, but this was neither the time nor place for an inquisition, annoying as that was. The man had disappeared once before; I didn't want him to leave before we had a chance to talk—to really talk.

I nodded, crossing my arms as the wind picked up.

Fitz shrugged out of his jacket before I could even protest and placed it around my shoulders.

"Let's get out of the cold. Can I take you to dinner?"

I was caught off-guard by the realization that I hadn't eaten all day—I'd been too nervous—and he mistook my pause for disinterest.

"I mean, no pressure. We don't have to. It's just—"

I laughed, interrupting his panic. "Let's get dinner."

"What a great idea, Hadley."

We wound through the thick crowd just outside the cathedral. Fitz turned toward me, placing his hand on the small of my back. The gesture felt comfortable, like we were assuming our previous roles. A twinge of apprehension hit the pit of my stomach.

A couple of streets over, the sidewalks were free of crowds, and I let out a deep sigh. The wind blew gently across the Seine, which served as our guide toward the café. We walked in silence only a moment before I broke the ice.

"I felt someone watching me before I saw you. It wasn't you, was it?" I asked, hoping maybe it *had* been Fitz watching me at Notre Dame.

"No. I had just climbed the steps when we met near the door," he said.

"So, it was someone else. I was really hoping I was wrong about that."

"Aye, but sometimes it isn't bad intent. Maybe the person was just curious about you."

"You think someone was watching both of us at the same time, and it was just a coincidence?"

"Did you just roll your eyes at me?"

I grinned. "Yes. But the question still stands."

"No. But it wasn't the government."

"And how do you know that?"

"I just do. I'm telling you this is different."

"You know we have to talk about all this, right?" I asked.

Fitz nodded. "I know. We have a great deal to discuss . . . and some decisions to make."

I waited patiently for him to continue.

"If it's all right with you, I'd like to talk about all that tomorrow, though."

"Tomorrow? Why?"

"I've looked forward to seeing you again for a very long time," he said. "I just want one night with you where we forget all the bullshite. Just one night, Hadley."

I couldn't pretend I didn't want the very same thing.

CHAPTER EIGHT

The café was charming. The host led us to a back corner, navigating mismatched, antique tables—products of a bygone era still serving as a catalyst for food and conversation. They looked at home amongst the sage walls, which were covered in mahogany shelves holding eclectic, vintage wine bottles. Although the restaurant was filled with patrons, the hum of conversation was soft, intimate.

Fitz pulled out my chair then proceeded to his seat. My eyes flickered across the table, wondering what it was about him that made every bit of my soul so incredibly aware of his presence.

His lips curved into a soft smile.

"What?" I asked, realizing my eyes had lingered far too long on my dinner partner.

"You. I forgot how observant you are. About everything."

"And you find it amusing?" I asked.

"I find it endearing."

I shook my head, butterflies dancing in my belly.

"Your mind is my favorite thing about you. There's always so much going on up there . . ." He trailed off, searching my eyes.

Silence fell. I would've felt embarrassed had it been anyone else.

The moment dissipated with the waiter's arrival at our table. We ordered a bottle of wine, and I suggested Fitz use his discretion to select food for the table. As I'd been in Paris only a day, it seemed wise to allow the veteran to take the wheel. Fitz was enthusiastic about sharing a couple of his favorite dishes with me.

He leaned forward. "Go ahead."

"What do you mean?"

"I can tell you have a burning question."

I pretended not to notice his amusement as I asked, "Why did you decide on Paris?"

"I didn't want to meet you in London, just in case Big Brother sorted out that you were going there next week. This is a close enough stop. And they think I'm in Budapest," he offered.

"You don't think they've figured out we're here?" I asked.

"I'd wager they've figured out I'm not in Budapest, but they have no trace to Paris."

"Nice."

"I needed to get away anyway, and Paris usually helps me sort out my head when I'm feeling stuck. You have impeccable timing."

"I remember that you love this city," I said. "I can already see why."

"Aye. It's a grand place for breaking monotony."

"What has you feeling stuck?"

Fitz's eyes grew distant, and an emotion stirred within me. Fear wasn't the right word for it, but something was troubling Fitz.

"My latest project," Fitz said. "Shall I bare my soul to you?"

I nodded in encouragement.

Though his words were lighthearted, he couldn't hide the tension that rose to the surface as he spoke. "I'm trying to solve a mystery surrounding my ancestor and an object they lost in 1662. I've hit a dead end."

"Is anyone helping you?"

"No," he admitted. "I haven't trusted anyone."

The look on my face must have betrayed my confusion.

"I don't want the government to know my family ever had possession of it, and I'm not sure who I can trust," Fitz said.

Why would it matter to anyone outside of his family if his ancestor had lost something hundreds of years ago? I'd spent far too much time on the mysteries of Fitz MacGregor and his family, and it seemed that pattern would continue.

"Is this about Esther?" I asked.

"You remember her?"

"Esther changed the course of your life. Do you think I'd forget something like that?"

He glanced down at his hands, his eyelashes fluttering as he smoothed out the tablecloth. When he looked up, his expression was unreadable. "I'm a slow learner."

I'd let his deflection go, at least for now. "Why are you telling me about it?"

"Because I trust you."

The waiter delivered our wine, and his request for Fitz to approve the Chateau de Ferrand broke our gaze. When we locked eyes, we could barely look away, as though we'd become aware of each other for the first time, a magical, invisible thread connecting us. It seemed to be some sort of communication we didn't yet understand—much like how we'd each developed the ability to feel the other's emotions and pain.

I felt his nerves across the dinner table, and I knew he felt mine.

The waiter poured the beautiful, deep burgundy liquid into my glass. After a brief swirl, I took a small, tentative sip, allowing it to trickle smoothly across my tongue.

"That's *delicious*," I said before taking another sip.

Fitz chuckled at my response and raised his glass in turn. "What do you taste?"

I closed my eyes, pulling another slow sip from the glass. "Dark fruit—black cherries. Spice. It'll open up nicely."

"Aye, it does want oxygen. It's a bit warm, which I fancy." He nodded appreciatively. "I'm glad you approve. Wine tasting has been a bit lackluster without you."

He deftly swirled the dark liquid, opening its full possibilities. There was something playful and unassuming in his manners. In his features, I'd found both a man that left me breathless and a boyish countenance that put me at ease.

I leaned forward. "You trusted me enough to talk about your secret project, so . . . let me help you."

"I'd be grateful for your help."

"How long have you been working on this?"

"Let's discuss more about the project later," Fitz said.

My eyes narrowed.

"Come on, Hadley. Let's save this conversation for another day. I don't really want to think about it right now."

"You know, there seems to be a lot of conversations being pushed to 'another day.'"

"You'll be here for a few days, so I think we'll have time to cover everything."

"Oh." My eyebrows raised playfully. "So, I can expect the pleasure of your company for several days?"

"If you'll have me."

I nodded. "Well, since we have several days in Paris, I have plenty of time to ask my questions."

"Here we go."

"Your good humor is appreciated. So, tell me more about what you're doing in Scotland now. You've been cryptic about your exact location—are you still in Edinburgh?"

"Aye. Conducting research and teaching a few Scottish history classes."

Edinburgh. Butterflies danced through me.

"Hold on. Are you teaching at the University of Edinburgh?" I asked in awe.

"Aye." Fitz smiled, clearly gratified by my response. The university was consistently ranked as one of the top in the world, and Fitz was only in his early thirties.

"I should have picked up on that. Your accent is stronger," I teased, pulling a laugh from him. "But that's incredible. This is how you landed back in Scotland?" I asked, reaching for . . . some sort of French cheese puff pastry at the center of the table.

"A couple of my mentors had asked me about my postdoctoral plans before I left for the States that summer, but I wasn't sure what I wanted. I doubted myself more than anything."

"So, what changed?"

"I came back to Edinburgh right after we left the lake that March, and I met with a few of those mentors. They thought I'd be a good fit for the history faculty. One thing led to another, and before I knew it, I was accepting a position as a lecturer."

He told the story nonchalantly, in his quintessential Fitz style, but I knew that accomplishment was no small feat, and I sensed the pride he took in his work.

"I teach in the School of Divinity, focusing on witchcraft and religion in Scotland during the 17th century."

"You seem happy with it," I said.

"Aye, and it's been nice to spend time in Scotland again. Seeing family is great too."

"I'm jealous. I have a long list of places in Scotland I want to explore, especially in the Highlands."

"I'd be honored to show you my country . . . if you'd like."

"I'd like that very much."

A broad grin spread across his face.

"Speaking of careers," I said, "I hinted at a change in my last letter, but I didn't want to put it in writing . . . I'm interviewing in London."

My heart skipped a beat as I omitted Edinburgh, but I wasn't ready to broach that conversation with Fitz just yet. If he noticed my nerves, he didn't show it.

"You'd be moving?" he asked.

"I need a change. Seems reasonable, right?"

"Perfectly reasonable I'd say, though I've never been the foremost scholar in reasonable."

I laughed knowing he was absolutely right, which I considered a mark in his favor.

"Are you staying in PR or looking into something different?" he asked.

"The same. I really enjoy working in PR. I just didn't want to be in Boston anymore." I shrugged.

"But why London?"

"The culture, the history, the architecture . . . it's always interested me. London has great career options—companies, museums, universities. I feel like it would be a good next step for my career."

"Aye, it's a good thought. I wonder—"

"What?" I asked, feeling a shift in his energy.

"I just wonder what's really drawn you to London. It's a proper Hadley story, but there's more to it."

"What makes you think there's more?"

"Because I know you, and I know when you aren't telling me something," Fitz said.

I thought about my father, my panic attacks, the emptiness that I thought might last forever. I thought of how I'd concealed all of this from my mom when she sought the same information only a few days ago. She and Fitz both knew me well enough to understand there was more to my decision . . .

I almost told him all of it, but the words stuck in my throat.

Not yet, I thought.

"Maybe you don't know me so well anymore," I said instead.

"I'll always know you," he responded, the soft smile fading from his face.

"You left, Fitz. I'm sure we've both changed. I know I have."

"I left? It's not quite so simple, is it?"

"Fine," I said. "We both moved, but I didn't end things."

"I didnae either. And you know this entire arrangement was for your protection."

"Do I?"

"Wow, Hadley. That's unfair."

I exhaled sharply.

"I dinnae want to argue right now. I just asked a simple question," Fitz said.

I closed my eyes in an effort to think clearly. "Truthfully, I thought about coming over here a couple days early, even before your note. I needed to . . . wrestle with my thoughts and process the past couple of years before jumping into interviews. With Dad . . ." I trailed off, willing the tears to stay in. "You know, I told you my dad died, and it changed nothing."

"My first priority was keeping you safe, and that's what I did."

"That's not what I needed most. I needed you there, Fitz."

"It would have caused a shite storm," he said. "It would have been far worse for you."

"You don't know that."

"I do know that. It would have been ugly, Hads. And what good what that have done you? You would've been dealing with the loss of your father, supporting your mother, and dodging the government? No." He shook his head. "You can be mad at me if you need to be. I'll take that. I *can* take that because you're here with me, and you're still safe."

I sighed. I was angry, but I couldn't decide if I was angrier at Fitz for what had passed or angrier at the fact that I couldn't stay mad at a man who was willing to sacrifice everything for my safety.

"How about we get out of here?" he asked.

"I could use a change of scenery. I think the jetlag is creeping in."

"We can go back to the hotel if you'd prefer."

"Absolutely not. I want to see Paris at night."

We wandered along the Seine, and the path was quieter than I expected. We strolled along in silence until I recalled a question I had about Fitz's research.

"How did you learn that the ring your ancestor lost was Esther's?"

"*Did I tell her about the ring?*" Fitz's voice echoed through my mind.

I froze.

What is happening to me?

Fitz laid a hand on my arm. "Are you all right?"

I was too confused to answer.

"Hads . . ."

"I'm sorry," I said.

"What's going on? Your energy feels panicked."

"I . . . You probably won't even believe this one."

"Hadley, have you met us? There's absolutely nothing normal about either one of us."

I hesitated still.

"There's no room for lies at this point—not between us. I'm not going anywhere, so you might as well be straight with me."

"I heard you thinking. I can hear people's thoughts now," I whispered shyly. "But it's not all the time. It just comes and goes. So, the random information I used to know about people?"

Fitz nodded.

My voice shook as I continued. "Now I can actually hear them thinking like they're talking in my head or see what they're seeing. I don't know what's wrong with me."

"There's nothing wrong with you. Please don't say that," he implored, his fingers sliding between my own, finding a firmer grip.

I nodded, not believing him, but unable to find the words I wanted to say. He rubbed the base of my thumb with his own, sending my feelings into battle with one another—pain, joy, anxiety, peace.

"When did it start?" Fitz asked.

"Right before I left for Paris."

"And no one knows about this?"

"No."

"Has anything else changed recently?"

I shook my head. "But things changed when Dad died. At first, I thought it was because I was grieving, but then . . ."

"What changed?"

"My hair thickened, and it changed color—from strawberry blonde to this auburn-ish shade that it is now. And it all happened so quickly, like in a week."

"That does seem odd."

I rambled further about the physical changes I encountered, the words tumbling out after seven months of secrecy. "My skin really smoothed out, and my complexion just . . . glows. And then I suddenly didn't need my contacts anymore. I know how this must sound, but it did happen all at once. I've been trying to find a connection, but it's difficult. I haven't talked to anyone about it."

"Don't you worry. We'll sort this out."

I nodded.

"Do you notice a pattern in what people are thinking?" Fitz asked.

"Is there any sort of trigger for the mind reading?"

"No. It truly is all over the map. The first time it happened was with my mom."

"Give me some examples."

"There was the detail with Esther. And then, on the flight over, the person next to me was upset, and suddenly, I was hearing thoughts about their divorce." I shook my head. "And I . . . saw myself through your eyes at Notre Dame. I was in your mind, Fitz. I'm so sorry."

"Hey," he said softly. "It's all right. You didn't mean to do that."

I couldn't find my response.

"I think there's a connection between them," he said.

"What do you mean?"

"Every instance you recall is because you wanted insight. Who's watching me? Why is this person upset? And so on. Random information isn't coming to you—you're controlling the information you receive. We just need to figure out how you're calling them."

"I'm not asking for information, Fitz. That's what I'm saying. I'm not controlling this."

"You hear information you're curious about. Is it so hard to reason that your brain is asking for the information it receives? It seems logical to me."

"I just didn't think it would be that simple."

"You're close to the problem, so you're overthinking it."

I nodded, considering the new possibilities.

"That still leaves us with the biggest problem, though," I said. "I have no clue how I'm calling this information to myself. And I need to figure out how I even have this ability. I need to understand how it works if I'm going to control it."

Though Fitz's speech was casual enough, his nerves were wild.

"I'm going to help you figure that part out relatively easily."

I paused momentarily taking a deep breath to dispel the nervous energy that rushed into my body.

"How are you going to do that?" I asked.

"Well, here goes our one night without the bullshite."

"What are you talking about?"

Fitz sighed deeply. "Hadley . . . I'm a witch. And so are you."

CHAPTER NINE

My stomach turned.

Fitz's words hung in the air, which suddenly seemed lifeless and stale.

Witches and witchcraft didn't exist. They were ideas created from the back of someone's mind many years ago. They were fabricated excuses used to persecute innocent women. They were Halloween stories and the subject of books and films, but they weren't real.

I looked at Fitz. The man who stood before me was no storyteller. He was a lucid, intelligent man who held an esteemed position at one of the foremost educational institutions in the world. I searched for the threads of a lie but found none. Fitz wasn't lying, but his statement couldn't be true. My mind wouldn't allow it.

"Fitz, do you realize what you just said to me?"

"Aye, I do. I think you're in shock. Here, drink some water," he countered. He pulled out a water bottle.

"Where the hell did that come from?"

"Don't worry about that." He twisted the cap and extended the bottle in my direction.

"I'm just fine, and I don't need water. You can't say something like that and then tell me how to respond. You can't just show up in Paris and casually throw out, 'Oh hey, I'm a witch, and so are you.'" I paused. "On second thought, do you want to take it back?"

"No, I don't. You *are* a witch."

"Yes, I heard you. Loud and clear."

He arched an eyebrow.

"Oh, Fitz," I whispered. "Listen, I just . . . my parents aren't witches. There's no way. I would know if they were. And I don't have some magical powers, okay? I can . . . read minds. I know it's strange, but not strange enough to call me a witch."

"You're right about your parents not being witches. Your mum can't know about this. Do you understand?"

I found myself nodding before I realized the harm in playing along.

"Good," Fitz said. "And there's nothing strange about mind-reading. Or witches."

I looked around us, hoping to god no one was eavesdropping.

"Don't worry about them. No one can hear us." His eyes were wild, full of something bordering excitement.

"You say that so confidently."

"Oh aye."

I let out a slow, loud sigh, wondering how I was even supposed to approach a conversation like this. Fitz seemed to think we were discussing something completely normal.

"What have I gotten myself into?" I whispered under my breath.

Fitz stifled a laugh. I was borderline angry, and he was amused. It would've been just another day had he not uttered those unbelievable words only moments ago.

"I'll explain everything to you. I understand it's difficult to believe this after living twenty-nine years believing witches are just made-up stories, but this is no fabrication."

I thought about walking away. But some inexplicable force seemed to hold me in place as curiosity took over.

"For argument's sake, let's say that I believe witches exist. Which I don't," I clarified. "And that I believe I have my abilities because I am one. How could I be a witch?"

"Traditionally, witches are born into families of other witches. However, there's an occasional witch born into a family of humans. You've felt the difference your entire life, aye? It's one of the reasons you're so comfortable around me—why you were so comfortable around Izzy."

He gauged my expression before continuing. "We're not sure why it happens, but it appears to be some sort of genetic anomaly that shows itself after years of human ancestry. Somewhere down the line, there was a witch in your family tree."

I didn't see how Fitz could be right about all this, but if he was . . . then there was another person in my family who was like me. I wanted it to be true so badly it made my heart ache, but I knew that was ridiculous. I shook off the thought.

"It's not allowed, but that family member must've mated a human," Fitz said.

Mated . . . something about the term tugged at me.

"I see," I returned skeptically. "What happens with these newbie witches?"

"When they first show a sign of harboring powers, other witches are assigned to look after them until their powers are mature enough to access them. At that point, we're allowed to mentor the new witch as their power develops."

"So, you've what? Followed me?" I asked.

"Everyone in the family has an avid interest in keeping you safe. We monitor you through spells. We use spells that reveal where you are and how you're doing, but we're not physically present. If you were to run into trouble, we'd know immediately. Witches developing their powers tend to get themselves into interesting situations."

"So, your family was assigned to babysit me?"

"We were assigned to help you. My dad really is a university professor, but he also receives monitoring assignments from our council—our Scottish witchkind government—to monitor witches developing their powers. Izzy and I have trained with him, and we work with him from time to time."

Was I just some project to him? Was everything between us a lie? I wasn't so sure I wanted to know the answer to that.

"I don't need your protection," I said, turning to leave.

"Where are you going?" he asked.

"The hotel," I hissed and then froze.

The prickle working up my spine was undeniable. We were being watched.

"Oh, come *on*," Fitz spit out.

"Perfect timing."

"Well, you're not walking back alone."

We hurried down the sidewalk, not yet certain of our destination. Whoever was watching us, they didn't have good intentions. I could tell that much.

"If we walk around long enough, they'll lose interest. I think," Fitz said.

"And if they approach us?"

"I'm not sure. I don't think they will, though."

We turned down a less trafficked alleyway and picked up our pace, noticing the lack of witnesses.

We rounded the corner into a busier street near the Champs Elysées. The sidewalks were thick with crowds, and cars zipped down the streets. We tucked ourselves into an arched cove near an old, wooden door and pretended to be otherwise engaged. I focused on steadying my breathing, which was difficult with adrenaline coursing wildly through my veins. The seconds ticked by slowly, and after a while, I wondered if we'd lost our pursuers. But just as the question crossed my mind, two people passed our shelter. Their hooded jackets concealed much of their features, but I knew it was the people who'd been watching us.

Fitz's breath caught, signaling that he'd felt the same knowledge settle in. He gripped my hand, and we stepped from the doorway as prepared as we could be for whatever might follow. I met the gaze of our stalkers unabashedly, refusing to give any sign that I was afraid.

Their faces were impassible, but not their minds. They weren't anticipating a standoff. They held our gazes for mere seconds before sprinting off.

"That was . . . easy," I said.

"Too easy," Fitz said. "I don't suppose you heard anything useful?"

"Not really. They were surprised and didn't want a confrontation, but I have no idea why—my reception got a little fuzzy."

Fitz nodded thoughtfully.

"I'd feel better if I knew what they're after," I said.

"I agree. Something's not right about all this."

"Either way, let's get out of here?"

We walked the final stretch to the hotel in silence.

"Tell me everything," I demanded as we entered my room. "Clearly, there's a lot more you need to tell me than I thought."

Fitz entered the room calmly and took a seat on the bench. I stationed myself in front of him and crossed my arms.

"Okay, what do you want to know?" Fitz asked.

"Anything, Fitz. Everything. *What am I?*"

His response wasn't immediate, which allowed enough time for me to change my mind.

"Actually . . . wait," I said. "Show me magic first. I want to see it. I need to see it."

"You believe me, then?"

I struggled with the words, and I finally just nodded.

He looked toward the small, built-in desk across the room, and his eyes rested on a half-peeled orange. With his thumb and first two fingers slightly extended, he flicked his wrist, and the orange hovered in the air.

A brief intake of air was all that betrayed my surprise—I felt the blank expression still resting on my face. He looked at me from the corner of his eye and then returned his focus to the orange. With another flick, the peel unwound itself, as if it were the work of invisible hands, and floated into the trash can.

And with one final flick, the perfectly peeled fruit floated across the room, stopping in front of me.

"Hold out your hand," Fitz said softly.

I followed his direction, and the orange dropped into my open palm.

"Good god," I said. It was all I could manage. And when I looked up, I was met by an inscrutable expression. "Okay now, tell me everything."

He sighed. "I think we should get some rest and pick this up tomorrow."

"You think I can fall asleep after your little display?" I said as I stifled a yawn, and Fitz narrowed his eyes at me.

"I'm done in, Hads. You're exhausted—and don't try to deny it."

I looked at the clock beside my bed. 3 a.m.

"Fine," I said. "But we're discussing this as soon as we wake up."

I walked Fitz to the door.

His eyes flickered to my lips, and I wondered if he was fighting against his willpower the same way I was struggling with mine. There was so much I needed to know, so much I needed to understand.

But in that moment, the only thing I could think about was how badly I wanted to feel his body pressed against mine, how badly I wanted reassurance that we were more than just a project to him.

Tension swirled through the air.

The desire consumed me. Fitz's head tilted slightly, and my eyes lingered across his face.

Fitz wrapped me in his arms, and the ache in my chest eased ever so slightly.

Progress, I thought.

As he released me, his hands slid to either side of my face, and a dull pulse echoed across my skin. He looked deeply into my eyes before planting a slow kiss on my forehead.

"Goodnight, Hadley."

Fitz released me into a restless night, sleep eluding my troubled mind. I wrestled with myself for hours before finally deciding that despite the lack of a true scientific explanation, everything pointed to Fitz being truthful.

I'd wondered my entire life why I was different.

Had Fitz finally given me the answer?

CHAPTER TEN

Fitz smiled as he entered my room the following morning, but he couldn't hide the tension radiating through our connection. Dressed in dark jeans and an ivory sweater, he was as put together as ever, though his disheveled hair was a telltale sign he'd been stressed. Fitz sank into the oversized chair in the corner of the room.

"So, what's on the agenda for today?" I asked.

"You and your wee agendas."

"Tease all you want. But I want to know."

"I thought about going through your questions over lunch. But I'm not sure if it's safe for us to go out or not. I think we should stay in."

"Well, we can't just lock ourselves in our rooms," I said.

"Right, but we had people stalk us around the city last night."

"Yeah, I was there."

"Check the attitude, Hads. You really think we should go back out there and risk it?"

"These aren't the government people who normally follow you?"

"Aye, and that worries me."

"I get that. But these people knew how to find us at Notre Dame and again after dinner. If they don't know where we're staying, it's only a matter of time. I don't think being out in public puts us at more risk."

Fitz narrowed his eyes in thought.

"I'm not saying this doesn't worry me—it does," I clarified. "But we're probably just as safe out in the crowds as we are sitting in this room."

Fitz nodded slowly.

"Tell me what you know about these people," I said.

"All I know is they're different," Fitz said.

"You're *certain* this isn't the government?"

"This isn't how they operate. They wouldn't be chasing us around Paris. Their visit would be much more . . . official."

A chill ran down my spine.

Fitz continued. "And I lost them when I left Edinburgh. They haven't found us."

"You said 'witchkind' government' yesterday . . ." I trailed off.

"Aye, we have our own government in witchkind. They're the ones who mandated we stay apart."

"Why?"

"They weren't certain your full set of powers would materialize," he said. "They told me to stay away from you unless that changed."

"Because?"

"Because humans aren't allowed to know about us. Until we knew you'd come into your powers, they thought I was putting witchkind at risk."

"That's ridiculous."

"I'm fully aware, trust me."

His nerves resurfaced in my body. My mind was spinning as we both danced around the things we needed to say but didn't yet know how.

"Whatever it is that's holding you back . . . let go of it. Please, just talk to me," I said.

Fitz sat forward in the chair and rested his chin on his hand. I leaned against the wall granting him time to roll through his thoughts, and when he raised his gaze to mine, the resolve in his eyes was clear.

"I've thought through this a million times trying to decide the best way to explain it all. Turns out, there isn't one." I nodded in encouragement for him to continue. "The truth is you need to understand what we're facing. And you need to decide if you're willing to take this risk."

"Okay . . ."

"You're safe from the government right now. I'm confident they haven't found us. But that won't last." He paused. "Until you match with your powers, you're still considered a human by the councils' definition."

"What do you mean by match?" I asked.

"Your powers are trying to settle into you—that's why you have your abilities. But to become a true witch, your power needs to fully enmesh with your mind and body."

"You think I'll match," I said.

"I feel it, Hadley. You'll match."

I nodded.

"But if the councils catch us before you match, they'll erase your memories of me."

"*What?*"

Fitz shook his head. "I know how that sounds. But it's true. And if they were to do that to you . . . I'm afraid it would meddle with other memories I'm associated with."

"All of our time at the lake . . ." The first time Fitz had met Daddy; that night we stayed up to see the sunrise with Izzy; the base camp hike we did with Jordan and Tanner.

"And I don't know how far they'd take it . . . But they wouldn't take the risk of your family and friends bringing up my name, I don't think."

"So, they'd erase their memories of you too? We'd forget it all?"

"Aye. Or they might leave their memories intact and relocate you after erasing your memories. It's impossible to say which option they'd lean toward."

"They can't do that."

"They can," Fitz said. "If they catch us, they'll do whatever they deem necessary to protect witchkind."

Erasing my memories was bad enough, but I couldn't allow that to happen to my loved ones.

"And what about you?" I asked.

"It depends," Fitz said. "There have been many different penalties given in the past from imprisonment to mandatory government service, but . . . they've also spellbound witches. If they feel it fits the crime."

"Spellbind? They'd take your powers?"

Fitz's gaze dropped to the ground. "They'd ensure I couldn't access them."

I shook my head. "No. That can't happen. I need to match to my powers. That's the solution to all this."

"Hadley . . . there's no guarantee that they wouldn't spellbind both of us as punishment."

I paused. "I see."

"There's little that's worse for a witch than to be separated from our magic. I won't lie to you: It would be horrific. It would be losing a vital part of yourself." Fitz's nerves fluttered through me. "Think about all this and what you want."

I started to speak, but Fitz was faster. "No . . . don't answer right now. Really think about it. This is your future, Hadley."

I sighed. "Fine."

"I'll bet you have loads of questions. And rightfully so. You should learn everything possible, so you'll make an informed decision." He sighed, and his brows knitted together. "But I'm having trouble concentrating in here. Your energy is everywhere."

"Let's go somewhere else then."

"I know a place for lunch. Let's get a proper meal—and some caffeine, and I'll answer all your questions."

I chose an open-air café for our excursion, and it turned out to be the perfect spot to work our way through lunch. The bittersweet changing of the seasons was apparent in the crisp air, and I tilted my face toward the sky seeking the direction of the sun. I refilled my coffee cup, realizing it was my only hope to combat the jetlag that compounded my lack of sleep, as I watched the passersby stroll along the old stone street.

Though the conversation with Fitz had been sobering, I was eager to leave the hotel and see more of Paris. I wanted to commit the feel of Paris to memory, knowing I would miss the energy of the city when I left.

I reached for a croissant and leveled my gaze at Fitz. "I have questions."

"Let's hear them."

"I guess my biggest question right now is . . ." I studied the man across from me, searching his eyes, wondering again if the feelings between us were real. The question almost escaped my lips, but I asked about witchcraft instead. "What am I? I mean, what am I capable of? What can I do?"

"Well, truthfully, I can't answer that question. Every witch has different abilities. You're very close to matching with your magic—I feel your power so clearly—and once you do, we'll test your abilities and see where your strengths lie. But based on the feel of your energy, you're an elemental witch."

"What does that mean—elemental?"

"There are two types of witches: elemental witches and spell casters. Spell casters are exactly what they sound like. They're witches who use spells to work their magic. But you and I are elementals. We don't require spells to connect with the elements. We're in constant communion with them, and our powers link directly with the elements to work our magic."

"The elements . . . like air or water?" I asked.

"Air, water, fire, earth, the moon . . . witches gather power from all the elements, but elemental witches are especially influenced by one particular element. Mine is earth—once you match to your powers, we'll know yours,"

"So, I'll connect to the elements, and I won't use spells?"

"In certain cases, you will. Elemental magic isn't the best choice for every need."

"Oh, right. You said you used spells to keep an eye on me," I recalled.

"Aye. It was easier and less invasive that way."

"Is one type of witch more powerful than the other?"

"Elementals are usually more powerful than casters," Fitz said. "A caster can't work elemental magic, but an elemental can work spells."

I nodded. "Do we need . . . wands?"

Fitz chuckled. "No, Hollywood. No wands required for either type of witch."

"Pointy black hats?"

"Myth. Do I look like a pointy hat-wearing witch to you?"

"I'm sure you'd look dashing in a pointy black hat."

Fitz shook his head playfully.

"Brooms?" I asked.

"Only for sweeping the floors."

"Are you a warlock? A wizard? Or is 'witch' the correct term?"

"Please never ask me that again." Fitz grimaced. "A wizard sounds like an eccentric old bloke with a celestial robe who reads spell books covered with cobwebs."

I laughed. "What about crystals, palm readers, tarot cards—all that stuff?"

A frown blanketed his features. "Crystals are accurately represented in human culture, but the rest . . . it's all tied to potential witches who never matched to their powers. Gifted humans, essentially."

"Basically, me if I don't match."

"You'll match."

His certainty gave me a little hope, but I couldn't ignore the doubts that nipped at the back of my mind.

What if he was wrong about me and I couldn't match to my power? What if he was forced to leave again? What if he left anyway?

I sighed. "Any of the witch legend true?"

"We're powerful," Fitz said. "We can manipulate the elements and bring fantasy to life. But we're as diverse as humans. We're not stereotypes."

I nodded. "What are some of the things elemental witches can do?"

"We control the elements to a certain degree—produce fire, work the air around us. Some are like you and hear thoughts, others are are time-walkers. Some speak with spirits of the departed or influence the weather—the list goes on."

"Time-walkers, like time travel? Speaking with spirits? Seriously?"

"Mm-hmm."

I was dumbfounded.

"This is loads of information, I know."

I nodded thoughtfully.

Fitz placed his hand on top of mine, and a surge from our unspoken connection flowed between us.

"Seriously, Fitz, why do we feel this energy? And don't you *dare* tell me you don't know."

"You won't like this," he began, his lip twitching. "But I don't know. I always feel when I'm coming into contact with another witch.

I feel the difference in the air, and my chemistry reacts differently than when I interact with a human—and that's normal. But when I make contact with you, it's electric."

I nodded.

"I researched this while we were apart."

"Did you find anything?"

He shook his head. "I think it has to do with your powers stirring. I still don't understand why, but there must be a correlation."

I opened my mouth to respond, but I couldn't seem to find the words. A prickle worked its way up my spine like an assault of hundreds of tiny needles. Fitz's eyes widened before he regained his composure.

"This feels like more than one person watching us."

"Aye, and their energy is familiar."

"Oh," I said, as the realization settled in. "It's the same people from before."

Fitz nodded. "Let's go."

CHAPTER ELEVEN

We slid into the backseat of a gray taxicab waiting just outside of a nearby museum. The driver set down his newspaper and asked for our destination.

"We need to drive toward Sacré-Cœur but without taking a direct route."

Our driver glanced suspiciously at Fitz in the rearview mirror.

"We're being followed," Fitz said. "If that makes you uncomfortable, we'll call another car."

"It's been a while since I've had some fun."

And there it was again—the driver's thoughts entered my mind as if he'd spoken aloud. A slew of memories flashed through my mind of cars zipping through the streets of Paris.

"Oh, damn," I muttered under my breath.

Fitz shot a questioning glance my way.

The driver slammed on the gas, and we sped away from the museum.

A sign hung from the front passenger seat. The second row of text was in English. "Welcome. Your driver is Adebayo."

I hoped Adebayo was up for a challenge.

"What are they driving?" Adebayo questioned, a heavy accent rolling from his lips.

"The silver Peugeot," I answered, garnering a raised eyebrow from Fitz. "What? You think you're the only observant one in this car?"

"Can you make that turn?" Fitz asked.

Our driver laughed, shaking his head. "Can I make that turn? Of course, I can."

And indeed, he did—at a record speed, I was sure. I slid across the seat into Fitz. He shouted, laughing, and braced himself against the door, his head nearly slamming into the window.

As we rounded the block, a farmer's market came into view. Pedestrians were scattered through the street browsing the market. Shoppers' hands were full of everything from paper bags to ice cream cones as they dawdled along the stalls. I scanned the block searching for an exit but came up short.

Adebayo's eyes narrowed in concentration. "Brace yourselves!"

Fitz pulled me closer and prepared for whatever followed.

Several things happened at once.

Mass chaos ensued in the market. A young woman holding a tasting cup in front of a stall selling honey released a blood-curdling scream. Shoppers ran toward what they hoped was safety as Adebayo pumped the breaks and turned the wheel. The tires screeched as they slid against the pavement, but the car made a U-turn in the the middle of the street. Adebayo's execution was nearly flawless, but the backend of the car clipped the corner of a stall. The car made impact with a loud bang that echoed through the street.

Several small thuds sounded against the roof of the car before lemons, oranges, and berries rolled down the windshield and into the street.

"Did we just hit a fruit stand?" I asked incredulously.

Fitz chuckled. "Here we go!"

"Hold on tight!" Adebayo called.

Adebayo slammed on the gas once again, and the tires spun out. We took off in the direction from which we'd come.

The silver Peugeot was speeding down the street, but it slammed on brakes and angled itself in an attempt to halt our progress. Adebayo sped up and clipped the front corner of the Peugeot. The car spun, and we turned down the nearest street. Fitz and I turned to watch the corner, and sure enough: the dented silver car came into view.

Adebayo smirked. "Don't worry. I have the perfect spot to lose them."

I held tighter to Fitz's arm, which was wrapped around me, and he rested his hand on mine. The shock was uncomfortable at first, but I adjusted quicker than expected. Apprehension hit the pit of my stomach as I looked at our hands. What were we doing?

A tight alleyway came into focus, and I instantly knew the plan. Fitz and I braced ourselves as best we could, and Adebayo turned our car into the small space with precision. The Peugeot, however, was less fortunate. The driver couldn't make the turn and slammed unceremoniously into the building. Smoke rose from the car, and before I could even react, we were back on a main road.

"Brilliant," Fitz said. "I don't know how you pulled that off."

Adebayo smiled. "I grew up racing these streets with my cousins. I've outdriven many cars."

Our fearless driver turned down a narrow alleyway and positioned the car out of sight.

"We lost them. But you should walk through this building and call a different car to pick you up on that next street."

"Adebayo, my friend. A job well done," Fitz exclaimed.

He grinned. "It's been a while since I had excitement like that. Just like James Bond."

Fitz slid a card into Adebayo's hand. "Call this number, and we'll set things right with your motor."

They shook hands warmly before we followed his instructions. Since we'd lost our pursuers, we requested that the new driver take us straight back to our hotel in the 1st arrondissement.

We entered the hotel through a back entrance, making our way quietly to my room. Fitz secured the extra lock on the door, and I pulled the curtains closed.

"Maybe we should cancel our dinner plans," Fitz said.

I sighed as I slid into a nearby chair. "I hate this."

Fitz eyed me sympathetically. His energy stirred.

"What is it?" I asked.

"I've known what I wanted from the beginning, and everything

I'm going through is worth it to protect you. But the stakes are high—you don't have to do this, Hadley. You can walk away from all this at any point."

"You might like that," I said.

"What are you talking about?"

"Would it make it easier on you if I did?" I asked. "Or would it just mess up your 'project?'"

"Do you really think you're a project to me?"

"Aren't I? I mean, you were assigned to monitor me."

"And what? I can't have fallen for you?" He laughed, but there was little humor in it. "Don't give me that much credit."

I shook my head. "I'm so confused."

Fitz's eyes softened. He knelt in front of the chair and took my hands in his. The shock was less intense than before. I was about to let go when a tremor worked its way from my fingertips throughout my body. I looked up from our linked hands to find Fitz's quizzical brow. Then energy blew through my veins like a gust of wind, momentarily stealing my breath. Fitz's emotions settled deep within me, and his pain was jarring.

I doubled over. "What the hell is going on?"

"I have no idea." Fitz said, his voice strained.

Fitz moved toward the gray linen bench and rested his elbows on his knees and breathed deeply. I followed his rhythm of breathing, and our heart rates slowed.

"I feel you so clearly," he said.

"It wasn't as strong as it used to be . . . until now."

"Aye. I noticed that too."

"I was worried. I guess I still am. I don't know what all this means."

Fitz nodded. "There's one source I haven't consulted. I could ask the government about it."

"No."

"I could phrase it as a lingering question from our previous time together. It might be worth the risk."

"We changed our lives for how long? For you to compromise yourself now? They'll know why you're asking. No, we won't go to the government. We'll find another way."

"There might not be another."

Silence fell.

"Does it bother you? Or scare you? That you can feel me so clearly?" he asked.

"Maybe it should, but . . ."

"What is it?"

"It's probably going to sound too weird," I said.

"Well, now you have to say it."

I groaned. "Okay. It's just that . . . whatever this connection is that we have, well, it feels normal to me. Natural, even. Feeling your emotions inside of me, carrying that knowledge of you . . . it just feels like it should be that way. When our connection was strained during our time apart, honestly, it freaked me out."

"It's the same for me. Don't you know that?"

I closed my eyes briefly, thinking.

"I know you're confused," Fitz went on. "I know this is unbelievable. But please don't question how I feel about you. My feelings for you have never faltered—not once."

There was no lie in his statement, not even the tiniest wisp of a thread. Fitz was being truthful, and finally, I decided I had to trust in his words.

I crossed the room and sat near Fitz. I timidly reached for his hand. The surge lessened, and I tightened my grip.

"This is our normal, I guess."

Fitz nodded. "Perhaps."

"We'll figure it out eventually."

"I want to find a way around the whole shocking bit. If we can navigate that, then I'm good," he said.

"Me too."

Fitz stood. "I'll be back. I'm going to have the hotel move our rooms next to each other."

"Speaking of which, the front desk wouldn't let me add a card to my room," I said.

"Aye, it's taken care of," Fitz said.

"Let me know the cost. I need to pay you back."

"Nae bother. We're good."

Fitz hadn't let me pay for anything . . . not since I'd met him. I wondered how money never seemed to be an issue for him.

"Oh, and I do think if we go out to dinner, it'll throw off whoever is watching us," Fitz said. "If we don't make sense to them, all the better for us. We'll be vigilant."

"Do you think they'll expect us to carry on like normal?"

He tapped his finger on the wooden desk. "I'd wager they're waiting for us to run."

"Eventually, though . . . that's what we'll have to do, isn't it?"

"Truthfully, I don't know. But you and I will decide what comes next—together."

CHAPTER TWELVE

Fitz would only share that we'd dine at a Parisian staple that evening—and that he planned to wear a suit. It took longer to dress than I cared to admit. I studied my reflection in the bathroom mirror, nervous about my newly acquired little black dress and how snugly it fit against my body.

I wondered if Fitz and I were making a mistake by going out for the evening. A deep breath escaped my lips as I tugged at the sleeves around my wrists and the hemline hugging my thighs, knowing my anxiety would flare higher the longer I sat idle. I slipped on the black heels I'd packed for job interviews and touched up my eyeliner and lipstick, keeping both my hands and mind occupied. A knock at the adjoining door startled me.

My heart rate quickened, and I opened the large, wooden door to find Fitz leaning against the doorframe. Dressed in a gray suit and a black cashmere sweater, he looked as handsome as ever. This man would be the death of me.

"You are . . . stunning," he said.

I was gratified by the dumbfounded look on his face. "Thank you. You look pretty good yourself."

"I had a witty line prepared, but I've lost it just now," he said.

"Well, hurry up and find it. I want to hear this."

"Oh aye?" He straightened up, cleared his throat, and offered me his hand. "Hi, I'm Fitz. I'll be your tour guide this evening."

I laughed, shaking his hand, and the afternoon's tension seemed to dissipate with our touch.

Soon we were again exploring the streets of Paris, the lights of Rue de Rivoli guiding us toward our destination. We walked in companionable silence, taking in the bustling streets saturated with happy tourists and well-dressed diners.

The night was intoxicating with the hum of activity, the sights around the Louvre, the cool breeze against our skin, and no signs of being under watch. Fitz carefully placed my hand in the crook of his arm and offered a timid smile in my direction.

"Gentleman," I said.

We turned down a heavily trafficked street which was illuminated by the warm light of streetlamps and the lanterns lining the buildings on either side.

And in a sea of beige, one section stood out amongst the rest: a dark wooden facade with a red banner. As we neared the entrance, I gasped. Maxim's de Paris. A Parisian staple indeed. The distractions of modern-day Paris fell away as we entered the world of Art Nouveau, a timeless dream.

I looked around distractedly. From writers to actors to musicians, this space had captivated the imagination of creatives for over a century. I'd dreamed about visiting the famed restaurant for years—and Fitz knew it.

Beautiful murals decorated the walls, intricately detailed columns and molding adorned the dining rooms, white tablecloths were spread across small tables . . . all cast in a dim haze of soft crimson. It was overwhelming.

"I'm not big on surprises, but this one . . . well done, Fitz," I said as we took our seats.

"I'm glad we could check this one off your list. I've not been here before either. This is grand."

Our waiter pointed out the table where President and First Lady Kennedy had dined during their visit, and he shared stories about everyone from Grace Kelly to Marion Cotillard, all of whom had dined in the magnificent establishment. A tuxedo-clad man crooned classic jazz tunes from a stage across the room, and soon enough, the music of Frank Sinatra and the Rat Pack morphed into the soundtrack of our evening.

"What's in this dish?" I asked, stabbing at one of the mysterious ingredients with my fork. I'd asked Fitz to choose an appetizer, but I was questioning whether that might have been a poor choice.

Fitz grinned at my reaction. "Go on. Take a wee bite."

"Absolutely not. I'm not putting that in my mouth until you tell me what it is."

"Stubborn as always."

"Part of my charm, right?" I asked.

"Oh, sure."

The waiter approached our table. "And how is everything tasting?"

"It's wonderful," Fitz said.

"And the appetizer? Is it to your satisfaction?" he asked, his gaze settling on me.

"Oh, absolutely." I smiled.

"Very well. Please, enjoy."

"*Escargots aux noix*" sounded through my mind.

"You sneak," I said. "I should've paid more attention when you were ordering."

"What?" Fitz asked.

"It has snails in it," I whispered.

"How did . . ." He paused. "Did you read the waiter's mind?"

"Don't look at me like that. It's not like I meant to."

Fitz laughed. "Aye, it has snails in it. But it also has walnuts, white wine, lemon juice . . . It's a fine dish."

I sighed and took another sip of wine. "When in Paris, I guess."

I took a tentative bite, and surprisingly, I couldn't argue with Fitz.

"Okay, it's pretty good," I conceded. "I think I mostly taste the lemon and spices. Parsley and . . . nutmeg, I think."

"Look at you being adventurous."

I narrowed my eyes, but he only smirked.

Food and wine kept our conversation light while we finished the appetizer, but once we ate our way into the main course, I decided to learn more about our situation.

"So, your dad doesn't know where we are?" The thought of Ian potentially knowing our location unnerved me. I didn't think he would betray his own son, but his work with the government bothered me.

"No, and it's to protect us both. It would place him in a compromising position if he knew more. Henry is the only one aware of our location."

"Your mysterious best friend." Fitz had mentioned Henry several times at the lake, and I longed to meet him.

"Aye, that's him. We've been running our own reconnaissance."

"What do you mean by that exactly?"

"Since we parted at the lake, I've built a network. Dad, Henry, and our friend Isaac partnered with me to research everything about witches acquiring their powers and about the witchkind government. Henry works in finance, so he also helped me with investments and properly allocating resources to fall off the government's radar. We knew the only way I could break the government's rules was to know them well and to be prepared for anything that followed."

"Wow . . ."

Fitz nodded. "We have loads of information."

"It still bothers me that you didn't tell me all this at the lake. I wish I had known."

Fitz sighed, setting his wine glass on the table. "I'm sorry. I was sorting things out as I went along. I didn't know what knowledge might put you in more danger, and I didn't want to risk the councils erasing your memories. And I didn't know what would make you more anxious, or even fearful. To lay that burden on you and then have to separate . . ." He paused, pursing his lips while deep in thought.

"Still," I said, "I think it would have been better for me to know the complete truth."

"Hadley, if I had crossed that line before I had the proper resources in place, we would have sunken quickly. So, what was the alternative? I tell you you're a witch who can't match to her powers yet and I'm leaving but don't worry because the witchkind government won't come after you to erase your memories as long as I'm gone, but they'll be watching us to ensure we stay apart?"

I squeezed my eyes shut.

"You forget how well I know you," Fitz said. "That would not have ended well. I know this was still a disruption to your life, but the alternative . . ."

I pushed my risotto around absentmindedly with my fork. "Fine. I see your point."

"I am truly sorry for what this did to you. I'm sorry that I didn't tell you. But I hope you know that every decision I've made has been for you. I would do anything to keep you safe, no matter the cost."

Fitz's honesty softened my anger.

He continued. "I can't say that I'd do everything the same way again—of course, I wouldn't—but what's done is done. In some instances, there were no better choices than the ones that I made. But for the others I could have handled better, all I ask now is that you forgive me."

"Forgiven. I know it was a big burden to carry. But don't keep things from me in the future."

"You have my word."

Dessert came and, in the midst of chocolate cake, I posed my next question. "Fitz, what happens next? My time here is almost over. I board the train tomorrow afternoon for London."

"Right. I'd like to travel with you and begin your training if you're comfortable with it? Help you get matched to your power."

"Yeah. I'd like that," I said.

"Good. I'll make my arrangements."

"How are you able to take time off like this during the semester?"

"I'm not teaching this semester," Fitz said. "I've been doing loads of field research in the Highlands, working from there or from Edinburgh. Or Paris, as it were. I'm building a new course exploring the policies of King James I and how his prejudice polluted his kingdom for centuries."

"I'll bet there's a connection to witchcraft," I said.

"He had a lot of blood on his hands. We'll explore the effects he had on 16th and 17th century life in Scotland, along with his influence on religion."

"I'll be the first to sign up for your class, Dr. MacGregor."

"I'd be honored, Ms. Weston."

"But for now, I think it's time for a change in scenery. You still have an Eiffel Tower to show me."

"Let's go."

The cab deposited us below one of the most iconic structures in the world. The Eiffel Tower stretched high above us, and I craned my neck to take in the sight. Luckily, the line was short, and I soon found myself ascending the attraction with my adventurous escort. My breath was labored when we reached our destination, but not only from the exercise. I'd seen countless photos of the historic landmark, but nothing prepared me for the grandeur of the experience. We gazed at the countless lights of the city, the cool evening air granting us vitality as we soaked in the view.

We wandered around the top of the tower, navigating past the summit's champagne bar and the line of excited patrons awaiting their celebratory flutes. The wind was a bit cold, and I regretted leaving my warmer coat behind. No sooner had I expressed that sentiment to Fitz than he had us huddled in a corner.

"What are we doing?" I whispered.

"Just wait," he said.

He glanced around casually and once he was satisfied no one was watching, he moved his hand in a circular motion.

Then, he extended his arm, which turned transparent, and he pulled my coat out of thin air.

My jaw dropped. When I'd slightly recovered, I looked around. Fitz found my response thoroughly amusing.

"What if someone saw you?" I asked.

"No one saw. I used concealment. A human wouldn't have any idea unless they were standing right here with us."

I was speechless.

"Here," he said, holding out my coat.

I turned, and he helped me slide my arms into the sleeves. He then pulled me into his arms, and I rested my head on his chest.

My body was wired from the excitement of watching him use his magic, but as he held me in his arms, I was lulled into a state of perfect happiness, calm and sure. I smiled as we created a memory I would always remember, the type of moment people tell their grandchildren about, eyes closed, recalling how alive they felt.

Fitz and I grabbed drinks from the Bar à Champagne and found a less crowded corner to enjoy the views. We shared more about our time apart, both hungry for details of the other's lives, completely lost in the stories only we could tell. And eventually, our conversation meandered to the first moments of our reunion at Notre Dame.

"I dreamed about that moment for a long time," Fitz said.

"And did you also dream about us lighting each other up like a Christmas tree?" I asked, recalling the intensity of the shock.

"Well, I must say, things went a little smoother in my dreams."

"How boring then. I guess reality really is better than fantasy sometimes."

Fitz's laugh was genuine and unguarded, and a piece of my soul healed at the sound.

"I dreamed about that moment too. More than I should have," I admitted.

Silence fell, and Fitz reached for my hand, holding it in both of his own. A surge of energy followed our contact, but I found that it wasn't painful, as though we were readjusting to each other.

Fitz ran his fingers across the moonstone on my finger. "You kept the ring. It's one of the first things I noticed."

"I couldn't seem to take it off. I . . . feel better when I wear it."

He nodded. "It's charged with my energy."

"What do you mean?"

"The day I gifted it to you, Izzy suggested I channel some of my energy into the stone. She thought it might bring you comfort while we were apart."

"She was right . . . as usual." I paused. "You thought of every-thing, didn't you?"

"I did what I could. It wasn't enough, but it was all I could offer you."

His eyes were troubled—filled with memories—and I leaned into him, hoping my touch might quiet his pain. He wrapped his arms around me, and we fell silent as we gazed at the lights scattered on the horizon.

I wasn't sure how long we stood there, suspended above the city, reveling in the rediscovery of our long-lost companionship. At some late hour, we paused to appreciate the light show sparkling all around us before descending the tower in search of a sweet nighttime snack.

We were close to abandoning our search when we finally happened upon a small bakery. The owner was pleased to pause his closing tasks, supply us with end-of-day chocolate croissants, and bid us adieu as we wandered back into the dim evening streets. We ate in comfortable silence, happy to stay in that moment as long as it would allow, until the gold and maroon hallways of our hotel welcomed us home.

Fitz and I did a quick sweep of our rooms before deciding we were safe for the evening.

Anxiety bubbled as I thought about parting ways for the night.

"What's wrong, Hads?"

"Nothing's wrong. Are you tired, or do you want a nightcap?" I questioned.

"I have a bottle of Glenfiddich in my room. Care for a wee dram?"

"Yes, please."

Fitz retrieved the bottle while I rounded up a couple glasses, and we ended up on a blanket on the floor, leaned up against the bed, glasses in hand.

"I didn't want to bring this up at dinner the other night, but I want to clarify something," he said.

My heartbeat quickened—and so did Fitz's.

"When you mentioned your dad's passing . . . I didn't stay away. I came to the funeral home."

"You what?"

"I did. I needed to see you, to do what I could to help you. But I never made it inside." He laughed without humor. "I even saw you in there." He paused, clearing his throat. "I'm sorry I couldn't be there."

I scooted closer and placed my hand on his. He held on to it tightly, a flurry of anguish and regret floating through our connection.

"What happened?" I asked.

"A few of my father's colleagues showed up. They'd foreseen my decision and were waiting to see if I would go in or if I'd change my mind. As I was reaching for the handle, one of them called my name."

"They came to stop you."

"Aye. According to them, I let things go a little too far at the lake."

"How did they know that?" I asked.

"The councils are eager to understand how situations like yours occur, so our evaluations were detailed, and the councils agents checked in daily." Fitz sighed. "From one of Dad's reports, an agent realized members of the family were growing closer to you than normal."

"They figured out it was a relationship between us."

"And an agent was on our doorstep within a day of that report being submitted. Truthfully, we didn't realize it would be an issue. We believed you'd match—we never saw you as human. But the councils clearly didn't see it that way and they reminded me that a witch and a human being together is strictly forbidden."

"So, they tried to remove you from my case and separate us."

"Aye. They wanted me to leave and allow Dad and Izzy to finish the observation after I felt our connection. The councils expected I'd try to see you again if you went through a major trial before your powers developed, or even if they didn't."

"Well, they were right about one thing, then. They knew we'd eventually do what we've done."

"They knew I couldn't help it, the bastards."

"So, what happened at the funeral?" I asked.

"They reiterated the *reasons* to keep my distance and told me to be patient, to let things run their course. It was harder to walk away from the funeral home than it was to watch you leave for Boston. I thought that was going to kill me."

I paused, collecting my thoughts.

"Thank you," I finally said.

"For?"

"For trying to be there. For being honest with me."

Fitz nodded.

"I don't like that the councils try to dictate who we're involved with," I said. "Just look at our situation; it was pointless. Why do they do this?"

His expression darkened. "As long as it isn't a human, they don't care. They're terrified about our secret getting out."

"Do you think they're right about that?"

"I understand their worry, and at the same time, I don't," Fitz said. "Humans are unpredictable. I understand the councils' fear of them, but you can't control the lives of witches and humans like this. They were wrong about us—that's a fact."

"It feels like they paid special attention to us. I mean, showing up at my dad's funeral was disrespectful. I just don't understand why our relationship bothered them so much."

"They *really* want me to follow in my father's footsteps. I need to be the kind of witch who adheres to the rules for that to happen."

"Is that what you want?"

"Doesn't matter. They haven't forced anything yet, but I've had a feeling for a long time that it'll all come to a head one day. Now I'm sure of it."

I squeezed his hand. "Well, if it happens, I'll support you no matter what—as long as you want me in your life."

"The only way you'll get rid of me now is if you send me away," he said.

"I've been waiting for you to tell me this is temporary," I admitted, "that you're going to have to disappear again."

He paused. "Hadley, I'm not strong enough to go through that again."

Our emotions muddled together as they swirled through me.

"It still worries me," I said.

"I didn't have a choice back then, but I do now."

"And that's not going to change?"

"No, it won't," Fitz said. "I've been ready for a fight since the beginning. But we weren't prepared—we didn't have the resources, and I didn't fully understand what we were up against. But being here, together, this will change everything."

"I'm ready for whatever comes. I'm exhausted from the secrecy—from being apart."

"To be clear, I still don't know the full consequences of all this. They might go easy on us; they might not. But either way, you know the risk we're taking now."

"To hell with the consequences," I said. "We'll find a way to beat the councils."

"It's easy to say that now."

"Maybe. But this phase of our lives is over. It has to be."

Fitz nodded.

"You said something that's been on my mind," I said. "You keep using the word 'mates.'. . .Fitz, is that what's happening between us?"

Fitz exhaled slowly, and as his eyes narrowed in concentration, his energy fluttered wildly through me. "Aye. I've thought that was the case since the moment I laid eyes on you."

"What does that mean exactly?"

"Witches often refer to their partners as mates, though it's really the same thing—only amplified."

"Amplified how?"

"When we find the person we're meant to be with, it's an incredibly strong connection."

"Is that why we feel each other's emotions?" I asked.

"Aye, I've observed it with other mates. The emotions seem normal."

"But not the shocking?"

"No," Fitz said.

I nodded.

He continued. "I think when you match to your power, our connection will intensify."

I placed my hand behind his neck and looked squarely into his eyes. "Good."

Fitz kissed my forehead tenderly, but when he pulled back, his features grew stormy. He tugged my body closer to him, one hand resting on my waist as the other cradled the base of my skull. My arms slid across his back, and instead of the jarring shock I anticipated, warmth pulsed through my veins like a vibrant life-source was channeling between the two of us. My heart raced as his eyes searched mine. He slipped a finger under my chin—holding my gaze until I was certain of his intentions—before dipping his head slowly and deliberately, as though he knew the prolonged moment would only make me want it more. To his credit, it was working.

As his lips found mine, electricity coursed through my body, chills rippling across my skin. My eyes popped open, and I found that his had done the same, both of us wired with the shock. My senses were heightened. Every touch, every feeling intensified until they outweighed the pain. Our grip tightened, and we continued to explore each other a few moments longer. He drew back as gently and deliberately as he had approached, eyes closed as he drank in the last intimacies of the moment.

"I'll remind you every single day just how much I want you in my life, even after you finally come to believe it," he whispered.

CHAPTER THIRTEEN

The following afternoon, I was seated next to Fitz somewhere high above Paris. The train had been my humble suggestion, but Henry had arranged a private flight for us. Though it felt extravagant, it had provided Fitz with the means to lose the witchkind spies in Edinburgh. Whoever was following us in Paris was about to receive the same treatment.

Sipping whisky on our brief path over the English Channel, my thoughts darted mercilessly around my exhausted mind. I was nervous to open my eyes and see the world for what it truly was and not for what I previously believed it to be.

But another feeling beat fiercely against the first for control. It bubbled up, refusing defeat: I was excited.

I recalled the little girl I once had been—the girl who was confident there was more to her than her human facade. A twinge of sadness accompanied the recollection.

By the time I'd reached adulthood, cynicism had crept into my bones and stolen my sense of wonder.

"What are you thinking about?" Fitz asked.

"My childhood."

Fitz swirled the whisky in his glass, his eyes distant. "You always knew who you were, Hads. You and your power have been trying to connect with each other for years. Your magic was already awakening you."

"Awakening me?"

"From an ordinary life. You were never meant to be normal."

Perhaps he was right. I needed to search inside myself to uncover that little girl and her unwavering belief.

Fitz leaned over, whispering. "Once you find that faith in yourself again, you'll be unstoppable."

"Stop doing that! It's so unnerving when you're in my head like that. You said you can't read minds."

"I can't. But I can sense your feelings and read your facial expressions. You smell doubtful, and you look like you're trying to solve a puzzle that's got the best of you."

"You can smell me thinking?" I asked, my face scrunched in full disbelief.

"Oh aye. It sort of smells like smoke."

I punched his shoulder playfully, though I was grateful for the comedic relief.

"Did I ever tell you about my favorite cat I had growing up?" I asked.

"Never."

"She was a large, fluffy black cat with these beautiful green eyes—almost the color of yours."

"What was her name?" he asked.

". . .Midnight."

"A witch-obsessed child naming her black cat after the witching hour . . . Oh, that's proper," he countered, amused.

"Can you see her?" I asked.

"Only if I bring that memory to the surface. We can do that if you'd like."

"Maybe later. I don't think I'm ready to revisit my childhood that vividly." I recalled how intense my memories were when Fitz recreated them.

Fitz's phone lit up, and his expression grew serious as he read whatever was on the screen.

"What now?" I asked.

"Dad said a council member called him this morning to ask for any information he might have on our whereabouts."

"They know we're together now."

"Aye. When we both slipped off the radar . . ." He trailed off.

"But they don't know we're headed to London."

"Which means we were successful in keeping things quiet when we booked your travel."

"How did my travel escape their notice?"

Fitz smirked. "There's a particular report that customs and border patrol send to witchkind government. Henry might have paid off a few people to prevent your information from being included."

My eyes widened. "How did he manage that?"

"That's a query for Henry, I'm afraid."

I shook off the thought and returned my focus to our current travel. "Okay. And you were right about the Parisian spies—they definitely weren't linked to the witchkind watchers."

Fitz nodded thoughtfully. "At least we're staying ahead of them."

"And our Parisian stalkers think we're headed to Istanbul—nice choice, by the way."

"See, there are a few perks to private air travel."

"There's something I don't understand, though. Can't the watchers find us using their powers?"

"That would typically be the case," he said.

"Why not in this instance?"

"Magic."

I groaned, which only humored him further. Then I asked, "When do I start trying to match to my magic?"

"Tomorrow."

"You've known for years about my powers. Why didn't I start this process sooner?"

"Your power materialized slowly due to human DNA obstructing its growth. When I first met you, you knew things about others because you were essentially pulling information from their minds, but you weren't yet hearing their thoughts like you do now. There are even humans, though rare, who have this ability. You simply weren't ready," Fitz said.

"How can humans have that ability?"

"It's like I mentioned the other day. They have magic somewhere in their lineage," he answered. "After a family mixes with humans, the power weakens with each generation until there's very little chance a descendant could match to their power. Every so often, that former magic shows back up in someone's DNA.

"Sometimes," he continued, "these people are like you and their mind and power can combine. For others, they'll possess some ability, but they'll always remain more human than witch."

"Do you know why my magic is matching with me? Like, my witch ancestor isn't too far back or . . . ?"

"My suspicion is you have recent magical ancestry on each side of your lineage. It would explain why none of your living relatives have abilities. It might just be the combination of your mum's and your dad's lineages."

"I've been wondering a lot about my family. I wish I knew who my magical ancestors were," I said. "I know Gram isn't a witch, but she's not too far removed from having some sort of power. There's just something about her. She has this . . . awareness about her, and her intuition is uncanny."

"We'll work on that mystery soon."

After years of countless questions, I was thrilled I would finally have my long-awaited answers. And the sooner I matched with my magic, the sooner I'd have them.

"Look," he said, pointing toward the window.

The city of London lay beneath us, a blend of generations of architecture stretching as far as the eye could see. I'd visited the city before, but there was something about it that always took me by surprise.

Fitz gently grazed my face with his fingertips. "When you're happy, excited . . . my god, do you take my breath away."

"How's my energy now?"

He lifted his arm, directing my attention to the goosebumps rippling across his skin.

A smirk pulled at his lips. "Electric."

The next few days were spent in interviews. I'd always held an interest in European history, and options like The British Museum and The Institute of Historical Research were at the top of my list.

Not only would they be a good career advancement for me, but I was genuinely interested in the work they did.

My career had developed at private firms, continuously pulled on to various projects, always consulting with multiple clients. Although the fast-moving environment had taught me a great deal, a steady partnership within an institution sounded like a fresh challenge and a desirable change of pace.

But after my recent interviews, I was unsure if that's what I still wanted.

After my interview with the sole private firm on my list, I traipsed my way out of the crowded ground floor of the modern high rise into the bustling streets of London. There was no city in the world quite like London, with its unique mix of palaces, tube stations, teahouses, and pubs. Fitz was waiting in a less trafficked area along the front steps of the building, and I settled next to him. We sat amongst office dwellers, most of whom sought to eat their lunches in the late September sunlight. As a native Seattleite, I understood their desire to soak up the last of the golden rays before the cold, rainy season set in.

"How did it go?" Fitz asked.

"It went well."

"You don't seem excited."

"The hiring manager talked about company culture and how great the benefits are, and the team seemed great . . ."

"This sounds positive," he said.

"Yeah, it is," I said. "I should be seriously considering this role."

"But you aren't, are you? Why is that?"

"I don't want to work in a firm anymore. I think I knew that before I even applied for the position, but now, I'm sure."

"You want to work somewhere like the museum instead," he guessed.

I had met with them the day prior. The museum seemed like a good fit, and they'd shared that the professional retiring from the position was more than willing to wrap up early—meaning I could start in less than a month.

"I thought I did, but now I'm not so sure," I confessed.

Fitz's questioning glance pulled more from me.

"I just . . . I'm different than I was a few weeks ago when I started this job search. My circumstances are different. I guess I'm really just questioning what I want for myself now that I know I'm a . . . you know," I said, glancing around to register how close our neighbors were.

"Aye, that's understandable."

I paused before pressing on. "There's another interview I haven't told you about yet."

"Let's hear it, then."

"When I was researching openings in London, another option came up."

"This last option isn't in London?" Fitz asked.

"No."

"Where then?"

"Edinburgh, at the castle."

I expected the words to elicit some sort of response from Fitz. Instead, he sat there quietly, eyes transfixed on the street below us.

Finally, I broke the silence. "I don't have to look into the castle if you prefer I don't come to Edinburgh."

"No, that's not it at all—I promise," he said, reaching his hand across to mine. "To have you in Edinburgh . . . don't you know how badly I want that?"

"Tell me what it is, then."

Picking at the square patch on his leather bag with his free hand, Fitz led into his explanation. "I don't want to influence your decision. Of course, I want you in Edinburgh, but that isn't fair. I don't want you to feel pressure about coming to Edinburgh if it doesn't feel right."

"I—" The words stuck in my throat.

"Out with it," Fitz prompted.

"I can't do long distance at this point. Not after what we've already been through."

"Long distance never crossed my mind."

"And what's the alternative?" I asked. "You leave Edinburgh?"

His eyes flickered to mine. "Aye. I'd do that for you."

"Fitz." I laid my hand tenderly against his cheek. "You're finally home. You belong there. I wouldn't want you to leave."

"I want you happy."

"I'll go to the interview, and we'll sort it out from there," I said. "Let's take this one step at a time."

"It'll be tricky going back to Edinburgh with you."

"Because of the government?" I guessed.

"We'll sort it. I believe in us."

CHAPTER FOURTEEN

"No, come on, Hadley. You need to still your mind!"

Apparently, I was off to a rough start unlocking my magic. We sat near the floor-to-ceiling windows in our hotel room as I navigated the complexities of my mind. My current task was to meditate—but what for was unclear. When I squinted, Fitz knew I wasn't exactly following his guidelines.

"Your powers will never settle with all those bloody thoughts buzzing around in your mind. It's a wonder you get anything done. And I told you that when you do this, I can't concentrate either."

"Fine. Tell me how to do this."

"Quiet your mind. Stop thinking."

"I'm going to punch you again."

A slight tug at the corner of his mouth threatened to break his demeanor into a full smile.

"I can't stop thinking," I said. "How on earth am I supposed to just make it all stop?"

"You are actually overthinking the process of not thinking, aren't you?"

"Yes, hi. I'm Hadley. Have we met?" I quipped, extending my hand.

"You can control your mind, Hadley," Fitz said. "Our minds are one of the most powerful things in the universe, and you can control yours. You want magic? Power? This is the key to unlocking an entirely new world."

"I still don't understand how to do this."

"You'll have to sort it. Only you know the answer to this."

"Fantastic."

With my determination, Fitz's coaching, and the knowledge of everything at stake, I hadn't stirred from our two-bedroom suite for hours, and I wasn't going anywhere until some sort of breakthrough occurred. My focus shifted outside, searching for anything that would quiet my raging mind.

Shangri-La held an incredible view of London.

Gazing through the large windowpanes, I traced the path of the River Thames rolling ceaselessly through the city. Vessels floated brightly against the murky water, and countless buildings shot up on either bank. The blinking glow of the London Eye captured my attention. I focused on the wheel, studying its bright lights and steady, circular motion. As I followed the slow, rhythmic spinning, my mind stopped.

For a split second, I panicked at the loss of vision. Fitz had warned me not to fear its onset, and with the reminder that my condition was normal, I adjusted. The darkness took my mind, leaving a complete absence of everything else.

Then, slowly, a large eye materialized. An eyelid swept upward revealing an iris that swirled with fire—orange, red, and yellow flames roared to life. The eye's gaze darted about, as if it sought something in the abyss. Something stirred behind the eye, and I squinted, curious what might lie beyond the pupil, before everything evaporated like smoke winding its way into the night sky.

I gasped, and Fitz ran to my side.

"What's happened?"

"I found the darkness," was all I could manage as I scanned the room, my sight restored.

"That's good. What else?"

"There was an eye."

"Where was it?"

"I don't know, just in the darkness. It was huge—the only thing I could see."

His eyes lit up, though my own thoughts remained puzzled.

"What on earth was it?"

"You did good, Hadley," he began, reaching toward me before quickly pulling his hand back. "You saw your mind's eye."

"What exactly does that mean?"

"Your mind's eye is your witch's eye. It couples with your magic to show you the things you can't see with those baby blues of yours." He paused, his gaze suddenly curious. "What color was the eye?"

"It was several colors—it looked like fire dancing inside of the iris."

Fitz grinned. "Well, aren't you lucky?"

"What? Why?"

"You're a fire witch."

"Does that mean what I think it does?"

"Your power is fueled by fire. It'll be one of your most advanced skills, then."

My happiness was palpable—I couldn't contain it, and my cheerful energy zipped around the room.

"I saw something else too. It was past the pupil of the eye. I could only see movement. When I tried to see past the eye, the vision dissipated."

"You saw your magic."

My head snapped up, meeting his gaze. Butterflies danced in my belly, fluttering about violently. "Why did it disappear?"

"Why do you think it disappeared?"

I thought for only a moment before the disappointing answer surfaced. "Because I started thinking about what it was."

"You have to still your mind long enough for the interaction to occur between mind and power. You've only been meditating a few hours. Keep trying. It will happen."

I broke out into what must've been the goofiest grin of my life.

Fitz shot me a questioning glance.

"I saw my powers."

"Pretty damn cool, isn't it? I'm so proud of you."

"I'm a witch."

The outline of my witch's eye danced freshly in my mind, and my skin prickled at the proximity of my power. I swung my legs toward the window and closed my eyes, eager to answer my magic's beckoning call.

"Let's get a bit of scran before you start again."

"But I want to try again now," I whined.

"What you need is nourishment to help sustain you . . . especially before you get hangry." He eyed me dubiously. "Then, you can try again."

He was right, but the call of the witch's eye consumed me. Fitz reached for my hand and pulled me from the ground.

"So, just now," I said, "when I came back to this reality . . . ?"

"When you returned from the depths of your mind."

"Right. You reached for me, but then you pulled back. Why?"

"Oh, that. My instinct was to reach for you—to make sure you were all right. Then I decided you might need a minute. The mix of our energies after your encounter with your mind's eye might have hurt you more than it comforted you."

"Makes sense."

"You thought . . . what? I didn't want to touch you?"

"Well, of course, I went straight to the worst-case scenario!" I exclaimed, pulling a laugh from Fitz.

"It's going to take a long time for you to believe that I never wanted us to be apart. We'll never be forced away again."

"Promise?"

"Promise. And, Hadley? I'm always wanting to touch you."

Fitz pulled me closer and slid his hand behind my neck, illustrating his point, before kissing me longingly. He then extended his hand, and my jacket floated from a chair near the door to where I stood, hovering until I extended my arm.

"Ready?"

"Oh, I need to learn how to do that."

"Just think, magic could be at your disposal very soon."

I decided the break was worth it considering we wandered into Ye Olde Cheshire Cheese, taking in the history and good beer. A pub since 1538, and rumored to have been a 13th-century monastery prior to that, it had been rebuilt shortly after the Great Fire of 1666. It was relatively busy given that it was a Friday, and the chatter was nearly deafening as we navigated the upper floors. Luckily, we found a spot in the lowest level of the structure, which was far less chaotic.

Our meal was set to dim lighting, a roaring fire, and wooden tables set on cold, stone flooring. Literary legends like Charles Dickens and Sir Arthur Conan Doyle had enjoyed the food, drink, and company of this very establishment, and I was happy to do the same.

Fitz's phone lit up for about the millionth time since we'd sat down.

Henry was calling him again.

"Maybe you should answer that. It could be important," I said.

"We have a code for that sort of thing. Whatever he's calling about, it can wait until after dinner."

"Another text just came through," I observed, eyeing him pointedly.

Fitz sighed before reading Henry's text and turning the phone around for me to read.

Ignore me all you want, mate. You're the one who'll be pissed later.

Another text popped up: *I know the bartenders at the Cheese well.*

I gazed over Fitz's shoulder and found a handsome man dressed in a suit leaning against the bar, humor spreading across his lips.

"Uh . . . Fitz. You need to turn around."

Fitz's expression darkened before following my instructions.

The man crossed the room casually, never dropping that gloating smile.

"Henry Stuart," the man said by way of introduction. He extended his hand. "I'm glad to finally meet you."

"Likewise," I said.

When our skin made contact, a small tremor moved through my hand. Fitz was right—I certainly sensed contact with another witch.

But unlike the intensity I felt with Fitz, a dull energy pulsed just under the surface at Henry's touch and then quickly passed. A peaceful sensation rested briefly within me, and I couldn't make sense of it.

After shaking hands, Henry squeezed Fitz's shoulder and took a seat next to him.

"What the hell are you doing here?" Fitz asked.

"Good to see you too, Fitz."

I wondered if Henry could feel the annoyance pouring from my dinner partner. I took a sip of my beer and studied this dear old friend of Fitz's. His mischievous hazel eyes were set below a strong brow and hair the color of champagne. Combed into a deep side part, I found it reminiscent of old Hollywood, like Cary Grant. Henry appeared young, maybe younger than his actual age, and his thin figure was draped in an expensive and well-tailored suit. Though he appeared a bit aristocratic, his countenance was deeply warm and inviting, and I gave myself permission to like him straight away.

"Question still stands, Henry."

"I thought I could be useful." Henry shrugged, clearly unfazed.

"That wasn't part of the plan. What if someone followed you?"

"Come on, mate." He scoffed. "Give me some credit."

Fitz sat back in his seat though he held Henry's gaze firmly. "You are so bloody annoying."

"Aye, and you're a walk in the park," Henry countered.

Fitz pinched the bridge of his nose, and Henry caught my gaze and smiled. I couldn't help but laugh.

"And what exactly is so funny to you?" Fitz tried to keep his composure, but the edges of his lips were threatening a smile.

"I have no idea what you mean," I quipped.

"You might as well tell me why you're really here," Fitz said.

Henry considered his question for a moment before launching into an explanation. "A few reasons. Curiosity, a need to be helpful, but mainly: your update on the trackers in Paris worried me. I wanted to be nearby in case they come to London."

Fitz's expression softened.

"Isaac is keen to meet this one, as well." Henry nodded in my direction.

"And how much time do we have before Isaac arrives?" Fitz asked.

"He said you'd be pissed, so he was thinking he'd wait until you're ready. But considering I texted him to let him know I was about to meet Hadley . . . five minutes at best."

Fitz laughed, followed by Henry.

"Isaac . . ." I mused. "You've mentioned him before. He's a lawyer?"

"Indeed, he is," Henry answered. "He's also consulted for the English council for years. He's a talented reader."

"It's a magical skill. Isaac is damn good at reading the intentions of both humans and witches," Fitz explained.

"He's one of our closest friends," Henry said.

"Aye. He's helping us, same as Henry," Fitz said, refreshing my memory.

"That's right," I said, recalling our conversation about his network. "Thank you for that," I said meaningfully to Henry.

"Dinnae mention it, lass. I'd do more if I could."

"And there he is," Fitz said. He nodded toward a witch sporting a navy fedora, a long houndstooth overcoat, and navy slacks with thin pinstripes.

The overcoat was unbuttoned, perched atop his shoulders, and he shed the layer in one rolling motion, revealing the rest of his three-piece suit. He was tall like Fitz and Henry and had the lithe, muscular build of an athlete. Isaac and I shook hands, and the same odd sensation came over me. Suddenly, his connection to Fitz echoed through me, and I recognized a pattern—their bond of friendship sent a signal of peace quickly through my veins. Fitz had shared that as I neared matching with my magic that my instincts would grow stronger, and my intuition was growing stronger by the day. The feeling was odd, and *that* was going to take some getting used to.

Isaac removed his hat and embraced Fitz before sliding onto the old wooden bench next to me. His dark complexion suited his chocolate-colored hair that was combed into a pompadour. He smoothed back a few loose strands as a waiter set a plate in front of him.

"Thank you, Martin," Isaac said. His accent was identifiably Italian. "That was fast."

"You can thank Henry," Fitz said. "He let us know you were on your way."

"I didn't tell you I was coming."

Henry shrugged. "I knew you couldnae resist."

Isaac sighed before settling a striking pair of dark eyes on to mine. They were complex like the fallen leaves of November and filled with an endless depth, and Isaac carried himself with a certain wisdom. I was excited to get to know him better.

"*Carissima*, how is your power-matching going?" he asked.

While I described my experience, I was struck by the significance of that moment. Observing the three men gathered around the table, I realized their friendship knew none of the usual barriers that mine often held. I had concealed parts of myself for so long, and I was overwhelmed by the simple fact that, for the first time in my life, I wasn't hiding who I was. I had no reason to keep a secret. As far as that group was concerned, I was *normal*. When I shared the sentiment aloud, Fitz reached for my hand.

"That's over for you, lass. You're with us now," Henry said.

"That's true," Isaac agreed. "I already know you and I are going to be buddies—isn't that what you say in America?"

"Isaac is convinced your friendship was 'written in the stars.'" Henry rolled his eyes playfully.

"I'm assuming you already know a lot about me," I guessed.

Isaac grimaced. "A professional hazard I'm afraid."

"Well, if we're future besties, it's time to level the playing field," I said.

He grinned.

"So, you're Italian. Clearly."

He laughed. "Yes, darling. I was born in Iran, but my parents moved us to Italy when I was a baby. I grew up in Genova. It's a coastal city in the North of Italy. You might know it by its English name—Genoa."

"Oh, I'm going to have so many follow up questions to that."

"I'm bracing myself."

Henry chuckled and looked to Fitz, who shrugged, though he was equally amused. I ignored them both and continued my questions.

"And you're a lawyer . . . ?"

"Yes. I've just made partner at my firm, so I plan to stay here a while, much to Fitz and Henry's dismay."

"Dismay or not, staying here is to your own detriment, mate. I mean, London is nothing to Edinburgh," Fitz argued.

"Too true," Henry added before plucking a Scotch egg from Isaac's plate.

"Spoken like true Scots," Isaac said. "And I *was* going to eat that."

Henry shrugged, a sly grin on his face. He sliced through the egg before depositing half back onto Isaac's plate.

"Making partner is big. Congrats," I said. "You must like London then. Or does the job just hold you here?"

"It's not London so much as his mate," Henry interjected.

"Now I need details."

"Well, there isn't anyone yet," Isaac said. "A seer told me a few months ago that I'll meet my mate in London and gave me a description. I'm keeping my eyes open."

"Hopeless romantic, this one." Henry winked.

"I just worry, you know? What if I don't know he's 'the one?'"

"*You'll know,*" Fitz and Henry responded in unison.

"Either way, that's not keeping me in London—Fate will take care of things one way or the other. I know her that well," Isaac added drily, eyeing Henry meaningfully.

"That was a joke, mate."

Isaac punched Henry's arm playfully.

"Come on, guys. We're in *civilized* company," Fitz interrupted, looking at me.

"Aye. Better make a braw first impression with your new best friend, Isaac," Henry said.

My phone vibrated the table, startling me. I flipped it over and sighed.

Jordan.

I know you're busy, but I'd really like to catch up and hear about your interviews. I miss you.

For the first time in seventeen years, Jordan and I had gone days without talking. I wanted to call her more than anything, but I didn't know how to talk to my best friend when I couldn't tell her everything. I knew she'd ask, "What's wrong?" the moment she picked up, and I couldn't be honest with her. I needed to protect her from the mess I was tangled in. I needed to . . .

"Shit."

"What's wrong?" Fitz asked.

I shook my head. I wasn't ready to talk to Fitz about the fact that I was willing to do whatever necessary to protect Jordan, the same way he had protected me.

As we worked our way through dinner, I found myself relaxing at the change of scenery, which allowed me to free my thoughts from the last few hours. I ran a finger around the rim of my glass, watching the dark beer swirl in tandem with it. The liquid ceased its movement only after my finger did the same. Stunned, I looked up to find a smirk on Fitz's face.

"When did that start?" Fitz asked.

"I guess right now?"

"You're close, Hads. Your power is so close."

I smiled, returning my attention to the glass. A small jolt of electricity pulsed through me, and as my finger resumed its previous path around the rim, the beer again answered the call of my magic.

CHAPTER FIFTEEN

We surrendered to the night, emerging from dim lighting and roaring fireplaces at Ye Old Cheshire Cheese into the cold air of the evening. The contrast between the warm pub and the night air jolted me from my relaxed state, and I felt invigorated as I scanned the scene just outside the door. Fitz instinctively reached for my hand as we wandered through the crowds in the courtyard, packed despite the weather.

Henry and Isaac returned to our suite with us to talk through the latest data they and Ian had collected regarding the Scottish and U.S. councils' search for us. Isaac proposed we create a barrier with the elements. Apparently, this would allow me to focus on matching to my magic undisturbed, and the guys could keep an eye on me while they worked through the updates. I couldn't quite wrap my mind around that one, but I sat and watched in awe as Fitz performed the honors.

He held my gaze and smiled, and I saw the tiniest ripple in the air around me—the kind of movement you'd never notice if you weren't paying close attention. He turned his head so his eyes could trace from one wall to the other, and then his gaze fell on me.

His lips moved, but I couldn't hear him. An awe-struck laugh escaped my lips, and I wondered if he could hear it. Fitz laughed in turn, waved, and joined Henry and Isaac's discussion.

I tried my best to push the scene from my mind so I could focus on acquiring my own power. I settled slowly into my former meditative state and began the process of quieting my mind. When I'd observed Fitz's daily meditation, it had seemed so natural for him—so necessary—and I was uncertain I could integrate it so effortlessly into my life. Fitz had been quick to remind me he'd been meditating since childhood, and once I matched with my powers, I would feel its draw and its promise to ease my mind's burden.

Even if I wasn't certain about that, I did feel more confident after seeing my mind's eye. And more determined. I knew what I was working toward, and my mind stilled with considerably less effort.

As I focused again on the large wheel and its bright circular motion, the rest of the world slowly faded to black. I reminded myself to remain neutral before I slipped into the abyss.

Darkness took hold, and I fought back against the rising hysteria, recalling that panic would pull me away from my magic. I breathed deeply, drawing in the positive and exhaling the negative. Peace wiggled inside, slipping from the pit of my stomach through the rest of my body, as though a healing power swept through my bloodstream.

On the coattails of the calmness came a heightened sense of awareness, and a dim shape wavered in the darkness. A large, translucent eye stared back at me, and I waited patiently as it regained its strength. It was a painting coming to fruition, each brushstroke breathing life into the unblinking object as the colors intensified.

Simply observe. Let the moment be.

The eyelid closed, slowly and deliberately, before lifting to reveal the flame-filled iris. A movement behind the eye shifted my gaze, and my power grew more distinct than before, drifting in an untamable cloud, all the while intensifying into the same mesmerizing colors as the eye.

It gathered itself together and slinked through the pupil of the eye, like smoke billows from a chimney. Rolling tentatively through the air, the cloud whirled closer, and its edges shimmered as they danced to some imperceptible tune. The hair on my body prickled, standing on end.

My curiosity almost got the better of me as a thought nearly slipped across my mind. My magic halted mid-air, threatening to disappear altogether, but I recovered quickly, dropping back into thoughtless observation. The cloud continued its forward movement. My mind and body both grew serene, increasingly at peace as the gap between us and my power—something I needed as much as the air filling my lungs—diminished. My arm instinctively greeted the cloud, closing the final space between us.

My fingers burned at the initial contact before a surge of electricity ripped through my fingers, consuming my hands, arms, chest, and eventually my entire body. My limbs contorted in pain, and my body fell to the ground, my legs unable to support my weight. Shrieks escaped my lips, a feeble attempt to relieve the pain building inside of me. The crippling ache lingered as power coursed through me, adjusting to its newfound home.

A throbbing sensation replaced the pain, like the dull beating pulse after stubbing your toe. Weightlessness followed, gradually radiating throughout my entire body from my fingertips, leaving behind no trace of the former discomfort. I perceived the air in a new way, freshly aware of its interconnectedness, understanding its relationship to the electricity snapping inside of me.

The air lifted me from the ground, suspending me.

My body lay limp for only a moment before my limbs began twitching, my entire body spinning and sputtering in the darkness. Once the twisting subsided, I floated back to the ground in utter exhaustion.

A heavy weight settled in my lungs, and I focused on inhaling and exhaling, finding comfort in the familiar rise and fall of my chest. I mustered the energy to sit up and looked in the direction of my mind's eye. The ever-present eye stared, expressionless, and I crawled timidly in its direction, proceeding slowly until I was mere inches away. I hadn't fully appreciated its breadth.

It stood at least fifteen feet tall, and the pupil was so large, I could step right through it.

As I studied the intricate detail of the iris, my proximity awakened its power, and the entire eye began to shimmer. I drew myself up and stood with my quivering legs before slowly raising my right foot and stepping through the center.

As my foot made contact with the ground, an explosion flung me across the empty space. I turned in the midst of the blast and inexplicably floated to the ground. Though my landing was graceful, the ringing in my ears proved the explosion was real. I turned to my witch's eye but found only darkness.

The final infusion had occurred, and both my magic and mind's eye rested comfortably inside my body, each in harmony with one another.

With my task completed, I woke from my reverie.

Fitz's usual carefree expression was replaced with creased brows and worried eyes. "Say something."

"Like what?" I asked grumpily.

"There you are. How do you feel?"

"Like a train toppled over me."

"Here, take these—they'll help with the headache." He handed me medicine and a glass of water. Even though I felt like I'd been run over, his preparedness demonstrated at least the discomfort was expected.

"Are Henry and Isaac still here?"

"We felt the shift when you matched to your power. They left to give you a bit of space, but they're just next door in Henry's room."

"Henry's room?" I asked.

"Aye, he booked a room next to ours in case we run into any trouble."

I looked around the room, hoping to orient myself, feeling the full weight of my dazed stupor. I was still sitting on the floor of our hotel room. The river and the gray skyline still lay beyond the windowpanes. And the London Eye still flashed brightly, though it wasn't quite as easy to gaze upon with the pounding in my head.

Fitz knelt before me and pressed a cold, damp washcloth against my forehead. I placed my hand at the base of his skull, twisting my fingers into his hair.

And for the first time since I'd met Fitz, we didn't shock each other.

I tugged until he moved his body closer to mine, our faces only a few inches apart. I closed my eyes, drinking in his deep scent, which was heightened after receiving my powers. His presence was tangible all around me, and I felt everything about him—his heartbeat, his energy, and his power. He was far more powerful than he'd ever let on.

I allowed the connection to navigate where it willed, and through my witch's eye, I saw a small stream of energy forming between the two of us. I couldn't fully comprehend it. It resembled the brilliant glow of vintage light bulb wires in a dark room. The connection I'd thought to be imaginary turned out to be real. Even though magic was fantastical to me, I had begun to understand it, innate as it truly was. I followed the length of the stream and found Fitz at the other end. It was only then that I noticed a second stream of light from Fitz back to myself. I opened my eyes to Fitz, who was still bent forward with his eyes closed.

"You let me in."

"What do you mean?" I asked.

"The streams. You saw them?"

I nodded.

"You found a stream that led to me—a path I created for you. I've waited a long time for you to find it. The other stream just formed between us . . . it came from you. You created a path for me to find you, as well."

"How did I do that? I don't understand what's happening."

Fitz crossed his legs and scooted closer until our knees touched. He took my hands in his. "I know this all must seem a bit scary, but this is normal for us. All right?"

I nodded. "What are these streams exactly?"

"Our energies formed a connection between the two of us. This type of connection—it only forms between mates," he said.

I paused. "You were right about us being mates, then."

"Are you good, Hads?" he asked. "I know this is quite a bit to sort through at once."

"I'm good."

He squeezed my hand.

"What causes the streams to form?" I asked. "You said yours has existed for a while, and mine just formed."

"They form as feelings and trust for someone develops. Once you trusted me, the connection formed. With the assistance of your magic, you created a path for me to find you."

His fingertips brushed the side of my face gently until my cheek rested in his palm.

"This connection is formidable, Hadley. These streams are life and vitality flowing between us. You have a direct line to my soul, and I to yours. You'll know immediately if I'm upset. I'll know if you're ever in danger."

"I've felt that already."

"Aye. I think that's partly due to mine forming so early on."

"Fitz, mine would have formed a lot sooner if I had my powers. I think part of it already existed from my side."

"I think that's why we've been shocking each other. That's gone now—for you too?"

I nodded.

"This connection was instantaneous," Fitz said. "I think your magic has been trying to match with you, and it's been trying to connect us."

The gravity of our connection hit me with full force, and the vulnerability that came with our interconnectedness left me feeling exposed.

"What's wrong?" Fitz questioned.

"It's nothing really. It's just that I feel naked—internally."

Fitz nodded.

"What if you don't like what you find in our connection?"

"Not even a possibility."

My heart raced.

Fitz's brows furrowed, and his eyes shut tightly. "Never worry again that I'll leave you."

"You feel that?"

"Aye, of course I do," Fitz said. "And god only knows why you feel that way."

"What if there's something about me that you can't deal with?"

"You're forgetting something: I know you, Hads. I know you better than anyone else, and I want you—all of you." He paused. "I have my flaws too. You know that. But you'll learn that it isn't our nature to run away from the tough bits."

Fitz's words were comforting, though his energy unnerved me— it was agitated.

"What's wrong?" I asked.

"I can't bear the feeling of your fear inside me. It's . . . painful."

I'd caused Fitz pain, and I didn't know how to remedy that. Closing my eyes, I succumbed to my instincts and allowed it to guide my actions. I closed the gap between us, pressing my lips firmly to his.

A slew of memories raced through my mind: the moment our eyes met at the lake, the electricity that drummed through me as we shook hands, the feel of his kiss the first time he pressed his lips to mine, the look in his eyes when we met atop Notre Dame. My emotions built with each memory, and warm desire pumped through my veins.

I anticipated the charge of the kiss, the final fusion of our connection. But the emotional intensity surprised me—it propelled me forward.

Unlike his slow, deliberate movements before, Fitz was consumed with need. One of his hands laced tightly to mine, and he cupped my face with the other. I responded by placing my free hand behind his back and tugged him closer to me.

He rocked back, pulling me onto his lap, and he stared into my eyes as his hands raked through my hair. He found his grip in the long, auburn strands and tugged my head back gently to expose my neck. His lips found the tender spot just under my jaw, and I sighed. He worked his way toward my chest before pulling at the left side of my V-neck sweater.

He paused.

"What is it?" I whispered.

"I feel you so deeply . . . much stronger than before."

"It's the same for me."

"My heartbeat—can you feel it inside of you?"

I nodded. I traced a path along his sweater and paused right where his heart lay. I pressed my palm to his chest, but it wasn't enough. I followed my instincts and pushed his sweater toward his head. He acknowledged my silent request and helped me with its removal. I unbuttoned his white dress shirt and tossed that barrier next to us on the floor before scanning the lean muscle of his sculpted torso. My breath caught when his eyes flickered back to mine. Fitz's gaze was intense.

I pressed my hand against his solid, bare chest, and his heartbeat intensified. The thump radiated through my body, and my own heartbeat raced to match his. Fitz slipped my sweater off my left shoulder and grazed his fingertips along the edge of the fabric until he found the soft skin over my heart. I closed my eyes as I tilted my head back, both reveling in the feel of his touch and willing my heart to not leap from my chest. Fitz leaned forward and pressed his lips to the spot his fingertips had just touched. I then tilted his head to meet my gaze, and whatever he found in my eyes—it lit a fire inside of him.

He slipped his hand behind my neck and pulled me forward, kissing me deeply before returning to my neck and lower. When he found my lips again, our motions grew in intensity, and I savored the feeling of our connection finally flowing freely. I'd never felt more connected to anyone or anything in my life. We lost ourselves to the intoxication of each other until I pulled back to search his face for any signs of its former distress.

Fitz grinned as he stretched out on the cool floor, dragging in the deep breaths his body sought. "I don't think I'll survive that again," he mumbled, pulling a hearty laugh from me.

"Well, I don't have to touch you."

"Oh, like hell you don't. You might kill me, but I suspect I'll enjoy every bit of it," he responded, leaning on to his elbows.

"I—" I paused, searching for the words. "I never could have imagined something like that. The feelings that channeled through that connection . . ."

"Aye, it's intense. Are you good?"

"More than good."

He laughed. "Well, that's grand."

"This is so different from the way humans approach relationships, though. I mean, it never felt right to me, and now I finally understand why."

"Aye," Fitz said. "We're programmed a bit differently. Once we find our missing half, we lose little time in starting our lives together."

"Desire is different for us?"

"Oh aye. Because we do have desire, but the impulse to find our mate is always just under the surface—always palpable—and we don't typically quell the loneliness by just hooking up randomly."

"But it happens sometimes?"

"There's an exception to every rule, but when there's such a strong urge to find your other half, anyone else just feels like a distraction—like someone who could throw you off course."

"You really feel this way about me?"

"You know exactly how I feel about you. You've known since the first day I met you—when I wandered into that clearing with you and Izzy. That was it for me."

My heart warmed at his confession.

He continued, "So, to answer your question: Aye, I really feel this way about you. I consider us bound together. Forever. Don't you?"

I ran my fingers along his jawline, and he rested his forehead against mine.

"Yes," I whispered.

Finally. A longstanding tightness released from my chest.

Fitz pulled back, a strange look blanketing his features.

"What is it?"

"There's nothing wrong." He paused momentarily. "It's just . . . I love you, Hadley."

"I love you too. I always have."

He couldn't keep the broad smile from his face, though I thought he was trying. His hand rested at the base of my skull, his thumb gently gliding back and forth, chills rising behind the warmth of his touch.

"Do couples separate in the witch world? Do they break this connection?" I asked.

"Not that I know of . . . it's just not in our nature to find our other half and then give up when things get tough. We mess up, we get angry, we have problems, but we fight for the love we've been given."

His words were comforting, and I released some of my previous anxiety.

"I could sit here forever with you, but perhaps we should have a little change of pace?" Fitz asked.

"What do you have in mind?"

"Power training?" he suggested.

I was on my feet before he could blink, my headache nearly forgotten. "What are you waiting for? Get up!"

Fitz rolled to his feet and slid his hands around my waist, pulling me back to him. "Yes, ma'am."

He kissed me quickly, a happy gleam in his eyes.

CHAPTER SIXTEEN

Fitz paced the room, his phone glued to his ear. Ian had finally called with more information, and my foot tapped nervously, awaiting the update. Ian's voice was bold and deep, and though I couldn't make out his words, the rise and fall of his cadence was distinct. His voice held as much presence as it would if he were standing in the room, and my reaction surprised me. Ian unnerved me, and even though I knew I owed it to our circumstances at the lake, the pit of my stomach still tightened.

Henry and Isaac didn't look any less anxious than I felt, and though the call was brief, it seemed to last an eternity. When Fitz punched the button to end his call, my stomach flipped.

"Dad says we need to meet with the Scottish Council, and if we give them what they want, he thinks things will be fine."

"Fine?" Isaac asked.

"He said he received a visit from the council this morning. They told him they've suspected Hadley and I were together ever since we both gave them the slip."

My breath hitched. Fitz sat next to me and took my hand in his.

"Dad told them that Hadley acquired her powers. After some back and forth, the council member left. They phoned this afternoon and said they want proof that she's a fully functioning witch now."

"Do you agree with that—that things will be okay?" I asked.

"No," Fitz, Henry, and Isaac responded in unison.

My eyebrows rose.

"Here's the thing . . . the councils work in strange ways. If they do let this go, there's a reason." Isaac said.

"Well, that sounds ominous," I said.

"I reckon it could be . . . they might want you for something in particular," Henry said.

"I don't understand."

"They might want to leverage a particular skill set for something. That's fairly common," said Fitz.

"I don't doubt that. This feels suspicious," Isaac said.

"I agree," Fitz said. "But I . . . I do think we should give them what they asked for, at least for now."

"How so?" I asked.

"We should provide proof that you have your powers."

"What if they decide to punish us? What if they spellbind us, Fitz?" My voice shook. I'd finally found myself, and the thought of losing my magic so quickly tore violently through me.

"I don't think they'll do that. And neither does Dad."

"I think it's more likely they'll ask something of you," Isaac said.

"We already know they want Fitz to work with them," Henry added. "I doubt that's changed."

"The only way to find out is to meet with them—and I think we should. If that's all right with you?" Fitz asked me.

"I don't think we have much choice unless we decide to run," I said. "But what are the odds they wouldn't eventually find us anyway?"

"Slim. We'd have to change our entire lives—give up our connection to everyone and everything," Fitz said.

"I don't want to live that way—not unless it's a last resort," I said. "Let's go and face this."

"Dad said this meeting is to discuss what's happened, and the council will collect whatever information they're seeking. If they decide there should be consequences, the courts will convene before a sentence is reached."

The room fell quiet. It was Isaac who first broke the silence.

"It's real now. We've prepared for this moment for a long time, and now we will see if we're ready."

"Aye, and if I'm being transparent, I'm nervous," Henry admitted.

Fitz nodded. "Same, mate."

"If anything goes wrong, we have contingency plans," Henry said.

"Which consists of Fitz and I disappearing?"

"Aye," said Henry sadly. "But if they move to spellbind you, your choices are to live a painful existence without magic or to run from the councils and disappear forever. I know it doesn't sound appealing, but you'd have each other—and your magic."

"Whatever happens . . . We'll be ready for anything." Isaac nodded once in our direction.

"You're good friends." I said. "I'm sure you know how much Fitz appreciates that, but I haven't thanked you properly. I want you to both know how much this means to me."

Henry smiled shyly. "You're a part of our wee family. We protect one another—no questions."

"We'll always have your back," Isaac added. The room fell quiet once again as we felt the weight of what was to come. I squeezed Fitz's hand reassuringly.

"Well, not to break up this tender moment, but it's getting late, and I promised Hadley one last evening stroll in London."

We were leaving for Edinburgh the following morning, as Monday's interview at the castle was only two days away.

"I won't see you in the morning before you leave, but I'll be in Edinburgh in a couple weeks. Sooner if the councils give you trouble." Isaac embraced me warmly. "Take care of yourself, Hadley."

"You too, Isaac. Miss you already."

He planted a quick kiss on the top of my head before embracing Fitz and then Henry. And as we dispersed for the evening, my heart tugged at me slightly. The spell was broken.

I was happy to learn Henry would meet us in Edinburgh, but it wouldn't be quite the same without Isaac. This small group of brothers had seen me through one of the most important and vulnerable moments of my life. And in our short time together, I'd learned just how much they'd contributed—and were still contributing—to help Fitz and me through this situation with the government. Though I was only just getting to know them, it felt as though they'd known me as long as Fitz had.

I waved goodbye to Isaac as we parted outside the hotel lobby. I didn't know much with any certainty, but of one thing I was sure: the next time I saw him, everything would be different.

PART TWO

CHAPTER SEVENTEEN

Forfar, Scotland
January 1662
Esther

I peered through the hazy windowpane, observing the snow drifting to blanket the earth in white. It was an exceptionally cold day, even for January, but I loved the way snow transformed the world into something new. As a wee bairn, the excitement had been almost unbearable when I woke to the brightly covered hills, and as an adult, the sense of nostalgia was strong. My husband Hamish wasnae fond of snow, which reminded me the fire needed tending before his return. Hamish had left for the village in the wee morning hours and hadna yet returned; my thoughts were further at war with one another the longer his absence stretched.

The fire roared with the crackle of fresh wood. Two figures materialized in the flames. My visions had troubled Hamish, but it had taken little time to discover who they were. I stared into the eyes of my many times great-grandson, as confused by his appearance as ever. Though I had grown accustomed to frequent visions, this one vexed me.

My foresight manifested as images in the elements—water, fire, earth, air, moonlight—as my power mixed with the spirit of the land. Oftentimes, I recognized those I saw—my kin, neighbors, and acquaintances—as I observed their futures, transfixed by their stories. Occasionally, my witch's eye watched the future for me. I'd foreseen the melancholy battle of Culloden Moor, the colonization of the New World as it headed west, and the invention of a horseless buggy—an automobile, I believed. With my mind preoccupied in times that had yet to pass, I had to be mindful of my speech—Hamish often said I spoke in strange ways. Perhaps I'd no been mindful of that as of late.

The flames grew restless, and I lost Fitz MacGregor and Hadley Weston in the all-consuming blaze. Their appearances set my nerves on end. Frequent manifestations meant I had a connection with their futures, and I felt Fitz and Hadley were in trouble. Their bodies floated through the in-between, an indication that they were on a lengthy journey through time or space. Long passages were tricky, and even with Fitz's power, I prayed they wouldnae attempt a dangerous expedition without a pressing reason. Perhaps I was wrong. Or perhaps they had caught my witch's eye for this very reason. Perhaps I was meant to assist them on their journey.

The light in the room brightened, and Hamish's figure filled the doorway.

"Did ye succeed?" I asked.

He eyed me dubiously as he shook the fresh powder from his overcoat.

"The truth, Hamish," I said.

"I pleaded with every witch in the area."

"None will help us, then."

Hamish cut his eyes sharply—he was searching for the right words, but he wouldnae find any. I reached out my hand, beckoning Hamish to my side.

"Damn them all to hell," Hamish said.

"Aye, and what would that do for ye?"

"I cannae understand, Esther. The council would do the same for their families if it came to it, and yet, none will stand now and fight."

"Come to me, *mo ghaol.*"

Hamish obeyed, my rising nerves undoubtedly registering in his body.

"Ye've done well, Hamish," I said. "There's nothing left to be done. Now, we must wait."

Tears welled in his eyes as he held me close. I rested my head on his chest, watching the flurry of activity on the other side of the panes. Icy flakes floated upon an invisible force, making their slow, winding descent to the ground, where they burst into flames. A chill ran down my spine.

Fate beckoned, and ere long, I would be forced to answer.

Edinburgh, Scotland
Present Day
Hadley

Scotland took my breath away. I surveyed what lay beyond the train window, already in love with the hauntingly beautiful land. The hills stretched as far as I could see, greeting the rolling fog like old friends. The land's beauty mixed with the nation's historical tragedies to create the perfect backdrop for fairy tales, legends, and the accounts of heroes. I wondered what my story might become in such a place. Perhaps it wasn't quite the substance of legend, but I was lost in my own fairy tale. How many people discovered one day that their childhood fantasy had been fulfilled? Even though Fitz and I would soon face the Scottish Council, I had to believe everything would turn out all right.

I felt the warmth of Fitz's hand on mine and turned to him, a man formed of this land. His strong figure seemed crafted to survive the harsh environment, and the magic about him was palpable. That magic transformed him into someone who'd stepped straight from the stories that his characteristically superstitious culture passed from generation to generation. Though the more I learned, the less superstitious I found those who heeded the warnings and tales of the past.

"We coexist much more easily with the humans now that they're, as a culture, more enthralled with their limited version of science," Fitz explained. "Most humans don't believe magic to be real, so they've turned to what they consider a more reasonable explanation of the mysterious. They certainly live less magical and informed lives than their ancestors. But to be honest, I think it's nice no one is trying to burn us at the stake. Let them have their science."

"It's unfortunate it has to be this way. It seems like witches could help humans quite a bit."

"Aye, but we can't tip the balance, anyway."

"And we keep this balance because . . ."

"Anything that significantly alters humanity must be left to Fate. There are consequences for pissing off Fate. She's a tricky mistress," he answered.

"You talk about Fate like it's an animate being."

"She is. Trust me, you'll see that. She can't really be explained or even fully comprehended, but she's there."

"What about God? Do most witches believe in a higher being?"

"In some form," Fitz said. "Our religious beliefs are as varied as humans', but with the power to see the world so clearly, it's hard to reason a higher being doesn't exist."

"So many people act like witches are all evil," I said. "Like we're devil worshippers."

"Aye. I'm not trying to commune with the devil myself."

"Really? I hear hell is nice this time of year," I said, pulling laughter from Fitz.

"I can't lay all the blame on the humans. We've had witches contribute to that narrative. But humans have posed as witches over the years, causing harm to our reputation."

"I'll bet some of the humans aggravated their captors with wild confessions."

"Devil's advocate, though. Some of them were just doing what they could to end things," Fitz countered.

"Because of the torture?" I asked.

"Days of sleep deprivation, the absence of food and light, and being held in freezing conditions would cause most anyone to confess, just to put an end to the torture. And that's only the beginning of what some of those poor men and women endured. Death seemed better than living."

"That honestly makes me sick to my stomach," I said. "I know there are still people today who want to cast a negative portrayal of the craft, and they're basing their judgments on false information. The overzealous witch-hunters might be dead, but the stigma lives on."

"It's frustrating that humans have turned us into caricatures. But the general belief in magical beings has faded. We've hidden ourselves, so we have to accept this version humans have created for their own amusement."

"How superstitious are people around here?"

"It's a modern city with modern people, but you'll be in contact with historians, English professors, archaeologists, and the like. Those humans are close to the past. They're researchers, observers of humanity. Superstitious, no. Perceptive, aye."

Fitz checked his phone, which quickened my pulse. I was wary of bad news.

"It's Henry," he said, undoubtedly feeling my nerves. "He's reminding me to use his estate outside Edinburgh for your magic training that's best suited for the outdoors."

"Estate?" I asked.

Fitz's lips tugged into a half smile. "Aye. His parents left him the family estate. His dad has some health concerns, and moving to a villa overlooking the ocean in Greece is his method of coping."

That was some coping mechanism.

"Are our health risks the same as humans'?"

"Serious risks like heart attack or stroke are exceedingly rare until we're quite old, as are the minor aches and pains. And cancer is almost non-existent in our world."

"How old is Henry's dad?"

Fitz hesitated before answering. "One hundred twenty-three."

"How is that possible? He would've been eighty-five when Henry was born? What am I missing?"

"Most witches choose to have children earlier than Henry's parents to stay on a more human timeline, but there are loads of witches who don't choose a traditional lifestyle. If you saw Henry's dad, you'd think he was in his late sixties now."

My curiosity got the better of me before I could halt my mind, and my eyes must've been the size of saucers.

"Hadley?"

"Oh my god. I'm so sorry."

"You're inside my head, aren't you?"

"I promise I didn't mean to. I just . . . lost control."

He exhaled slowly, requiring a moment to check his feelings.

"It's okay. You're new at this, and honestly, you won't develop proper control until I track down someone to help you with that power."

"Thank you for understanding."

He nodded.

"Do we really live to two hundred?"

"Aye, somewhere between two hundred and two-twenty-five typically. Our magical energy slows aging. It prevents major diseases from taking root. As our bodies finally age out, they become more susceptible to illness, but it takes longer."

"Wait, so how old are you?"

"Thirty-three. Don't worry, you're not with an old bloke."

"Thank god."

Fitz laughed, amused with my concern.

"Okay, so Henry's dad is ill much earlier than he should be?"

"Oh aye, and when Henry's ready, he'll relay his dad's tale to you. He was active in the First World War. Because of the damage, his body invited illness early. Luckily, what ails him now isn't life-threatening."

The train pulled to a stop, and Fitz smiled, the buzz of my energy swirling all around us. As we exited the bustling Waverly Station, the fresh air felt unusual—animated somehow—as its tiny movements danced wildly across my skin. My feet greeted the earth of Scotland and were immediately met by a burst of energy, which climbed rapidly, humming throughout my body. My energy, my blood, everything within me responded to an invisible force in the elements. I hesitated, glancing at Fitz.

"Magic grows stronger in certain areas of the world. Our spirits return to the places we called home, regardless of where we die. We feel that concentration of their power, and our own powers strengthen because of it." He grinned, bursts of his euphoria hitting me in waves. "Edinburgh has a rich, magical history. Your body is feeding on the collection of energy and spirit. Paris and London have strong footholds as well—you're becoming more in tune with yourself since you perceive the magic here."

The feeling of power pulsing through my body was sensation enough, but this knowledge was exhilarating. Standing in the midst of the historic city, my magical brothers and sisters across countless generations were granting me vitality.

People passed by us, consumed with their daily lives, completely unaware of the life transforming before their eyes. For the first time, I felt like I belonged to something on a grand scale. After years of searching in vain for others like myself, feeling ill at ease in my own body . . . I was no longer alone.

CHAPTER EIGHTEEN

Edinburgh exceeded my expectations, idyllic and dramatic as the city was. Throughout Old Town—fittingly the oldest part of the city—remarkable architecture, cobblestone streets, small pubs, and charming tourist shops filled with tartans and Scottish trinkets all culminated into a uniquely Scottish experience.

And if that was somehow insufficient, the expansive and ever-present Edinburgh Castle sat atop Old Town, granting a glimpse into the ingenuity and realities of medieval times. Researchers believed it had been besieged twenty-six times in the castle's 1,100-year history. The massive structure had previously housed everyone from royalty to prisoners, but its seemingly final role was preserving history, educating and entertaining tourists, and adding jobs to the

Edinburgh economy.

I strolled down the esplanade near the castle entrance. The gray stonework rose high above my head, and the thick, impenetrable walls held two large wooden doors in place, which opened to a court-yard filled with tourists. My chest swelled as I considered joining the ranks of the castle employees, preserving history and architecture for generations to come.

An hour later, I had lost myself to the castle, which was grander than I'd expected. The sights were breathtaking from the outer walls, granting an unparalleled view of Arthur's Seat, the ancient volcano credited as the main peak in Edinburgh's group of hills. St Giles' Cathedral stood out along the Royal Mile, the main street of Edin-burgh's Old Town, which was filled with centuries-old buildings and throngs of tourists.

My eyes scanned from Old Town to New Town over to the Firth of Forth, the estuary where several Scottish rivers rolled toward the North Sea. I wondered if this magical city might be the place I would soon call home. I wandered through the Great Hall, learning about Oliver Cromwell's army laying siege to the castle in 1650, and I couldn't help but think of generations past—and of witches like Esther. Her story had come to life for me, and that only brought the history of the castle further to life as well.

Engrossed in the history as I was, a small jolt of panic hit me when I realized only a few minutes separated me from my impending interview with Mr. Murray.

I rushed through the doors of the Great Hall and navigated around the crowds of tourists scattered about the sunny courtyard. I thought I might have received some assistance from the supernatural in reaching his office on time.

Mr. Murray was a distinguished gentleman in his early sixties, if my appraisal was correct. A white button-up, a charcoal waistcoat with matching slacks, and expensive leather shoes accompanied his tartan-inspired jacket. As he drew closer, I took stock of his handsome features and the twinkle in the blue eyes shining brightly above a fluffy, gray beard. I found it odd when he didn't shake my hand, lightly nudging my elbow instead, guiding me toward his office. There was something protective in the gesture—almost fatherly. I settled into the leather chair opposite the desk from him and looked around the office.

"Not too shabby, aye?" he smirked, a thick Highlander accent rolling off his tongue.

Although not large, the space was comfortable. Two leather chairs nestled into a corner, and a nearby wooden table held two glasses with a bottle of Scotch cozied between them.

"My assistant wants to throttle me half the time." His hand swept over the stacks of books, magazines, and loose papers covering most of the mahogany desk.

I rather doubted that. Mr. Murray had a lot going on, but he was equally organized if the appearance of his desk bore any true reflection of his character—and in my years in the workforce, I found it usually did. Each stack appeared orderly, an organized system in play. The window near his desk opened to the center courtyard, his office perfectly positioned to observe the happenings of the castle. Not too shabby, indeed.

Mr. Murray asked various questions about my career path and what I sought from my next position. I, in turn, asked about the company culture and Mr. Murray's experience working for the castle.

"I was a bit surprised this job posting was open to international applicants," I said once Mr. Murray had finished sharing about his tenure with the castle.

"Oh? Well, I'm keen to find the proper fit, Ms. Weston. Your areas of focus in your previous positions are a good match for the needs in this one. And you mentioned your love for history. That's something I always look for in a candidate."

"Areas of focus, like my event work," I guessed.

"Aye. We dinnae have the budget for a fundraising manager, so that role is spread across several positions. The PR manager is head of the annual donor event. I was glad to see your experience in that area."

Running an annual event . . . though I'd worked on event teams in the past, this would be my first opportunity to head an event. And that sounded like the type of challenge I was looking for in my next move.

"Speaking of international applicants," Mr. Murray said, "perhaps I should have led in with this, but what has you interested in leaving the States to pursue a career in Edinburgh?"

And at that precise moment, a tingle worked its way up my spine. It was fleeting, but the signal was clear—this man was no human.

Out of all the job opportunities I'd explored, I was banking on the one where I'd report to another witch. My mind raced wondering if he realized I was a witch, but of course, odds favored that he did. Surely, he knew. I suddenly understood why he hadn't shaken my hand at the beginning of the interview.

The thought unnerved me, but I responded as calmly as I could. "I'm ready for a new challenge and am very interested in expanding my horizons in another country. Scotland has such a rich culture and wonderful outdoor community. I think it's the perfect place for me."

"Oh, you're keen on the outdoors then?" he asked, stroking his neatly trimmed beard.

"Hiking and kayaking are both avid interests of mine."

"You're sure to have endless adventures here, especially through the Highlands."

I smiled, hoping to hide my growing apprehension.

"Well, if you dinnae have additional questions, I'll let you get on with your day, Ms. Weston. I plan to call your references this afternoon."

"That sounds great. I really appreciate your time."

I extended my hand, my eyes intently awaiting his reaction. He followed my lead, and a small tremor moved through my hand. Mr. Murray was certainly a witch, and a powerful one at that.

Walking down the corridor, I wondered if others of our kind worked within the castle. Could they determine I was a witch from afar, just as Mr. Murray had? I stepped into the courtyard and found Fitz.

"You know," I said, "If it weren't for your modern clothing, you'd fit right into this medieval place, you bloody Scot."

"You're a real charmer, you know that?" Fitz leaned over, planting a kiss on the top of my head. "Finally. I thought you were going to stay in there forever," he murmured, tugging me closer to him.

His warmth was inviting against the lingering nip of fall. I slipped my hand in his and told him about my experience with Mr. Murray.

"I'll ask Isaac to do a background check on him—he has access to those witchkind resources," Fitz said. "What's Murray's first name?"

"James."

"James Murray . . . that sounds familiar." Fitz's eyes widened, though he recovered quickly.

"What's that about?" I asked.

"Well," Fitz said, "there's a James Murray on the Scottish National

169

Coven Council, but I don't know if they're one and the same."

"He works for the *government*?" I didn't like that at all.

"We don't know that yet," Fitz said. "Let me do a bit of research, and I'll let you know what I find out."

"I don't know how I feel about working for another witch, and if he's a part of the council . . ."

"Why are you unsure about working for a witch?" Fitz asked.

"I don't know. I'm not comfortable with my magic yet, and I guess I'm just nervous."

"That will change, though. Faster if you allow yourself to spend more time with other witches."

"Point taken," I said. "You know, I sensed the energy of the stalkers in Paris, but I didn't feel anything from Mr. Murray until we were nearly finished with the interview."

"You sensed them because they were tracking us—they were actively using magic," Fitz said.

"Murray definitely knew I was a witch though. How did he do that?"

"As your skills develop, you'll be able to determine if another witch is close, even if they aren't expending magic. Every witch has varying levels of power. You'll learn to pick up on their energy. It'll be even stronger between the two of us, though—I know you're not far by simply feeling your energy or catching your scent on the breeze."

"What do I feel like? How far away can you feel me?"

"A respectable distance, I suppose. When I walked through the castle gates, I knew you were still inside," Fitz said. "Your energy feels like sunlight dancing on my skin when you're at a distance. Similar to standing beneath the canopy of a tree on a day like today. The wind moves through the leaves, and I catch glimpses of your light and warmth. And as the gap between us closes, it grows warmer, more pleasant."

My grip instinctively tightened on his hand. "And my scent?"

He rested his face against the top of my head and inhaled slowly.

"Your scent is caramel." He paused. "Your scent is sweet, your warmth is palpable, and you're miraculously standing in front of me with your hand linked through mine. Who forgot to tell you that you deserve the whole world?"

I shook my head lightly, though his praise sent butterflies through me. "It's come on gradually, but I know your scent and feel as well."

"Like you're downwind from a farm?"

"Way to ruin the moment!" I laughed, pausing briefly to collect my thoughts. "You smell of oak . . . of a whisky with hints of fruit and spice. I noticed it when you hugged me that first moment in Paris. I assumed it was the scent of drink and cologne, but now I know it's you. It's comforting . . . You make me feel at ease."

That elicited a shy smile from Fitz.

"And the feeling your energy gives me," I said, "well, I'd liken it to your description. That feels just right."

"It's amazing, isn't it? That this sort of thing is real."

"It honestly feels unbreakable."

Fitz nodded. "Damn near it, I think."

The hair on our necks suddenly bristled. Though Fitz's expression remained blank, the shift in his energy buzzed in tandem with mine. We were being watched.

"*I don't know who this is,*" his voice whispered in my mind. "*We should go.*"

It seemed our exploration of the castle would have to wait for another day.

CHAPTER NINETEEN

The following afternoon, I sat cross-legged on the floor of my hotel room after meditating. Elemental witches may have been more powerful than casters, but we also carried a heavier burden. Because of this, Fitz placed a real emphasis on meditation becoming a part of my daily routine. I'd already recognized its necessity to ease my mind and release my excess energy.

I stretched lazily across the floor and reveled in the few moments when I felt perfectly centered.

I gazed up at the castle, smiling despite my recent protests with Fitz. The fact that he had upgraded my room to a castle view suite was something we were still fighting over. He wouldn't allow me to spend a dime—or, well, pence—as long as he was around.

The hotel was beautifully appointed, and the bathroom bigger than mine at home.

I jumped at the sound of my ringing phone. The number was local, and I answered quickly.

"Good afternoon, Ms. Weston. This is James Murray calling from Edinburgh Castle. I'm calling to let you know you'll hear from our head of HR later today with an official offer for our PR manager position. I hope you'll consider joining our team."

"Wow, that's great news," I said, hoping my voice was enthusiastic.

"I'm glad to hear it. I just have to say, you'll be a fine match for the role."

"Thank you so much. I look forward to hearing from the team."

After I hung up, I stared blankly at the castle, allowing my mind to roll through my thoughts. I wanted this job. Honestly, I wanted this life: living in this city with Fitz and working for an Edinburgh landmark.

But apprehension still channeled through me. Mr. Murray had done nothing wrong. In fact, he had done everything right. But Fitz and I hadn't yet met with the council, and I wasn't as honed into my newfound skills as I'd like to be prior to working closely with another witch.

And besides all that, Fitz had confirmed that James Murray did, in fact, sit on the National Coven Council for Scotland.

Fitz attempted to assuage my fears by telling me that James wasn't like the council members who had kept us apart and that Ian held him in high regard.

I was distracted as I readied myself for the evening. I was having dinner with Fitz at his flat, and though I was thrilled to see his place, the weight of this upcoming decision pulled at my good humor.

I had just poured a cup of tea when my phone rang for the second time that afternoon. It was the same number Mr. Murray had called from. I took a deep breath and answered.

Despite it being my idea, I was nervous as I walked over to Fitz's home. Fitz had offered to pick me up, but I argued against his need to protect me.

"At least call a car. Don't walk over alone," he'd said, after reminding me about the witch who'd watched us at the castle.

I shook my head and checked the directions on my phone again. Fitz would be angry if he knew I was indeed walking alone, but my desire to stretch my legs and admire the city at night was acute.

A shiver ran the length of my spine. I almost paused before instinct smothered my curiosity. Realizing I was about halfway to my destination, I picked up the pace. Although the night air was crisp with the chill of autumn, it wasn't the culprit of the sudden cold in my bones or the pinpricks of a glare assaulting my skin. I was being watched, and not by someone with mild curiosity either.

I glanced around confidently, remembering the advice I'd been given over the years: when alone at night, appear confident and alert. I hoped that advice was applicable to witches as I pressed onward. My heart beat wildly against my chest, and my sense of time was distorted. The minutes seemed to tick away slowly. Thoughts danced through my mind. Had our Parisian stalkers returned? Was it the council? *Was I in danger?*

My balance wavered as a silhouette took shape in my mind.

From the beige wool coat to the auburn hair, it was clear I was watching myself through my stalker's eyes. It took intense focus to keep moving forward as the scene grew more vivid, and even though my pace slowed, I threw my shoulders back and walked more confidently than I felt, all the while praying I wouldn't stumble and fall. From the stalker's point of view, I determined they weren't close, and perhaps they thought they were far enough away that I wouldn't notice their observation.

I shook my curiosity from my mind and focused on the path ahead of me. There was no discernible energy near me. Still, I feared the watcher would overtake me before I reached the street's next intersection, even though the Royal Mile was already in view. I reminded myself to breathe, releasing a deep sigh of relief upon rounding the corner on to Old Town's bustling main drag. The witch's stare faded along with the darkness of the street I left behind, and I focused on propelling myself closer to Fitz. Deciding I was safer amongst the crowd of people, my pulse slowed, and I checked the map a final time.

If I was reading the map correctly, Fitz's flat lay within one of the most impressive addresses in Old Town. Ramsay Garden towered over the city and only drew shadows from its western neighbor, Edinburgh Castle. I'd walked right past his home as I strolled down the esplanade to my interview. The majestic Scots Baronial-style building was beautifully adorned with white and beige stonework and trimmed in a contrasting red.

"What's wrong?" Fitz asked as he threw open the door.

"Nothing."

"I was about to call you. I felt your nerves."

"Well, there's no need for that now," I said.

"Hadley."

"Fitz."

He eyed me warily, and I reached for him instinctively, knowing his touch would quiet my agitated energy. "Don't worry about it. I'm just happy to be with you."

He ushered me through the doorway and kissed me quickly.

"So, what's on the menu?" I asked.

"We're making Scotch pies."

His answer made me smile.

"I know you're not keen on mutton, so I bought chicken instead."

My sigh of relief made him laugh.

Fitz gave me a brief tour of his flat, which was stunning. The wood floors were walnut, complementing the stormy gray walls of the living room. Large bay windows adorned the west-facing wall, allowing for ample light during the day, but were just then flaunting their view of the castle, all lit up for the evening. His furniture held deep, rich colors in the woods and warm brown leathers, rustic like a beautifully worn saddle. Books, new and old alike, were randomly stacked on most surfaces, and a half-empty decanter held a golden liquid, sure to be single malt Scotch.

The distant sound of jazz grew in volume as Fitz led me into the kitchen. My eyes flickered around the space, surprised by the comfortable size of it. Since his flat was housed in an older European building, I had expected a smaller kitchen.

"I decided on this flat solely for the kitchen. It was the largest I saw—the former owner was a chef and expanded it. You should've seen the rest of the place, though. It was tragic but completely worth the work for this setup."

"This place suits you."

The kitchen cabinets were mahogany and the counters a gray concrete. Copper and stainless steel hardware completed the look. His flat was warm and comfortable, just like him. I grinned as he set the ingredients on the counter, the thought of passing many an evening in this manner flitting across my mind.

Soon, my hands were buried in dough, and I relaxed into the rhythm of the evening. Fitz was preparing the filling. He set an onion on the cutting board and turned to me.

"Help me dice the onion?"

"Um, sure," I said. "Let me just wash my hands."

"No need. Just come over here for a second."

I followed his instructions, and he stood behind me wrapping his arms around my waist.

"Try to levitate the knife."

I craned my neck to face him. "Seriously?"

"Aye. Mind how you connect to the elements. Ask them for what you want."

"You're pretty distracting right now. You know that, right?" I asked.

He smirked. "I can move."

"No," I protested, holding firmly to his hands.

He chuckled and reached for a dish towel to wipe away the traces of dough.

"Go on," he prompted.

I scanned the materials the knife laid against—the gray counter, the worn, oak cutting board—before studying the knife. Its handle was made of dark wood, and the steel blade gleamed in the light that shone from beneath the upper cabinets.

My mind willed the knife to move.

Nothing.

"Feel the air with your energy," Fitz said. "Feel the elements that surround the knife."

I navigated the molecules surrounding me and felt my way slowly toward the knife. I jumped when my energy met the impermeable object.

"Now connect to the air around it."

The experience was more visual than I anticipated, but the air rippled as my magic infused with it. I timidly tugged my energy upward, and though it was wobbly, the knife rose from the counter.

When the knife fell with a clatter a few seconds later, I couldn't even be disappointed. I turned to Fitz.

"Did you see that?" I exclaimed.

"Aye. You're a proper witch."

Fitz kissed me, and goosebumps spread across my skin. I ran my hands along his neck, finding my grip along his shoulders. He cupped my face gently before resting his forehead against mine.

"I'm sorry," I said.

"For?"

"Pretty sure your shoulders are covered in dough now."

"Oh. Nae bother."

I ran water over a dish towel and Fitz lifted me onto the counter. He leaned into me as I wiped his shoulders clean, and my pulse quickened. He kissed me quickly before depositing me back on to solid ground.

I finished the dough distractedly as I watched Fitz command the knife to magically cut the onion for him.

"Do you do that often?" I asked.

"Cook with magic? No, but I hate chopping onions . . . the burning, watery eyes and all that. If I were ever captured, there's no need for waterboarding, just give me a hundred onions to dice."

"Oh, I really need to learn how to prep food with magic."

"You'll get there," Fitz said. "Patience."

"One of my strong suits."

The navy, ceramic plates looked beautiful as I set them onto the wooden dinner table. Fitz refilled our glasses with cabernet and took a seat, his face softly illuminated by the dim lighting.

"This is incredible," I said, savoring the first bite. The double-crusted pie was filled with chicken and just the right amount of gravy. "The combination of herbs and gravy create such a great flavor."

"Aye. And the onions too. It's a controversial choice in some households, but I prefer mine with it."

I was about to comment on the onion controversy. Then I remembered. "Oh, I have news."

"I feel your nerves. Put me out of my misery, Hads."

"I accepted a job offer this afternoon."

Fitz set his fork down and paused briefly before his eyes flitted to mine. I couldn't place what I found in them . . . apprehension, maybe.

"Oh aye? What did you settle on?" he asked.

"Well, I'm moving to Edinburgh."

Fitz's gaze dropped momentarily, and a flood of relief washed through me—his relief. When he looked up again, a heartfelt smile graced his lips.

"Do you know how happy that makes me?"

I nodded. "I think I do."

Fitz laughed softly, a kind of laugh that captured perfect happiness, before rising from the table. He slid my chair back and pulled me into an embrace. I wrapped my arms around him and held him close, content to stay in that moment forever. I pulled his face to mine, kissing him deeply.

After dinner, we moved to the couch by the fireplace. Curled up under a blanket, I was relaxed and happy.

"How's Izzy?" I asked, taking another appreciative sip of wine.

"You like this one, don't you?"

"You have good taste in women and wine," I countered, pulling a deep laugh from Fitz.

"Aye, that I do."

His fingers skimmed the length of my thigh, taking their time in meandering back to my knee. "Izzy's good. She was in her last year at the University of Washington when you moved?"

"Yep," I said.

"She accepted a job in grant writing with Seattle Children's Hospital."

"That sounds like a good fit for her."

"She's always wanted to help others, and this is a good opportunity for her. I don't know how long it'll last, though," Fitz said. "It's hard on her to be indoors at a desk for so long. She told me just yesterday she'd like to open a shop to sell plants and herbs, teas, that sort of thing."

"Okay, now *that* sounds perfect for her."

"Aye, her heart's always been in nature."

I recalled the teas, salves, and whatnot she'd brought to Daddy while he was sick and how much that had meant to us.

"I'd like to see her," I said.

"She's anxious to see you again. We should arrange that."

"Really? That would be amazing!"

"I'll call her tomorrow and ask about her holiday time. She'll hop a plane in a heartbeat."

"I can't believe how long it's been since I last saw her," I said.

"That's partially my fault. She would have come sooner, but I didn't want to pull her further into this mess while you and I were breaking the rules."

"You were right to do that."

"There's no harm in it now," Fitz said. "You have her number. Call her any time you'd like."

Fitz insisted on walking with me back to the hotel, although I didn't need any convincing. Anxiety rolled through my body as we crossed the hotel lobby. I hadn't yet mentioned my earlier encounter. Fitz would overreact, but the thought of being alone haunted me. Fitz's internal battle raged, and his warring energy washed over me. We were feeding into the other's negative energy and leading each other down a rocky path. He'd known something was wrong before I even arrived at his home, and he clearly felt the emotions that now raced through me. As the elevator propelled us toward my floor, my internal struggle came to a halt. It was time to end our game.

"Someone was watching me again tonight."

"Excuse me?" he returned, his eyes immediately wild.

"Don't overreact."

"I'm not overreacting."

"Really?" I asked.

"First of all, *really*. You know I can't help it. And this sort of thing just isn't done. You don't watch other witches."

"Okay, fine."

"Where were you when this happened?"

"When I walked over to your place."

"I told you not to walk over," he growled.

"I told you not to boss me around."

"You still don't grasp how dangerous this is, do you?"

"I do."

"Then why did you put yourself at risk?"

"I thought it would be fine—it was a short distance, and I thought it would be more crowded than it was."

He met my eyes sternly.

"Look, they didn't get close enough for me to know for sure, but I think it was the same witch from the courtyard at the castle. They never made contact or anything and trailed off right before your place."

Fitz pulled me through the door, throwing a glance at the lock. It secured itself. He then nodded toward the far side of the room, and the curtains moved to obstruct our view of the outside world.

"I'd like to stay here tonight," Fitz said.

"Sounds good to me. You could probably call the front desk for a toothbrush. Unless . . ."

"Unless what?"

"Can you just produce that sort of thing with a snap of your fingers or something?"

"I'll call the front desk," he said, reaching into the air. Without warning, the phone flew across the room and into his impatient grasp.

"Oh god. Please teach me how to do that," I said.

"All in good time. You performed levitation tonight. You'll be calling up objects in no time."

Getting ready for bed was infinitely more fun as I considered the objects I could call into my reach, wondering if I could brush my teeth without using my hands. Upon entering the bedroom, I initially reached for my leggings, but after some debate, I settled on my pajamas. They outranked my leggings on the cute scale, and much of the top was a transparent lace. It wasn't an attempt to seduce Fitz necessarily, but I thought he might shoot down the request I was about to make, and I needed all of the ammunition I could muster. I marched into the living room to find Fitz lying on the couch.

"Well, don't you look adorable?"

"Are you coming in here or what?" I asked.

"*Hadley.*"

"What? Please, don't be a prude tonight. Besides, you're able to offer more reliable protection at a closer range."

"You are something else."

"Come to bed, Fitz."

I expected resistance, but he crossed the room, stopping just in front of me. My eyes searched his, hoping for an opening into his thoughts, but to no avail; he remained carefully impassable. He turned me around and led me into the bedroom. We held each other's gaze as we climbed onto the bed.

"What are you afraid of, Fitz?"

"I'm afraid of handling this wrong."

"What do you mean?"

"Our past is complicated, and I don't want that for our future. I'm being mindful of the changes you're working through," he said.

"Which I appreciate, but . . ." I trailed off.

"You asked me to not be a prude . . . have I really not made my desires clear to you? If you read my mind right now, my thoughts would make you blush."

My heart quickened, and Fitz let out an irritated groan, rolling on to his back.

"What now?"

"The last thing I need is your body responding to my confession."

I laughed lightly, taking hold of Fitz's arm and tugging him to face me again. "Okay. I'm calm."

His eyebrows rose at my response.

"Just . . . continue. Please."

"It's important that you and I do what we can to cultivate our relationship," Fitz said. "I don't want to rush things and then realize we should have taken time to let other aspects of our relationship develop first."

"I get that. There's so much going on between us, but also just with me. With my powers, my mind, my body. I agree."

"I don't want you flying into everything headfirst, and then regretting it later."

"I don't think that would happen," I said, "but I also appreciate that we're trying to take things at a reasonable pace. There's a balance, though, and we're currently tipping the scale."

"Are you comfortable with this? With me staying over?"

"This feels better already—more comfortable than being without you. If you still need some space, that's fine, but don't stay away on my account," I said.

"Have you gone mad, then? I had to talk myself down last night, so I wouldn't come over here and sleep outside your door."

"That worried?"

"You have no idea," Fitz said.

"No more of that."

"Deal."

I slid my body closer to his and rested my head against his chest. We shimmied ourselves until we fit snugly together, clinging tightly to our rediscovered territory. Peace radiated through me, and I closed my eyes, allowing foggy calmness to take hold.

CHAPTER TWENTY

On Wednesday, Fitz and I walked up the steps of the Scottish National Coven Council's main campus. The beautiful beige building towered high above us, its stonework contrasting little against the gray sky. As we neared the entrance and people became visible on the other side of the glass doors, I froze. My muscles tensed, my heart raced, and the overwhelming urge to run took hold.

"Oh no," I muttered.

Fitz turned quickly. "It's okay, Hads. Let's take a deep breath, aye?"

I nodded.

He led me through a few breathing exercises until my body eased. Then, he wrapped his arms around me and held me until I was calm.

"Sorry about that," I said.

"A bit overwhelmed?"

"My anxiety has been better over here, even with everything happening. But . . ."

"I understand," Fitz said. "But we'll face this together . . . we'll be all right."

Fitz's energy fluttered through me. I knew he was worried too, but I accepted his encouragement gratefully.

"I'm sorry to say this, but we're tight on time." Fitz said. "Ready, you reckon?"

I swallowed hard and nodded. Fitz reached for the door handle.

Perhaps it was my prior experiences with government buildings, but I'd painted the witchkind government offices as old, dilapidated buildings with buzzing, flickering fluorescent bulbs. A carefully curated space both preserving the building's history and boasting modern comforts awaited me instead. An attractive brunette's heels clicked down the hardwood hallway as she led us past large, black pane windows. I was struck by both the grandeur and the tastefulness of the offices. Everyone smiled or nodded as we passed them in the hallway, and they seemed genuinely pleasant. Several witches spoke to our guide, who was full of banter and laughter. She knew everyone by name.

Our guide left us seated by a desk in a small room surrounded by beige stone walls and a large picture window, massive trees full of red and yellow leaves swaying gently on the other side of the glass. The table was sturdy, good quality, and topped with a large Apple monitor. I tapped my fingers nervously on the wooden desk, and Fitz slid his hand over mine.

A petite woman with gray hair and framed Prada glasses entered the room, gliding effortlessly toward the desk.

"Hadley. Fitz. Such a pleasure to meet you both." She shook our hands, and her eyes widened. "Oh my. Such power you *both* have!"

I shifted in my seat, and Fitz once again reached for my hand. His nervous current of energy coursed through me, reminding me of our earlier conversation—how the Scottish Council had been trying to recruit him for years. He'd avoided a meeting like this for a long time. This must have been a worst-case scenario for him in more ways than one.

"Mrs. Cameron," Fitz said. "It's nice to meet you."

"Please, you can both call me Olivia." She smiled broadly.

I was surprised by her friendly nature, though it felt forced. Something was off.

I caught Fitz's glance through the corner of my eye.

"Oh, good," Olivia said. Olivia's eyes were fixed behind us. I turned to find a small witch in the doorway. "Thank you for joining us, Mia."

Strong waves of energy fired off her snowy skin and crackled through the still air like lightning warning of an approaching storm. Her eyes were as soft a blue as Lake Crescent's glacial-fed waters, and they were starkly contrasted by her raven hair. She felt equal parts ethereal and threatening.

"This is a rare treat," Olivia explained. "We don't often have Cardinal Court members join these types of meetings. But I'm pleased to introduce you to Mia Davies."

"A court member?" Fitz questioned.

"That's of little consequence," Mia said. "I'm only here to observe your meeting today."

Her soprano voice was melodic, though it held a tone of authority. She was used to giving orders, I thought.

Fitz's energy grew tight, and it was clear we both felt how strange the situation was.

"First things first. We need to verify Hadley's power," Olivia said, rising from her seat.

A flurry of nerves shot through me. "What does that mean? What do I have to do?"

"Oh, this will go quite quickly," Olivia said. "Hadley, I'll just place my palm on your forehead, and then I'll feel the palm of your right hand. Will that be all right?"

"I don't have much choice, do I?" I suddenly felt trapped, and my tone was harsher than I'd intended.

Olivia smiled, and my skin crawled.

"She's happy to oblige," Fitz intervened.

"*This is a dangerous situation. Try to remain calm,*" Fitz whispered into my mind.

My eyes flickered with uncertainty. I wished I knew how to respond telepathically.

"No need to be nervous, Fitz," Olivia said. "I imagine I'd have the same response if I were in Hadley's position."

Olivia was, indeed, quick. She stood next to me and closed her eyes, muttering unintelligibly under her breath. Her palm rested gently on my forehead before she took my hand, palm up, in hers. She grazed and circled my open palm.

After a few minutes, she opened her eyes and smiled before turning to Mia, who was leaning against the brick wall near the window with both her arms and legs crossed. Olivia nodded, and Mia stepped forward, still studying me.

Olivia returned to the opposite side of the table, typing rapidly before hitting the enter key with force and meeting my gaze. "You certainly have matched with your power. There's no doubt about that. The power you each possess is extraordinary."

Fitz nodded once. My stomach flipped. The council knowing the extent of our power felt more dangerous than defying their orders had.

"Fitz, you were right about Hadley, but you both understand our concern?"

I felt like a child in the principal's office. Olivia's tone was coercive, like we should see her point of view, and it didn't sit well with me.

After all they'd put us through, they weren't allowed to tell us how to feel about it.

"I'm afraid I don't," I returned, meeting her eyes unabashedly.

"Hadley."

"No, Fitz. I don't understand, and I won't sit here and pretend I do." I returned my focus to Olivia. "I am a witch. I always have been. Fitz was able to see that. If the councils are so wise and use such discernment ruling over us, how could you miss that?"

Fitz shifted uncomfortably in his seat.

"We didn't miss anything," Mia countered.

"Are you kidding me? You kept us apart because you didn't realize I was a witch. That sounds like missing something to me."

"We kept you apart because it was uncertain you'd match," Mia said. "And in the end, you defied orders anyway. You should answer for what you've done."

"That was on me," Fitz interjected. "If anyone is to answer for these actions, that should be me, and me alone. I made these choices, and Hadley had no part in that."

"Fitz, no," I said.

He kept his gaze fixed on Mia.

"Fitz kept our secret until it was time for me to match to my power. He didn't do anything wrong," I continued. I wouldn't let him take the fall alone.

"There is an order to things. He stepped out of line doing this without the council's involvement," Mia shot back.

Fitz's energy stirred through me. I was making him nervous, but I was so angry I couldn't seem to stop.

"But it was time for me to match—clearly. Your order didn't make sense."

"It's worked perfectly for years. Our rules are in place to protect everyone—even yourselves."

"You protected us from nothing. You served your own self-interests, sure. But can you honestly tell me you did anything in my best interest?"

"This line of thinking demonstrates how much you don't know—which is a lot, by the way," Mia answered.

"Is that so? Please, enlighten me."

Mia shook her head. "That time hasn't come."

"What does that even mean? I'm tired of this, of hiding information. I think you're just trying to cover your tracks because you realized you were wrong."

"It's not that simple, I'm afraid," Olivia interjected.

"Oh, but it is," I said. "Things either are, or they aren't. I am a witch. The councils forcing us apart was wrong. You made the wrong call."

"We made the best decision we could, and we did it to keep everyone safe," Olivia said. "I know this must have been a difficult season for you."

"Do you? Tell me something: can you really understand what I've been through?"

Olivia quietly held my gaze, and if I wasn't so angry, perhaps her intensity would have made me uncomfortable. Mia's features were cross, but she held her tongue.

"No. I guess I don't," Olivia finally acknowledged, sighing.

"You have no idea what you did to us." I hated the strain I heard in my voice, but I kept my eyes firmly on Olivia before shifting my gaze to Mia. "You sit in here and makes rules for the witches you govern, but do you truly understand the consequences of those choices?"

"Of course, we do," Mia said.

"Sometimes we're forced to make decisions that are best for witch-kind as a whole," Olivia said. "There may be negative side effects, but we can't always control every factor. It's impossible."

"Is that what I was? A factor?" I shook my head.

"You're quiet, Fitz. What do you think of all this?" Olivia asked. Perhaps she thought Fitz would see the sense in their faulty logic, but she was mistaken.

"Of course, I don't agree with the council's choices regarding our relationship. I think we're all clear on that. But this moment isn't about me." He cleared his throat, and I didn't miss the way he pushed back his shoulders and sat straighter. "It's about what's been done to Hadley and about how you forced us apart unnecessarily. Hadley doesn't need me to speak for her."

"This truly was meant to protect everyone," Olivia said. "Humans are too dangerous. They can't know about us."

I met Fitz's eyes meaningfully. I wouldn't be coerced into believing the councils had intended to protect me.

"But here we all are. Hadley has come into her powers. There are no rules being broken now. You are free to move forward with your relationship without any further involvement from us."

"We're glad to hear that," Fitz said. "One more question, though."

Olivia nodded for him to continue.

"Someone watched us while we were in Paris, and now someone has been watching us from the shadows here in Edinburgh. Is it the council?"

"No, we haven't had anyone watching since you've been back—and we didn't even know of your whereabouts when you were in Paris. We trusted you to come forward and meet with us, as you and your father said you would, so we stopped trying to find you, truthfully."

"You're certain?"

"Quite. Do you have reason to believe they're related?"

"It would be quite the coincidence if they aren't, but we have no hard evidence either way except that they have different energies."

"We'll find out who it is and ensure your safety." Olivia turned to Mia, who nodded.

"Thank you," Fitz said.

"We can assign an agent to you if you feel threatened," Olivia said.

"I don't think that's necessary," Fitz said.

He looked to me, and I shook my head. "We'll pass on that for now. But we appreciate the offer."

"We do need to assign a council trainer to meet with Hadley and assess her powers, though," Mia said.

"Why?" Fitz asked.

"It's standard procedure when a witch of . . . uncertain ancestry matches with their power, especially if it happens in adulthood," Mia said.

"What do you mean by 'uncertain ancestry?'" I asked.

"We don't know where your magical lineage comes from," Mia said. "But we'll find out."

"I'd like to know the answer to that myself," I said.

"Then you should cooperate with us."

"This assessment process isn't invasive," Olivia said. "They'll run Hadley through different spells, observe her using her magic, that sort of thing. We're continually improving our research so we may better assist witches in this situation in the future."

Fitz sat back in his chair, though he didn't immediately respond. His energy tightened.

Olivia broke the silence. "It'll be helpful to Hadley as well. The trainer will prepare a report with information regarding her best abilities and those you'll want to hone during training to improve on."

Fitz looked to me, and I shrugged.

Truthfully, I didn't love the idea, even if they were able to provide answers, but I wasn't sure if refusing the trainer would land us in trouble.

"On one condition," Fitz said.

"That being?"

"The assessment doesn't happen here. I think Hadley would be more comfortable elsewhere."

Mia stiffened, and Olivia turned her head slightly and nodded to Mia. Whatever occurred in their silent exchange prompted Mia to sigh . . . and then agree.

"Pick a location that suits both parties. We look forward to working with you both," Olivia said.

"So, that's it, then? We're free to go?" I asked.

"I think we can all agree on leaving the past behind us and moving forward." Olivia smiled warmly.

A chill ran down my spine. The guys were right: they wanted something from us.

"Aren't you a feisty one today?" Fitz quipped as we exited the council building.

"One minute I was panicked, and the next I was angry."

"Oh, that much I sorted out."

"You won't have to just 'sort it out' once you teach me how to communicate telepathically."

"Patience, Hads."

I groaned and then my mind turned back to the meeting. "I don't like Mia's involvement. I think she had something to do with our separation," I said.

"Because she was a part of this meeting or is it something else pulling at you?"

"Yeah. I mean, the Cardinal Court sounds like a big deal. And one of their members was present for our meeting? It seems odd."

"Aye, it does seem a bit much."

"So, do you think we're done now?" I asked, hoping he'd disagree with my instincts.

"No."

"Oh, great," I said.

"We'll hear from them again. Did you see her reaction to our power? Her surprise wasn't genuine. I think she already knew what she'd find."

"Fitz, why do they want you to join them so badly?"

"It's my abilities. They want me to utilize them for the council's purposes."

"I know you're powerful. I know you can bring my memories to life and all that . . . but what else can you do?"

Fitz hesitated. "Do you want me to tell you about them, or show you?"

"Show me. Definitely."

CHAPTER TWENTY-ONE

Henry's estate was straight out of a fairytale. A lengthy driveway wound across the rolling hills of the countryside, crossing property so extensive that no neighbors were visible, even with the lack of foliage. The Palladian-style home was grand, sitting atop a hill in the center of his acreage. The home had been constructed in the late 17th century by Henry's wealthy ancestors and had remained in his family for hundreds of years. It had recently been left to Henry after his parents moved to Greece.

We stepped through the French doors from the patio into a large sitting room. Two of the walls were covered in bookshelves that held countless volumes of literature. Paintings covered another wall with what I assumed were the likenesses of Henry's ancestors.

Though the suit jackets betrayed the time period of each portrait, the red Stuart tartan clearly spanned across generations. The far side of the room held antique maps and a stone fireplace that appeared to be just getting started for the afternoon. Tufted chairs and a large leather couch were near the fireside, and end tables were decorated with stacks of books and lamps emitting a warm glow.

"Happy birthday, Hadley!" Henry exclaimed happily as he entered the room. He enveloped me in a warm hug.

"It's so good to see you again, Henry," I said.

"It's lovely to see you, as well."

Henry had returned to Edinburgh the day prior.

"How's your special day been?" Henry asked.

"Well, let's see. Fitz woke me up with breakfast. And then I opened presents from him—look at my new watch," I said, showing off one of the gifts.

"Oh, that's bonnie," Henry said.

"Then we hiked Arthur's Seat and grabbed lunch."

"Gonnae train on your birthday?"

"She insisted," Fitz said.

"What better present is there than learning more about my magic? I mean, seriously."

"You have a point, lass," Henry said.

"Speaking of which, we should get started," Fitz said, laying a hand on Henry's shoulder. "She has loads of training ahead of her."

Henry nodded. "I'll be just here if you need me."

Fitz led me outside to my designated training location, and the afternoon passed as I learned to command my fire magic.

I dug the heels of my baby blue rainboots against the Scottish soil and pulled my body into the proper form . . . or so I thought.

The wind nipped at my bare fingers, but it was of little consequence. My fingers burst with flames, and I shot a fireball toward the target.

"Are you joking?" Fitz shouted from behind a small fir tree.

"Obviously not."

"I ought to send one back, so you know how it feels."

"I can take it."

"Seriously, please don't set me on fire. It would ruin the afternoon."

I snickered, pulling a smile from him as well.

Mastering the skill of fire creation was a huge step in my training. Once I'd understood how to commune with the elements, asking them for what I sought was easier and more intuitive than I'd anticipated, for which I was grateful. It made me feel like a real, certified witch, and that was a true confidence booster this early in training.

The next step was creating fire with my body and then using that fire to protect myself. I never could have imagined there were so many ways to command fire. I could throw it like a baseball, wield it through a bow and arrow, shoot it from my fingertips, and radiate it from my entire body. I was basically a dragon, I observed to Fitz, who rolled his eyes.

Throwing had taken little practice. Fitz had noted it was one of my most natural skills, with an appreciative nod. The bow and arrow had worked out quite nicely as well. My father had taught me to wield a bow and arrow long ago. Apparently, that was skill enough. Radiating fire from my entire body? Evidently, I wasn't half bad at that either. I had gasped as the air ignited all around me, absolutely in awe at the way the flames responded to my request.

However, using my fingers like a gun to shoot fire was an issue. I'd almost set Fitz ablaze with a misfire. Twice. Though he was trying to maintain his humor, I was sure nearly being lit on fire was a harrowing experience. He walked over to demonstrate again how my form should appear.

"One more time. Legs here. Back straight. Arms tight and slightly bent."

"Do I really need both arms out?"

"Your ability is still materializing, and you'll have twice the strength with both hands. It should fully develop in the next week," Fitz said.

"Best news I've heard all day."

"Arms just a little lower. It's a slightly different form from shooting a firearm. Aye, perfect."

I adjusted per his instructions and shot. My flames landed at the edge of the target.

"Now, that's better," Fitz said.

"I was a lot closer on that one."

"Try it again. Focus on what you want."

I took a deep breath, mindful of my form, and reveled in my desire to set the target ablaze, envisioning how flames would lick the air. I closed my eyes briefly and asked my magic to guide my efforts.

"Fire," I breathed, and took my shot. Flames leapt from my fingertips, brilliant against the waning daylight. "Oh my god," I whispered, mesmerized by the target, ablaze in magical desire made real.

"That was braw!" Fitz was beaming as he lifted me from the ground. My lips found his, both of us alight with excitement. "Let's see that again."

Firing off shots one by one, I hit my mark, my energy bursting at the seams. Finally, I paused, a sudden urge for Fitz taking hold.

"Damn," he breathed. "Your eyes."

My head tilted in curiosity.

"They're on fire, Hads," he explained, his hand resting at the base of my skull.

"I don't understand."

"They're red, orange, yellow . . . the same as your fire magic."

Like my mind's eye, I realized.

"Is that . . . normal?" I asked.

"Aye, I think it is for you." His heart rate doubled as he met me in a kiss, fiery in its own right.

"I wish I had a mirror," I said.

"Call one up."

I grimaced. I wasn't excelling in calling objects as quickly as I was with my fire magic. One of the main rules with calling forth an object was that we could never risk a human catching us in the act, so we had to work a concealment around us to hide the fact that we were pulling something from thin air.

"The concealment part of the spell is still giving me trouble," I said.

"There's no one around—I'm certain—so don't worry with the concealment. Just call it up."

I thought of the compact mirror in my makeup bag: the antique brass one that Gram had given to me years ago. I visualized the etched floral pattern on the lid. I could almost feel it under my fingertips. I reached my hand into the air and when I pulled my hand back, the mirror rested in my palm.

"That's brilliant. Nice work," Fitz praised.

I flipped open the lid, and sure enough, just above my bright smile, my irises danced with flames. I gasped.

"You good, Hads?"

It was an unnerving sight, but it was fresh proof of the power I held inside of me. "More than good."

"Why don't we head inside? You need to rest."

I groaned.

"Fine. I won't show you my powers then."

My eyes lit up. I'd forgotten. "You should have led in with that. Come on. Time to show me what you can do, Dr. MacGregor."

"Shall I pour drinks?" Henry asked as we entered the sitting room. Henry had a "no shoes" rule in his home, so I swapped my boots for a pair of cozy slippers—which Henry had bought me—before making a beeline for the warm hearth.

"That does sound grand. But something else vies for my attention this evening," Fitz said.

Henry's gaze turned curious.

"Hadley's asked to see the rest of my powers."

A grin spread across Henry's lips. "Oh aye? Well, prepare your-self, lass."

Henry padded to the kitchen, and I settled onto the couch next to Fitz.

"You remember at the lake when I pulled your memories to the surface?"

I nodded.

"There's more to that power."

"Show me."

Fitz turned his head, and I followed his gaze to find a familiar face staring back at me.

"Momma?" I asked, thoroughly confused. She couldn't be here, could she?

My mother walked toward me. "Hello, honey."

I tentatively moved closer, not realizing until that moment just how much I missed her. After everything that had happened—that was still happening—I wanted nothing more than to see her, to tell her everything about the witch I was becoming.

I touched my mom's arm, and she dissipated right before my eyes.

I stared blankly at where my mother had been.

"I apologize if that was too much—with your mum. When you asked me to show you, I just pulled out the first person I could find in your memories."

"She was an apparition?" I asked.

"Aye. My power mixes with your memories and recreates them like they're real . . . and they play out in front of your eyes."

"That wasn't like the mind trick before. That was . . . real."

"It's jarring, I know."

"Damn, that was incredible. You're *really* talented, Fitz. That took a lot of power—I can feel it."

"Oh aye. There's nothing much to it," Fitz said.

"Wait, are you blushing?"

"Don't look at me," he countered playfully, walking off to the kitchen. Though his remarks were lighthearted, I knew it was difficult for Fitz to be praised. I thought he would be used to it considering the vast amount of power he possessed, but Fitz was humble, and for that, I was inordinately grateful.

When he returned, he was flanked by Henry and holding two glasses of water. Henry settled into the armchair in the corner and began rummaging through papers and magazines on the side table.

"I have something else to show you," Fitz announced as he passed a glass of water to me.

"Bring it on," I said.

"Pick a place."

"What?"

"Just pick a place. Name somewhere that fascinates you. Anywhere."

"Why? Oh my god." My eyes must have been huge. "Can you . . ."

"I'm a time-walker, Hadley."

"Are you kidding me?"

A snicker from the corner of the room was the only sign Henry was listening to our conversation. His face was hidden behind the latest edition of *The Times*, one of the only London-based newspapers still offering print copies, but I didn't need to see past the paper to envision the grin on his face.

"Careful, lass. You'll catch flies with your mouth open like that," Henry said.

"How do you know what my expression looks like?"

Another snicker from Henry was all I could expect in answer. I redirected my attention to Fitz.

"We're about to transport?" I asked.

Fitz chuckled. "Go on, then. Tell me where we're going."

"The Virgin Islands."

"*Nice*, Hadley." He smirked. "Okay, chug that water."

I followed his instruction quickly.

"Now come here."

With one arm secured around my waist, he urged me to remove my slippers and pulled me snugly against his body.

"Hold on tightly," he whispered, his breath warm on my ear. "And whatever you do, do not let go of me while we're in the in-between."

I was about to ask what he meant when the world spun, sliding away from the light, and weightlessness consumed our bodies. Ever so slowly, stars came into focus, their illumination momentarily jarring after the absolute darkness. Mesmerized, I extended an arm before Fitz reminded me to hold on to him. The stars faded away, replaced by many indiscernible objects, each swimming around us. Color returned, bringing shades of blue and green into my vision, along with the oppressive weight of gravity.

The spinning ceased, revealing ocean, sun, and land. I gasped when my toes met smooth, warm sand.

Unlike the beaches I'd visited in my short lifetime, the lush tree line mingled with the sand, the palm trees providing a welcome refuge from the bright rays of the sun.

"Welcome to St. John."

Stunned, I grasped his hand tighter and walked toward the crystal-clear water, mesmerized as it sparkled like hundreds of diamonds in the afternoon sun.

"How long can we stay?" I asked.

"We don't have to be back in Edinburgh until tomorrow morning."

"Will Henry be worried?"

"Not in the slightest."

"This is the best birthday gift I've ever received."

We journeyed over to Cruz Bay, securing essentials for an afternoon by the sea. We traded our warm clothes for swimsuits and staked our claim on a deserted stretch of sand. As I sank into a beach chair, Fitz floated a Corona in my direction, and I fired off my first question.

"Does it always happen like that?" I asked.

"Like what exactly?"

"The darkness, the stars, the spinning."

"Oh aye. It's always been like that. We're navigating through elements and time in order to find another place."

"How difficult is that for you?"

"Very," Fitz said. "It takes loads of practice and concentration. It's my most difficult power to control."

"Can you go anywhere?"

"Anywhere on Earth. Any further and you begin to deal with gravity in a different way. The distance alone is pretty troubling."

"You say you're navigating through time," I said. "Can you visit the future or the past?"

"I can visit the past, not the future. Though witches can see the future, it isn't a certain track. We're not omniscient, so we only see the future in a limited way."

"What do you mean?"

"There are unknowns," Fitz said. "Everyone changes their mind. When we make a decision, we alter the future. If we change our mind, we alter the future again. Then there's Fate . . . and God."

"So, with varying levels of power mixing with God and Fate, witches have limited future vision," I said.

"Right. You might set out to travel to one particular part of the future, but with the threads of time and humanity changing, you could land in some type of non-reality, basically trapped in time."

"That sounds like my worst nightmare."

"It would be anyone's worst nightmare," Fitz said.

"So, the future is an ever-changing beast, best left alone."

"It isn't stable enough for someone to physically transport themselves, especially with how quickly it changes."

"This is so fascinating!" I said. "Do you transport often?"

"No. It's tiring, especially when I bring someone along. Of course, that depends on the distance or how far into the past I'm traveling. But sometimes I take off on a whim."

"What about the past? Have you visited it much?"

"Some. I only stay for a short period of time. I don't want to accidentally alter the past. It's tricky and tiring, but the experience is truly incredible," Fitz said. "We'll pick a year and go when we have more time."

The sun descended, announcing the approaching evening, and I envied its calm path, sinking into the arms of the night. It was a stark contrast to the thoughts pinging around my mind. The past swirled all around me. My mate could transport us to anywhere in the world, and to any time in the past. We were witches. I'd fallen for him at twenty-seven, nearly lost him, and found him once more.

I climbed out of my chair and waded knee-deep into the gentle water of the Caribbean. I questioned who was nearby, awakening my mind's eye. A boat lay far off the coast, loaded with wealthy college students on school break. Around the corner—separated from us by large, slippery rocks—were two newlyweds, caught up in each other. Outside these few people, Fitz and I were alone on this tiny portion of the island, for which I was grateful.

I felt Fitz's presence behind me. His hands found my waist as his face nestled into the crook of my shoulder, planting a kiss on the sensitive skin. A low sigh escaped my lips, encouraging him as he slid his hand across my abdomen, leaving a trail of goosebumps in the wake of his fingers. Magic brought his desire to life as it twirled my body around slowly to face him. He searched my eyes, his fingers tracing the length of my cheek before planting a slow, long-awaited kiss on my parted lips.

Even though forming our connection had solidified our relationship and crafted a profound intimacy between us, everything felt more precious after facing the council together. But regardless of the cause, desire coursed through me even stronger than before. Fitz paused, his eyes searching mine.

"Do you know how much I love you?" I asked, running my fingers along the stubble on his jaw.

Fitz leaned into my palm, kissing it. "I can't even think straight. Our desire is clouding my mind, and I . . . Hadley, I know we've tried to pace ourselves, but my god, do I want you."

"Then don't hold back," I whispered.

A shift sounded through our connection, and for a few seconds, I struggled to identify what it was. Then, exhilaration pulsed through me, and I identified the former feeling—happiness had replaced a restrained tension that had existed from the very moment we'd met. It was so familiar that I had thought the sensation normal, and the newfound freedom in Fitz's energy was intoxicating.

He lifted me into his embrace. I wrapped my legs tightly around his waist as he walked us toward the dense tree line. He flicked his wrist, and a large blanket appeared under the canopy of the palm trees. Fitz dropped to his knees, lowering us onto the blanket.

Fitz scanned the area around us, and the air shifted. He was creating a privacy shield.

I took stock of my mate, and he watched as my eyes swept his body. I traced the muscular outlines along his chest with my fingertips and further down to his sculpted abdomen. His head tilted back, eyes closed, before a smirk formed on his lips. A burst of euphoria hit me as our connection intensified.

I slipped my hands through his hair as he leaned forward and kissed me. I tried to tug him closer to me, but he pulled away. He shook his head playfully before reaching behind my back to untie the strings of my swimsuit and tossed it aside. His eyes lingered, and his attention quickened my pulse.

Fitz ran his fingers across my collarbone to my shoulder, then lightly down my spine before tracing lower to my hips where he found his grip. His lips took their time studying the curves of my body, like he meant to learn every inch of it through touch. Goosebumps spread across my skin, and my mind grew thick. I was operating on instinct as the final threads of our connection began to take shape.

When Fitz's eyes returned to mine, a small intake of air rushed through his lips.

"What is it?" I whispered.

"Your eyes," he returned softly. "They're in flames again."

"Fitting."

"Aye. Fiery you are." He ran his thumb across my bottom lip. "My wee firecracker."

I looked deeply into his eyes, and my breath hitched. "I would have waited forever for you. Lifetimes, even. This—what we have—it was worth the risk," I said.

Fitz's gaze softened, and as I leaned in to kiss him, he wrapped his strong arms around me. His touch was filled with desire, but it was his energy I noticed most. For the first time since I'd known Fitz, all of our troubles melted away, and our bodies released the last of our tension, our anxieties. We were perfectly at peace with each other, and I finally knew Fitz in his purest form.

As our desire propelled us forward, a fire raged within me, and the warmth pumping through my veins grew until I thought it might consume me from the inside out. I moved against Fitz, and he rolled us to the ground. We were beyond words now, and the air was quiet except for our quickening breath. I was no longer in command of my body, my mind lost in the haze, and instincts took full control.

I arched my back as we embarked into the last of our unknown territory. Sparks floated lazily in the space surrounding us like fireflies lighting a horizon at dusk. I was certain I had lost myself in a dream as we cradled each other in magic, untamed and infinite. Time seemed to stand still as we held tightly to pink sunsets, warm breezes, and the most devoted hearts.

CHAPTER TWENTY-TWO

The following afternoon found us back at Henry's. Fitz and I continued our work on my fire skills, and eventually, we decided to retire to Henry's sitting room to relax.

Henry grinned broadly before passing wine glasses to Fitz and me.

"Hadley, I hear this is a favorite of yours, so I ordered a few bottles for the bar," Henry announced, his large, hazel eyes twinkling mischievously. My mouth gaped as I sniffed the dark liquid.

"This is the Chateau de Ferrand we had in Paris."

I looked to Fitz, who nodded in affirmation.

"Henry!" I said. "I can't tell you how appreciative I am of all this, and not only the wine. Thank you for letting me practice here."

"Oh, dinnae mention it, lass. You know you're welcome anytime."

Henry raised his glass, and we followed suit. "*Slàinte mhath!*"

We sank into large, leather chairs near the unlit fireplace.

"Hadley, perhaps you could do the honors," Henry said.

I inhaled deeply and envisioned the neatly stacked wood alight in flames . . . and it was.

"Nicely done," Fitz said, a proud gleam in his eyes.

"Brilliant," Henry concurred.

I settled deeper into the couch, allowing the sounds of the crackling fire and the taste of good drink to relax me as my toes warmed from the nearby heat.

"Well," Henry began. "The council called. They're sending out that trainer."

"Today?" I asked.

"Aye. They phoned about ten minutes ago and said he would be here soon."

"Ready or not," I muttered.

"If you're no ready, I'll request he come back another time," Henry said. "You've had a busy few days, and this is last minute."

"I'm fine to meet him today. I don't think we'll be doing any training this afternoon."

Fitz nodded.

A noise in the hallway disturbed the quiet of the sitting room. I turned toward the door, noting the extra wine glass sitting on the table. I had missed that earlier. Soon enough, Henry's housekeeper, Olga, shuffled into the room to announce a visitor. Henry requested she bring our guest in, and she smiled softly before nodding and disappearing through the entryway.

I wasn't sure what I had expected, but it surely wasn't what followed. A tall, muscular frame filled the doorway, and though I recognized his face instantly, I wasn't prepared for the charge of energy that accompanied him.

"Holy shit. You're a witch."

Tanner. He was one of the few people I thought I knew like the back of my hand, but I had clearly missed one very important detail.

Tanner ran a hand through his dark hair and crossed the room, lifting my rigid body off the ground and into a warm embrace. "Nice to see you too, Hads."

"You've got to be kidding."

"Now, is it the witch part or the council part that's throwing you off here?"

"Uh, both. Obviously," I said.

"Right, *obviously*." Tanner grinned. "The witch part does make sense when you think about it, right? I mean, didn't you ever wonder about us? Everyone else did. How we could be so close, spend all that time together, but with nothing happening in the romance department?"

He was right—we were magnets, but there was never any sort of romantic chemistry between us. Everything was starting to make sense.

"Everyone found our relationship odd, except for us," I said.

"We were kindred spirits—the same species surrounded by a lot of humans."

"Jordan . . ."

"Jordan was used to your oddities years before I ever entered the picture," Tanner said. "I probably make about as much sense to her as you do, but it works somehow."

"Well, I declare."

"You sound just like Gram!"

"You do know how to compliment a girl," I said, beaming ear to ear.

Staring at my companion of many years, the urge to give him a nice smack to the back of the head overwhelmed me, and I acted on that desire.

"What was that for?" Tanner asked, rubbing the back of his head.

"For keeping a secret from me," I said.

"Because I had a choice?"

I gave him an amused look.

Fitz interjected into the conversation, and he and Tanner shook hands. I couldn't help but think of all that had passed since I'd witnessed their first meeting over that very gesture. Tanner's expression dulled. I didn't expect him to have the same reaction to Fitz as he did to me, but something seemed off between them.

An introduction to Henry followed. Henry offered Tanner a drink, and we settled back by the fire.

"Is our friendship organic?" I asked.

"What do you mean?" Tanner asked.

"She's wondering if the council prompted you to make friends with her," Fitz clarified.

"This might be difficult to believe, but no. Our friendship was totally organic. I had no idea I'd be asked to assess you one day."

"But you knew I was a witch coming into my powers, right?" I asked.

"Yeah, absolutely. I figured that out pretty fast. I wanted to be careful around you, but we just bonded, you know? I didn't think our friendship would be a problem, but I got the MacGregors' blessing once they entered the picture."

"Really?" I turned toward Fitz.

"Dad told him to be careful around you, but he didn't see any harm in it."

"Okay, wait . . ." I said, trailing off.

"Yes, detective?"

"You started training hard right before I left the lake for Boston."

"Yeah," Tanner said. "The council hired a buddy of mine—you remember Slingshot?"

"How could I forget?" I returned drily. He'd never been a good influence on Tanner.

"Yeah, so they hired him as a trainer around that time, and he knew another position was going to open up in about a year or so. These positions are the kind you work your ass off to get a shot at because they don't come up very often, so I decided to go for it."

"When did the council hire you?"

"You remember that interview I was telling you about on the way to the airport?"

"No way," I said.

"Yep," Tanner said. "Apparently, they canceled the rest of the candidate interviews after meeting with me and offered me the job. Pretty strange actually."

"Are you moving to Edinburgh then?" Fitz asked.

"I don't know. I started working with the Washington council, and they asked me to consult on a 'special project,' so I got on a flight two days ago, and now I'm here . . . to assess your powers."

Silence fell, and truthfully, we were all a bit shellshocked.

"Well," Henry finally began. "I dinnae know about you, but none of this sounds like happenstance to me."

Fitz shook his head. "It can't be. The councils know about their connection. That's why they transferred Tanner over here."

Tanner nodded slowly. "Are you comfortable with this, Hads?"

"I wouldn't trust anyone else. You know that."

We decided Tanner would begin his assessment the following day, and with that, we allowed the conversation to meander toward everyone growing better acquainted. Touching on the subject of acquiring our powers, Henry shared his own story of coming into the craft.

"You caused an *earthquake?*" I marveled.

"Aye."

"What on earth were you doing to cause an earthquake?"

"Oh, that's the best part, isn't it, mate? He was planting a garden for his mother," Fitz answered, howling with laughter.

"And, of course, earth witches think this story is quite funny," Henry said eyeing Fitz. "It was a minor occurrence, but an earthquake nonetheless. It takes air witches a bit longer to command the earth elements, but eventually, I sorted it out."

"I heard that," Tanner said.

"You're an air witch too?" I asked.

"Yeah," Tanner confirmed. "It's the most common for elemental witches."

Henry took notice of Fitz's lingering amusement, and his eyes narrowed. A book then flew from a nearby table, its trajectory set for the back of Fitz's head. Just as I thought it would make contact, Fitz caught the book mid-flight, and with minimal effort.

"Fitz is annoyingly proficient in his magic—almost impossible to catch off guard," Henry offered, rolling his eyes.

"He's quick too," I said. "You should've seen him *move* when I almost lit him up with my fire pistols."

It was Henry's turn to laugh. "Maybe I should join your training after all."

"I'll inevitably entertain you with my witchy antics."

"Of that, you may be certain," Fitz added, a boyish grin spreading across his lips.

I took Fitz's hand in mine, and our energies relaxed. After tying our threads together in every possible way, I found our connection was stronger—and more palpable—than ever.

"Oh, shit," Tanner said.

"What is it?" I asked.

"You two are mated."

I laughed softly and nodded.

"When did that go down?"

"A week ago."

"It's pretty intense," Tanner observed.

"Aye," Henry agreed. "They have a strong bond. It's impossible to find where one energy ends and the other begins. It's all tangled up, and I cannae sort it."

"That's quick."

"I think she's known subconsciously since we met," Fitz said. "A part of our connection formed long ago."

Tanner whistled.

"Aye, muddles your brain, doesn't it?" Henry said.

Tanner nodded. "Well, I'm happy for you, Hads."

Tanner's energy didn't match his words, but I decided to let it slide until I had a chance to speak with him alone. His eyes flickered to mine, and I nodded, reassuring him that I was fine. Tanner's eyes were noticeably lighter than normal, seemingly russet and rimmed in gold. They brought a long-standing observation to mind.

"Tanner, why do your eyes change color?" I asked.

"You noticed that?" he asked. "Damn, I thought I was so careful with you."

"Not much gets past her," Fitz said, shaking his head lightly.

"Electrokinesis is one of my powers. When I use it, my eyes get lighter—something to do with the electricity. Anyway, it takes a while for them to fade back to a darker brown."

"So, you can . . . manipulate electricity?" I clarified.

"Yeah. I mean, it's nothing crazy. The same way you have fire, I have electricity." He shrugged.

The look on my face made him smile, and I was glad to see him release some of the tension from our previous conversation.

"How does that work if you're an air witch?" I asked.

"Electricity is energy. The way that the air fuels my magical energy generates electricity."

My mind reeled in complete wonderment.

We spent a few more hours beside the fire, and eventually our energies all settled into one another. Tension faded from the air, allowing me to breathe easily again. At some late hour, we began trading stories of our magical experiences and laughing like old friends. And for those few hours, I was content to let myself believe everything would turn out all right.

As we drove back to town, I asked Fitz about a couple of observations I made about Tanner.

"Is my energy off, or was it Tanner's?"

"What are you asking exactly?"

"I felt a tension between the two of you," I said.

Fitz sighed. "Aye."

"Care to expand on that?"

Fitz shot a look from the corner of his eyes.

"Please," I said.

"It's complicated. It all started at the lake."

I nodded.

"Dad was following orders, and Tanner disagreed with the way your case was being handled. He didn't like having to hide who he was from you. And we agreed with that—none of us wanted to conceal our true selves from you."

"Did he know your plan?" I asked.

"Not for a long while. But the day you left for Boston, Tanner paid me a visit." He paused. "It wasn't pleasant."

"What happened?"

"We argued, but eventually, I shared my plans with him. And he offered to help."

"*Really?*"

Fitz nodded. "I didn't think you would be keen on it since you care for Tanner like a brother, so I was hesitant. But he was persistent. If you want to know the god-honest truth, he applied to that position for you. It was his way to break into the councils' ranks."

"And no one thought to tell me this?" My voice rose.

"His tale isn't mine to tell. He asked me not to say anything so he could share everything with you himself. I think that's a conversation he'd like to have with you one on one, and I've already said too much."

I sighed, perhaps a bit dramatically, but Fitz kept his focus on the road. "Is there anything else you know that's going to blindside me? Because if you do, tell me right now. I'm tired of this."

"Hadley . . ."

"Are you keeping something from me? Anything at all?"

"Hadley, I've told you that you're a witch, what the councils knew, how I was feeling, all that. This is different though. I'm not even keeping my promise to Tanner by telling you this much. Damned if I do, damned if I don't."

"This is so messed up," I said. "I hate what the government has done to us."

Silence fell. I watched the rain streak down the passenger side window as I allowed my thoughts to roll through the new information about Tanner.

"Just tell me this . . ."

"Hadley."

"Did he already know I was meeting you in Paris before I told him?" I asked.

"No. Henry was the only one who knew ahead of time. I wanted someone to know where we were, but I was worried about the councils finding out, so I kept those details from everyone else. Of course, Tanner called me as soon as his best mate shared the secret with him . . ."

"Yeah, that one was my bad. But I only told Tanner because—"

Fitz waved his hand. "I'm not angry with you, Hads. You don't have to explain it to me."

I sank further into my seat, focusing on the patter of rain falling outside the car, and wished for the millionth time that these circumstances had never found us.

—CHAPTER TWENTY-THREE—

We'd just finished breakfast the following morning at Fitz's flat when I pushed for more information on Esther's ring.

Fitz topped off his coffee and settled onto the couch beside me. His finger circled the smooth surface of the moonstone in my ring. I leaned forward.

"I told you Esther was murdered in the witch trials. She wore the ring until the end of her life. Her husband Hamish was meant to retrieve the ring immediately after her death, but he was consumed with grief . . . Our family thought after strangulation, the captors would burn her remains at the stake. When collecting the ashes, he would also collect the ring . . ."

He trailed off momentarily.

"But they didn't?"

"They decided to burn the bodies in barrels of hot tar."

"Holy hell," I said. "I mean, I know it's all horrible, but that feels even more barbaric? I mean, it honestly just feels weirder somehow."

"Aye, it was."

"So, he didn't have any remains to collect," I gathered.

"Right. Then he wasn't sure about the ring, whether or not it was still in the tar or if it was taken before that. So, he and another witch combined forces and discovered someone removed it right after she was strangled."

My stomach turned as I considered how horrible an end those poor souls had endured, and my heart sank thinking of Esther.

"I feel so badly for Hamish. I can't imagine."

"Right. Hamish had already been through hell before he even lost Esther."

"Like what?" I asked.

"Oh, I'll give you a history lesson later," Fitz offered with a wink. "The MacGregors were outlawed by the king. Esther and Hamish assumed the last name Lockie for a time."

"So, you come from a distinguished line of outlaws?"

"Aye, just like me." He smiled. "We found his journal in the attic at my great-grandparents' house when we were organizing a few years back. Hamish never forgave himself for not solving the mystery of the ring. He felt like he dishonored Esther by not carrying out her final wish."

"Fitz, there were a lot of innocent souls lost to the trials, and most of them weren't even witches. But Esther was. Why didn't she resist or flee?"

"She had a good reason," Fitz said. "The most powerful witch in

Scotland sat on the witch-hunting committee."

I gasped.

"He infiltrated them to prevent as many deaths as he could, but he had to remain inconspicuous. He couldn't be overzealous."

"This witch couldn't save Esther?"

"No, and he wouldn't allow Esther to resist by utilizing magic. She was quite powerful, but not powerful enough to stand against him. She also had three children to consider."

"He would've leveraged the children against her," I said.

"In a heartbeat. She had no choice but to bow to Fate. So, she didn't resist arrest, endured torture, and was brutally murdered."

"How was she compromised?" I asked.

"There was a woman named Helen Guthrie at the heart of the Forfar witch trials," Fitz explained. "She was arrested along with her thirteen-year-old daughter. Helen realized that as long as she remained useful to her captors, she would stay alive and have the chance to protect her daughter."

"It would be easy to hate her if it weren't for the fact that she was a mother protecting her daughter—no matter the cost."

"Harsh times, harsh measures I suppose. Helen told all she knew and all she could imagine. She implicated several women: some witches, some humans. Helen exaggerated Esther's ability of fore-sight and claimed she used it to alter the future in evil ways, doing the bidding of the devil. Esther didn't stand a chance."

"How did she know about Esther being a witch?" I asked.

"I can't say for sure, but I imagine it was the result of Esther slipping up in front of the wrong person. Or another witch sharing information on Esther to protect themselves."

"Makes sense."

"Hamish searched tirelessly for the ring," Fitz continued. "He scoured the village, used locator spells, but the ring was gone. Another witch must've taken it; a human couldn't have concealed it from Hamish. I'd like to honor Esther and Hamish by finding that ring."

Esther and Hamish MacGregor. Though I couldn't alter the past, I could at least ensure they weren't forgotten.

"What has you worried?" I asked.

"You feel that, huh?"

"Of course, I do."

"Esther saw her fate as a young woman, and it haunted her family until their last days. Her parents, aunts, and uncles all channeled their powers into the ring right before their deaths. Before Esther's capture, her only living aunt brought the ring to her. There was nothing Esther could do, and her aunt Annabel was left with a big responsibility."

"This was their attempt to save her life?"

"Aye, the ring held immense power—power that was forbidden. One of our laws states that you aren't allowed to host or harbor a witch's power in an object."

"Why?"

"Two reasons: taking power from another witch is a heinous act," Fitz said. "But it would also make anyone too powerful if they controlled the power of multiple witches. You see how your strength grows in certain areas, and that's only from our energies reacting with each other's. Can you imagine controlling the power of five witches?"

You'd be unstoppable, I realized.

"The ring could fall into the wrong hands. Maybe it already has . . . I think of the evil our kind has battled over the years and wonder if my family's power is being used by the wrong team."

"I know you have meetings to prep for, but show me your re-search later? After all, you did agree to let me help you, remember?"

"Aye. Thanks, Hads."

CHAPTER TWENTY-FOUR

With Fitz's afternoon schedule full of meetings at the university, I used the time to pack the last of my neglected belongings in my hotel room. We hadn't spent a night apart since the evening the witch followed me, and it seemed like staying at his place was a natural progression in our relationship.

I walked halfway through the room before realizing my suitcase was propped open near the window—not where I'd left it. Housekeeping might have moved it, I reasoned, though I'd declined service for days. I tiptoed the final distance, holding my breath as I peeked into the bathroom. Unused towels were strewn about the floor and vanity.

Not housekeeping.

I assessed the remainder of the room, prepared to shriek and run for the door should I find someone lurking under the bed or in the closet—I'd watched one too many horror movies when I was younger. I came up empty-handed and fell onto the bed in relief, allowing my heart rate to steady.

Realizing I'd forgotten my phone on Fitz's coffee table, I scanned each of the misplaced items, committing them to memory. I closed my eyes and searched the energy of the room, seeking any sign that it had been the work of the Parisian stalkers. The energy slowly registered, and though it felt familiar, I was certain it wasn't them.

I tossed my belongings into the suitcase, tugged at the zipper, and made a mad dash for the lobby, strong waves of anxiety rolling through my body. I rushed through checkout as the prickle of another witch hung heavily in the air, a warning that I was under watch. Unlike the previous occasions, no witch's glance chilled my back, but though the witch attempted to mask their stare, my witch's eye perceived their presence.

I paused at the front door, allowing the bellman to load my belongings into the cab. Standing in the cool afternoon light, I sensed an energy shift, and slowly but surely, an icy chill ran up my spine.

The bellman opened the cab door, and I slid into the backseat of the taxi, taking the opportunity to follow the trail of energy.

A man stood in the hotel doorway, unmistakably witch, and the chill grew stronger as I met his eyes. His pale, icy blue eyes glowed against his light brown skin and dark hair. His triangular face was chiseled and covered in dark stubble, and his light V-neck tee showed off a strong body. He would have been attractive if not for the uneasy feeling his gaze sent through me.

The slamming of the car door did little to dispel my growing anxiety. I held the witch's gaze firmly, refusing to release him as the cab drove away.

Fitz was waiting at home when I arrived. He must have felt my nerves; he was wearing holes in the hardwood as I entered the living room. When I shared that a witch was watching me at the hotel, his eyes darkened.

"Again?" Fitz yelled.

"You don't have to yell," I said. "You're such a brute when you're pissed."

"That's what this witch is about to learn."

"Oh god."

The look he sent in my direction could have killed someone, but he took a deep breath and exhaled slowly as I stared unfazed in his direction.

"I don't know what the hell they want, and it worries me," Fitz said.

"He."

"What?"

"You don't know what the hell *he* wants."

"You saw him?"

"Yeah, or I saw someone," I said. "I can't say for sure it was the same witch all three times, but I think so."

"What did he look like?"

"Tall, built, maybe mid-thirties? Light brown skin. And blue eyes."

I shuddered. "They were this icy, transparent blue. When our eyes met, I felt cold."

"I don't know anyone who fits that description. If this isn't the council, then I have no idea who it is. I'll call my dad and see if he might know him."

"That's a good start. We need to figure this out."

"We'll sort it, but for now, maybe you shouldn't be alone unless necessary."

"You think he'd approach me?" I asked.

"Maybe. He probably wouldn't cause a scene in public. If he caught you off guard with no one around, though . . ." He trailed off, his knuckles white from clenching.

"He was pretty brazen, like he wanted me to see him, but if he had any intention of approaching me, he had his chance."

"Hadley. What are you not telling me?"

I paused, taken aback by the venom in his voice.

"Please," he whispered, squeezing his eyes shut. "Just tell me."

"Someone ransacked my hotel room."

Fitz's eyes flew open, though he remained silent.

"I thought maybe it was housekeeping at first. But it wasn't. Someone moved my stuff, threw towels around—I guess to see if I'd hidden anything? And there was a . . . strange energy in the room."

"So, this bastard went into your room."

"It seems that way," I said.

"Seems that way?"

"Well, I don't have hard evidence it was him. It just seems highly likely considering he was watching me."

"I'll kill him," Fitz said.

"You'll do no such thing!"

"You'll no sit here and defend this bastard," he returned, teeth gritted.

"I'm not defending him."

"If you dinnae want him harmed, you'll be disappointed if I see him, if I *ever* feel his presence again."

"Fitz . . . You'll *have* to show some restraint."

"I cannae help myself. My instincts will be too strong."

"You'll control yourself. I know you can be smart about this."

Fitz shook his head, his gaze fixed on the open window.

"Look at me," I said.

He made no effort to do so. I closed the gap between us and reached for his jaw. He caught my hand in his, and his eyes were stormy as they met mine.

"Do you no want my protection?" he asked, though his voice was losing its edge. "You may no want it, but you need it. You're still learning. You're still growing in your magic."

I sighed.

"I told you my stream formed long ago, and with it, I gave you my love, my loyalty, my protection. I've focused on shielding you from harm for so long . . ." He trailed off. A breathy laugh escaped his lips humorlessly. "I'm content to be your sword and your shield for as long as you have need of it. Truthfully, I dinnae know how to be anything other than this."

His confession filled my veins with tender warmth. I'd been so caught up in what he'd hidden from me that I hadn't truly understood the toll our situation had taken on him or the role it had forced him into.

With my free hand, I ran my thumb along his lips. He raised my hand that he still held in his and leaned forward to kiss my wrist.

Goosebumps rippled across the tender skin.

"I want all of you, Fitz. Every little bit that makes you who you are. But I'm growing into my power. I'm not the lost girl you fell in love with at the lake."

Fitz nodded. "I know."

"There's a freedom in that," I said. "A freedom for us to find our balance. We'll both want to protect each other, but that's not your identity. That's not your sole purpose."

"My purpose is to love you. I protected you because that's what you needed most."

"Now, I need a partner in life. And I know that's what we'll be to each other."

"Aye." He pressed his forehead to mine. "But when it comes to this witch who's watching you . . . I don't think you should be alone. It's not wise."

"I'll text Mia," I said, inwardly groaning at the thought of our partnership with her.

"Good."

"We'll figure this out. This witch won't win."

"You might be right, but if it's all right with you, I think I'll act as your shadow for a wee bit longer—until you're further along in your training." He slid his arm around me absentmindedly, pulling me tightly against his chest.

"Fitz," I whispered, warm adrenaline pulsing just under the surface even though the thought of my supernatural stalker was far away.

Fitz rested his hands on either side of my shoulders and placed his forehead against mine. We stood motionless, suspended in time, closing our eyes to savor the moment.

Then he tilted my face upward to meet his gaze before kissing underneath my jawline. He worked his way to my lips, kissing me thoroughly. My sigh encouraged him further. He pinned my hands above my head, and I stood on my tiptoes to kiss him again. Our energy flowed freely between us—witch to witch—until we found what we sought and ended up tangled on the floor, watching the rise and fall of our chests moving in time with each other.

I wrapped my leg around his and pushed myself against him, my head tucking tenderly under his chin.

"The way I feel for you, Hadley . . . words aren't sufficient."

"I hope you know I feel the same. Never doubt my love for you."

CHAPTER TWENTY-FIVE

The next day, I sat on the back porch of Henry's estate, waiting for Tanner to wrap his mind around how to explain everything to me. He'd listened to my long-winded argument about how unfair I found the situation without interruption.

Finally, he broke the silence.

"I understand how you're feeling. I'd feel the same way. It feels like we've bamboozled you, right? But I want you to know something. We only did this to protect you, and I know we would do it all over again if it means you're safe."

I leaned back in my seat. I knew that, and I appreciated it, though I wasn't ready to let him know that.

"I don't like that I'm just finding all this out," I said.

"I know. But you needed to know you were a witch before you could understand the reason behind any of this."

"I get that. But learning that so many witches were keeping me safe while I didn't understand a damn thing about it is not a fun feeling."

"Yeah, I bet," Tanner said. "No one ever wanted to hide anything. I promise you that. We just wanted to figure this all out so you could move on and be who you were meant to be."

I nodded, parsing slowly through the information.

"We tried to make the right decisions," Tanner said. "I mean, I was against it at first, but once I understood everything, it was an easy decision to help."

"What changed your mind?" I asked.

"When we were at the lake, I fought a lot with Ian. I felt like it was unfair that you were being observed without your knowledge. I didn't get how complicated your status was. I'd never spent time around someone in your situation. If the councils didn't do this, you might have gotten yourself into a lot of trouble or hurt yourself. But it still felt wrong."

He paused. "I fought with Fitz too. I'm sure he told you that. But he was the one who helped me understand how dangerous your situation was. I didn't understand the stakes. And once I understood, I stopped fighting and started helping. All we wanted was to find a way for you to match to your power and live a good life."

"And you thought it was best that I didn't know too," I said.

"Yeah. You can't sit there and tell me that if you knew the truth, it wouldn't have wrecked everything. I know you better than that, Hads. Fitz does too. You would have obsessed over it. Plus, we knew the government might wipe your memories. So, I decided to help him figure out how to beat the councils."

I thought about the time I'd spent apart from Fitz: the panic attacks, the heartbreak, wondering who I was—*what* I was. Not knowing the facts had caused a fair amount of worry. I wondered if it would have been better—easier—if I had known the complete truth. I thought so, though if I was being fair, I couldn't know that for sure. It was irrelevant now, anyway.

"I know you'll be angry at all of us for a while," Tanner said. "That's okay. I'm just happy you're safe and that we can be open about everything now."

"You're right. I'll have to work through it. But even if I'm angry, just know that I understand the weight you carried—all of you."

Tanner nodded. "Fitz most of all. Go easy on him. I didn't at first, and I still regret that."

"You do?" I asked.

"I don't regret pushing him to a point where he let me in. But when he did, I realized how much of a toll it was taking on him . . . and that it would continue for however long it took us to sort all this shit out."

"Thank you for telling me that."

"It's something you should know."

"I'm sure I'll have more questions later. But for now, I guess we shouldn't keep Henry waiting much longer."

"Let's go get you assessed, woman," Tanner said.

Tanner, Henry, and I were sprawled out in front of a fire in Henry's sitting room in the midst of a training session while Fitz worked on his family research in Henry's office. As Tanner and I progressed through my assessment, we learned that I was gifted with mental transport. Though it felt like being a spirit-traveler was far less exciting than Fitz's abilities as a time-walker, mental transport did have one benefit over time-walking. I could travel through time and space, much like Fitz, but I couldn't be observed by the naked eye.

"Do you think spirit-travelers are to blame when humans think a ghost is around?" I asked.

Tanner and Henry looked to each other, their expressions quizzical.

"I've never thought about that before," Tanner said.

"Aye, me neither. That's a good question, lass." Henry paused, lost in thought.

"Some of their energy would be in the room. I learned that my first day on the job in Seattle," Tanner said. "We were assessing another spirit-traveler, and I felt the shift of energy when her spirit came in the room."

"Do you think a human would notice it?" I asked.

"That's the million-dollar question," Tanner said.

"We should test the theory sometime," I said.

"Aye, but you'll need to learn about the skill first," Henry said.

Henry wasn't gifted with mental transport but knew a great deal about it. After a fair amount of discussion on the subject, he agreed he'd provide training to the best of his ability while Tanner worked alongside him to assess the power. I'd need a couple of trainers to help me through my new skill set, and Tanner agreed Henry was a good fit.

"We'll start by identifying what you want," Henry said.

"Food."

He laughed.

"That is the most Hadley line I've heard in a long time." Tanner shook his head but smiled.

"A girl after my own heart, but I dinnae think that's going to help us here," Henry said.

"Right." I thought hard. "I want to see Gram."

"See her right now or in years past?"

"That's an option?" I asked.

"Aye. You can see her now, or you can see her at any point in her past. You have the power for it."

You have the power for it. I liked the sound of that.

"Do you have anything of hers on you?" Henry asked.

"These earrings." I tugged at the back and slipped an earring from my ear. "My granddad gave them to her when they first married."

"Just one is sufficient. Hold it in your hand where you can see it."

"Like this?" I asked. The gold button earring sat upright in my palm, a delicate chain holding a diamond in place at the center.

"Perfect," Henry said. "You won't always need an object, but it's helpful when you have it, especially until you're proficient in the craft. Take a few deep breaths and relax."

I followed his instruction and fell into the steady rhythm of breathing.

"I can feel that you're trying to relax," Tanner said, "but your mind is too excited. Forget everything. Just breathe and listen to Henry's voice."

I closed my eyes and focused intently on my breath, pushing everything else from my mind. This was no different than my regular meditation, I reminded myself. My magic was instinctive, fueled by both need and strong desire. It had no use for frivolous thoughts.

"Connect with the earring and tell me what you feel," Henry instructed.

"I feel its strength . . . the ridges from how it's cut. The gold that keeps the diamond in place."

"Ask your witch's eye about the person who created it."

Nothing.

"Let everything else go," Henry prompted, sensing my difficulty.

The darkness faded as I focused, my curiosity taking root and revealing a dim, windowless room where a jeweler peered through a microscope. A cut jewel lay on the table in front of him, ready to be set.

My eyes popped open, pulling a smirk from Henry. "I saw the jeweler. He was looking at the diamond."

"Well done, you!"

"Nice job, Weston," Tanner said, typing notes on to the tablet resting on his lap.

Henry requested I navigate to the same vision once more before we moved to my next task. I did so dutifully, my sights set on mastery of another skill.

"Now you'll repeat the process, but I want you to find the day they were sold to your grandfather. Once you're in that vision, ask it to navigate to the time the earrings were given as a gift to your grandmother."

"Got it."

"Dinnae lose focus. Ask your vision for what you want to know—breathe. You have full control over where time takes you. It answers to *you*."

Time revealed a salesman standing behind a jewelry counter filled with rows of gold, silver, and precious stones on a maroon bed of velvet. The salesman placed cash into the register while speaking with a handsome man in a navy suit. I recognized my young grandfather instantly, having seen his likeness in a frame by Gram's desk for as long as I could recall. The salesman handed a box topped with a big white bow over to Granddad, who ran his hand nervously through his short, blond hair before accepting it.

As he disappeared through the doorway, I asked time for a glimpse
of Granddad gifting the earrings to Gram. The edges of my vision blurred, and the darkness grew until it was once again all I could see. I waited quietly, attempting to maintain focus, hoping I hadn't failed. I tore my interest away from the thought, returning to peaceful nothingness.

Light dawned, and Granddad walked into a room where a woman sat in a satin dress the color of pearls. Her long, auburn hair was curled about her face, which was carefully painted for the festive occasion, her blue eyes bright against her porcelain skin. Gram was beautiful, and I was grateful to catch a glimpse of an event I couldn't imagine if I tried. Their wedding photos had been destroyed in a fire years ago.

Granddad handed the box to Gram, who opened it slowly, as though she already knew what precious treasure lay inside. Once opened, a single tear ran the length of her cheek, and she embraced Granddad tightly. When Gram had gifted the set to me, she'd shared that Granddad was living on a small wage at the time and had gone without quite a few comforts in order to afford the gift.

I slowly navigated to the present and opened my eyes to Henry's studious face.

"How was it?"

"I don't have words . . . amazing."

"Think you're up for one more tonight?" Henry said.

"Yes, of course!"

"I dinnae want to overtax you."

"Henry, you two made me rest all day," I accused, pointing in Fitz's general direction in the adjoining room. "An entire day without magic! I'm going to explode magical energy everywhere if you don't let me do this."

Henry turned. "Tanner?"

"She's doing good, and her energy levels seem good too. I think it's fine to keep going."

I looked to Henry, a gloating smile on my lips.

"You were telling us earlier about the first time you accidentally read Izzy's mind. What if you traveled to that day? You can pick a scene from your own past," Henry said.

"That's going to be strange," I said.

"To say the least. But you need a recent destination after the last journey. Fitz has the watch Izzy gave him that summer."

Henry held the item in his open palm, a mischievous grin on his face. "You sneak."

He passed the watch to me, and I sat motionless for a moment, preparing for another venture in time.

"Focus on what you want. Ask time to take you there."

I clutched the watch tightly and listened for the ripples of time, more aware of the experience than before.

I opened my eyes to a summer day in June. Everything was spectacularly clear through the kitchen window—giant spruce trees, swaying ferns, the sparkling lake.

I took a deep breath, trying not to lose my nerve.

Gram was working in the kitchen. She narrowed her big, blue eyes in concentration and reached for another mason jar. For as long as I could remember, she'd worn her hair cropped above her shoulders, warm auburn with sun-kissed strands, a testament to the amount of time she spent in her garden. Someone bounded down the stairs, pulling her focus away from her task, and my former self strolled into the kitchen.

The scene was vivid, and I could've sworn I was living the moment all over again.

"Where are you headed off to, Priss?" Gram asked, her southern accent thick. My heart swelled at the sound of her familiar, gravelly voice, which sparked countless treasured memories.

"I'm riding bikes with Izzy this afternoon."

"Nice girl."

"She *is* nice. There's something about her, though, that just doesn't . . ."

"Doesn't what, honey?" Gram questioned, a coy look on her face.

"This is going to sound stupid, but there's something about her that just doesn't seem quite human. She's too ethereal, too graceful."

Gram chuckled at my response, but an odd note rested in her laughter.

"What is it, Gram?"

"Oh, nothing. It's a silly thought, but I do know what you mean about her. The whole family is that way."

"You met the rest of her family?" I asked.

"Sure did."

"Did her family seem—I don't know—like her?" I recalled how desperate I was for information on the family. I had hoped to make sense of what I thought had happened the night before in my dream—or dreamlike state.

"I'd say so. Both kids were handsome, and how did you put it? Ethereal and plenty smart, too." With Gram that usually meant they had a quick sense of humor, one of the traits she admired most in a person.

Fitz and Izzy had stopped by that morning, just as Fitz promised, and I was thrilled when Izzy had asked me to hang out that afternoon. I wanted another chance to observe her—to make sense of her. I recalled the way Fitz had filled my mind with possibilities from the moment our eyes met. He was the first person to see me for who I really was. The girl before me had no idea about the love and magic that awaited her.

"What did you think about her parents?"

"Smart, funny, both seem pretty successful."

"I wonder what's up with them," I said, my mind spinning with possibilities.

"Maybe nothing, maybe something," she remarked, a twinkle in her eye.

Gram was more superstitious than anyone I'd ever met. There was rarely an old wives' tale or nontraditional remedy she didn't heed and pass along for future reference. As a child, I'd found it fascinating about her. As an adult, I'd found it quirky and endearing. And as a witch, I suspected that part of my power must have been passed down through her.

A rap on the door disturbed our conversation.

"I've got it," I said.

I was met by Izzy's bright smile when I swung open the door.

"I come bearing gifts." She passed through the door holding up a brown paper bag in one hand and a vase full of greenery in the other.

"What's all this?" I asked, eyeing the bag suspiciously.

"Your grandmother mentioned your dad's illness earlier and how she's been trying natural remedies to help him feel better in between treatments." She set the bag on the old, wooden buffet and pulled a large glass jar from it. "This is a blend of herbs that makes a nice tea. It'll help with the fatigue and with the nausea, too."

"Is that Izzy I hear?" Gram's voice floated in from the kitchen.

"Hi, Mrs. Weston!" she called. "I brought those herbs we talked about this morning."

Gram's eyes lit up as she entered the room. "Oh, that was fast. Thank you! And call me Gram—everyone does."

"Very well, Gram." She grinned.

"Izzy said she grows these herself, so I'll bet they have twice the healing power of what I've been getting at the store," Gram said.

"You grow this where you live in Seattle?" I asked.

"Aye. My roommate and I live in a townhome near the university, and we have a bit of yard. It's not nearly as much as I'd like, but it's a grand little space."

"What about this?" I asked, pointing toward the vase. Ferns were arranged beautifully around small branches of lush evergreen trees and expertly draped bunches of moss. A piece of burlap was topped with a sage ribbon and tied around the vase.

"Oh! These are for your dad's room. I harvested responsibly, but I wanted to bring a wee bit of nature to him. I know some days it's tough on him to be outside."

My eyes misted, and I caught Gram's gaze. She nodded. While my mind had been tied up in suspicion about my odd dream, Izzy had gone out of her way to be kind to my dad.

"That was really thoughtful. Izzy, thank you," I said.

"Don't mention it. Oh! And one last thing." She reached into the paper bag and pulled out a large mason jar filled with tiny crystal-like rocks. "These bath salts are the best I've found. All the way from Scotland." She winked. "But they smell lovely and soothe aches and pains. If they help, I have loads more at the house."

"Oh yeah, these'll do fine," Gram said, unscrewing the lid and taking an appreciative sniff. "Thank you, Izzy. This is mighty kind of you."

"Nae bother at all."

And in that moment, I didn't care about what had happened the night before.

I couldn't help but to hug her. She wrapped me in a tight embrace—the kind where you know the other person understands, the kind that stitches you back together when you're falling apart. She granted me comfort and validation in the way that only another woman could.

"Okay, let's get going?" I asked. "I could use some fresh air."

June was a tricky month on the Olympic Peninsula. One day might be hot and dry, while the next was cool and rainy. Izzy and I peddled along the gravel path until the tree line gave way to a clear view of the lake. We hopped down and walked to the end of a nearby pier. We sat in silence for a few moments, watching the cars zip along the 101 across the lake from us. Izzy laid back, stretching her arms and legs as far apart as possible.

"Do you think you'll take that job?" I asked.

"Which job?"

"The one your dad wants you to take after graduating?"

After a brief silence, Izzy pulled herself forward, leaning back on to her elbows. Her expression was indecipherable, but I already knew what I'd done.

"Or at least I thought you mentioned that yesterday. I must've made that up."

"You didn't make it up," she said.

"We don't have to talk about it. I'm sorry I brought it up."

"No, it's fine. I don't mind talking about it. I just don't remember telling you."

"You must have," I said. "I mean, how else would I know that?"

"How indeed," she pondered. I recalled how her gaze had lingered on me long enough to make me uncomfortable, but the end of her internal battle was clear in her eyes. "Well, if you know about it, I must have said something."

I had allowed my mind to grow too preoccupied with an event that must have been a dream . . . and I'd slipped with my very real oddity because of that.

I followed our path back to the cabin where Gram had fresh lemonade waiting for us. A man's voice filtered through the front door, and I froze in recognition. Daddy. My thoughts raced around haphazardly. I knew I wasn't ready to see him—not like this. Tears welled as I asked time to release me back to my rightful place.

Tanner's eyes met mine, and he gave me a soft smile.

"I think I'll join Fitz and type up my report. Let's call it a wrap for the day." Tanner grabbed his tablet and left the room.

"Henry?"

"Aye, lass?" he asked.

"You said you don't have this power. How do you know so much about it?"

He sighed and reached for the nearest bottle of Scotch. "Fancy a glass?"

"I'm fine, thank you."

He poured a healthy serving, taking a sip of the amber liquid, and I waited patiently for him to begin. I came to the idea that perhaps I shouldn't pry, but then he began.

"I haven't talked about this much, but it'll be good to tell you. My mate, Emily, possessed your ability. I was with her during her training—that's why I know so much about it."

"I haven't heard you mention Emily before," I observed, leaning forward curiously. Neither Henry nor Fitz had ever talked about Henry's mate.

"It's no a story with a happy ending. I'll tell you nonetheless if you'd like."

I nodded sheepishly.

"I was thirteen when I met Emily. It's pretty rare, you know, for witches to find their mate so young, but we were lucky. Emily was beautiful and smart, with a quick, dry wit." He laughed, though without humor. "I was hopelessly in love with her. Our parents let us wed at sixteen. Our family and witch friends celebrated with us, but the humans wouldn't understand, not with our age."

He paused, pulling slowly from the glass.

"We did everything together. Studying, school, traveling. She loved to travel, and after we completed secondary school, we took a few years off, traveling and working around the world. We decided to come back to Scotland for uni. Dinnae get me wrong; things weren't perfect, but we were happy.

"Then a business trip to Inverness changed everything. We made a short holiday of her work trip. We drove up the Friday before and enjoyed the weekend. We were driving home—just outside the city. We were so close."

He hung his head quietly, breathing deeply. I placed my hand on his free one, and he held it for some time before pressing on.

"A drunk driver hit us. Nasty pig. Our bodies can withstand a great deal, Hadley. We can push past loads of human limits, but Emily couldnae do it. He was flying eighty miles an hour down the old lane. He slammed into us, pinning our car between his and a nearby building. Emily and I were both crushed. She died instantly."

"Henry . . . I am *so* sorry," I whispered. "I am so sorry this happened to you."

"I was a real mess after," Henry said. "Almost died myself. Broke most of the bones in my body, went into cardiac arrest, was in a coma for two days. I had a long road to recovery, and that was only physically. I didnae give a shite about anyone for a long time."

"You clearly do now."

"Aye. I was twenty-eight when Emily died. After about a year, I met Fitz. Best thing that could've happened to me. He helped me turn things around, go on to pursue my graduate degree, and honestly helped me become the man I wanted to be for Emily."

I smiled. That sounded like Fitz all right.

"I've been over it time and time again, punishing myself. Convinced there was something I could've done differently. I wish every day I had died instead of her. I'll never understand why it had to be her."

A tear rolled slowly toward his jaw.

I could have told him he lived for a reason. How grateful Fitz and I were to have him in our lives, or how Fate gave him a second chance, but none of it would change the fact that Emily was gone.

Instead, I wrapped my arms around him, locking us quietly in an embrace.

"I'm sorry," Henry said.

"What on earth are you apologizing for?" I asked, releasing him.

"You didnae ask me for all that."

"I'm sorry if bringing it up was too much," I said.

"No, I need to think about it sometimes. It ultimately helps, I think. I need to remember all of it—even the worst part of our story."

"Thank you for telling me about Emily. I'm glad you felt like you could."

"I had fifteen years with her," Henry said. "It was far too brief . . . but I know what it is to love someone with everything in me, and I'll carry that with me always."

"That's a gift for sure. And to have experienced so much life with her. A lot of people never have that."

"But you do—and you'll continue to grow. There are so many good things to come, Hadley."

"I'm a lucky girl," I said.

"Aye, and Fitz is one lucky bastard. He knows it too."

It was good to hear Henry laugh.

I couldn't begin to imagine what a loss like Henry's felt like, but my admiration for him grew. Those like him were special—the ones who loved, lost, and found the will to live again after tremendous tragedy.

Right on cue, Fitz entered the room, embracing Henry in an overly dramatic hug, pulling laughter from us all. Tanner followed shortly after, and we all stayed at Henry's late into the evening talking and laughing in a way that's only possible once you've opened yourself up to one another. When we left for the evening, I held Fitz tighter and dearer to me than before.

CHAPTER TWENTY-SIX

I sat on the edge of the bed the following morning while Fitz showered, reflecting on the many changes that had occurred over the past couple of years. I tried not to think of the past too often, following my therapist's advice that it was healthy to allow myself to feel and process grief, but it wasn't healthy to dwell. With all that had occurred since Paris, it had become difficult not to think about the summer I met Fitz. And in doing so, countless memories with my dad also bubbled up.

As my head sank into the soft pillow, I allowed my mind to return to a day I'd tried to forget for a long time. I closed my eyes, allowing the onrush of pain . . . but also the happiness of seeing Daddy's face again.

November 22, 2021 was a date I'd never forget. While my friends' families prepared for the upcoming holiday season, mine was focused on keeping my dad comfortable and in good spirits. He'd decided that morning that he wanted to go outside, and we had helped him walk to the back deck. He'd turned his face to the mist that drifted from the gray rainclouds and asked to sit in the doorway wrapped in a blanket.

But on his way back to bed, my dad had fallen in the hallway, unable to stand, and we had helped him to the bedroom. I'd never forget the pained look on Gram's face or my mother's strained response.

"Oh—Matt!"

It was her voice that had pierced me the most. It was almost a whisper . . . the whisper of a woman who felt completely defeated.

The chemo dragged on for months, the promise of it extricating the cancer turning to ash in our mouths. After each treatment, Dad felt increasingly weak for the following few days. My own mental strength withered with him, but I couldn't give up—my hope wasn't yet gone. After all, my dad was a tough guy, and growing up with him had been a splendid adventure. We'd spent countless days on the trails, chasing the mystique of the mountains. He'd always split his own firewood and fixed anything that broke around the house. As a child, I was convinced he could do anything.

But his illness finally forced me to acknowledge how completely helpless I felt.

I noticed the change of expression on his face, how his features seemed less bright and his skin less vibrant. I could no longer ignore the hollowness of his face, the loss of his beautiful dirty blond hair, and how his thick, athletic figure was wasting away. His structured jawline and gray eyes were the only familiar features I recognized in this foreign face.

Once we settled him into bed that afternoon, he was too weak to get up on his own again. His joints ached, he struggled to keep food down, and my entire world was crashing all around me. Mom, Gram, and I rotated sitting with him, helping him out of bed as needed and procuring anything that might make him more comfortable.

We discovered that if I made dinner, he wouldn't refuse to eat. So I handed Dad a bowl of pasta and sat at the foot of the bed to have dinner with him. He smiled before focusing on his food, and my heart warmed.

"I need you to make a promise to me," he said.

"Anything."

"You need to find a way to stop worrying so much about me."

"Dad . . ."

"I'm serious, Hadley." He leaned over in pain, even the act of conversing taking its toll on his energy, but I knew better than to tell him to rest. The man had always done just as he damn well pleased.

"Dad, you always put yourself last, but now isn't the time for that."

"I know you can't understand this now, but everything your mom and I have done from the moment we knew we were expecting you has been for you. Every decision with our home, our careers, our lifestyle . . . it's all been for you," he said. "You are my life's work. Having you put your life on hold for me would be the opposite of what I've wanted for you for the past twenty-eight years."

I had been debating my career decisions for post-grad school, and my dad encouraged me to look outside of Washington. I'd always dreamed of moving around but had decided against it when I learned of my father's diagnosis.

With this talk, he finally convinced me to follow my instincts and find the right fit for me, no matter the location.

When the job offer in Boston came up three months later, I discussed the offer with him. My dad told me I needed to take it. I'd never seen him prouder of me.

"I'm going to get better, and I'm going to come see you in Boston, Pumpkin," he said. "We'll have a blast."

I knew if I stayed in Washington rather than accept it, I'd not only let my father down, but I'd take away from any happiness he had while battling that monster.

It was with renewed purpose that I faced the soft glow of my laptop one late February evening, replying to the offer that had changed the course of my life.

In the couple of months after my move, he rallied, and we all felt real hope again. He somehow convinced my mother to drive him across the country in their camper. The doctors advised against it. My mom fretted the entire trip. I nearly had a stroke over it.

It took them two weeks because my mom worried about him being on the road. We meticulously planned the road trip so they could stop for his treatments. We didn't want to risk his health with the trip, but Dad was insistent. And he was extraordinarily happy sitting in my living room, a wide grin highlighting his features.

His miraculous turn continued for a couple of months, but he'd declined quickly last December. And that was that.

He never healed. I never had the chance to show him the harbor, the Freedom Trail, or my favorite parks—the particularly verdant ones that reminded me of home. We'd mourned beside his casket in January. But he had made it to Boston because he was my dad, and he was a man of his word.

CHAPTER TWENTY-SEVEN

"I think I found something," Fitz yelled across the room.

We'd practically, or perhaps not so practically, torn apart Henry's attic over the span of the past three days.

I was starting my new job on Monday, and we wanted to make some real progress on Fitz's family project over the next week before my attention was divided.

With Fitz delving further into his research, his dad sent over all the family records: journals, grimoires, enchanted objects, and the like. And by sent over, I meant that I stood in Henry's attic one afternoon with Fitz and Henry while the items suddenly materialized in the space.

The three of them felt the collection would be more difficult to locate in Henry's home should someone come snooping for inform-ation on the ring. All information regarding how to access the vast power held inside the ring needed to be carefully concealed. I had expressed concern over such a treasure lying in someone's attic, but Fitz was quick to point out how heavily protected it was.

"There's no need to worry. This protection spell Dad and I worked up is intricate. It would take someone a considerable amount of time and effort—enough that we'd feel it. And with the alarm spell, if they ever did sort it out, we'd know immediately."

"Sounds like you've thought of everything," I said.

"Almost."

As we turned most of our attention to the MacGregor family mystery, Fitz's dad partnered with the Scottish Council to investi-gate our problematic witch's identity. Divide and conquer, as they said. Between spending most of my time with Henry and Tanner, and with Fitz indeed acting as my shadow, I hadn't seen nor felt the snooping witch over the last week.

The three of us worked our way into the middle of a large, wood-en chest and discovered a grimoire and a corresponding 1662 journal wrapped neatly in linen. The fabric alone betrayed their age, its color resembling that of the leather-bound books that surrounded it. Both had belonged to Esther's aunt, Annabel. Since she was the last living relative in the family pact and had gifted the ring directly to Esther, if there were any details surrounding spells for the ring, we'd find them in either of the two books.

Though Henry had assisted us in tearing through the attic earlier in the day, he drove to town for the evening and gave his housekeep-er the night off—meaning Fitz and I would be able to examine the materials undisturbed by Olga, who was sweet but intrusive.

The oversized leather couch in the sitting room was to be our stage for further investigation of the books, and I bounded down the stairs, happy to leave the drafty attic behind.

The sitting room was a bit cool itself, and I extended my arm, tossing flames toward the neatly stacked logs in the fireplace.

They burst into a roaring fire, and I sank into the couch next to Fitz feeling quite satisfied. I'd never tire of fire bursting to life at my fingertips.

As an afterthought, Fitz nodded his head and a bottle of Glenfiddich and two glasses landed on the table in front of us.

"Henry keeps a few bottles around for me," Fitz said. "He prefers Bunnahabhain 25 Year, but I find I'm just not that extravagant."

I smiled at Henry's innate taste for the finer things and floated Annabel's journal to Fitz's side. In return, a crystal glass landed in my open palm, a thistle pattern distinct against the generous amber pour, and we settled down to the task of solving the mystery.

We found ourselves engrossed in Annabel's writings.

She'd left very specific incantations for her magic in the grimoire, and her journal held a fascinating account of life in 17th-century Scotland. Although the objective might have been searching for specific spells, we couldn't help but relay various spells and passages back and forth to each other.

The fire crackled through the evening, a soft soundtrack to the slow sipping of Scotch and the happy conversation between two history buffs combing through 17th-century artifacts.

Fitz was reading aloud from the journal, enjoying a particularly humorous account of Annabel's conversation with the local butcher, when the next passage caught his attention.

Took the wee item to E today while H and the bairns were away. Exceedingly surprised and angry at first, claiming we broke our word and wronged our brothers and sisters. She refused. I advised hir of the great sacrifices we experienced to pass this to hir. Said she would be unable to use this item to hir benefit at any account. Eventually relented. Showed her S and P.

"'S' and 'P' . . . do you think she's referring to the spells?" I asked.

"Let's find out." Fitz lifted the grimoire on to the table and flipped back to the first page.

Each witch had a unique method for casting their own incantations, which ranged in complexity and strength. Though magic wasn't always worked through spells, Annabel had certainly cast a spell on this occasion. She would have taught Esther her spells in the hopes that only she would be able to access, use, and summon the ring—Esther, and her bloodline.

We carefully made our way through the incantations, and as we identified spells that were potential fits, I recorded them on my laptop. Then, Fitz recited the spell, and we waited. The spells worked, but the ring remained to be seen.

After four attempts and hours of study, we were losing steam.

"We'll find it," I said.

"Aye. Of course, we will." He placed his hand at the base of my neck and kissed me. "I'm glad to be doing this with you."

I smiled and squeezed his hand. "Here's the next spell." I turned the laptop to face him.

He sighed.

"We need a bell and fire. Luckily, we have fire right here." I called my magic forward and my forefinger blazed hot with flames.

Fitz chuckled.

"Where are we going to find a bell?" I asked, my eyes darting across the room.

"That's an easy one."

Fitz disappeared, and when he returned, he held an antique gold bell roughly the size of my hand.

"What is that?"

"A bell with the Stuart Clan Crest on top. Excuse me, the *Stuart of Bute* Clan Crest. Henry keeps it in his office—he rings it when something good happens."

"Why?"

"Don't ask me. Have you met Henry?" Fitz retorted, shrugging his shoulders.

He handed the object to me, and I turned it over for further inspection. The handle had been crafted into a lion, its upper limbs positioned in attack. The bell itself was simple, except for the inscription at the bottom: "Nobilis Est Ira Leonis."

"What does this say?" I asked.

"The lion's anger is noble."

"Sounds about right." I passed the bell back to Fitz. "Let's do this."

Fitz performed each spell twice. Once with an ordinary object in mind to test the spell. The second time was to summon the ring.

"*Light the fire and hearken the bell . . .*" Fitz began.

I called forward my flames as Fitz rang the bell.

"*Bring forth the object I remember well.*"

The pen I had set in the adjoining room materialized. We repeated the spell, and this time . . . Nothing.

"Onward, it seems," he said.

Hours passed, and we finally reached the end of the grimoire.

"Ready to give this last one a try?" I asked.

He scanned the instructions once more.

"We need two candles, a topaz stone, cinnamon, and sage." He scoffed. "This one is *no* gonnae work."

"Not with that attitude it isn't," I quipped. "You're cute when you get worked up. Your accent gets so thick."

"Cute, am I? Well, I'll be keeping that in mind."

"Okay, now focus!"

"To the kitchen we go," he said, laughing.

Olga kept a well-stocked kitchen, and we found cinnamon immediately.

"Candles and sage," I repeated, tapping my fingers on the counter.

"In that pantry there."

I opened the nearby door to a room as large as my childhood bedroom. The shelves were stocked with countless dried herbs and spices, and rows of drying plants hung from the ceiling. At the far end of the pantry were candles of all colors, shapes, and sizes.

"Whoa," I muttered.

"Aye, he has an impressive collection."

I meandered to the end of the pantry, scanning the labels. Bay leaves, mandrake root, yarrow, belladonna, and the list went on. An impressive collection, indeed.

"Which colors?" I asked.

"White for protection and blue for communication."

I grabbed each color in the smallest size and turned to find Fitz leaned against the doorway, his arms crossed and his eyes mischievous.

"What?" I asked, walking toward him.

He wrapped his arms around my waist, slipping one hand in my back pocket. "You make me very happy," he said.

I tilted my head to face him, and he met me in a deep kiss. His hands wandered, and I broke away. "No, do not distract me right now. You're going to make me drop the candles."

"Who cares about the candles?" He reached for me, but I eluded his grasp.

"This is not focusing!"

He caught me and pulled my body to his. His kiss left me breathless, and for a second, I forgot about the spell.

"After you." He signaled toward the doorway.

When we returned to the sitting room, I felt hopeful again.

"Her spells are so many different forms," I said. "Some are just words and thoughts, others require objects, and then there are others that are sentences long."

"Usually, witches create spells in whatever form works best with their magic," Fitz said. "They also vary depending on what they're asking of the elements. But you're right—Annabel's are all over the map. This is the grimoire of a witch who was trying to throw others off."

"She suspected someone would come snooping."

"Aye. And she didn't make it easy on us."

Fitz scattered cinnamon across the coffee table, and I lit the sage and handed it to him. He waved the bundle through the air, and the fragrant smoke wafted through the room. He placed the sage at the center of the cinnamon base and placed the two candles at the top. I tossed fire at the wicks, which promptly burst to life.

"We forgot the topaz," I realized.

"Nae bother." Fitz closed his eyes and opened his hand. A topaz stone materialized in his palm. "What's the spell again?"

"You tell me," I said, pointing to the words.

"*Ghairm mi*. It means 'I summon.'"

I nodded. "And you'll need to think about the object you want to send for while you say it."

"I hate spell work," he said, his face cross. I stifled a laugh.

"I'll start with another crystal from Henry's collection to test the spell, and then I'll try the ring." He paused. "*Ghairm mi.*"

A moonstone materialized in his open palm.

"How clever," I said.

He smiled. He then repeated the spell.

Nothing.

"I'll just cross that one off the list then," I said.

He narrowed his eyes at me and reached toward the grimoire. It flew into his expectant grasp. He ran his fingers slowly over the book before feeling the air around it.

"Come feel this," he said.

I crossed the room quickly, feeling the return of his excitement. I ran my fingers across the book but felt nothing.

"I think Annabel left me a clue. We were so focused on the spells, I didn't investigate the energy as I should have."

"What do you mean?"

He flipped the book open and turned the pages until a smile spread across his features. "She hid a page of the book. Feel again."

A small twinge of energy nipped at my fingertips. I gasped.

"She enchanted the grimoire." He pointed to a small brown smudge on one of the corners. "This is her blood. She enchanted the book, so only her blood kin would recognize it."

"And I can feel it weakly because of our connection," I concluded.

"Exactly."

"Let's see what she hid from prying eyes."

Fitz laid his finger on the blood mark and closed his eyes. The other pages fluttered, and a soft illumination grew from where Fitz's finger met the page. He reached between the pages and tugged—and a new page pulled from the center of the book.

"You did it," I said, breathless.

"Annabel, you crafty witch."

Fitz read the summoning spell aloud:

> *That which was lost*
> *Soon shall be found*
> *Desire in your heart*
> *Bring the ring*
> *Here and now.*

Flames leapt in the fireplace, and the hair on my neck stood on end.

"The elements," I said.

Although no ring appeared in our midst, it was clear the elements understood Fitz's request.

"Aye, it seems the spell recognizes my blood, but I think something was omitted."

"You think Annabel left something out on purpose?" I asked.

"If she was this meticulous in crafting her spells, and in hiding the correct spell in the grimoire, she'd have made the spell itself difficult, too."

"May I?"

Fitz placed the grimoire in my open palms, a curious expression on his face. This was intricate and required focus and strength, but my lessons with Henry were going well, and I felt confident. This was the purpose of my magic, after all.

I sat and placed the book on the worn, wooden planks in front of my crossed legs, as Fitz retreated quietly to the couch, sensing my need for space. I simply stared at the pages, which were illuminated by the fire. I felt life within the grimoire, and I drew closer, taking an experimental sniff. The scent of aged paper and long-dried ink rose from the book as I searched for details of the woman who'd put ink to paper. The scent grew stronger still, and I rode the waves until I found the path I sought. My fingers traced the text, seeking the subtle changes of the page.

The air grew musty and damp and heavy with smoke, along with the nostalgia of a distant memory. Everything was fuzzy, like I was peering through foggy glass, and I closed my eyes briefly as my sight cleared.

I found myself in a rustic cottage. The walls and flooring were simple wood planks and stone with visibly rough craftsmanship, though the walls were in good shape. The counters were heavily marked, the result of the wear of sharp knives over the span of many years. No fridge, no dishwasher, no electricity . . . I was searching for any sign of modern convenience when a woman emerged from an open doorway. I jumped at her sudden appearance, but my presence didn't register with her.

"I'll be with ye soon enough, Alannah," the woman barked out over her shoulder. "The mistress will be none the happier for it either!"

Alannah's counterpart was a plain, middle-aged woman draped in a simple period dress. Her chestnut hair held streaks of gray, and a severe expression hardened her worn face. As she cleared dishes from the counter into a large wooden bucket, I thought how pleasant her features might be should she allow even a hint of softness. But times must have been difficult for many people, especially those in her line of work.

"Murdina!" a voice rang through the doorway.

My newfound companion turned quickly on her heel, clamoring

out that she would be a moment more. Murdina's eyes then landed in my direction, and as her quick footsteps brought her closer, I held my breath. To my great delight, she walked right through me.

"I did it," I exclaimed under my breath. Recalling the events Annabel recorded in her journal, I gazed through the open window at the early morning light. Annabel would prepare for the day in a less trafficked area of the house.

Though simple, the house was larger than I expected, and I wound through several rooms and one lengthy hallway before perceiving hushed voices on the other side of an upstairs door.

I proceeded timidly, calculating the odds that I could transport myself through the door. I touched the door softly and asked my magic to deposit me on the other side.

A small but tidy bedroom was brightly lit, the morning sun pouring through the east-facing windows. A large, four-poster bed stood boldly in the middle of the room, covered in thick, wool blankets.

My eyes scanned over the few items crammed beside the bed and landed on an oak desk in the far corner of the room. Annabel sat at the desk, deep in discussion with a man I discovered was her husband.

What, is he human? I marveled. My heart softened as I thought of Fitz's and my challenges before I'd matched to my power. I could only imagine what this couple had faced.

My mind wandered to my human-witch ancestry. What challenges might my own family have encountered?

The man jumped from his seat, and his brows furrowed angrily as he stalked out of the room, slamming the door behind him. Annabel's left hand extended toward the ceiling, her journal materializing into her open palm. She set the book gently on the old, wooden surface, and the pages flew open to a blank sheet. Her hair fell loosely past her shoulders, the gray strands not yet smoothed back for the day. I moved closer to peer over her shoulder when my vision dissipated like smoke on the wind, and I was left staring at Fitz.

"No! I was so close."

"You lost concentration, that's all."

"How long was I gone?" I asked.

"Maybe ten minutes."

"Ugh."

"Just focus. You've got this," Fitz said.

Miraculously, I returned to where I left off, peering over Annabel's left shoulder. The passage was a few days prior to her encounter of passing the ring to Esther. I was close, but not quite close enough. I closed my eyes, asking my witch's eye to work with time to guide me forward.

The world went dark, and I was sucked into a wind tunnel, billowing around with total loss of control.

I'd once endured a tornado with Gram. We weren't far from her home when a large, swirling funnel appeared on the horizon. We had little time to react, jumping from Gram's car and running frantically toward a ditch behind other carloads of people, clinging to the hope that they knew what was best. I'd never forget those few horrifying moments when the elements betrayed us, and objects flew impossibly through the air. That experience was the closest to which I could liken this moment, but even that didn't feel quite sufficient.

When the wind died down, my sight was restored, and I watched Annabel gather her belongings. Excitement coursed through my veins as I followed her into the streets of Forfar, Scotland circa 1662.

CHAPTER TWENTY-EIGHT

Annabel made her way down a dirty path, which was lined with horse dung and the contents of chamber pots, one of the less appealing attributes of the time.

Annabel's narrow lane was soon behind us, and we strolled down the main thoroughfare of town, greeted by the sounds of a marketplace in full swing.

Though she spoke to very few, Annabel was watched by all she encountered. Merchants, housewives, and children regarded her path through the busy street, and a few made eye contact. It seemed that Fitz's family was well known by the small town's human population. She even seemed to be watched by other witches, who undoubtedly knew the witchhunt was coming for Esther.

The sight provoked a fresh wave of gratitude for the lack of human observation in modern times.

Annabel, though simply dressed, was vibrant against the crowd and held a stately appearance—the woman demanded respect. Her gray hair was twisted away from her face and mostly covered by a linen cap. She held her head high, meeting the gazes of others unabashedly. Annabel turned down a wide lane lined with trees, and eventually made her final steps toward what I hoped was Esther's home.

A row of two-story homes lay ahead. It could've been a string of townhomes found in modern times, albeit a little rustic for our era. But they appeared sturdier and cleaner than the area around Annabel's home, everything indicating this row was more affluent than the main street of town.

A thick, arched wooden door swung open to reveal a large foyer. A young servant girl stood aside, allowing Annabel to pass into the grand, open space. The girl didn't speak, though her doe eyes flitted timidly back and forth. She then signaled for Annabel to follow her, allowing me the opportunity to view Esther's home.

The house spanned two floors, and a balcony emerged from the stairwell, stretching the length of all four corners of the room and revealing several doorways—almost as many as the ground floor. The room was mainly comprised of wood and stone, and though each had the rustic appearance of centuries past, the masonry and carpentry work were of good quality, the materials in the space all working together seamlessly and in harmony.

A sizable tapestry was suspended from the second floor's vaulted ceiling, lying flat against the far wall, the soft, faded tartan colors forming a backdrop to the clan crest. It must have served as a symbol of family loyalty for many generations. A crowned lion's head was at the center, and the Gaelic words "'*S Rioghal Mo Dhream*'" formed a half circle around it. I wondered if the tapestry had recently been added to the decor, or if it had been hung openly in defiance of the king's orders against the MacGregors. I thought of all the tartan-clad items I'd seen at Fitz's flat and at Ian and Ann's cabin at the lake. Esther and Hamish would have been proud to know the MacGregor pride lived on.

Stag antlers further decorated the solid wood half-wall of the balcony, and tables and chests alike were strewn against the backdrop of the stone walls, made from the same deep wood that constructed the stairwell and balcony. Esther's home was well-kept, and I wondered how many generations of Fitz's family had called these walls home before Hamish and Esther had come to know them.

A lady's maid walked Annabel into the sitting room without hesitation, where she received a warm greeting from Esther. Esther was beautiful, and I discerned both expressions and features I recognized from Izzy's fair skin, emerald eyes, and auburn hair. She was too ethereal to be human, and I was sure many humans in the small community were resentful.

"Aunt, I thought ye would never return," Esther said.

"Och aye. Same as I, truth be told."

"Well, I'm pleased to have ye home," Esther said. "Do take a seat."

Annabel looked down at her hands, an uneasy expression washing over her face. "Ye ken, my business that took me away, it was of a delicate nature."

"Oh aye?" Esther asked as she poured a dram of whisky, handing it over to Annabel.

"Aye, and I must speak to ye about it."

Esther narrowed her eyes in curiosity.

"Through the years, the family has endured torturous thoughts and visions, finding no rest even in sleep, even in death—"

"Aunt," Esther interrupted.

"Hear what I have to say."

"We struck an accord, or have ye forgotten?" Esther asked. "We are never to speak of these things."

"I remember well, child. Do not think because my body ages that my memory ages in turn."

"Why do ye trouble me then?"

"I have good reason, and ye must hear it," Annabel said.

"Make it brief. Hamish will return soon. I'll not trouble his mind today."

"Your parents believed they would pass before your vision came to fruition, and as such, they entrusted a grave task to me," Annabel fumbled along, her nerves clearly rising.

Esther shifted in her seat, taking a deep breath, but allowed Annabel to continue uninterrupted.

"Child, I do not speak of the past to harm ye, but to tell of our burden and our cause."

Esther nodded wordlessly.

"Before their deaths, your parents called each of the living family forth and held counsel on what could be done to prevent your early death. Each side of your family was heavily represented, as ye must ken that we each wanted to protect ye."

"I had no knowledge of this," Esther said.

"Oh, certainly not. It was arranged with great secrecy and maintained in such."

"When did this pass?"

"Some fifty years ago. We convened for days upon days. We considered every course of action. Somewhere in the deep of night, an idea emerged."

Annabel fidgeted slightly. This was it.

"This idea . . . this is why ye've come."

"Aye."

"I willnae like it."

"Nae, but there's no helping it. What's done is done." Annabel leaned forward, looking Esther in the eye, before proceeding. "Your own excellent parents wrestled with the idea, but in the end, there was nothing else to be done, and each of us would risk more than this to save ye."

"Aunt, what have ye done?" Esther asked, her voice barely audible.

Annabel reached into her pocket and removed an object neither of us could yet see. "Open your hand."

Esther obeyed, though slowly, just as a small, shiny object caught the sunlight and fell into her waiting grasp.

I gasped and instinctively ran my fingers over the moonstone on my own hand. They were practically identical. My mind raced. How had Fitz procured my ring? With their similarities, it couldn't be a coincidence.

Tearing my focus from my own finger, I gazed upon the horrified face of Esther.

She looked from the ring that lay in her grasp to her aunt before dropping the item to the floor. "Ye have brought great shame to this family!" Esther yelled, making no attempt to conceal her anger.

"Esther, my child."

"No, do not attempt to justify these perverse actions!" Esther said.

"Ye are too harsh. Hear what I have to say."

"This is a crime! I won't let my husband and bairns take part in the blame for this. They have endured enough."

"They dinnae have to endure any more suffering."

"What are ye saying, Aunt?" Esther questioned as she paced the room, walking off her violent energy.

"Hear what I have to say," Annabel responded softly, pointing toward Esther's seat.

After a moment's hesitation, Esther followed her instruction.

"Ye say this is a crime, and though that may be true, the law does no always dictate what is right. Humans have done a great evil to our kind. They fear the unfamiliar, but fear does no justify killing the innocent. Ye have done nae wrong, nae evil to them. Ye, who are blameless, do no deserve to be put to death. As such, we have placed our powers into this object."

"Surely no yours as well?"

"I have no yet done so. My death before your capture wasn't foretold, but I'll forfeit my power to this ring before ye are taken."

"Ye will do no such thing," Esther said. "Who still living knows of this?"

"Only I and your Uncle John." Annabel stooped to pick the ring up from the floor. "What is foretold is wrong, but we have provided a path to fight this evil. We will alter the future; we will make it right."

"We could suffer dire consequences changing the future in such a way," Esther said. "Fate would be none too pleased."

"Perhaps. What would ye have us do? We're your family. Would ye no do the same for your own bairns?"

Their arguments continued, but finally, Annabel made some headway.

"This was the dying wish of your parents, Esther." Annabel's eyes filled with tears. "Do ye no understand, child? Ye were their last thought. Think of your parents. Think of your bairns."

Esther hung her head.

"Ye dinnae need to make me any promises today, but accept this ring, Esther. It holds your parent's power. Hold them close."

Esther nodded. It was weak, but it was progress. Although Esther would ultimately refuse to utilize the enchanted object, I wondered if her family's power had given some measure of comfort to Esther in her final weeks.

As the initial shock passed, Annabel continued her mission, giving instruction to Esther on utilizing the ring. I wasn't sure I heard correctly at first, but Esther repeated the words back to Annabel:

That which was lost
Soon shall be found
Desire in your heart
Ignite with the moon
Bring the ring
Here and now.

"I only need to alter the word 'moon?'"

"Aye. My powers draw strength from the moon. Yours, from the earth. Alter only this word, and the right to summon is yours. Let's have a try, shall we?"

Annabel tapped the ring, muttering unintelligible words under her breath, resulting in its sudden disappearance. "Proceed."

Esther held up her hand and recited Annabel's incantation.

The ring materialized in Esther's open palm.

I could've easily lost myself for hours with these women, but it was time to return to the future . . . or the present, as it were. With my research complete, I envisioned Henry's sitting room. I thought of Fitz's anxious face and my desire to be with him once again.

The heat of a nearby fire warmed my face, and the familiar scent of Scotch welcomed me back to the present.

"I know what we need to do," I whispered.

CHAPTER TWENTY-NINE

We sat by Annabel's grimoire, and Fitz's hunger for knowledge was palpable. I squeezed his hand and focused on relaying my recently acquired information. Fitz's powers were fueled by the earth, just like Esther's. He repeated the modified incantation, and when the last word escaped his lips, the fire again roared. This time, the ground rumbled, and the lights flickered as well. But yet again, no ring appeared.

Fitz worked the spell several times, the fire flaring higher, the ground shaking harder, and the lights flickering longer with every attempt. Although the elements yielded a greater response, the ring remained to be seen. Fitz sighed, turning to me.

"Are you sure you saw this correctly?" Fitz asked. His tone was accusatory.

"Of course, I'm sure."

"Don't be snippy. It was only a question."

"Your tone speaks volumes."

"What tone?" he quipped, the tone in question still lingering in his voice.

I arched my eyebrow but remained silent.

Fitz sighed. "I don't mean to sound frustrated with you. I'm just disappointed this isn't working."

I slid my arm around his waist. "We're going to figure this out. It's not you. Your words are exactly as Annabel taught Esther."

Fitz nodded, and his face grew pensive.

"Would I be able to use the spell even though I'm a different bloodline?" I asked.

"It might work; it's less likely outside our bloodline, but possible. The spell might recognize you since we're mates."

"How about I try? It'll at least help us narrow down what's going on."

"A fine idea," Fitz said.

I ran my fingers along the enchanted page of the grimoire and closed my eyes thinking of the missing phrase that held the key to this spell. I'd commanded fire and used my mind to see past events, but this was my first spell. Excitement coursed through my veins, and I used the excess energy to fuel my efforts.

When I opened my eyes, I was ready to pull the ring to me.

"That which was lost
Soon shall be found"

An energy rumbled through me, and my heart raced.

"Desire in your heart

Ignite with the fire"

ɟertips glowed red.

"Bring the ring
Here and now"

As the last word escaped my lips, an unfamiliar room materialized around me. Dark gray walls spanned the space, and several large paintings popped brightly against the deep color. A large wooden door was closed at the far end of the room. I crossed the worn hardwood floors, curious about the maps hanging from the opposite wall, hoping they would lend some clue about my location. The largest map was a rendering of Europe dated 1648, along with a smaller map of 1600 Scotland and a 1650 version of Forfar and its surrounding area. Wondering if I had left Scotland, I rummaged around the room.

Two oversized mahogany chairs and a matching table were positioned in a corner of the room. Letters were strewn on the surface of the table, all addressed to a Dr. Belmonte. I sifted through the items, not even certain what I was seeking, but when I lifted the final letter, I gasped. Esther MacGregor's magical ring lay at the center of the table, glimmering like it hoped to be discovered. Upon seeing it up close, I was struck by the exact detail my replica held to the original. I reached for it hungrily, but I was met by an invisible force, sending a small shock through my fingertips.

The ring was enchanted by an unfamiliar energy. Though I tried, nothing would grant me access to the magical item, and there was precious little I could do about that. There was nothing I could do with the ring without my physical presence anyway. If I wasn't able to secure the ring, I could at least continue my search around the room.

I was unable to open the door, nor was I able to transport myself to the other side, and I was confident that whoever Dr. Belmonte was, they understood the treasure in their possession. The thought stopped me in my tracks. Would a witch so powerful be able to detect that I had been in the room? If only I could see outside or into the hallway, maybe I could learn a little more about where I was. I scanned the room yet again, hoping I missed something in my initial search. Another door lay at the opposite side of the room. There hadn't been a door along that wall before—I was certain. I tried the handle, but it was also locked.

I wondered why the room had no windows, but no sooner had the thought crossed my mind than a window appeared. I hesitated briefly, trying to wrap my mind around this odd room, before tossing the curtains open to find a mountain range just beyond a small, snow-covered valley. The range was impressive, answering my earlier question. I might have been gazing upon the Alps, but surely not Scotland.

Turning from the spectacular view, another map caught my eye. Rather than my having overlooked it the first time, my instincts whispered that the enchanted room chose what to reveal and when. To my great surprise, a map of the Olympic National Park in Washington State hung from the wall, covered in red ink. A large "X" marked the High Divide Trail, which wasn't far from my mom's home. There was no indication of what might be along the trail, and having spent a considerable amount of time there, I was at a loss. I committed the details to memory and combed over the room one last time before asking my powers to deposit me back in Henry's home.

I was surprised to see Henry waiting alongside Fitz for my spirit to return to my body. I practically choked on my words while relaying the details of my adventure, describing the room and the great power holding the ring in place.

"You actually saw the ring?" Fitz asked. The light in his eyes was enough to draw a wide smile across my lips. He'd committed so much time to finding the item, knowing that he might never discover what he sought. Here was his answer after years of research—and bursts of his excitement flowed through me. "I can't believe we finally have a lead on its whereabouts."

"I just hope this name leads us somewhere," I said. "I could find my way back to the room, but if I can't open the desk drawers or exit the room, I think we're at a standstill."

"Most of the maps were of Scotland, you said?" Henry asked.

"One of Europe, one of Scotland, and one of Forfar. All were dated from the 17th century and at least looked like original drawings. The good doctor is clearly interested in the time period when the ring was created."

"And Forfar," Fitz added. "That's where the ring was certainly forged, but I just can't make sense of all this."

"I think we need to keep in mind that there was an Olympic National Park map too," I said. "The others were a bigger focus, but something about it is tugging at me."

"You know the area well, aye?" Henry asked.

"I can't even count the number of long weekends and summer camping trips I took with my parents in the area when I was growing up. My . . . mom lives by a lake in the park."

I'd almost said "my parents." Would it ever get any easier?

Fitz slipped a hand onto my shoulder. "Henry, it's close to where Hadley and I first met."

"Have either of you been to the trail?"

"Yes, of course, but I don't remember anything out of the ordinary," I began, trying to recall any useful details. "The trail is pretty long. I think eighteen miles or something like that—diverse terrain."

"I think it's worth our notice," added Fitz. "Hads, think on it further and see if anything comes to mind."

"Fitz, show me the spell you've been using," Henry said.

Fitz performed the summoning spell, the elements answering in the same frustrated manner as before.

"Well, it's apparent the elements are irritated. Hadley's right: someone definitely has the wee thing under a potent protection spell."

"That means they've been waiting on someone to call the ring. Do you think this person knows who we are?" Fitz wondered.

"Not necessarily," Henry said. "But they realize this power can be called forth and are either using the ring for their own purposes or buying time until they figure out how to tap into its power. The incantations Annabel used are strong; not just any old bloke could hack into that power."

"Okay, so let's start researching Dr. Belmonte, cross-reference Scotland, Forfar, and Washington State, and see what we can come up with," I added.

"Aye," Henry agreed. "Great work, Hadley. You'll make one powerful witch yet."

CHAPTER THIRTY

Fitz arrived back at his flat from a day spent in the archives of the National Library of Scotland to find me prepping dinner. He kissed me quickly before throwing on an old sweater and helping me dice carrots for a stew.

"Your energy's off," Fitz observed.

"I'm nervous about my meeting tomorrow with the council."

"Did they confirm who you're meeting with?" he asked.

"Mia for a touch base about the Paris stalkers." I slid chopped onion into the pan. "Then I meet my new trainer."

"Do you want me to go with you?" Fitz asked.

"I don't want to pull you away from your research. I'll be fine."

"It's just computer work tomorrow. I'll work from the lobby so

I'm around . . . if it helps."

"Of course, it helps."

"It's settled then," he said.

Fitz reached for the bundle of celery on the counter and placed it on the cutting board.

"So, I hope you're ready for a little family bonding." Fitz raised an eyebrow.

"What do you mean?"

"Izzy is coming over on holiday. And so are my parents."

"Wait, really? The whole family?"

"Izzy is excited to see you. They all are. And Dad is interested in our progress with the ring."

"That's great, Fitz. I can't wait." I focused on choosing the right spices from the cabinet, hoping my forced smile only read as distraction.

I knew he must've felt my conflicting emotions, but he didn't pry. I was thrilled to see Izzy and Ann, but I was nervous to see Ian again, if I was being honest. Ian had always been polite but distant. For the longest time at the lake, I had been convinced he didn't like me . . . and then there was the observation. I still had a lot of complicated feelings to unpack when it came to Ian.

"When do they arrive?" I asked.

"Izzy arrives two weeks from today. Mum and Dad arrive the following Monday. They're staying for a couple weeks."

"How did they get that amount of time off work so last minute?"

Fitz eyed me meaningfully. "The councils."

"So, the councils have basically infiltrated everywhere."

"You have no idea," Fitz said.

"I'm starting to get an idea."

"Mum and Dad offered to bring items from your mum's place if that's helpful."

I was lucky on the move front. My mom had volunteered to oversee the process in the States, and I only needed to collect my belongings on the east side of the pond. My mom had always loved a project, but after Daddy died, they'd become somewhat of a saving grace for her—something she could pour all her attention into.

With that business settled, my next task was finding a place to live in Edinburgh. Though it seemed Fitz and I were headed in the direction of living together, this flat was his space. He hadn't yet asked me to officially move in, and I hadn't addressed it with him, but time was running out.

"I need to figure out where I'm going to live," I said.

Fitz set the knife on the counter and faced me.

"John is moving out." John lived right next door to Fitz. "He just accepted a new job in Glasgow. The two flats would make a grand space if they were opened up."

I eyed him.

"You might not want to move in with me," Fitz said, "but I've . . . gotten used to you being here. I don't want you going anywhere."

"It's not that I don't want to be here. Fitz, I'm not sure I can afford a place in your building."

"We could purchase it together," Fitz suggested.

I hesitated.

"There's also the council," Fitz said, "though I'm not sure you'll want to have any ties to them."

"What do you mean?" I asked.

"If you want the help, the government will send you monthly payments, plus they'll help you sort out wherever you want to live."

I turned the stovetop off before turning. "Excuse me?"

"Humans, as a whole, might not know about us, but the leaders of their countries do," Fitz said. "They understand secrecy is imperative, meaning there's a specific branch of their administrations that carries out business with witchkind. Only their highest levels of leadership are aware of our existence."

"What ensures their secrecy?"

"The knowledge that almost every country in the world has an agreement with us, so they don't need to make enemies. We could take down an entire nation if we so choose. If they blow our secret, our Cardinal Court could have it ordered to take them out. It's a pretty compelling reason to be discreet."

"My god. But how does that affect my bank account?" I asked.

"Each country funnels money into secret accounts that fund the supernatural within its borders. So, you'd be funded by lovely Great Britain." He paused briefly. "I told you Henry's father was involved in the First World War. And I mentioned how I think the council wants something from us. We're occasionally asked to support our government with our talents. It's rare in times of peace for regular citizens to be called into any major action, but every once in a while, it's warranted."

I was astonished.

"Countries vary in the amount they funnel, depending on their economic state and how many witches live within their borders. You'd be amazed at what else your tax dollars fund, but we won't get into that."

My head was already bursting with information.

"So," Fitz concluded, "the money would basically keep you on retainer. But if you were ever needed, they wouldn't hesitate to ask."

"That seems kind of . . . scary?"

"Aye. It's one of the reasons I'm worried about Olivia's reaction to us. I've thought a lot about it since our meeting. I think she already knew about my power. Yours took her by surprise a bit. But that gleam in her eye . . ."

"I don't know if I want that tie to them."

"I've declined their help ever since we left the lake."

"I understand why."

Fitz nodded distractedly.

"What is it?" I asked, his nerves present in the pit of my stomach.

"I told you about Henry helping me invest my money."

"Yes . . ."

"I have a decent amount stocked up."

I tapped my fingers against the concrete countertops.

"So, how do you feel about the flat next door?" Fitz asked. "I know you won't let me buy it for you, but we could buy it together. And I do think if we have this place and the one next door, we could open the spaces into one large flat. If you'd want to do that, that is . . ."

"I think it's a brilliant idea. I feel a little funny about you splitting the cost of the flat with me, but if you want the larger space anyway . . ." I paused.

"I want to build a home with you," Fitz said.

And I longed for the same thing. It was decided, then.

"Let's do it."

Fitz smiled, shaking his head softly.

"Are you ever going to stop being surprised I want to be near you?" I asked.

"Absolutely not. I'm beginning to think someone enchanted you. How else can I explain it?"

"Explain what?"

"You're intelligent, powerful, stunning, and funny," he rattled off, a mischievous twinkle in his eyes. "What are you doing with me unless it's enchantment? Oh god . . . or pity. I'd like to think it's enchantment myself. At least it makes for a more romantic story."

I pulled him closer to me. "Hmmm, what am I doing with you? Besides the fact that you have the body of a Norse legend, intellect, and humor, let's also not forget that the power you possess is far beyond reasonable."

I asked the air to close the final gap between us, and it silently responded, pressing Fitz's body against mine.

"*Very* nice, Hadley."

"Shhh . . ." I placed my finger across his lips. He proceeded to kiss my finger slowly before brushing his lips along my arm. As he reached the tender skin between my neck and shoulder, I released a satisfied sigh. In the past several weeks, I'd discovered a completely new world full of wonderment, but at that moment, the only marvel on my mind was calling Fitz undisputedly mine.

CHAPTER THIRTY-ONE

The following morning found me in the one place in Edinburgh I did not want to be: Mia's temp office at the Scottish Council's headquarters. Seated across the marble-topped desk from her, I was far from comfortable. My nerves were almost as high as the first time the stalkers had tracked us. I'd hoped she would be more pleasant at this meeting, but she remained as cold as her cryokinesis powers.

"You and Fitz haven't given us any useful information on your stalkers from Paris," said Mia, her tone bordering on accusatory.

"Trust me, we want to know who they are as much as you do," I said.

"Trust you? How am I supposed to know that you want this as much as we do?"

"Why wouldn't I want them caught? Being stalked is not one of my favorite pastimes."

"You'd be surprised," she responded tartly.

I was coming to the idea that I couldn't do anything right in Mia's eyes—she'd combat me at every turn.

"You know, for someone who's meant to help us, your annoyance with Fitz and me has been painfully clear from the beginning. You've turned our meetings into accusations rather than collaborations."

"That's fresh coming from you."

"Oh, please do expand upon your position, Mia."

"You clearly distrust witchkind government. You act like I'm your enemy when I have done nothing but help."

My blood boiled. "Help? Are you kidding me?"

"If you'd like to calm down now, that'd be great."

"I'm fine."

"Really? Cause deflecting your fire is not on my agenda today," Mia quipped, though her eyes shifted warily from my eyes to my fingers.

Crap. My fire magic. I closed my eyes, exhaling my anger with each breath.

"Okay, sorry. I didn't mean to get angry."

"Let's just focus on why I called you in today. The reality is we can't generate a lead in any form. We have no idea who these witches are," Mia continued.

"Where does that leave us?"

"You haven't felt them watching you again since you've come to Edinburgh? Not even the slightest hint of something odd?"

"Nothing. This new watcher—he's different."

"Have you felt him watching recently?"

"Not since I last messaged you, but we've been spending a lot of time at Henry's and at our flat." I thrill ran through me at my first mention of Fitz's place as ours. "We've been careful."

"And you still want to decline an agent being assigned to you."

"Yes, that feels more like imprisonment than help."

Mia's eyes flickered to mine, but she let my comment go.

"This is pretty rare, you know," she said.

"Being watched?"

"Not only that, but being watched by three witches the councils can't identify."

I nodded.

"We'll keep running searches, but if you think of anything else in the meantime, let us know. Something isn't right. And regardless of what you might think, your safety is important to us," said Mia.

"Thank you . . . seriously. The experience was nothing short of violating, and it's always in the back of my mind. Being watched gets under your skin. So, you can trust me when I say if I think of anything new, I'll let you know immediately."

"We'll do our very best with this."

"If that's all on that topic, I have another question."

Mia nodded for me to proceed.

"Did you have anything to do with my separation from Fitz?"

Mia's energy stirred, but her face was impassible. "Do you think I did?"

"You were involved in my first meeting with the council, so it seemed like you had an interest in it."

"That doesn't equate to my involvement."

"Correct. But you've made your opinion decidedly clear about it."

"Yes, because you broke the rules."

"I don't understand you."

"What is that supposed to mean?"

I ignored her question. "Did you have any involvement—any at all—in mine and Fitz's separation?"

She held my gaze, neither of us willing to look away first.

"I didn't give the order if that's what you're asking," Mia said.

"Then why do I feel like you were involved?"

"Spare me your questioning."

My blood boiled. "Did you give orders related to it? Consult on it?"

Mia sighed. "I was consulted, yes. The issue was raised to the U.S. National Coven Council—Ian fought hard for you and Fitz."

I nodded.

"No one wanted to vote against Ian, but they were conflicted because you were breaking our laws. One of the members called to consult with me."

"And what did you tell them?"

"That we govern based on the law."

I scoffed.

"Perhaps the laws need revisiting," Mia admitted, "but that is a different conversation. My duty is to uphold the law."

"That's shortsighted," I said.

"And you're judging the situation emotionally," Mia said. "Take emotion out of the equation and revisit it with fresh eyes. Everyone thinks they deserve to be the exception."

"Take my emotions out of it?" I repeated incredulously. "This is my life, Mia, not some textbook math equation!"

Mia's eyebrows rose.

"And Fitz wasn't a crush. We are mates. The council forced apart two witches who are mates. I think you have other laws that should have been considered."

"You made your position perfectly clear at our first meeting," Mia said. "We don't need to revisit it."

I shook my head and stood. "Do you need anything else for my statement?"

"No, we're done."

I stalked across the room but turned back before leaving.

"You know, I'm sure you're a talented witch, Mia. But you're as cold as the ice that spills from your fingertips. And that is your biggest detriment."

I raced from Mia's office and tumbled right into a young woman with dusky hair in the hallway.

"I am so sorry," I said, reaching for the woman as we balanced ourselves.

"Don't worry about it," she said, a hint of a smile crinkling the corners of her wide, umber eyes.

"I was just heading back to the training department's reception area, but I think I'm a bit turned around."

"Straight down that hallway on your right."

"Thanks," I said.

She nodded and dragged her black combat boots down the hall. I waited until she was out of sight and leaned against the wall, breathing deeply. My meeting with Mia had unsettled me. How could I accept help from this group of witches if I couldn't trust them? I took another deep breath and turned in the direction of the training department.

Tanner was waiting for me in the training reception area.

"You good, Weston?" he asked eyeing me suspiciously.

"Yeah. Just met with Mia," I offered in explanation.

That satisfied Tanner, and he escorted me into a training room.

Two new faces greeted us. One was short and slender, with bronzed skin and raven hair. Her dark eyes seemed to perceive everything, and I was struck by their intensity. Her physical being was almost otherworldly, and the lighthearted energy of a free spirit wafted casually around her.

The other had wavy, blonde hair that hung to her lower back, bleached by the sun, much in the same way her tanned skin had been kissed by it. She looked young, but her cunning blue eyes held wisdom and experience.

Tanner introduced the latter as Chloe—a Cardinal Court member, just like Mia. I groaned internally.

"Chloe is from Australia," he said. Tanner's energy was off, and there was something in his voice . . . strain, I thought.

I observed Chloe. There were few places in the world that made as much sense as Australia did for this woman. Her build was that of an athlete, and I wondered if perhaps she owed years of surfing for her sculpted, lean muscle.

Chloe had been assigned as my lead coach, meaning she was responsible for appointing and overseeing my training.

"Right on. I'm so happy to meet you, Hadley. I'm sorry I didn't make it over here to meet you sooner. I had some urgent business back home, but all is well now."

"Australian witchkind was on the brink of civil war about a year ago. But Chloe's been working to bring the two parties together," Tanner explained. "Really amazing work."

I didn't miss the admiration in his voice or the twinkle in his eye.

"It hasn't been easy, but we're finally in a good place—settling down and moving forward. Of course, that doesn't mean we don't have the occasional hiccup," Chloe said, winking.

An entire world existed within the one that I thought I had known so well . . . and everything I'd thought to be true was being challenged.

Chloe smiled. "Well, let's get started, shall we? This is Maka."

Chloe had chosen Maka from the Cheyenne River Sioux Tribe of the American Dakotas to improve my understanding of my abilities and to assist me in controlling them.

"I'm so happy to meet you," Maka said, extending her hand.

A warm energy traveled up my arm, and I returned her greeting.

"Maka will be working with you a few times a week until you master your mind reading and your mental transport," Chloe said.

"It sounds like your mind reading is your biggest challenge right now, so we'll start there," Maka said. "I'm excited to get started."

"Maka will send reports to me, and Tanner will continue to monitor your progress. We'll make sure you have the support you need until you're proficient in all of your abilities."

"Does that mean I won't be working with Mia any longer?"

Tanner had mentioned a rumor floating around headquarters that Mia was going to be assigned as my lead. Since she had been involved in my first meeting and on the stalker investigation, we gave some merit to the rumor, but I was thrilled to have this report disproven.

"She'll continue her work on the investigation, but the court decided I'd be a better fit for your training. I hope you're not too disappointed."

"No disappointment at all," I assured. "I look forward to working with you."

"Rad. Maka will meet you here tomorrow at nine. I know you start work on Monday, so we'll adjust your training sessions to fit your schedule."

They offered a chorus of niceties as I left the training room, and though I wanted to believe they had my best interest at heart, I left the room with a heavy amount of skepticism lingering in my mind.

Fitz was waiting for me in the main lobby. From the leather brief-case to the book in his hand to his wool waistcoat, he looked every bit of the scholar he was. Fitz kissed me quickly and gathered his belongings.

We were halfway to the apartment, and I was recounting the morning's chain of events to Fitz, when my breathing came short. I froze and cast a nervous glance to Fitz. Fitz's breathing grew labored for just a few seconds before he breathed deeply and reached for me.

"What's wrong?" he asked.

"I—I think I'm on the verge of a panic attack." I glanced around anxiously at the people who passed us along the sidewalk.

"Hey, look right here," Fitz said, his voice soft. "Keep your eyes on mine."

I followed his directions.

"Good. Don't worry about them. It's just you and me here, aye?"

I nodded.

"Breathe. Keep your eyes here and breathe."

I followed his directions. My heart still pounded in my chest, but I began to feel like I might catch my breath.

Fitz's eyes grew distant but before I could question it, a bit of peace flowed through my heart and into my bloodstream. A sense of calm seemed to glide through my veins, easing my nerves as it washed through me. My heart rate continued to slow and my breathing came easy.

Fitz extended his hand. "May I?" he asked.

"Of course," I said weakly.

He slid his arms around me, enveloping me in a safe, warm space. I leaned into him and closed my eyes. Edinburgh fell away—the people, the sights, the sounds. For a moment, only the two of us existed, and I had nothing to fear.

The wind whipped furiously as we worked our way to the top of Arthur's Seat. The ancient volcano boasted one of the best views in Edinburgh, being the highest peak in the hills surrounding the city. It was little wonder Robert Louis Stevenson had described it as "a hill for magnitude." Fitz and I were quiet on our ascent, content in each other's company and the sweeping views.

We found a seat near the edge facing the Royal Mile and pulled trail mix from his backpack.

"We should discuss your panic attack."

I dropped my gaze. Fitz had suggested a hike, knowing it often worked well to dispel my excess energy—and anxiety. But I knew the conversation wouldn't wait.

"You're not too keen on sharing this kind of information with me, but you expect that I tell you everything. That's hardly fair."

I wanted to tell him he was wrong, but I couldn't find an argument to support it.

"What do you want to know?" I asked.

"When did they start?"

"The moment I left the lake for Boston." I paused. "I felt like something was missing, like my gut was telling me something was wrong. I had a panic attack in the airport, but that was only the beginning. By the time I reached Boston, I felt a bit of hysteria. I can vividly remember sitting on the plane on the tarmac, waiting to exit, and feeling like my stomach was flipping."

"Do you have a theory on what triggered it?"

"I wondered if I was just nervous to move so far from home and leave my parents on the other side of the country, especially when Daddy was so ill, and I know there was some level of that. But . . ."

I gritted my teeth, hesitant to share more.

"What?"

"But I couldn't get you out of my head. I kept seeing your face, and I felt like I was missing something only you could give me."

Fitz's heartbeat raced through our streams.

"The first night in my new apartment, I was brushing my teeth when I was seized with hysterics. I basically fell to the bathroom floor and couldn't catch my breath. It was absolute panic and fear, which was only multiplied when I couldn't figure out why it was happening. Everything felt wrong. I was so worried about you."

"I'm so sorry." Fitz's face was downcast, but it wasn't my intention to make him feel bad about the past. I knew he had struggled too. "Sometimes, this anxious feeling would take hold of me. Since I didn't want to overstep in our relationship, I asked Izzy to work a spell to check on you when it felt like she'd be a better choice. She always said you were fine—that you were stressed about something— but she never told me the extent. She knew I'd take the next flight out. I didn't even know they were panic attacks until your last letter."

"Izzy did the right thing. You didn't need to worry about me with everything going on."

"There is nothing more important to me than you. You were all

I was worried about."

I leaned over and kissed his shoulder. I couldn't have asked for a more thoughtful mate.

"Can we calm others from a distance?" I asked.

"Any witch can craft a calming spell, but it takes a powerful and exceptionally intuitive witch to craft the spell and then send it across the country."

"I thought as much."

"Izzy cares for you like a sister."

"Sometimes, I'd be in the middle of an attack and then inexplicably feel fine. It was something I couldn't explain—until now. What you did earlier today . . . I'd felt that before."

"It was Izzy. I'm sure of it."

"Thank god for her," I said.

"And what about now? Have you had more that I don't know about since we've been together?"

"No. This is the first one since I matched to my powers—well, aside from the one I almost had the day we met the council. But today . . ."

"Today was intense. Arguing with Mia after you were already nervous to meet with her, being introduced to a new court member and your new trainer."

I nodded.

"We'll run through an extra meditation tonight and work on a few calming techniques for tomorrow. You've got this, Hads."

CHAPTER THIRTY-TWO

I stood across from Maka in her training room at the council head-quarters, readying myself for my first training session with her. I wanted to get to know her better. There was just something in Maka's energy inviting me to trust her.

"Maka, your name is beautiful. I've never heard it before."

"Oh, that's because it's a nickname. It essentially means earth. In Lakota mythology, it's related to our earth spirit. When my mom was pregnant with me, she knew my abilities would be strong. Since she could feel my power so clearly, she named me Hope. But because they didn't know definitively what we were, many members of my tribe only sensed my strong connection with our earth. The nick-name just stuck," she said with a smile and a shrug.

"Well, it's lovely, and I think you might just be an earth goddess after all."

Maka began by learning more about my struggles with mind-reading.

"I have so little control of that power," I said. "I've started before I even know I've begun. And sometimes the thoughts are a little fuzzy or in and out. I really need to get a handle on it."

"I hate to tell you this, but controlling your mind is a matter of practice," Maka said. "You'll make progress as you continue to focus on controlling it."

"I've tried to be cognizant around others, but it's difficult to maintain that focus in a crowd of people."

"When you first learned to ride a bike," Maka said, "you had to focus on your balance, peddling, and where you wanted to go, but at some point, balance and peddling became innate. This talent will be the same. Keep focusing on what you want, and together, we'll get there."

"It's been tough. I'm so happy to have help with this now," I lamented with a smile.

"Oh, I know exactly how you feel. I've been there too."

"It's encouraging to talk to someone who's been through this."

"It must seem overwhelming right now, but you haven't had the benefit of training since you were young. You're just now discovering the world the rest of us experienced since childhood. I know without a doubt that you'll master everything in the time we have together—you harbor such strong and unique magic inside you."

"Thank you, Maka."

"Okay, we're going to work on some basics today: meditation and setting your intentions with mind reading. Mastering these are the first steps toward controlling your mind, and we'll start each session this way."

I nodded.

"Have you been meditating?" Maka asked.

"Yes," I answered truthfully. Fitz meditated daily, and we'd fallen into a routine together.

"And yoga?"

I grimaced.

"It's all right; you aren't in trouble," Maka returned, laughing. "But I want you to make room for it. You carry a massive amount of anxiety in you. Other witches' and humans' negative thoughts and energy will linger in you. Regular yoga practice is just as important as meditation in your case. They'll work together to remove all the negativity from your body, your thoughts, and your spirit."

"I know," I said. "That's horrible, isn't it? I know it'll help me, and I still haven't made room for it . . . I'm just having trouble balancing everything. I want to do better."

"Oh, Hadley," Maka began. "You have so much going on right now. You discovered you're a witch only a couple of weeks ago, and you're mentally wading through those changes and what they mean. You're moving to a new country. You're in a relationship that, yes, began a couple years ago but is different now in many ways. And you're starting a new job."

I laughed softly, nodding my head.

"No one would find their balance quickly, and you shouldn't blame yourself for not getting there with the snap of your fingers."

"Thank you."

"You're tired," she stated. It wasn't a question, but I answered anyway.

"Yes."

Maka took my hand gently. "For someone with your talents, it's imperative you get into a routine. And once you do, you'll feel the anxiety peeling off, layer by layer. You'll feel yourself moving closer to your balance. Don't deprive yourself of inner peace."

I dutifully promised to adjust my routine. I wanted better for myself.

"Okay, look around the room and find where you're most comfortable," Maka instructed. "Settle into your meditation in whichever position feels best."

I looked around the carefully curated space. This training room was small, about the size of my living room, and it was cozily furnished. The stone walls held two windows at the north end, allowing pale light to filter on to the stone flooring. A large, cream-colored rug took up a sizable portion of the floor, bearing gold vines and burgundy flowers. There were egg-shaped lounge chairs tucked into a corner near the windows. Made of bamboo with plush cushions and draped with cozy blankets, they added to the relaxing atmosphere of the room. Natural sounds of rainfall drifted through the open windows, and the burning incense in the room was cinnamon—the scent was said to increase concentration and decrease muscle tension.

All the elements worked together to create a peaceful environment where I felt like I could achieve true connection between my mind, body, and magic.

I sank into one of the lounge chairs and tucked my feet underneath me. There would be much to learn, but meditation wasn't one of them. I already had the tools to be successful with this first step, and I was immensely grateful to Fitz for that. I closed my eyes, focused on my heartbeat, and allowed the outside world to fall away.

When I emerged from my reverie, Maka opened her eyes and rose from her chair across the room.

"How did you know I was done with my meditation?"

"I'm an energy reader," Maka said. "I felt your energy shift. Studying your energy while you meditate will help me make the most effective training program for you too."

"Being so attuned to people's energies, I bet you're proficient in feeling intentions."

"There are witches more specialized in that area, but yeah, I can usually figure out if someone has good intentions or not." Maka tilted her head curiously. "What is it, Hadley?"

"I was just wondering how Mia's energy feels to you."

Maka's eyes shifted warily, her face lost in thought. She pursed her lips. "I haven't really spent time with her. Anyway, let's get back to it. Let's move into setting your intentions."

I accepted her deflection—for the time being—and refocused my mind.

We deliberated the truest purpose of my skill and ultimately settled on this: the purpose of my mind reading was to only gather information that was necessary to me. I'd work daily to ingrain into my mind that I need only call upon this ability when appropriate.

"What constitutes it being necessary?"

"We usually say you shouldn't use it unless you're working with the council in some sort of official capacity. The mind is a sacred place. Outside of training, you shouldn't access someone else's mind unless it's truly necessary. But if you're ever in danger, you can use it to gain the upper hand."

"If the stalkers get brave."

"Exactly—if you're ever in danger, don't hesitate, Hadley. Use it to your advantage," Maka said.

"Understood."

"And if you ever find yourself in that situation, you might run into shielding, meaning you wouldn't be able to read your opponent's mind anyhow."

"Shielding?"

"It's when a witch protects their mind. It isn't something that's done and forgotten about. It takes constant energy to keep a shield in place, so most witches don't bother with it unless they really have something to hide or they're in a situation where they feel like someone is watching them."

"Is there a way around it?"

"Absolutely. It's difficult to break through a shield, and the witch will definitely know someone is doing it. So, proceed with caution."

CHAPTER THIRTY-THREE

On Monday morning, I stood in front of the bathroom mirror studying my reflection. I'd been meticulous in selecting my outfit for my first day at work, wanting to feel my most confident for the occasion. I pinned my hair away from my face and then smoothed out my new houndstooth blazer. I took a deep breath. I was ready for this.

My Oxford heels clicked against our hardwood floors, pulling Fitz's attention from the *The Student*, an independent newspaper produced by students at the University of Edinburgh. A broad grin spread across his lips.

"Oh, *there's* Edinburgh Castle's new PR manager."

I giggled. "And the outfit—first day at work approved?"

"Give me a proper spin."

I followed his instructions.

"Aye, very bonnie." He walked over and kissed me. "Now, come take a seat."

I checked my watch.

"You have plenty of time. I have a wee treat for you."

"Well, in that case." I took a seat, and Fitz wandered into the kitchen. When he returned, he set a steaming cup of tea and a chocolate croissant in front of me.

I gasped delightedly. "A croissant!"

"Your favorite. I found a local bakery owned by a French pastry chef."

"Oh," I said. "I'm going to be spending a lot of time there."

Fitz chuckled. He reached into his leather bag and pulled out a small box wrapped with a green bow.

"What's this?" I asked.

"Just a wee something for your desk."

I tugged at the bow and opened the box to find a small marble bowl with crystals inside of it. I pulled the crystals out to examine them—opal, citrine, moonstone, and rose quartz. I held up another. It was bright blue and speckled with gold.

"What's this one?" I asked, examining the stone.

"Lapis lazuli—it supports truth and helps with decisiveness. It seemed a good choice for your office."

Each of his selections was tied to something that would be beneficial to me, from my October birthstone to my truth-supporting crystal.

"This was thoughtful, Fitz. Thank you."

Fitz nodded. "I thought you might want to add your blue lace agate and black tourmaline."

"Great idea."

Post-breakfast, I attempted to call my coat forward from the closet, but I was still struggling with the concealment piece. When I reached through the air, I felt nothing. I sighed and reached for the coat again, foregoing the concealment. No one was around anyway—practice would have to wait.

Fitz walked with me to the castle gate, where we parted for the day.

"I'd wish you luck," Fitz began, "but you don't need it."

"Thank you—for all of it," I said.

He leaned forward and kissed my forehead. My heart fluttered.

"I'm proud of you. Go get 'em, firecracker."

The esplanade was already packed with tourists, and I navigated my way to the staff line and scanned my digital pass that HR had sent the night before. I turned as I reached the castle gate and found Fitz right where I'd left him. He didn't need to tell me he was proud of me—it was written on his face. He smiled and waved, and as I passed through the entrance, I carried the peace of the morning with me.

The HR office was compact, only a couple of small rooms that had been modestly decorated with modern desks and antique photos. The young woman at the reception desk was friendly, and the morning passed with new hire training and filling out paperwork. Soon enough, it was time to meet Fitz for lunch in the castle's tea rooms. I walked through the castle courtyard and into the restaurant, finding Fitz and Henry already seated.

"This is a nice surprise," I said as I took a seat next to Fitz.

"I had a last-minute meeting arise in town this morning and thought I'd have tea with Fitz if he had time. This is better," Henry said.

"I can't disagree with that," Fitz said. "So, how's the first day going?"

"Nothing exciting to report. Just routine stuff. I'm glad they left my lunch open. This is a nice break before the afternoon."

"First days are usually slow, I'd reckon," Henry said.

"And I'm good with that. I've had plenty of excitement in my life lately. I'm content with a slow start to my new job."

We chattered on aimlessly, talking about work and plans for the week. It was nice to decompress from visits to Dr. Belmonte's office and power training by passing the lunch hour in casual conversation. As we wrapped our lunch, a text from Isaac in our group chat turned our conversation in a different direction.

Conference call Friday at 7 p.m.? I should have all reports back on Dr. Belmonte by then, and we can discuss the findings.

"That'll work fine for me. You two?" Henry asked.

Fitz nodded as he placed his teacup back on the table.

"Me too. I'll text him back," I said.

I sent the message and grabbed my purse. "I'd better be going. Glad you could join us, Henry."

"Aye, I'm happy for you, lass. Enjoy the rest of your first day."

I was halfway across the courtyard when a prickle worked its way up my spine. The watcher. He had returned. I glanced back, but Fitz and Henry had already disappeared.

I pulled out my phone and sent a text to Mia.

The watcher is back. I'm in one of the castle courtyards. I'm heading back into new hire meetings, but maybe this can generate a lead?

I hit "send" and hastened my steps.

I knew I'd recognize the watcher if I saw him again. I scanned the crowds thoroughly but couldn't locate him. I searched for his mind, but I found nothing promising—there were far too many thoughts swirling through the area, and I found it completely overstimulating. The witch's gaze faded as I entered the building, and I ran up the steps, determined not to be late.

I took a deep breath and reached for the door.

The next item on my agenda was a tour of the castle offices, and I was thrilled at the prospect of moving around rather than sitting in an office for the rest of the day.

And I might catch sight of the snooping witch again, I thought.

A familiar face stepped into the office. Mr. Murray's assistant had offered to be my tour guide.

"Edna, it's great to see you again."

"It's lovely to see you too," she said.

Edna led me through all of the buildings, and it was strange to see the modern office life existing in such a historic structure. Once we worked our way into the building that housed PR, marketing, and the rest of the business team, I paid special attention to the layout where each team was located. We peered into the breakroom as a young man was vacating a small table on the far side of the room. He made eye contact, and I smiled. He met my gaze and then looked at Edna, who was sharing more about the space, before his expression turned sour. He picked up his bag and headed for the exit.

"Oh, this is Mark Cunningham," Edna said. "He's on the marketing team. Mark, this is Hadley Weston, our new PR manager."

"Nice to meet you, Mark," I said.

He looked at my extended hand for a few seconds too long before shaking it quickly and nodding curtly.

"I'm looking forward to working with you," I said.

Mark nodded again. "If you'll excuse me, I'm late for a meeting."

I was curious about his cool reception and my mind wandered into his. I caught myself before I'd heard much of anything, but I got just far enough to understand that he wasn't pleased about Mr.

Murray's decision to hire me.

"Did I do something to offend him?" I asked.

Edna hesitated.

"I don't mean to pry. If you don't want to answer the question, that's fine, but I just wanted to be sure I haven't done anything wrong."

"Oh no. You haven't," Edna said softly. She paused. "Mark recommended a good friend of his for your position."

"I see."

"Aye. A good friend who's native to Edinburgh. He felt a Scot would be best in the role. So, don't take it personally. He'll get over it." She smiled warmly. "You were the most qualified candidate, and you are the best fit."

"Thank you," I said.

"Let's keep going?" she asked.

I tried to forget about the interaction, but it stewed in the back of my mind. Mark was the first of my colleagues I'd met who I'd partner with in my responsibilities. And that wasn't a pleasant start.

As we neared my office, we bumped into Mr. Murray, and his face lit up.

"Ms. Weston! I am so pleased to see you."

"It's wonderful to see you again," I said.

"I was relieved when I heard you accepted our offer. You'll do great things here."

"I'm looking forward to it."

That Wednesday after work, I settled in front of our flat's roaring fireplace and set my laptop before me, taking a deep breath.

It was time to call Jordan.

When I'd texted her earlier in the day to schedule a time to talk, she'd proposed a call this evening. I thought about pushing it for a few more days, but I'd put off the call long enough. I needed to face this new reality with my best friend, whatever it was. Fitz kissed me on top of my head and padded down the hallway to the bedroom to grant me some privacy. The bedroom door closed with a soft click. I initiated the call and checked my expression, determined to wear a bright smile when she answered.

The call connected, and Jordan popped onto the screen.

She squealed in delight. "Hads! I'm so happy to see your pretty face."

I laughed. "I've missed you so much."

Jordan's midnight hair sat in a large bun atop her head, and she wore blue silk pajamas.

"But you know you really should be asleep right now. I know you have an early morning," I said. It was 11 p.m. on the East Coast.

"What? And miss this? Not a chance, sis."

"I'm glad we found some time to catch up," I said.

"I'm glad you decided to stop avoiding me."

"Jordan!"

She smiled mischievously. "Don't deny it."

"There's just been a lot going on."

"Yeah, yeah. So, how's the job?"

I filled her in on my first couple days, from Mr. Murray to Edna to Mark.

"Pretty sure Mark hates me."

"Who would dare hate you?" Jordan said. "That's messed up."

"Exactly what I thought."

We both laughed.

Jordan asked about my mom, and I, in turn, asked about her parents, and then her job.

"I've been pretty swamped myself. We lost the analyst I've been partnering with—her last day was yesterday—and they haven't replaced the position yet. I think they're hoping I'll absorb both caseloads, but I don't see how that's possible."

"Your hours are intense already. I can't imagine adding more to your plate," I said.

Jordan sighed. "Yeah, well. If you can convince the FBI that work life balance is a thing, let me know."

I shook my head lightly.

"My parents arrive on Friday for a visit, but I don't know how much I'll see of them. I asked for time off weeks ago, which was approved, but now that this analyst is gone . . ." She shrugged.

"It's tough finding a balance when you're in a different city than your family."

"Speaking of which, how is your mom handling the distance?" she asked.

"She's less than thrilled, but I think she'll be okay. Gram is spending some time with her."

"That's great," Jordan said. "How are you both holding up?"

I paused.

"We don't have to talk about it if you don't want to," Jordan said.

"I honestly don't know. I've been thinking of Daddy lately, and it's hard, you know? One minute I'm fine and the next . . ."

"I think that's normal, Hads."

"I think so too."

"So, it sounds like things are on again with you and Fitz?"

I nodded. "He met up with me in Paris, and . . ." I trailed off, smiling.

"Oh, damn. It's *really* on, isn't it?"

"It is. It's . . . serious."

Jordan's eyebrows raised. "I mean, that's good, I guess. But are y'all working through all this stuff from the past year?"

"It's complicated, but yes. We're sorting it all out."

"Does he have a good excuse for why he left?"

I hesitated. It was about to get tricky. "He does."

Jordan's expression was clear. She wanted an explanation.

"It's complicated and a bit . . . personal."

"I see," she said.

"I know that's not a great answer, but it's something that I can't really share with you."

Her lips twisted as her eyes dimmed in thought. "This is why you've been distant."

"Well, not exactly."

"Then what is it, Hads? What's going on?"

"I can't talk about it."

Jordan shook her head. "Nah."

"Jordan . . ."

"We're sisters, you and I. That's what we've always said, right? We tell each other everything. We always have each other's backs. But now, you're closing your life off from me. I don't understand it."

"That's not true."

"Is it because of Fitz? Are you doing this because of a guy? After everything we've been through . . ."

"That is absolutely not it."

"Seventeen years, Hadley Weston. That's how long it's been. And we've barely missed a day talking to each other. But you left for Paris and just dipped."

I sighed.

"Don't you start sighing on me, either. What you need to do is start talking."

Silence fell, and we held each other's gaze. Finally, I made my decision.

"You know I'm different," I said. "I've always been a bit . . . odd."

"Like knowing my thoughts," she said.

I nodded. "Well, turns out, there's something to that."

Her eyes narrowed. "What are you telling me?"

"There are other people who are like me. People that can do the same type of thing."

"Like the MacGregors," she said.

My surprise registered on my face.

"Oh, come on, Hads. I'd have to be pretty oblivious to miss the fact that they're an odd family."

Despite the serious nature of our conversation, I couldn't hold back my amusement. A smile nipped at Jordan's lips.

"So, what does that have to do with you and me?" she asked.

"I can't talk about the things I can do, or the things they can do. We can't tell anyone."

She eyed me suspiciously.

"It would put you at risk," I continued. "Major risk."

Jordan mulled over my words. "And who is the threat?"

"People like your employer." I eyed her pointedly.

She sat back in her chair and closed her eyes, releasing a deep sigh. "That is not what I wanted to hear."

"I know you understand my meaning. We can have a relationship—we're still sisters no matter what. But we can't ever talk about this stuff."

Jordan nodded her head slowly, her eyes shifting in consideration. Finally, she met my gaze. "I understand what you're saying."

"Jordan, you are one of the most important people in my life. You are family. I can't lose you, and I won't put you at risk. We *have* to be very careful. Do you understand?"

"Are you in danger?" she asked. "Because I have the resources to help you."

I smiled softly. "I appreciate that so much. But no, I'm not in danger—as long as we abide by this rule."

"You're sure I can't help you?"

I nodded.

"I need you to make me a promise," she said.

"Anything."

"I need you to promise me that if anything changes—if you find yourself in danger—you'll let me know immediately. Let me help you, Hadley, if I can."

I hesitated but then nodded.

"Tell me. I need to hear you say it."

"I promise, Jordan."

"I love you, Hadley. And I'll do anything to protect you."

I wondered if she truly understood that I was concealing information from her to keep her from harm.

"I know. I love you too, Jordan."

I returned from the office late on Friday evening. An all-staff meeting had run long, and I rubbed my aching neck as I passed through the doorway. I found Fitz in deep discussion with Henry. Isaac's voice sounded from the phone sitting on the coffee table.

Fitz rose from his seat and kissed me quickly.

"Sorry I'm late," I said.

"Tough day?" Henry asked.

"Just a long one. It's been a long week, actually."

"Did you have training tonight?" Henry asked.

"No, we're doing a Tuesday, Thursday, and Sunday schedule," I said, taking a seat next to Fitz.

"*Carissima*, is that you I hear?" Isaac asked warmly.

"It sure is. How are you?"

"I'd be better if I could figure out this Dr. Belmonte for you."

"Nothing?" I questioned.

"We've narrowed down our list, but it's still extensive. And we haven't found anything that matches all of our search criteria yet," Isaac said.

"Isaac mentioned one guy captured their attention, but his trail has gone cold," Fitz explained.

"I've consulted my best resources in the business. Ran background—nothing. Traced accounts—nothing. Looked into any and all documentation we could find—nothing. We found some old records, but they don't tell us much. Then he disappeared completely two years ago."

"If your team cannae find a lead on this guy, we have a problem," Henry groaned.

"If we search all of his connections, something is bound to turn up," Fitz said.

"Is it worth speaking with the councils about?" Isaac asked.

The group paused.

"Perhaps, but we shouldnae rush it," Henry said. "I think we should wait a bit. Fitz, Hadley?"

"I agree," Fitz said. "I'm not keen on bringing them into this yet."

"I'd prefer the councils not be involved if we can avoid it," I said.

"We'll hold off then," Isaac said.

"How many of his connections have you identified?" I asked.

"We have twelve decent leads to research," Isaac answered.

"And if none of the people on this list turn up anything useful? Where do we go from there?" I asked.

Isaac hesitated. "I think we'd need to ask you to pay Dr. Belmonte's office another visit if you were comfortable with it."

"Why don't I do that anyway?"

"Do you know if there's any risk associated with that, Henry?" Fitz asked.

Henry mulled over the question. "I dinnae think so."

Fitz turned to me.

I nodded. "I'll go back to Dr. Belmonte's office tomorrow."

CHAPTER THIRTY-FOUR

The following morning, I set Annabel's grimoire on the table in front of me and traced my fingertips lightly across the surface. Hundreds of years had passed, but this magical book still teemed with Annabel's magic. I felt its presence more clearly than I had when I'd first held the book. I wasn't sure if I owed that to my progress in training or if it was tied to me using her spell. Either way, I found a solace in her energy. There was something comforting in the fact that we existed so vibrantly even long after our deaths.

Fitz emerged shirtless from the bedroom, rubbing a towel over his damp hair, and effectively halted my process.

"What?" he asked.

"Nothing. Just admiring the view."

"Is that so?"

He crossed the room, and my pulse quickened. He knelt in front of me and pulled me forward. I wrapped my legs snugly around him, and he kissed me. When we pulled back, he flipped my wrist over and kissed it. The blood hummed under the surface, and I closed my eyes.

He ran a thumb over my ring, which reminded me: "Esther's ring looks just like the one I wear."

"It's a replica."

"How did you know what the ring looks like?"

"I don't know firsthand, but had it made based on a vision of my aunt's. Her mind's eye saw the ring, and she sketched it for us. That sketch is somewhere in Henry's attic actually."

"Why did you give this to me?" I asked.

"Because I believed you were my mate."

"And what does that have to do with Esther's ring?"

"Hads . . ." he whispered. "I risked everything to keep you safe, just like Esther's family did for her. It seemed a proper gift."

I ran my fingers along his jaw before pressing my lips to his.

"Okay, now get out of here," I teased. "I can't focus."

He chuckled. "I'm going for coffee. Earl Grey latte?"

"Yes, please."

With Fitz out of the room, I returned my focus to the grimoire.

The problem with being summoned by the ring was that I had no idea where I had traveled. Had I traveled through time to reach Dr. Belmonte's office, or had I remained in the present? To return, I'd have to rely solely on instinct, trusting the ring and my magic to guide me back.

We'd moved Annabel's grimoire and journal to Fitz's flat as it had become increasingly difficult for me to be apart from them. Henry said he'd seen it before with Emily—items used as a catalyst by spirit-travelers became a part of them.

I recited Annabel's summoning spell. A large map of Europe materialized . . . and then a room with dark gray walls. I crossed the room quickly, anxious to check if the ring still lay on the table. My sigh of relief disturbed the deafening quiet, though I still couldn't obtain the enchanted object.

Fitz and I had worked on my opening skills—or break-in skills, as I called them—after work over the previous couple of days, and I was ready to unlock Dr. Belmonte's sealed desk drawers. I sank into the rolling chair and placed my hands on the desk. Mental transport was such a strange experience. Though my body wasn't physically in the room, my hands felt as though they truly touched the desk, and my feet perceived the imperfections of the wooden planks on the floor. I ran my fingers across the cold surface of the desk, lingering along the coarse grain of the wood, allowing my mind to connect deeper with the elements.

Its life had begun in a lush, green forest with innumerable trees, alive with untouched vitality, and I watched as men cut the trees and hauled them to a mill. The tree became lumber, and the lumber was then worked into furniture before a young woman stained and sealed the desk, crafting it into a finished product. And finally, a staggeringly handsome man with dark eyes and a lithe but chiseled physique bought the desk and brought it home. This would be Dr. Belmonte, I reasoned.

Though Dr. Belmonte was attractive, something ominous rested in his features, and the longer I watched him, the more uncomfortable I became. Adrenaline coursed wildly through my system, and anxiety rested in the pit of my stomach. I momentarily rested my mind, contemplating my next move, before closing my eyes once more. I waited patiently, borrowing knowledge from the elements, asking them for intelligence on what had passed in this room.

Dr. Belmonte spent countless hours writing in code, making indecipherable calculations and hiding his work within this desk. His voice sounded in my ear, imparting the words that would open the drawers. I took a mental record of the spell, allowing the vision of Dr. Belmonte to dissipate, and promptly recited my new prize.

To my delight and amazement, four soft clicks fractured the silence as each of the locks unbolted themselves. I tugged at the top drawer.

But before I could look through the drawer, the click of another lock disturbed my progress. I froze.

I returned the desk to its former state and jumped from the chair just as the door swung open to reveal the man I'd begun investigating. He locked the door and tried the handle, ensuring no one else could access the room before leaning against the door for a moment, his eyes closing. His clothing was . . . odd. He shrugged out of a black velvet coat, which boasted a high collar and silver buttons. The ivory undershirt tucked into high-waisted trousers hid little of his toned figure. He looked as though he'd stepped off the set of a medieval film.

Dr. Belmonte crossed the space decidedly, though looking distractedly around him, before taking a seat in the chair I'd vacated only seconds before. He called for the locks to open and pulled at the bottom drawer. I was blanketed in security. I'd escaped his notice.

But suddenly, Belmonte paused. He slowly cocked his head in my direction, and a slight smile rolled across his parted lips.

"I can feel you, spirit-traveler. I know you're here," he stated plainly, as if he were offering to pick up the check for coffee.

Belmonte leaned back in his chair and placed his arms behind his head, clearly waiting for my next move. He wore a taunting smile, and my stomach turned as I realized he wanted a game. My mind ticked quickly through what I knew about spirit-travel, and I realized I didn't have an answer for my most pressing question: I didn't know if he could hurt me.

Think, Hadley.

I had crouched on the floor in my panicked dash from the chair, and I rose timidly, certain I'd hear the creak of floorboards even though I knew better. His eyes flickered in my direction and flitted around restlessly like he was trying to make sense of exactly where I stood.

I slinked around the room, catlike in my movements, and moved past the window, slowly circling the space to put distance between the two of us. He closed his eyes and brought his fingertips together in front of his chest. When he opened them, his gaze had found me again.

I gasped.

He chuckled. "Are you enjoying yourself? You may keep trying all you want, but you won't shake me, spirit-traveler."

An icy chill crawled through me. Something about the way he drew out his words was playful, and his speech unsettled me even more than his ability to follow my spirit. I didn't have a way to communicate with him, and I was too new in my powers to know any tricks.

We were at a stalemate.

"I may not know why you're here or who you are, but I will find out. No one enters my home without my permission, not even someone who smells as lovely as you. Make no mistake; I'll know you when we cross paths again."

"Hadley!"

"What is it?" I mumbled, struggling to regain consciousness.

"Thank god. Are you all right?"

"Of course. What's your problem?"

"My problem is I came home to find your limp body uninhabited, white as a ghost, and perspiration on your forehead. You scared the hell out of me."

"Crap, I'm sorry. I didn't mean to do that. It's just that I found the room again and I was finally on to something . . ."

He sighed. "It's all right, take your time."

"I figured out how to open the desk drawers, but then I was interrupted by Dr. Belmonte. Fitz, he couldn't see me, but he knew I was in the room. I mean, he didn't know it was me, but he knew someone was there."

Fitz held me, listening quietly until I related the chain of events.

"Dr. Belmonte knew where I was. His eyes followed me."

"That's odd," Fitz said. "I don't know how that's possible since it was only your spirit there."

"He said he could *smell* me."

"Now, that one I don't believe. Maybe he tried to unnerve you by saying something creepy like that."

"Well, it worked," I said.

"Hey, you don't have any reason to fear him. You know why?"

I shook my head.

"Because I'll never let anyone hurt you. And more importantly, you're a fiery, strong, mesmerizing witch. No one can mess with you unless you let them."

Fitz believed in me, and that counted for something.

CHAPTER THIRTY-FIVE

I hung up the phone and stared from my office window. Though the castle relied heavily on government funding, donations from members of the U.K.'s elite were equally vital. And I'd learned that because many of those donors were witches, only a witch could be chosen for the role I now filled.

Between phone calls with donors, meetings with the event planners, getting to know my new coworkers, Fitz's family mystery, and my magical training schedule, time was slipping away quickly.

Mark had emailed me last year's donor pamphlet that afternoon. Though the rest of my colleagues had been helpful and welcoming, Mark was still as distant as he was on my first day. I hoped time would benefit that relationship.

The phone rang again, and I checked the time: 6:15 p.m. I sighed and reached for the phone.

"Good evening, this is Hadley."

"Oh, hello there. Is this Edinburgh Castle's fancy new PR manager?"

I giggled. "What do you want, MacGregor?"

"When do you get off work? I miss you."

"Did I even give you this number?" I asked drily, though a smile nipped at my lips.

"No. But I'm a researcher. It wasn't much of a challenge, Ms. Weston."

"I see. Well, as it happens, I miss you too. But I'm very busy and important."

Fitz chuckled. "Oh aye. That much I know."

"I can head out soon—but I'll have to bring some work home."

"I'll be going quite late on this course material, as well. It's due for the Dean's review this week. I'll order in tonight?"

"See you soon."

I placed the phone back on the receiver and gathered my belongings from the wood-topped standing desk. According to Edna, Mr. Murray had insisted on a new desk when the castle hired me. He wanted me to feel well taken care of, Edna had shared. My space was small but comfortable. My window was smaller than Mr. Murray's expansive courtyard view, but it did boast a nice view of the Firth of Forth seascape, so I had no complaints.

I'd already added a few touches of my own to the space, and pops of green now contrasted against the stone walls and wooden doors—plants, courtesy of Izzy. A baby blue mini fridge was tucked in the corner, which Fitz had bought and stocked for me—lunch often appeared inside of it midday. I'd told him he didn't need to worry with it, but he consistently made lunch or had it delivered for me. With my magic training adding to an already busy schedule, he wanted to help where he could.

I waved goodnight to Edna, who never left before I did, and dashed home. Fitz was seated near the fire, and stacks of papers, a few books, a notepad, and his laptop were spread haphazardly around him. As I crossed the threshold, he rose to meet me. He hugged me tightly to him, and I pulled his face to mine.

We opted to eat near the fire and between the warmth of the flames and the taste of fish and chips, I relaxed into the evening.

"How's the event coming along?" Fitz asked before popping a fry in his mouth.

"Good. I think it'll be pretty swanky."

"Aye, I've always heard it's quite posh."

"Better get your tux ready," I said.

"Only if I'll have a hot date."

"You'll probably have a tired one, but I do hear she cleans up nice."

"She's *always* bonnie," he said, his features turning sweet.

"And how's your course coming along?" I asked. "Your students going to hate King James or what?"

"That man was a blight on humanity."

I nodded. Fitz had shared his research with me, and I couldn't disagree with his assessment.

"I need to get my hands on a particular book tonight at one of the libraries."

"How late are they open?" I asked.

"They're closed. But the director owes me a favor, so he's arranged access."

"Well, aren't you important."

"Aye, right. Didn't you know that already?"

All jokes aside, Fitz had an uncanny knack for being granted special access to academic institutions that didn't make exceptions for just anyone. I suspected, in Fitz's case, that had more to do with the distinction of his work than his network.

"Come with me?"

"Sounds like a perfect way to end the day."

Mahogany shelves stretched down a lengthy room with an arched ceiling, and the book covers were faded, dulled by the ravages of time. I walked slowly along the dimly lit center aisle and ran my fingers along the shelves. There was something innately romantic and timeless about libraries. While humans and witches would come and go, these volumes spanned the centuries. Long after I'd returned to dust, the stories in this very room would live on.

Fitz was seated at a small wooden desk, and he typed furiously at his laptop with an aged volume of literature open on a book stand. I peered over his shoulder and found an account of an accused witch during the North Berwick trials in Scotland in 1590. Fitz carefully turned the page of the book. He resumed typing, and a soft sort of heartache traveled through my chest. It wasn't only the thought of Esther's death that troubled us. Learning about the persecution of our kind was difficult, and a certain sorrow lingered within us as we dug deeper into the past.

I had wandered further into the archives by the time Fitz was done. He found me flipping through a book I'd found on Queen Victoria.

"This was so much more interesting than the work I brought with me," I said.

"And what do you have here? Ah, Victoria. One of the better monarchs this country has seen."

"Her story is fascinating—the reform she brought, the legacy she left."

"She was a powerful woman. Just like you, aye?"

"I can only hope."

I slid the book back into the empty slot.

"I love how she and Albert worked together. I always wanted a love like theirs," I mused.

"And did you find it, my love?" Fitz brushed his fingers along the side of my face.

"Even better," I whispered.

Fitz cradled my head in his hands before dipping his head to kiss me gently. Our lips worked slowly, passionately, as we sorted through our feelings together. Gradually, we grew in intensity, and Fitz lifted me from the ground. I wrapped my legs around his waist, and he pinned me against the wall. My hands ran through his hair, across his neck, down his back. He gripped me securely with one arm while his free hand slid up my shirt. The library was quiet, disturbed only by the distant ticking of a clock and the rise and fall of our labored breaths.

I dipped my head backward as his lips found my neck, and suddenly, another sound fractured the silence: the click of a door. We froze, our eyes wide. But we didn't sit in suspense for long.

"Dr. MacGregor, you in here?"

"It's Lawrence. He's with maintenance," Fitz whispered.

I tried to stifle a giggle unsuccessfully, and Fitz slid his hand over my mouth.

"Aye! What can I do for you, Lawrence?" he called in response.

"We're done for the day. Just checking on your progress."

"I'm returning the books now. I'll be just another minute."

"Very good. I'll be in my office if you'll let me know when you're heading out."

The door shut, and Fitz and I broke into laughter.

Fitz kissed me once more. "All right, firecracker. Let's not keep Lawrence waiting."

CHAPTER THIRTY-SIX

"Izzy!" I exclaimed, running for the door. I had still been at work when Fitz picked Izzy up at the airport, and I was pacing the living room impatiently by the time they arrived at our flat.

"Oh, Hadley! I've missed you!"

We embraced warmly—a hug that was years in the making—as two women who could finally be transparent about who they were. The last time we'd seen each other, too much couldn't be said aloud. It was exciting to be able to finally talk openly with her. I showed her around our new apartment, explaining our future plans regarding the space.

"The sale is still pending, but the seller is motivated to close quickly, and so are we. It's all happening so fast, my head is spinning,"

I said.

"This will be incredible. You'll have loads of space, and Fitz's flat could use a woman's touch," she said, winking.

"Not to interrupt, but are you two ready for a bit of scran? I'm starved."

"Oh aye," Izzy answered. "I'm famished."

We chatted about Izzy's trip as we made our way down the rain-soaked streets of Old Town. As we wandered into Whiski, our restaurant of choice for the evening, the warmth of the space was nearly jarring against the bite of late autumn that blustered through the city.

The pub was cozy and quaint, and something about it just felt like home. Tables were randomly strewn about the front room; a lovely bar was decorated with countless bottles and a busy bartender. The front door bordered a wall of windows, and I could see the charm of sitting amongst the window tables, watching tourists explore the Royal Mile. A traditional Scottish band sat in the front corner, their melodic stories tumbling out in Scots Gaelic alongside the captivating sounds pouring from the instruments in hand.

We settled into a corner booth, and I noticed Mr. Murray talking with the bartender. He waved and walked over.

"I trust you're enjoying your evening, Ms. Weston."

"Very much. Mr. Murray, this is my partner, Fitz, and his sister, Izzy."

"It's wonderful to meet you," Izzy said.

James shook her hand and then introduced himself to Fitz.

"I'm glad to meet you," Fitz said. "Hadley has spoken highly of you—and so has our father."

"Your father is Ian MacGregor?" Mr. Murray asked.

"Aye."

"Second to none, that one. Your father has been a huge asset to the Scottish Council. An honorable witch."

Fitz beamed at Mr. Murray's praise of his father.

We passed a few moments in idle chatter before Mr. Murray excused himself and moved closer to the band.

"He does seem like a nice fellow," Fitz said once he was out of earshot.

"He just looks like someone who'd sit on the national council, doesn't he?" Izzy said.

"Aye, he's distinguished all right."

"And he's also your manager at work?" Izzy asked.

"Right. I was nervous about that, but he's honestly been great."

Izzy inquired about how my new job was going.

"I was a little worried about the volume of work that came with this position, but I love it," I said. "I finally feel like I'm back in my element, you know?"

"I see that in your eyes."

Izzy went on to ask about Fitz's curriculum and, in turn, she told us about her career and the life she'd built in Seattle.

"Your work sounds incredible," I said, "but Fitz tells me you're missing nature."

"I'm a green witch through and through." She smiled. "I know the work I do at the hospital is important, but I miss growing things. I need more time to cultivate my garden properly. It pains me, Hadley."

"I understand just what you mean," I said. "That's what you were meant to do. It doesn't mean your other work is less important. It just means nature was meant for you, and the other job is meant for someone else."

"It sounds simple when you put it like that," Izzy said.

"Isn't it, though? We worry so much about letting others down or what's expected of us. But ultimately, this is your life and your gift. It's time to use it again, Izzy."

"A fine argument. Now I just have to save up for a shop."

"Do you think you'll stay in Seattle?" I asked.

"I don't know. I love Seattle, but I've thought of returning to Scotland, too."

"Oh, Iz. I didn't know that," Fitz said softly.

"Well, I didn't want to get your hopes up in case I couldn't sort it. But I'm quite serious about it."

"Well, I don't want to pressure you, but . . ." I trailed off, my eyebrows raised.

She giggled. "I understand your position on the subject perfectly. I'll take it into consideration, Ms. Weston."

"What will you sell?" I asked.

"A few plants, to be sure. Tea, herbs, salves, and the like. Oh, I was just thinking of your dad the other day. I perfected a salve that he would have loved."

Her eyes misted, and I took her hands in mine.

"I'll never forget your kindness to him," I said.

"He was a wonderful man, Hadley. I know you must miss him greatly, but just know that you aren't alone in that, aye?"

"Thank you," I managed.

The night wore on in conversation and good food, and sometime after dinner, I finally asked Izzy about a long-ago occurrence I always questioned: the night I thought I'd dreamed about wandering into the forest with her.

"You're right. That night wasn't a dream," she said.

"Even the night it happened, I knew deep down it wasn't a dream, but I couldn't make sense of it. I thought it couldn't have happened."

"I'm an earth witch, and my power is tied so closely to nature. I spend time healing the natural world and its wildlife when I can. When you stumbled into the forest with me, I had no idea what to do."

"You must have panicked a little."

"You have no idea."

I laughed. "Okay, but I have to know . . . was I hallucinating or was your skin glowing?"

Izzy grinned, and Fitz laughed heartily.

"Sorry," he said. "I can only imagine what went through your head when you saw Iz *glowing*."

"Oh aye. It took me quite a bit of practice to sort that one out, but essentially, I pull the elements to me in such a way that my energy reacts to the air by creating light. The light is far better than head-lamps and that sort of thing."

"That really freaked me out," I said. "But now that I understand everything, that's an impressive feat, Iz."

Izzy smiled shyly.

"The other thing that's been bothering me is why were we in danger," I said. "Who was it that showed up?"

"I can't say for sure. At the time, I just knew whoever it was, they didn't have good intentions, and I couldn't risk anything with you. Now that I know everything happening with yous, I wonder if it was one of the folks who've been watching you recently."

"What a terrifying thought."

"Iz and I did our best to find out who it was, but our research didn't yield any leads. We had so little to go on," Fitz said.

"It's strange they turned up in the woods with us like that," I said.

Izzy's face was distant, lost in reflection. "I wouldn't let it worry you considering that's the only time something like that has happened. That *is* the only time, right?"

"Yeah, you're right." I said, though the pit of my stomach twisted.

Rain misted through the city streets, lending a hazy dreamlike quality with the soft illumination against the stone buildings. Though the wind had quieted, the air was still cold with the promise of winter. The weather didn't dampen the mood of the countless groups of people bustling across the streets, and the mix of voices and distant bagpipes echoed down the Mile.

We wandered back toward our flat and as we reached St Giles' Cathedral, I tugged at my scarf, hoping to find the source of the draft at my neck. Fitz paused, helping me to adjust it.

Church bells rang through the square, announcing the eleventh hour. Izzy closed her eyes and turned toward the sound.

A prickle worked through me.

"Do you feel that?" I asked.

"Aye," Izzy said.

"And it's not a friendly gaze," Fitz observed.

"It feels . . . familiar." I glanced around us, attempting to appear nonchalant. I scanned across the Mile—tourists taking photos, groups of friends laughing as they meandered down the road, couples walking hand in hand—until I found the source.

His icy blue stare was just as unsettling as it had been the day he'd watched me outside my hotel.

"To your right," I said. "Green cable knit sweater. He's leaning against the building."

"He's the one you saw outside your hotel?" Fitz asked.

I nodded.

"You two stay here," Fitz said, walking toward him.

"Not likely," Izzy retorted, and we fell into step beside him.

My stalker noticed us and walked briskly down a nearby alleyway, the entrance reading "Roxburgh's Close." He was at the end of the close, and we chased behind him as quickly as possible. My adrenaline was high, and I felt Fitz's energy running through me. It was oddly invigorating.

Our suspect turned the corner, and we followed suit. The close opened to a small courtyard. I scanned the buildings, their varying shades of beige and gray stonework jutting up around us, hoping I'd find something useful.

A hotel was just in front of us, and Fitz walked over to peer through the large windowpanes. "Nothing over here."

"I'll look on the far side by the restaurant," Izzy suggested.

Our mystery witch darted from a hidden corner near the restaurant as Izzy grew near, and we scrambled to follow him. I couldn't stand the thought of him getting away, and that propelled me across the courtyard faster than I thought possible.

I grabbed on to a lamppost, using it to launch myself into a right turn, and I was soon on Izzy's heels.

Another close was positioned at the far side of the courtyard, and our guy neared the end of it. I bounded down the dark stairwell and tripped about halfway through. My body stabilized, though I couldn't take credit for the action.

"*Keep moving!*" Izzy said into my mind..

Fitz was already out of sight, and when I emerged into the bustling street, I ran right into an unsuspecting tourist.

"Hey, watch where—" The man cut himself off as his eyes scanned across my features. "Are you okay?"

"I'm fine. I'm so sorry," I called over my shoulder, already running in the direction where my connection knew Fitz would be.

I found Fitz and Izzy breathing hard as they looked around.

"Hadley," Fitz called. He wrapped his arm around me and kissed the top of my forehead.

"We lost him," I guessed.

"Aye," the MacGregor siblings answered in unison.

"On the bright side, we've all seen him now," Izzy said.

Fitz pulled out his phone. "I'll update Dad and the guys."

I nodded.

"Thanks for the hand back there," I said to Izzy, still panting.

She nodded.

"Let's get out of here?" I asked. "I think we should head home."

CHAPTER THIRTY-SEVEN

The distant sound of bagpipes and the chatter of friends and families filled the streets of Edinburgh. The culmination was distinct, and I knew the moment was a core memory that I would carry with me always. We spent the day popping in and out of shops, restaurants, coffee houses, and bars. Izzy was excited to return to all her favorite haunts, and she had Fitz and me try everything she ordered.

"Fitz! You *have* to try this," Izzy said.

"How are you still going? I don't think I can eat another bite, Iz."

"Well, you'll have to find room. Hadley, make him try this."

"You two are something else." I laughed, reaching for my buzzing phone.

"What's the matter?" Izzy asked, noting my expression.

"Oh, it's nothing. I was just responding to a text from Jordan."

"You don't seem too pleased."

I hesitated before nodding.

"Mind if I ask why?" Izzy asked.

"To be honest, I was ignoring her calls for a while."

"You have to conceal too much from her now," Izzy guessed.

I nodded.

"That's always a tricky balance with human friends. But Jordan is your best friend. It takes a bit of work, but you'll be happier with her still involved in your life."

"I let her know in a roundabout way that we can't talk about certain things. She understood."

"Aye, that I can imagine. Jordan has always known something was different with you. She's been understanding in the past."

Fitz eyed me.

"He was telling me the same thing. I finally listened." I nodded in Fitz's direction.

"He was right. This time."

Fitz wore an offended expression, and we laughed. He snatched the cranberry scone from Izzy's hand and took a bite.

"Now, was that so hard?" Izzy asked.

"I still like the blueberry better."

"Aye right. That's because you're wrong."

"Okay, you two. Behave."

They grinned.

"We need to get moving—it's time to meet Maka."

When we saw her, Maka's face was tilted expectantly toward the sun enjoying the cool sunlight that had broken from the clouds earlier that morning after several days of clouds and rain.

I made introductions before we headed inside the coffee shop. Fitz and Izzy secured a table while Maka and I ordered at the bar. The shop was darling, all stone walls and cream-colored paint with pops of pale blues and verdant plants.

While awaiting our Earl Grey tea, Maka issued a challenge telepathically. We'd been working on telepathic communication, and I felt like I was finally growing proficient.

"Okay, Hadley. I know it's crazy in here, so this will be a good test for you. Do you hear people just talking right now or do you hear their thoughts too?"

"No thoughts. I have them shut out."

The small shop was crammed with young professionals and tourists, and the noise was almost deafening, even without the extra clamor of their thoughts buzzing through the air.

"Open the flood gates. Let it all in."

Over our past few sessions, Maka had taught me how to open my mind to hear other thoughts, the same way my ears heard their voices in a crowd. It was miraculously simple. I only had to find that particular wave in my mind and open it. Though the action was easy, the result was terrifyingly overstimulating, and I only attempted it when instructed during training.

Suppressing the flow of information was the toughest part. I focused my mind and opened the wave. Suddenly, my brain filled with thoughts. From breakups to vacation plans to storylines as people read nearby, my head swirled with information.

"Whoa," I said aloud.

"It's okay, Hadley. Breathe through this. You hold the information, not the other way around."

I nodded.

"Find one train of thought and focus in on it."

Scanning the crowd, I picked through the voices and slowly shut out anything that didn't suit my objective, obeying Maka's orders dutifully. Someone was reading a familiar story, and I found their voice soothing. It was fascinating to me how some people had a voice inside of them that read aloud in their mind as their eyes scanned the pages. It was my favorite revelation to come from training my mind reading ability.

Pip.

It clicked.

They were reading one of my favorite classics—*Great Expectations*. I'd first read the book in college, and though it held its fair share of tragedy between its covers, Pip's dry humor had me laughing through the story.

"Now, shut out their thoughts again."

I tuned out every thought in the room, and as focused as I was, I barely registered the change as they all fell away.

"You are a true proficient," Maka said aloud.

"I have a wonderful tutor. I'll give you her number."

As it turned out, Maka was a blessing in more ways than one. Magnetic energy channeled between the two of us, strengthening what would have certainly been an already natural friendship, and that made training far more enjoyable than it would've been otherwise.

Finally, the council had done something right.

CHAPTER THIRTY-EIGHT

When Monday arrived, it was the first day I felt disappointed by going to the castle. I rolled my eyes when Fitz insisted on walking with me to work, even after I argued that it was only a two-minute trek. I couldn't withhold my good humor when he promised he and Izzy would meet me at the castle restaurant for lunch. The day turned out to be quite busy—lunch was delightful—and before I knew it, the workday was gone.

I tapped my foot nervously as I leaned forward on our sofa and swirled my whisky glass a bit aggressively. Fitz's hand landed on mine, attempting to steady my movements. Izzy eyed me sympathetically.

"There's no need to be nervous, Hadley," Izzy said.

"I've been trying to tell her that," Fitz said.

"Easy for you two to say," I quipped.

Fitz pulled me closer and wrapped his arms around me. "Dad likes you, you know."

I scoffed.

"He does," Izzy echoed. "He always says he maintains a professional distance when it comes to our cases."

Her tone was clearly meant to mimic Ian's, and Fitz and I chuckled.

"He's nervous to see you again too," she offered seriously.

The knock on the door startled us all, and as I rose from the sofa, a montage of memories flashed before my eyes: the curtains moving in the upstairs window when I was outside with Izzy, his cool reception when I entered their home, his distant side glances when he noticed me walking through the yard, his expression the afternoon I saw him talking with Tanner in his office.

Fitz swung open the door, and my heart stopped. Then Tanner strolled in.

"Oh, you've got to be kidding me."

"A warm welcome, as always," Tanner said.

"Sorry," I muttered.

"She thought you were Dad," Izzy explained.

"Ah, she's nervous."

"Yeah, and we don't need to unpack that right now, just so we're all clear," I said.

Tanner raised his hands. "Wasn't gonna."

A rap on the door sounded through the flat once again, and this time, the party didn't wait before entering. Henry walked through the door, a huge grin on his face. I was just about to complain when two figures filed in behind him.

"Look who I found," Henry said.

A slew of exclamations followed his statement, but my eyes darted straight for Ian MacGregor. We made eye contact instantly . . . and then he smiled. And just like that, I could breathe again.

Ann hugged Izzy before pulling her over to Fitz and embracing him too.

"Both of my wee bairns under one roof again! Oh, I think I might greet."

"Mum, come on," Fitz teased, though he planted a quick kiss on the top of her head. Izzy beamed before making a beeline for her dad.

I took the opportunity to greet Ann while Ian reunited with his children. It made me happy to see the admiration in Fitz's eyes when he looked at his dad.

"Hadley, we are so glad to see you!" Ann began. "You have no idea how happy I am to be here with all you kids again."

Ann was right—the tears spilled out, and I hugged her tightly, grateful to meet her again under far better circumstances than when I'd last seen her.

Ian made his way over to us, and I turned to face him. I thought, somehow, he and Fitz looked even more similar than before. He dropped his blue eyes to the ground momentarily.

"Hadley, I want you to ken how happy we are for you and Fitz. And I hope we can spend some time together while I'm here, so I can have the opportunity to ken you better . . . firsthand." His lips dropped into a lopsided smile.

"I'd like that."

We shook hands warmly. There were conversations to come and feelings to sort through, but I knew in that moment that we'd be all right in the end.

Henry set a couple bottles of whisky on the table as we settled in. While Ann wanted a full report on my time in Scotland, Ian had questions about my experience working at the castle and Tanner's work with the council. Conversation was smoother and less tense than I had anticipated, and I grew more comfortable as the evening progressed.

I worked a few projects with a bloke over at the castle," Ian said. "James Murray—you might ken him?"

"He's my manager. He didn't mention that you worked together directly, but he did speak highly of you."

"No kidding," Ian marveled. "You ken he sits on the Scottish National Coven Council?"

"I didn't at first, but Fitz figured that out."

"It doesn't surprise me that James didn't mention it. He's humble when it comes to his work, but it's good for you to keep his work with the council in mind."

"What type of work does he do in a position like that?" I asked.

"We haven't fully covered government structure yet," Fitz clarified to his father.

Ian nodded. "The Scottish Council seats are elected positions. He put in countless years at local levels before even being considered for nomination. One representative from each national council is sent to the European Coven Council—that's held monthly in Vienna. Then two representatives from each continental coven council are sent to the United Covens Affairs quarterly on the Island of Little Cumbrae."

"Where is that?"

"Here in Scotland," Henry answered.

"Aye, a wee island west of Glasgow," Ian said. "The owners are a part of the Scottish National Coven and offer the estate for their meetings."

"We're an organized bunch, huh?" I asked.

"You have no idea," Izzy said.

"I've been a bit nervous about working with James because of his seat on the council," I said.

"Dinnae let it trouble you, kiddo," Ian said. "Murray is a good guy. He's one of the few members of the councils that I respect completely."

"He's still a part of the council," I argued.

"Aye, but he had nothing to do with our separation. We need to give him a fair chance," Fitz said.

I still resented the councils for their actions against us, but my time with Maka had shown me that there was good to be found as well. And my experience working with Mr. Murray had been positive so far.

"I'll give it my best shot."

"That's all we could ask," Henry said.

"Tanner, Fitz mentioned that you're helping Hadley?" Ian asked.

"The council has me assessing Hadley's powers."

"I thought you were hired as a fitness coach," Ian said.

"Yeah, I was. They're teaching me to assess powers because they want me to create training regimens that best supplement agents' powers to make them as strong as possible across the board."

Ian shook his head. "Usually, they have someone specialized in that area onsite with you, and you build the plan together."

"That's how they explained things in Seattle," Tanner said. "But when I got here . . . they sent me out solo."

"Doesn't make sense, does it?" Henry questioned.

"Not at all," Ian said. "I'll do some digging into this. I'm not sure what they're playing at."

"Thanks, Dad," Fitz said.

"Of course."

"I should be going—I have an early morning," Henry began. "But, Hadley, I wanted to hear everyone's thoughts on your encounter with Belmonte."

"Oh, right."

I recounted the series of events.

"My experience is that spirit-travelers can't be harmed while they're outside of their bodies. Have you ever heard any different, Ian?" Tanner asked.

"No," Ian said. "Their spirit is separated from their physical body, so you cannae harm them."

"But how can I move things around if he can't harm me?" I asked. "How can I feel the desk and the floor but walk through a door?"

"You're focusing your energy into moving objects. You aren't moving them with physical force. You're asking the elements to move them for you."

"I swear I can feel them on my fingertips."

"Have you ever heard of phantom limb syndrome?" Ian asked.

I nodded.

"This is similar biologically," he said. "Your spirit has stepped outside of your body, but there's still a connection. Your mind is walking through the process of your movements, and your brain and your nerves are still speaking to each other."

"How did he figure out I was there?" I asked.

"Your energy. If you've attuned yourself to energy shifts, you can identify them."

"What about him saying he smelled me?"

Izzy visibly shuddered.

"Rubbish," Ian said. "He was trying to get under your skin."

"There would be minimal risk in Hadley returning to his office then?" Henry asked.

Ian considered Henry's question for a moment. "I'd say so. The risk is low, but keep in mind that we dinnae ken how powerful Belmonte is. There are no guarantees when it comes to magic."

"I want to go back—I want to try again."

"Let's give it a go tomorrow," Ian said. We can walk you through some exercises that might be helpful. If you play your cards right, you can sort through his protection spells. You have that in you, Hadley."

"Tomorrow then." I smiled even though my blood ran cold.

CHAPTER THIRTY-NINE

The next evening, our small crew gathered around the living room coffee table ready to learn more about Dr. Belmonte. Ian had located a few council records with matching names, and only one set had been sealed. We had a hunch that he was our guy. Ian submitted a request for the records, but in the meantime, Isaac began a new background search based on Ian's findings while I focused on a successful third trip to Dr. Belmonte's home.

"When you finish your initial assessment of the type of magic he used for his protection spell, feel your way around the energy. If he's good, there will only be the tiniest wisp indicating where the spell was sealed," Ian explained.

"You'll need to really focus, Hads. Push everything else out of your brain," Tanner added. "True focus is the only way you'll recognize the edge of the spell."

"Then what?"

"Let your mind and your energy connect to the edge," Ian said. "You can either ask the air to disperse the energy, or you can use your own energy to tug it loose. Either way, the spell should unravel."

"How would a caster do this, Dad?" Izzy asked.

"They probably wouldnae, Iz. They might be able to work a spell to have the air pull at the edges, but unless they're lucky, I doubt they'd find a way to be in tune with the elements enough to tug open the seams."

"Are you ready, Hads?" Fitz questioned.

I nodded. "Yeah, I think I'm ready."

"Let's give her a little space, then," he instructed.

Everyone dispersed to the edges of the room aside from Fitz and Ian, who remained close by to monitor me. Ian wasn't positive they could pull my spirit back into my body if I ran into trouble, but he was confident Fitz could follow my path physically to help sort things out.

I closed my eyes, a bit distracted by my audience. But recalling that I was attempting a tricky passage, I cleansed the day from my mind and fell into my own abyss. Sensing I was in the right state to travel, I whispered the summoning spell to myself, and when I opened my eyes, the gray walls of Dr. Belmonte's office welcomed me back.

My first order of business was to check for the ring. I searched the table where I'd found it just over a week prior, but the ring was gone. I rummaged around the room and in the desk drawers, but again, came up short. The desk drawers were empty, and I realized

Dr. Belmonte wasn't taking any chances with me. I walked toward the door and tried the handle, as if I expected anything to be different from last time, but my hand tingled as it met the invisible force protecting the exit. I took a step back and closed my eyes, feeling out the energy in the room.

The room was deafeningly quiet. Nothing stirred, and I couldn't even detect the sounds of electricity. I finally detected a hum of energy overhead and looked in its direction. For the first time, I realized the room's light came from torches mounted on the walls. I couldn't imagine having missed them on my first two visits, and I suspected the magical room was playing tricks on me once again.

I stared at the light, contemplating what I was seeing. The light didn't seem to be fire exactly, but instead some sort of glow that closely resembled it. I shook my head and moved on. The secondary hum radiated from the doorway. I paused in front of it and focused my mind on the energy circling it.

I sat cross-legged on the worn wooden floor and allowed my energy to saturate the space. I found that it was easier to focus on the energy's makeup by closing my eyes and allowing all of my senses to focus on the feel of it. I pushed my way around, poking and prodding until I found a tiny wisp floating at a far edge.

It was flitting about elusively, and it took several attempts before I was able to grab on to it. I didn't expect the charge of electricity that seared through my fingertips. My eyes flew open at the pain, and I released it quickly.

I breathed deeply, willing the sensation to pass. I reminded myself that my fingers didn't actually hurt, and my nerves calmed. I closed my eyes again and refocused on my task. The wisp was easier to locate the second time around, and I braced myself for impact as

I again gripped it between my fingers. My chest tightened with the contact, but I pushed through the pain and tugged until the opening widened.

The further I pulled the spell, the less it hurt, and I jumped to my feet and ran for the opposite wall, pulling as hard as I possibly could. The spell unwound, the energy dispersing through the space like tiny fireflies all around me, and I walked timidly to the doorway.

I held my breath as I reached for the old, wooden door, but there was no need for hesitation. I walked right through.

The hallway was dimmer than the magical room, and my eyes adjusted slowly to the lack of light. Torches lined the space, and their flickering revealed gray stone walls and flooring. An ornate floor runner provided the only color to the space. The cream-colored base was decorated with swirling patterns of indigo, forest green, and flowers of rusty red. Nothing indicated which direction I should investigate first, so I decided to head to my right. After a few steps, I noted a door to my left and pressed my ear to it in silent request.

Nothing.

The next doorway yielded something more interesting. Though I couldn't make out the words, the rise and fall of voices filtered through the large, arched door. Half of my body leaned through the door, and I found two women sitting by a fireplace. I debated if I should risk them perceiving my presence or not, but they appeared deep in conversation, so I decided to cross into the space. The stone fireplace took up most of the wall to my left while rows of windows took up most of the space on the far wall. A large painting hung from the wall to my right, and I moved closer to investigate.

The painting reminded me of the Italian Renaissance works I'd studied in my college art history class. The scene was unfamiliar.

Countless figures were draped in Renaissance-style cloaks, and they were gathered around roaring firepits and mounted torches. A figure stood in a red cloak near the center of the painting, and he was pointing toward a woman whose back was turned. She had cascading auburn hair and a navy cloak with whimsical swirling patterns stitched in silver. Something about the painting felt ominous, and I studied it thoroughly, unable to look away. Finally, I tore my eyes from the painting and moved on.

Encouraged by their lack of observation, I moved closer to the women warming themselves near the fire. They were both ethereal, and their energy radiated through the space; they were powerful. But that was where their similarities ended. One of them had her honey-colored hair pulled into a neat chignon, and her eyes were the palest blue I'd ever seen. She was poised and held a teacup between her delicate fingers. Her energy was reserved, and I realized it would take time to read her.

The second woman sat across the fire from the other, and it was her energy I noticed most. It zipped around the space wildly, and her nerves pricked at the edges of my own anxiety. I breathed deeply before proceeding. Dark hair spilled down her back, cloaking it with strands the color of a midnight sky. There was something in her hazel eyes I couldn't quite discern, a wisdom. And a sadness. She leaned against the stone wall, and she rested her arm across her knees, a teacup hanging lazily from her fingertips. One of her legs was exposed through the slit of her floral dress, and a jagged scar ran the length of her calf.

The scene felt off . . . something was wrong. From the strange flaming torches to the women's medieval inspired clothing, it was an odd scene. Was I at some sort of Renaissance Faire?

I miss freedom, Camille," the black-haired woman said. "I long to return to Thalassa."

"Give it time."

"It's unnatural for me to be away from the sea this long. My heart is frozen like the wasteland outside those windows." She shivered, though I didn't suspect it was from the cold. "Don't you miss France?"

Camille swirled the black tea in her cup, considering the question. "I'm not like you. I don't miss anything I've left behind."

The black-haired woman sighed and leaned her head against the stones. "I should like to see France. I'd give anything to see Earth."

The world seemed to tilt on its axis as my stomach flipped.

"I'm fonder of Opimae myself," Camille said.

"Anything would be better than this frozen hell."

"Mind your tongue, Gabriella."

The room fell quiet. Camille finished her tea in silence while Gabriella stared wordlessly toward the windows. A blizzard raged outside, causing total whiteout conditions. I turned back to my newfound companions to find Gabriella's gaze settling on me. I thought perhaps she was watching the storm, but as I moved around the space, her hazel eyes traced my progress. I froze.

Camille snapped her fingers, and her teacup disappeared.

"He's back."

She rose from her seat and headed for the door. It closed softly behind her, and I returned my focus to Gabriella. Her dress billowed in her wake, and my breath came short as she stopped just in front of me.

"You'd better go. You wouldn't want him to catch you lurking again." She closed her eyes briefly. "Are you well-intentioned? I feel that you are. I hope I'm right about that."

She made her way to the door and her fingers rested lightly on the handle for a few long seconds before she turned back to me.

Her brows knitted in concentration. "I should be more careful than this, but . . . if you're the one from the prophecy . . . his name is Lorenzo Belmonte. Come quickly, before he learns how to use that ring."

And with that, she was gone.

I awoke in my living room feeling confused and unnerved. My heart raced and perspiration peppered my body. I looked around and registered the worried expressions of six faces I knew well.

"Hadley, my love. Are you all right?"
I focused on Fitz and wrapped my arms around his neck. He held me tightly until I was more composed, and I pulled back nodding.

"I'm okay."

Fitz lifted me from the ground and placed me carefully in a comfy chair near the fire. Henry slid a dram of whisky toward me. I nodded in gratitude and took a sip, allowing the fiery single malt to warm my belly before launching into my explanation.

"Sorry about that. The return was incredibly disorienting this time."

"Your body was stressed almost the whole time you were gone," Tanner said.

"Whatever it is that happened to you in Belmonte's realm, it agitated your body and spirit to a point that the reinfusion was jarring for you," Ian explained.

"That makes sense," I said.

"Take your time, but Hadley . . . what happened?" Izzy asked as she knelt to the ground in front of me. She touched her hands to my feet, and calm energy pushed through my veins, quieting my agitation.

I started from the beginning and ran the group through the chain of events. The story was littered with gasps and questions, but we finally made our way to the end, and the room went silent for a moment before Ann broke the quiet.

"I was a historian before I retired, you ken? I spent years in the archives researching a legend that most witches discredited. But for whatever reason, I couldnae seem to let it go."

Ian's head snapped to Ann, his eyes wide.

"Oh god," he whispered.

Ann nodded before continuing. "You see, there are a few records that turned up from the late 18th century that reference another world—a world where witches were allowed to travel to and from."

Her gaze shifted to me. "That world was called Opimae."

A gasp escaped Izzy's lips. Tanner rose from his seat and began pacing the room. Fitz and I locked eyes.

Ann continued. "I dinnae ken what I believe. Even after years of research, I've found the evidence is conflicting. But . . . I wouldnae discredit what Hadley heard in that room."

"I'd like to see your research, Ann," Henry said.

"Me too." Tanner turned to face us again.

"I think I need to talk to James Murray," I said.

"Are you sure about that, Hads?" Fitz asked.

"No. But he's on the council. If I tell him I heard about a world called Opimae, I'll at least know if his response is truthful or not."

"I dinnae think there's a risk with James. He might not reveal anything, but I foresee no danger," Ian added.

"I'll talk to him soon, then."

"I'll come to the castle in case you run into any trouble," Fitz said. "And Isaac arrives Friday, so if you meet with Murray then, I'll bring Isaac with me."

With Fitz's family in town and the chaos of my spirit-travel, I'd forgotten Isaac was coming for a long weekend. That was a bit of good news, at least.

"We could meet before then to review Ann's research?" Henry suggested.

A round of affirmatives filled the air.

"This started as research into a family mystery, and now we're discussing prophecies and foreign planets," Izzy marveled. "I can hardly believe it."

She was right. Life was about to get a lot more interesting—and fast.

CHAPTER FORTY

I asked for a meeting with James Murray on Friday. Apparently, his day was packed, but Edna had sent him a note to check in with me if he found some time in between meetings. I decided to go about my day as usual while Fitz and Isaac spent the afternoon at the castle exploring in hopes that I'd have a chance to connect about Opimae.

I crossed the castle's Great Hall to photograph a recently repaired wall near a suit of armor when footsteps echoed behind me. For a moment I froze, worried my supernatural stalker had returned, but almost as quickly, I recognized the energy.

"Mr. Murray, it's nice to see you."

"Good afternoon, Ms. Weston. Might I ask what you're working on this fine afternoon?"

"I'm gathering material for a pamphlet Marketing and I are pulling together. It's for donors attending next year's function. The new year will be here before we know it."

"Brilliant. I cannae wait to see what you pull together."

"I'm hoping Mark and I will make some strides together on this project. I don't think he's pleased that I'm here."

A soft smile tugged at the corner of Mr. Murray's lips. "He'll warm to you. Give it time, Ms. Weston."

I nodded.

"Well, I'm guessing the reason for your visit is due to my request for some of your time?" I asked.

"Indeed, it is. I have about thirty minutes open."

"Great. Could we head to your office? It's not something I'd like to discuss out here."

Mr. Murray signaled for me to lead the way. We stepped from the warmth of the Great Hall into a blustery scene. The wind gusts were excessively cold and strong, and I slipped my camera strap over my shoulder before pulling my hair back and braiding it as we crossed the courtyard toward our offices. Tourists were laughing as their hair blew straight up, and one gentleman was running after his ballcap, which was tumbling toward a castle wall.

I was relieved when I took my seat across the desk from Mr. Murray, warming my hands on a steaming mug filled with tea. But my relief was short-lived. Mr. Murray's energy was off, and something about it prickled at my witch's eye.

I cleared my throat and began.

"There are a few things I wanted to ask you about. They aren't related to castle business."

Mr. Murray arched his eyebrow but nodded for me to proceed.

"What do you know about Lorenzo Belmonte?"

He hesitated before answering. "A fair amount I suppose. I sit on the Scottish National Coven Council—I assume you've grown familiar with the witchkind government structure?"

I nodded. "So, is Dr. Belmonte involved in the council with you?"

His voice rose. "He no longer deserves the title doctor. He violated his oath to do no harm many years ago."

"So, that's a no, then."

Mr. Murray sighed. "Why are you asking me about Lorenzo? You shouldnae be looking into him."

"It's too late for that."

"Ms. Weston, please. There's so much you cannae possibly understand."

I paused, considering my next move. I decided to take a gamble.

"That's actually what I wanted to talk to you about. I . . . well, I gathered some information that doesn't quite make sense."

"What do you mean?"

"Have you heard of a place called Opimae, by chance?"

Mr. Murray sat back in his seat and rested his chin on his linked hands. "Do you ken what you're asking?"

"I do. Or at least, I think I do."

He eyed me suspiciously. "What are you getting at, Ms. Weston?"

"I believe that's where Lorenzo is—in Opimae."

"How did you arrive at that conclusion?"

"All signs pointed in that direction," I said.

"And what signs were those?"

I gave no answer.

"You shouldnae be researching this. And whatever you do, do *no* return to Lorenzo's home."

My blood ran cold. "Excuse me?"

Confusion flashed across Mr. Murray's features for only a second before recognition sank in. He knew what he'd done.

"How did you know I was in Lorenzo's home?" I asked. "Have you been watching me?"

Mr. Murray gave no answer, but his eyes were distant. I waited until he found his explanation.

"I'm a seer," he stated with some resignation. "I admit I was looking into you more than necessary. I apologize, but your position is important to the success of the castle and our restoration project. I care about this place immensely."

"What did you see?"

"I saw you in an office. Hadley, Lorenzo Belmonte is dangerous. He *will* find out who you are, just as he told you. I ken you haven't calculated your next move, but I'm concerned."

"I can't believe you were watching me."

"I apologize—truly. Hear me out?"

I nodded.

"You are still adjusting to your magic, and I worried about an issue arising around the castle. Our secrecy is imperative. And truthfully, I didnae have time to await information from the lower councils—not if we were going to make an offer quickly.

"With your . . . history, I've checked in occasionally. I wanted to warn you, but I need approval to discuss it. The councils are effective, but we're not always the most expedient."

"Approval?"

"From the upper council and the Cardinal Court."

"If Lorenzo is dangerous, I have to wonder why you waited to warn me regardless of their approval."

"That wasn't my call. There would be consequences if I stepped out of line."

"Then you and Fitz's father are more similar than I'd like," I said.

His eyebrow arched, though he remained silent.

"This isn't just about me being a newly matched witch, is it? You know about me and Fitz."

"Aye," he returned through pursed lips.

"Did you know our story when you hired me?"

"I thought you two were quite brave."

As much as I appreciated his sentiments, I didn't have much time with him, and I needed to return our focus to the reason I had requested this meeting.

"I need more information on Lorenzo."

Mr. Murray sighed. "I cannae talk any further—not yet."

"I think we could reach some sort of mutual disclosure. I think we could help each other."

"I'm as interested in Lorenzo as you are. But I'll need approval from the Cardinal Court to discuss this any further."

"If I may offer a suggestion?"

He nodded for me to continue.

"Chloe Wilson is overseeing my training. Raise this question to her."

Mr. Murray hesitated and then said, "Aye . . . I'll do it."

I had one last effort to give. "I know you're limited in what you can share, but Mr. Murray . . . I transported to a strange place. Please, can you just confirm this for me? Did I travel to Opimae?"

He held my gaze, and I thought for a brief moment that I had won him over.

He finally responded. "I'll speak with Chloe immediately, and hopefully, I can reveal more information soon."

I thanked Mr. Murray for his time and headed for the door.

"Ms. Weston?" he called as I reached for the handle.

"Yes?"

"It would not be wise to return to Lorenzo's home. He is a danger to you."

I checked my phone as I exited the building—a text from Jordan.

Still on for our FaceTime date tomorrow? she asked.

Wouldn't miss it, I replied.

And I wouldn't.

We'd talk about our jobs, how much we missed each other, my relationship with Fitz, her parents' recent visit; and I would continue to carefully avoid talking with her about the changes that I most wanted to share, the secret that burned inside of me like a searing hot knife in the pit of my stomach.

But I was learning the balance of my new life, and I was grateful Jordan could still be a part of it, even if our relationship had to look a little different than it had in the past.

I slid my phone back into my bag and headed for the castle exit.

Fitz and Isaac were waiting just outside the castle to walk home with me. Isaac lifted me from the ground and spun me around.

"I am so happy to see you, *Carissima*."

When we entered our flat, the whole gang was there, and I was glad we were closing on the adjoining apartment. I had the distinct feeling we were going to need the space.

I recapped the meeting for them. "I'm trying to be open-minded here, but this is still strange to me. I can't believe he was watching me."

"I understand why he did it, but typically, we need clearance from the councils to engage in any sort of surveillance," Ian said.

"From what I understand, James Murray is a rule follower, so this was a huge risk on his part and—honestly—out of character."

"The councils have been riding that line for years though," Isaac added. "This does not surprise me."

"Let's not forget that because Murray has a seat on the council, he knows a great deal more than he's letting on," Fitz said. "As soon as a witch of human lineage who, along with her mate, defied council orders and then crossed this border, you can bet the Scottish Council did everything in their power to find details on us."

"That's true. I wonder what he's been plotting," Henry wondered.

"That's an eerie thought. Just when I thought things were settling down," I said.

"Being a witch is different from being a human in a lot of ways. This is just another example. We're all so connected, it's harder to keep secrets. It's just our nature," Tanner said.

"Speaking of secrets, do you think he believes in the existence of Opimae?" Ann said absentmindedly.

"He chose his words carefully, but I'm certain that's why he's seeking Chloe's approval. I think he wants to talk to me about it."

Izzy reached for her mom's hand. "You will keep us updated, won't you?"

"Of course, Iz," Fitz answered.

"And I dinnae ken what type of partnership he might try to build, but keep us updated on that as well," Ian said. "You ken as well as I do that the council doesn't offer information like this unless they intend on recruiting you."

"I know, Dad."

My chest grew tight.

My mind began ticking through all the little signs: the council offering us an olive branch, their long-time desire for Fitz to join them, their decision to bring Tanner to evaluate me, James Murray hiring me for my position at the castle . . . and I knew Ian was right.

James wouldn't share this information unless he wanted something from us.

This was it. This must have been the reason the council had gone easy on us.

"In the meantime, I think we should do a bit of our own information gathering," Henry said.

"What do you have in mind?" Ian asked.

"I propose Hadley return to Lorenzo's home. Each time she's gone, she's gathered new intelligence."

"It's a good idea," Fitz agreed as he turned to me. "But it's solely your decision, Hadley."

I looked around the room at the faces anxiously awaiting my decision. "I'll do it. Tomorrow."

CHAPTER FORTY-ONE

The following evening, I sat in our apartment, flanked by our friends and family. James had spoken with Chloe and was awaiting an answer from the court, but we decided to push forward with my return to Lorenzo's home instead of waiting for a final decision.

I closed my eyes and asked time to take me to Lorenzo's kingdom.

I expected to open my eyes to the office, but instead, the room appeared distantly before me, like I was peering through a snow globe. At first, I saw nothing but darkness around me, the scene floating in an abyss, but as my sight adjusted, weak light took shape in the depths of the void. I'd seen the swirling constellations of the in-between with Fitz while transporting, but I'd never encountered it during my spirit-travels, nor had I ever seen the stars so dim. I returned my focus to Lorenzo's office as I pushed back against the anxiety nipping at the edges of my consciousness. I willed myself closer to the scene and ran headfirst into an invisible barrier.

I instinctively reached for my aching head before realizing it would do me no good and reminded myself that my spirit and my body were less connected than normal: *mind over matter.* I reached timidly toward the room, and my fingers sent waves of energy rippling through the air.

Lorenzo had increased his protection spells.

But my training was going well, and it would take more than that to stop me. I closed my eyes and ran my fingers across the edges of his spell, picking at anything that felt suspicious. Eventually, I found the wisp that tied the energy strands together and tugged.

The energy unraveled, though it lingered through the air like it was searching for something. I paused, suddenly understanding the energy was meant to cling to the witch who unraveled it—it was meant to tie them to Lorenzo. A shiver ran through the core of my spirit, and I held my breath until the curious energy drifted through me. It continued onward in its search for the physical manifestation of me that it wouldn't find.

The air shifted, and an opening into Lorenzo's office appeared before me. I stepped through and fell to my hands and knees. A sigh of relief escaped my lungs.

I worked my way around the room, searching for anything that might be helpful. The ring was nowhere in sight, but since the summoning spell had brought me to Lorenzo's office, I knew it must be nearby. I scanned the stone walls. The maps were missing, and the windows were gone.

Windows, I thought, and they appeared.

At least I was getting something right. Though the skies were gray, visibility was decent, and I scanned snow-covered peaks that stretched as far as I could see.

I turned back to the room and decided to try Lorenzo's desk drawers again. I was standing in an enchanted room, after all. Perhaps the answer had been right in front of me this entire time.

I sat in his chair and shuddered. He'd been there recently—the chair was still charged with his energy. I shook off the thought and searched for the edges of a protection spell. And sure enough, it was there. It took only a few seconds to find the opening, and I tugged. I repeated the process of unwinding his spell. With the final tug, the drawers opened.

Finally.

"Files," I whispered.

Countless files materialized, and I set to work. About halfway through, a page caught my attention.

Though the paper was dulled by time, the ink hadn't faded. I swept my fingers across the pages, searching for anything useful. I was met by the magic that had been intertwined into the ink by the letter's author. The text was foreign to me—Latin, maybe—but I recalled a spell Maka taught me that would translate languages and recited it quickly.

The letters faded, and my heart dropped, but then, the words materialized in English. I read the page twice trying to commit the information to memory.

Lorenzo,

Take your mother to Opimae. Unexpected issues hold me in London, but I'll join you as soon as I'm able. The plans for the fortress are enclosed. The modifications needed are slight, but they're necessary. With the ring, the councils won't be able to stand against us, and we can finally overturn their faulty thinking.

May Fate grant us favor as you carry forward our plans. Remember what I told you about the in-between—vary your threads. I'll be with you soon.

- Father

I thumbed through the attached floor plans for the layout of the fortress before stumbling across a map of Opimae. A mountain range rose from Opimae City toward the northwest and near the top of the range someone had drawn a red "X". I checked the elevation charts: 22,438 feet. The nearest mountain town was Terra Firma, and per the scale, it looked like the fortress was located roughly ten miles north.

I felt my heartbeat quicken somewhere . . . *on Earth.*

If these papers were correct, then I'd confirmed Lorenzo's location was in Opimae—and I'd found his *exact* location. I sat flabbergasted for a moment before returning the paperwork to the desk. I rushed to the window under a compulsion to look once more at the landscape. I threw open the arched pane window and was met by jagged, snow-covered mountains.

I closed the window and turned.

Lorenzo stood near the doorway with his eyes fixed indisputably on me. I studied him quickly, noting that he was again dressed in black, though his attire seemed to echo a medieval warrior. His overcoat held four large buckles that secured dark leather straps into place, and my eyes traced a dark leather strap to a quiver resting on his back. He moved slowly to the desk where he pulled the quiver over his head and rested it gently on the wooden surface.

I scanned the closed door, wondering how he had entered the space, before returning my gaze to the face of my opponent. His dark eyes remained fixed on me, and though I couldn't wonder why his eyes held so much anger within them, their intensity sent a chill through the pit of my stomach.

He moved toward me slowly, and I froze, remembering that he couldn't harm my spirit. I thought he might walk straight through me, but when he was merely inches from my face, he paused and closed his eyes.

"Ah." He fractured the silence and opened his eyes. "It's you again. I thought as much."

The slightest hint of a smile tugged at his lips, and he linked his hands behind his back before he paced the room seemingly lost in thought.

"Why don't you tell me a few things? You could begin with your name, for instance." He looked again in my direction, and my heart rate grew perceptible in my chest. He'd be handsome if it weren't for the ominous energy lingering around him like a cloud. Something about him felt . . . unnerving.

A noise escaped my lips—more breath than laugh—and unbelievably, it didn't seem to escape his notice.

"Impossible," I muttered.

Lorenzo's grin widened. "No. I'm afraid nothing is impossible. Didn't the councils tell you that?"

"How can you hear me?"

"You aren't the only gifted witch in this room. You might have penetrated my spells, but don't believe even for a second that you're more powerful than I am."

"How would you know?" I asked.

Lorenzo paused as he cocked his head in my direction. "Oh," he whispered. "It *is* you, isn't it, Hadley?"

My blood ran cold. How could he possibly know my name?

"I thought so. Who else would it be?" He nodded thoughtfully. "Why have you come here?"

I hesitated, choosing my words carefully. "I wanted to know if Opimae was real. Is that where I am?"

"Surely, you already know the answer to that."

"I want to hear you say it."

He laughed. "Then you'll remain in want."

I stayed silent.

"See, you've broken into my home before. Why should I tell you anything when you're sneaking around looking for things that don't belong to you?"

"Fine. I want to understand why you took Esther MacGregor's ring. What do you want with it?"

Lorenzo tilted his head considering my question. "I want to fix what the councils have broken. The ring will help me set things right."

"Like what?"

"The councils force witches to live in secrecy. We hide from the humans like we are ashamed of ourselves." Lorenzo shook his head. "And for what? Because we fear their persecution? It does not make good sense," he said.

I hesitated.

"We need a revolution. Reform won't come to us unless we demand it," he said. "The councils have overstepped, and they must answer for the injustices they've inflicted on to the very group of magical beings they've vowed to protect."

I thought of their threat to wipe my memories. I thought of Fitz's fear that they'd spellbind us, our speculation that they'd force us to partner with them . . . on something related to Lorenzo.

"The councils are trying to help me. They said they'd protect me,"

I said weakly.

"Is that so? But you know better than that, don't you?" he asked. "They only protect themselves."

Hadn't I expressed the same sentiment to Mia the first day I'd met her?

"They don't care about witchkind. I wish to change that," he continued.

"The councils say this arrangement protects us, that it would be detrimental to us if humans knew we existed." The words tasted bitter on my tongue. They echoed the very sentiment Mia and Olivia had expressed to me. But I needed to push Lorenzo—keep him talking until I could figure a way out.

"And have they protected you?"

I didn't answer.

"They're all liars, Hadley. Have you not learned that by now?"

"No."

"But that's not quite true, is it?" He came closer. "What does it feel like when someone lies to you, Hadley? To me, the truth feels like cool water trickling across my tongue. But lies? They run me dry. And right now . . . I thirst."

His eyes were like inky pools that longed to pull me under.

In the buzz of the moment, I'd forgotten to shield myself against my enemy, and Lorenzo stood so close that my head grew thick at the intensity of his energy. His scent permeated my senses with frankincense and amber. There was something else—vanilla, I thought. The ancient scent was too strong, overwhelming in some way, but I still needed a deep breath to push back against the ambush of his energy.

I steadied myself before drawing in the deep breath I sought, and upon my exhale, I asked the air to disperse the sweet, musky scent, and the effect was immediate. My head cleared, and I prepared myself for what would follow.

"You want some truth? You got it. I don't believe a thing you say. For you to have that ring . . . you've stolen power from another family. You disgust me."

Lorenzo tilted his head back ever so slightly, and as he mulled over his response, I took the opportunity to pick at the edges of his mind. Like his home, his mind was protected, but I was growing proficient in recognizing the patterns in his magic.

"What are you doing with the ring, anyway?"

Lorenzo's mind ticked through a myriad of thoughts, and so quickly that they didn't quite make sense. But soon enough, I heard something useful.

"Oh," I whispered. "You haven't found a way to access the power of the ring."

The anger burning through Lorenzo's eyes was palpable. He grabbed my wrist and pulled me mere inches from his face. "No one can read my mind."

My mind was frantic. How was he touching me?

"How did you do that?" Lorenzo asked.

I tried to pull myself free.

Lorenzo shook his head. "Answer me!"

"Let go of me!"

"Hadley," he growled.

"Don't you dare speak to me that way."

"I don't take orders from anyone," he spat. "You better remember that, fire witch."

I attempted again to pull myself loose from his grasp, but he grabbed my other arm and held them together. I wasn't thinking clearly. I'd let the shock of the moment get the best of me and that needed to change if I was going to make it out of that room. I looked around, orienting myself, grounding myself back to the scene around me.

"Stop looking around and talk to me," Lorenzo said sternly.

"How do you know I'm looking around?" I asked.

"The outline of your energy shimmers. I can see you; I can feel you. Now, how can you read my mind?"

I shook my head. "I don't know. I just can."

"Don't toy with me. It won't end well for you."

My mind finally caught up. I needed to return to my body. I just needed to call myself home. I closed my eyes and thought of the room where my body lay.

I thought of Fitz and the feel of his touch rather than the uncomfortable grip of Lorenzo's. The air shifted, and I opened my eyes to a hazy scene. The details of the room mingled with those of Lorenzo's office, and I knew it—I was suspended somewhere between the two places. I thought of my home, of the roaring fireplace, the smile on Fitz's face, but suddenly, the scene disappeared, and I was back in Lorenzo's office.

"We're not done here." It was a demand. "And if you'll stop being stubborn, I'll tell you why you should come to Opimae."

"What are you talking about?"

"Join me, Hadley."

"*What?*"

"We shouldn't be fighting against each other. You belong on the right side of things—not the councils' side."

His eyes were wild as they searched mine.

"What are you talking about?"

"You're working with the councils, yes?"

"They're helping me."

Lorenzo chuckled. "That is so naïve, it's almost endearing."

"Well, they aren't holding me against my will, so that's a start."

"And you think they wouldn't have wiped your memories clean to protect themselves? They say they're protecting us." Lorenzo scoffed. "Are you working with them? Are you here to spy for them?"

"What? No. I just want the ring back. And I want to understand what's happening."

Lorenzo's eyes narrowed in thought.

"Join my side, Hadley. I have forces greater than you can imagine. Together, we will ensure the councils will never punish another witch for who they love."

I hesitated, and Lorenzo smiled.

"You know I'm right. Work with me, and we'll set things right in the witch world."

I paused, unsure of my next move, before pulling back from him. He tightened his grasp and shook his head. "Stop doing that."

I gathered all my courage and settled my gaze squarely on Lorenzo before pulling my energy into a whirlwind all around me. The energy pushed violently against Lorenzo, and despite his best efforts, I pulled myself free. He knelt and struck his hand to the floor. The ground beneath me rippled. As the disturbance met my feet, a burst of energy slammed me against the wall. Before I could recover, Lorenzo was in front of me.

He pressed me against the stone that crept from behind the crumbling plaster wall.

His hand rested on my collarbone, and his fingertips pressed uncomfortably into my neck. His eyes flickered across me, and he moved closer until his breath was warm on my ear.

"You will not win this fight, Hadley." His voice was filled with venom. "You have no idea what you're up against."

"Neither do you," I whispered. I gathered every bit of energy that channeled within me. I called to the air and asked for her favor. I pulled at every stray energy in the room, and I worked them into a growing funnel within me. When the force of the motion threatened to overtake me from the inside out, I whispered to the threads of time, and I asked to return to safety. The energy spilled out, and Lorenzo released me in utter confusion. Wind whipped through the room, and when he reached for me again, the shock between us was so intense, I screamed.

A spark lit the space between us. Lorenzo cradled his hand protectively against his chest, but I could make out the fresh burn marks. His brows knitted in pain, and his wide eyes were the last thing I saw before darkness overtook me.

"Hadley, please." It was barely a whisper, but Fitz's voice echoed through the stillness.

Why is he worried? I wondered before my mind caught up. *Lorenzo.* I needed to wake up. I needed to tell everyone what he was trying to do, and what he could do. I needed to tuck myself safely against Fitz's chest until I'd steadied myself again. I focused on pulling my spirit back into my body and found the constellations of the in-between.

I searched for anything of substance, anything that gave me a sense of direction, but it was fruitless. Panic would make everything worse, I realized.

I closed my eyes and focused on my breathing until my heart returned to a normal pace. Then, I set my intention. I would find my way home. It was that simple. The stars began to swirl, and I navigated through them until I ran into a soft glow. I could go no further, but suddenly, a familiar energy washed over me.

Fitz.

I focused on Fitz: his energy, his soft smile, his voice. The illumination grew brighter until I could see nothing else, and my mind grew heavy. Just when I thought my mind was slipping under, Fitz appeared.

"Fitz! What are you doing here?" I asked.

He looked around curiously. His face lit when he found my energy.

"I can hear you in my mind. That's a good sign," he said. "Are you okay?"

"I think so. How did you get here?"

"I felt you panic, so we decided I should follow your path," Fitz said. "The threads were fragile, but our connection wasn't. I was able to follow it through the in-between and straight to you. It was quite the journey."

"What do you mean?"

"Hadley, this was a ridiculously far journey for a time-walker. I think it's true. This is a whole different universe."

A whole different universe.

"Then I'm surprised either of us made it here."

"You still don't understand how powerful we are."

I nodded before remembering he couldn't see me. "I've landed in the in-between twice. We need to get out of here."

"Aye, but can you leave? Your power feels weak, and I can't carry your spirit like I can with your body. I think you need a bit of help."

"I'm not taking a boost from you, Fitz. You need all of your strength to return to Earth."

"I'll return home and channel my power toward your physical form."

I considered that. "Okay, then."

"I'll see you soon," he said.

Fitz closed his eyes and his brows knit, and soon . . . he was gone. After a few seconds, bursts of energy channeled through the connection and into my system. The feel of his power inside of me created a sense of euphoria, and I thought I'd be delirious by the time he was finished. When the transfer was complete, I knew what to do.

I closed my eyes and envisioned my home. The faces of our friends. The cool air that leaked from the old windowpane near my favorite leather chair. The scent of whisky welcomed me to safety.

My eyes flew open, and I immediately turned to Fitz. His worried eyes were already studying me. I flew into his arms, crashing into him with a thud. He chuckled and held me tightly in his strong arms.

"Oof," I muttered.

"Aye," Fitz said. "You took a beating in Lorenzo's office."

"I'll help," Izzy said as she moved closer.

Izzy squeezed me gently before resting her hand on the side of my face. She whispered words that were lost on me, but a warm, fuzzy state of serenity took hold.

A calming spell.

"Thank you."

"We can't keep the questions at bay for long, but hopefully this will help you get through it all."

I nodded and looked at Fitz. "Your power is unbelievable," I muttered. "It was good for me to experience it like that."

"Like what?" Ian asked, bringing me back to the world around us.

"Oh," I said, pulling back.

I found Tanner at the opposite side of the room. His eyes were flooded with concern, but when I met his gaze, his features relaxed.

I tore my focus back to Ian's question. Fitz had already shared some information, but we explained the rest of the encounter.

Ann shook her head. "You two make a great team."

"Fitz's power has always been a marvel. I never thought anyone would come along who could be seen as his equal . . . not until you," Ian said.

"You're pretty powerful yourself, Ian," I countered.

"The MacGregors are legendary," Isaac said. "Their magical lineage is distinguished."

"The earth has granted us favor. But none are as distinguished as Fitz, though," his dad said. "He's the most powerful living Mac-Gregor."

"All right, enough of all that," Fitz muttered.

"Allergic to compliments." Izzy rolled her eyes.

"We need to discuss our next move," I said, pulling our focus back to our situation.

"We need more information on Lorenzo, plain and simple," Isaac said. "There's more information for me to go on, so I can continue my searches. But Opimae complicates things."

"Surely, we'll have an answer from the court soon," Henry said.

Fitz nodded. "They have the information we need—they're our most viable information source."

"Aye, I think it's time to put pressure on James," Ian said, his gaze resting on me. "You spoke directly to Lorenzo. James—and the rest of the councils—will want to hear about that. You just found your leverage."

CHAPTER FORTY-TWO

Ian was right about the leverage. Monday after work, Fitz and I found ourselves at Whiski ready to meet with James Murray. When I had demanded to see him that morning and shared that I had encountered Lorenzo again, James asked to meet with Fitz and me at 7 p.m.

The warmth of the pub was a relief as we filtered through the doorway. It took little effort to follow Mr. Murray's energy trail to the back of the bar where he sat nursing a dark beer and scanning the crowd through its narrow opening.

"Can you feel that?" Fitz asked.

An invisible barrier hung around Murray's table, and the air was heavy with the sign of protection. I was becoming quite proficient at identifying privacy spells.

Though the front of the restaurant was cramped, empty tables surrounded Mr. Murray's booth. We took a seat across from him.

"Hadley. Fitz. I'm so glad you both made it."

It was the first time he'd ever called me by my given name.

"Of course. It's a pleasure to see you again, Mr. Murray," Fitz said.

"The pleasure is all mine. Please take a seat, and you both can call me James."

We ordered drinks and dove right into the conversation.

"I paid Lorenzo another visit."

"I told you to stay away from him."

"Yes, I know. You were right about him being dangerous."

"Are you all right?" His eyes swept over me.

I nodded.

"As it happens, I received approval from the court last night to speak with you two." James sipped his drink and sat forward in his chair. His eyebrows knit tightly. "The word '*opimae*' is Latin, you ken? It means luxurious or lush, and the terrain is certainly that."

I nodded, though it didn't make sense. The landscape I'd seen from the windows hadn't exactly matched that description. And what did this have to do with anything?

"You noticed the maps on the walls in Lorenzo's office, I'm sure?"

"I did."

"We've been trying to make sense of them, James, but we haven't found a correlation in all of the locations," Fitz said.

"You wouldnae—not without access to council records. You see, Lorenzo acquired those maps while on the run, and he plotted the perfect escape from the councils. The area he sought refuge in is located in the Olympic National Park—right in the midst of your homeland, Hadley."

"Why there?" I asked.

"There was a particular area he needed to find."

"I saw markings along the High Divide Trail. Why would he go there? Easier to lose the councils?"

"There's a portal located off the trail."

"A portal? Where does it lead?"

Mr. Murray leveled his gaze. His eyes met Fitz's, and then mine. "To another world. The portal leads to another universe."

Silence fell momentarily.

"So, Opimae truly is another world?" I asked.

"Aye."

"How is that possible?" Fitz asked.

"It's magic," he quipped.

"I've heard rumors of another universe inhabited by magical beings, but until now, I discredited those accounts," Fitz said.

"The UCA—United Covens Affairs—gained knowledge of a portal around two hundred B.C. The portal was adjusted to what is now Washington, and it was a secret shared with no one outside witchkind, not even the human leaders of the day." He smiled. "As you can imagine, it seemed a safe location at the time, and it has remained one of the most discreet locations in the world. Shortly after its creation, we began to patrol the portal to ensure no one entered or exited who shouldnae."

"What do you know about this world?" I asked.

"Magic is practiced freely and openly, without fear or repercussion. Their convention is similar to our structure, and much of our knowledge and communication is through them. We've maintained a peaceful relationship over the centuries. Unlike Earth, their world is made up of many magical beings—witches, elves, dragons, and even water witches, or mermaids, as we call them here."

Fitz and I caught each other's gaze, marveling at the new intelligence.

"How is it possible?" I asked. "That so many mythical beings exist . . ."

"Well, for one, there aren't humans in Opimae. The beings all once existed here but were run close to extinction. Those left on this side were sent through the portal for protection. Another reason the portal has fallen to myth, even in witchkind."

"Fear anything that's different: the human motto," Fitz stated plainly.

"Unfortunate, but true. We saved those we could. It's imperative we maintain control of entrances and departures. Any magical beings, apart from witches, are not allowed to cross the portal into Earth. It's simply too dangerous at this time."

They'd never stand a chance here, I realized. They'd be captured, poked, and prodded until humans pulled every bit of information possible from them. Our way of life would end.

"But witches may cross openly? Most of us don't even know the world exists," Fitz said.

"The portal has been closed for about two hundred years to anyone outside of government business," James said. "It was a request from the Opimae government. But that recently changed. We haven't yet decided how to share this information at large. It could cause chaos."

"How did Lorenzo ever make it through?" I wondered.

"The answer to that question has evaded us for years—it's a mystery. There are no records of his passage through the portal that we can find. But the Opimae government has confirmation that he is on their planet."

"What I'd like to understand is why the council has decided to trust us with this information and what you hope to gain from it," Fitz said.

"We dinnae ken what Lorenzo is capable of, and that must change. Hadley wandered her way into Lorenzo's *home*—do you understand that no one with the UCA has been able to do that? The councils have searched for years for a witch who could do what Hadley has done. You clearly seek him for a reason of your own, something of immense value to you. We would like to partner with you to combine our efforts to pinpoint his exact location. Then, we'd like to bring him to justice for crimes he has committed."

Fitz nodded to me, confirming he felt truth in what James said.

I thought of my conversation with Lorenzo. I thought of his belief that the witchkind governments were the ones in the wrong.

"What are his crimes?" I asked.

Mr. Murray sighed. "Lorenzo went rogue years ago. He claimed our government prevents witches from reaching our full potential. He believes we should rule over the humans rather than coexist. He caused quite a stir and almost exposed us to humankind. It's all rubbish, of course, and we were able to stomp out his wee movement before it escalated beyond repair."

"And then?"

"We called him to trial, then he disappeared. We have reason to believe he is planning another uprising, and that would end in tragedy—he cares little for the carnage he creates."

I mulled over the information.

"And he has no regard for human life." James shook his head.

I found James's statement odd considering he was high-ranking in a government that would have erased my memories when I was considered a human.

"So, if we were to join you . . . is this working behind the scenes, or are we talking fieldwork?" Fitz asked.

I had suspected the conversation would lean in this direction, but I wasn't sure I was prepared for what may follow.

"It would be both, and I'm afraid the fieldwork has a real level of danger. It's one of the reasons we've spent years searching for the proper individuals to fill these positions."

"What exactly do you mean by fieldwork?" I asked.

"You'd both play major roles in the mission against Lorenzo," he began, clearing his throat. "With that being said, you'd be essential in the planning phase, and during this time you'd also undergo some training. This would happen in Opimae with their council, though members of our government would also accompany you—you wouldnae be alone in this. But you would be key players in enacting our strategy to stop Lorenzo. You could be preventing war."

"You believe we can do that?" I asked.

"Look at what the two of you were able to do on your own. The councils tried but couldnae prove you two were even in contact, even with the most skilled seers available. When you decided to slip off the radar, you did. And you weren't located until you allowed yourselves to be found. You believed in something, and you accomplished it. Then you broke through Lorenzo's spells and entered his home—something we've been unsuccessful in doing for years. If you can do that alone, imagine what you'll accomplish with the councils' resources."

"Well, when you put it that way."

James chuckled. "And that's in addition to your power, your intuition, and your innate sense of good—of right and wrong. You're the type of witches others will follow, which is immensely important."

Fitz nodded absentmindedly.

"Maka's reports have been undisputedly favorable," James added. "Chloe recommends you for this role. And Fitz, it's no secret the Scottish Council has desired a partnership with you for years. We'd be thrilled to have you finally join us."

I took a deep breath. "Can you see the future of this mission?"

"No," James said, "but I've done extensive research on what is needed to defeat Lorenzo. There's a . . . prophecy about this mission."

"A prophecy?" I asked, though Gabriella's words echoed through my mind.

"*If you're the one from the prophecy . . .*" she'd said.

"The Opimaeans have a prophecy of old. It tells of a great conflict that is brought to their peaceful planet. The Opimaean folk partner with Earth and a team of crusaders. Two of these crusaders have a strong connection to one another, and Fate ultimately leads them to the conflict. They possess great power and hold the key to bringing peace once again to the nations of Opimae."

"And you believe we're those crusaders," Fitz said.

"Aye, I do. And I believe that together, we can accomplish what the prophecy has foretold."

Fitz and I looked to one another.

"You have exactly what we're looking for in our crusade leaders. Even though Hadley is new to this world, she's demonstrating great mastery of her skills, and clearly, we have need of her abilities. And when I discovered you two were mates, I thought perhaps this was the connection referenced in the prophecy."

I nodded, still at a loss for words.

"And beyond that, you two are more powerful than most witches I've known. Your powers exceed normal standards alone, but together . . . well, it's extraordinary." He paused and looked between the two of us. "I believe Fate led you to the council for this reason—she has prepared you for what lies ahead."

"*Came to dinner with my boss. Might join a crusade to fight evil on a foreign planet,*" I said to Fitz's mind.

"*Aye just another day.*"

"Lorenzo must be stopped," James continued. "And I believe we need both of you to do so. Will you join forces?"

Lorenzo had posed the same question to me only two days prior, and now I was tasked with deciding which side was right and which was wrong.

Fitz and I exchanged a glance.

"*I think we need to take a moment to really sort this,*" Fitz said to my mind.

"James, would you mind if we take just a few minutes to talk?" I asked.

"Absolutely not. This is a lot to process. I need to make a call anyway."

James exited the room, his phone in hand, granting us privacy to discuss our future.

Fitz swirled his drink, the Scotch trickling back down the length of the glass. It was a sign I knew well—he was about to share something he found no pleasure in. "You know we don't have a choice?"

"About joining?"

"Aye."

"This is one of those moments where we're called and have to answer."

He nodded. "Right."

"And what happens if we refuse?"

"I think we'll face the consequences of our previous actions."

"Spellbinding," I said.

"Aye. This is why the council played nice when we returned to Scotland. Think about it: Olivia Cameron's reaction, Mia—a Cardinal Court member—attending the meeting and working on our case. Chloe being assigned as lead over your training."

"They were already curious about me because of the way I came into my powers, and they've wanted to work with you for years," I said.

"Then we defied their orders and effectively dropped off their radar. They realized we weren't their average case," Fitz said.

"And when we showed up in that office and Olivia felt our power . . ."

"Exactly," Fitz said.

"Shit."

"Aye . . . shite."

"So, James probably had his eyes on us from the beginning, and then I paid a visit to Lorenzo's home . . ."

"Right. Your break-in sealed the deal."

"And here I thought I wowed him with my PR skills."

"Of course, you did. But that wasn't the only thing about you that wowed him."

"I don't trust the council," I said.

"How could you?" he agreed, shrugging. "We take it a day at a time. James wasn't responsible for what happened to us. He's a good guy. That's as far as I can see right now."

"That's a good way to look at it. We take things a step at a time and assess as we go."

"And some of the members have helped you—Maka, Chloe."

I couldn't disagree.

I thought of our only alternative: run. I thought of Jordan's offer to help. I thought of Henry and Isaac's backup plan they'd put in to place when we first met with the council. But our alternative plan wouldn't bring us closer to the ring . . .

"Regardless of any of the rest of this crap, you need your family's ring back. Lorenzo can't have it. We have to fight this."

"I want that ring back more than I resent helping the councils."

"And there's larger implications to consider . . . the unrest Lorenzo could cause."

"Aye. This rebellion could affect countless lives in both worlds."

"We can't allow that to happen," I said.

Fitz agreed.

"Why are you looking at me like that?" I questioned.

"Oh . . ." His smile widened. "Honestly, I'm just in awe of you sometimes."

"What? Why?"

"You're so sure. Courageous."

"No. I'm scared, Fitz."

"Me too. But we're facing this head-on, my brave lass." Fitz took a sip of whisky, his face turning pensive. "I'm debating how much we should share of what you learned from Lorenzo."

"We both believe Lorenzo is wrong, correct?"

"Aye."

"Then I think we tell James the location of the fortress. Maybe it helps shorten this whole partnership if I'm just forthcoming from the beginning. Speed this thing along."

Fitz paused momentarily, and then nodded.

We knew what we had to do. I gripped Fitz's hand tightly. Fitz waved to James, who was waiting patiently near the front door pretending to be otherwise engaged.

"Well then? You've reached a decision?"

"Aye, we'll join you."

"Oh brilliant! I cannae tell you how pleased I am to hear that," James returned, clasping his hands together happily. "Come to the the Scottish National Coven Council meeting at the castle on Saturday. We'll discuss the particulars of your travel."

I'd come to dinner with my manager and had somehow agreed to travel to a magical land in another universe to fight a warmongering witch. Was I making a mistake?

No, I knew I wasn't. I wasn't human; I was a witch. With my power and intuition, I knew we were right to trust James, and we needed to honor Fitz's family.

"There's only one condition," Fitz said.

"Anything," James replied sincerely.

"He—Lorenzo—has something that belongs to my family. I want it back."

"And what is that?"

"He has a ring that belongs to my family," Fitz said.

James's face lit in recognition, which was quickly followed by his eyes growing wide. "You mean . . . your ancestor's ring?"

"You know about that?"

"We've known about the ring for a long time. You see, we were the ones who first took the ring after your grandmother's death. The local coven knew what she possessed but believed she wouldnae fight her way free. The leaders decided there was no danger in leaving it in her possession until her death unless her decision changed. They hoped it would grant her some comfort as she suffered in her last days.

"The council leaders sent representatives to collect the ring with the intention of locking it away until your grandfather was composed enough to release the powers. They thought it would give him closure. But the ring mysteriously vanished one night under careful watch. The guards were incapacitated, and all the spells meant to protect the ring were disarmed."

"Oh my god," I whispered.

James nodded. "It requires vast aptitude and force to undo the work of so many other powerful witches. When the guards awoke, the ring was gone."

"And you have no idea who took it?" I asked.

"It appears our investigation has yielded nothing of significance. When I looked into council records earlier this week, I found the file on the MacGregor ring. It seems the search for it was abandoned. The case was marked as suspended."

"And now Lorenzo has the ring. God only knows what his plans for it are," I said.

"And you're certain it's the proper ring?" James asked.

Fitz and I shared the details of our investigation and my experience with the ring.

"We've been unable to penetrate the perimeter of his home—that is until Hadley broke in," James said. "That's the only reason I was able to see inside. You casually discovered something we've been unable to for years, my dear."

"I didn't do anything special," I said. "I talked to the elements the way I always do."

"It seems Hadley disarms others' spell," Fitz said. "When I

couldn't utilize Annabel's summoning spell but Hadley immediately transported to the ring, I realized her powers find the loopholes in others' spells and latch on. She couldn't call the ring to her either, but the ring somehow summoned her. It's incredible actually."

"Extraordinary!"

I took a deep breath before I shared the last of my major news with James.

"There's something else," I began. "James, I think I know where Lorenzo is located. It's a fortress in the northern mountains on Opimae's portal continent. If you provide me with a map, I think I can find it again—or at least I can get close."

James exhaled deeply, his expression blank. He looked down for a few seconds, and when his gaze met mine, the determination in them was clear.

"Incredible," he mumbled. He pulled out his phone and typed furiously before sliding it back into his jacket pocket. "You'll have maps sent your way immediately."

I nodded.

"Is there any further intelligence you gathered?" James asked.

"Nothing of importance. Lorenzo was cagey with me, but I think you're right to suspect a rebellion from him."

"If you think of anything else, you ken how to reach me. We'll have you give an official statement on Saturday at the council meeting."

I nodded.

"Hadley, take the rest of the week off from the castle. If my suspicions are correct, you'll be in Opimae before the end of the year."

My breath came short. The new year was only six weeks away—only six weeks and then my life would look completely different.

"Is everything all right?" James asked, his brows creasing.

"It's nothing. Just . . . I feel like I finally found my place here in Edinburgh, and it's all about to change. And honestly, my work at the castle has a lot to do with that."

James's face relaxed, and he nodded. "Your position will be waiting for you when you return."

"Who will fill my role in my absence?" I asked. "Who will head the event?"

James hesitated, which told me exactly what I needed to know.

"You're thinking of asking Mark's friend—the one who applied for this position," I guessed.

"He was the most qualified candidate, after you."

I had to wonder if James was being truthful about me being the most qualified. Or had he only hired me to recruit me for this mission?

"It's only temporary, Hadley. The position is yours."

Mark will hate me more than ever when I return, I thought.

"And the ring?" I asked. "Will it be returned to Fitz?"

"Aye. The ring will be released to Fitz once we free the power from it. Consider it as a part of your reward for helping us."

"Is that something Fitz will be able to help with? Releasing the power?"

"Of course."

James insisted on picking up the check, citing council business. He took his leave, turning on his heel before pausing.

"Oh, and one last thing . . ." James called back, over his shoulder. "Welcome to the crusade."

CHAPTER FORTY-THREE

The following morning, our group gathered at Henry's to discuss the new information we'd received from James. The room fell into chaos.

"You *agreed* to that?" Ann asked. Her soft features were scrunched in horror.

"And what if they had refused?" Ian returned. "Would it have done any good?"

"You think the council would have really called them on it?" Tanner asked.

"This is huge. Of course, they would have," Isaac answered. He sank into a nearby chair. "This is bad. This is very bad."

"So, we're past the point of questioning this as reality?" Henry asked. "We truly believe Fitz and Hadley are traveling to another universe?"

The room fell silent.

"Murray is highly regarded amongst the ranks of witchkind government. He's a sensible fellow. If he says Opimae exists, then it does," Ian said.

"How can this be?" Izzy asked almost to herself. She met my gaze frowning. "You're sure about doing this?"

I considered her question, my mind rolling through the past twenty-four hours. "Even if I'm not . . . it doesn't matter, Iz."

"It matters to me."

"Thank you." I squeezed her hand lightly. Her gaze fell on her brother. He nodded softly.

"Okay, so . . . we're doing this, right? I mean, we're all going to fight for a spot on this mission in some form or another?" Tanner asked.

"Aye," Henry answered.

"No," Fitz said taking on an authoritative tone.

"And why not?"

"You've been able to elude the councils. Don't mix yourself up now."

"That's no your call to make."

"*Think*, Henry."

"Fitz . . ." I began.

"Hadley, this is dangerous. I'm already up to my eyeballs in anxiety over you. I won't have your back like I normally would, Henry. I'll be focused on protecting Hadley."

"I can handle myself, mate. Besides, you'll need me in Opimae to help protect Hadley, keep her power hidden from Lorenzo."

His gaze shifted to me. "We'll all be in some level of danger. But Hadley . . . none of us are able to locate the loopholes like she can, and Lorenzo is already sorting that out. I'll do my part to protect her."

"You truly want a part in this?"

"I hail from a long line of warriors, and though I have seen little battle, their valor rests in my veins. I'll do what I was born to do."

Fitz exhaled slowly.

Henry continued. "Hadley needs me too. She's family now, and even you willnae prevent me from protecting our family."

Fitz placed his right hand on Henry's shoulder.

Though his energy was tight, he knew Henry well enough to know he'd made up his mind. "Then I'm proud to have you fight with me, brother."

Ian cleared his throat. "I'll join, as well."

"Ian," Ann whispered.

His face grew tender as he gazed toward his wife. "I'll not let Fitz and Hadley run headfirst into danger on their own. Besides, what's the likelihood the council willnae ask this of me anyway?"

Ann's face fell. "Slim," she answered.

"I can feel it coming. But I'll make this decision for myself. For our family."

Ann dropped her gaze. The room was suspended in silence.

When Ann raised her head, the resolution in her eyes was clear. "I'll volunteer my services on the intelligence teams," Ann responded. "I'm not meant for battle, but I'll do my part."

"A fine offer," Ian returned as he slipped his arm around her.

"This group will need a reader. Reading others' intentions has never been more imperative," Isaac chimed in. "Count me in."

"I'll join mum and offer my hand at research," Izzy said. "My plants can wait.”

I had to laugh. It was such a classically Izzy line.

“And I’ll ask for a transfer to this project,” Tanner said. “Either as a trainer or a team member—as long as I get to help somehow.”

I smiled. “Wouldn’t want anyone else kicking my ass.”

And there we were: a family willing to risk it all for one another and for the greater good.

Later that night, Fitz and I lay in bed as we talked though the implications of our decision.

“I don’t know what to tell my mom,” I admitted to Fitz.

“Stick as closely to the truth as possible. The closer to the truth, the better you’ll feel, and it’ll be easier to remember your story.”

“I don’t think she’ll understand that I’m tangled up in some mission that won’t allow me to communicate for a while. She’s just getting used to me being over here, and now I have to tell her this.”

“Look, Hads. I don’t know how much your mother already knows . . .”

“What?” I sat up, my elbow sinking into my pillow.

“I saw your dad before he died. He asked for a good portion of our conversation to stay between us, so I’m not going to share much with you—I’m sorry.”

“Fitz. Shit . . . you say something like that, and then you can’t tell me much?”

“Aye, this is why I haven’t said anything. I know you’ll be pissed at me, but it’s a promise I intend to keep, and you’ll have to get over it, unfortunately."

"You have a way with words sometimes, you know that?"

"Here's why I brought it up—I told your dad what I am . . . that I'm a witch."

"How did *that* go?"

"The man looked me dead in the eyes and asked if you were a witch too—if that's what was going on between us."

I laughed, caught off-guard.

"I told him what you were and how you didn't know yet. I showed him magic. Hadley, I broke every damn rule in the book. I told the man everything."

"Why?" I drawled out.

"Because I knew he wouldn't make it much longer," Fitz said. "You were heartbroken—he knew that. I wanted him to know his little girl would be all right. That one way or the other, you would be fine and happy. I wanted him to know the councils wouldn't keep us apart in the end."

"Oh my god . . ." I whispered.

"Hads, he died knowing who you are, and with a couple of promises from me . . . which will stay between him and me."

I nodded, not trusting my voice.

"I'm telling you this because he said he wasn't sure if he'd share anything with your mum—a fair amount he promised he wouldn't. But some of it, he might have found a way to share with her cryptically. She might not be all that surprised by what you tell her."

"So . . . there are things she might know, others she definitely doesn't?"

"Your dad wouldn't have told her you're a witch . . . but maybe that you're different, and I'm the same kind of different."

"But you wouldn't have known about any of this . . ."

"No, *but* my dad sensed something strange for years before I met you. He said I'd find someone to equal my power. And my mate and I would embark on something grand . . . something unbelievable. I told your dad I knew we had a big calling in life.

"So, back to your mum. I'd say you have until the day we cross through the portal to talk to her, but the longer you allow this to sit in the back of your mind, the worse you'll feel."

"I guess I should call her tomorrow."

"I think that's wise," he said, brushing his thumb across my cheek.

"I can't believe I'm going to leave her completely alone." A tear spilled down my cheek.

"Hads," Fitz whispered.

"My dad leaves her. I leave her." I shook my head. "I feel awful about this."

"I'd tell you not to worry, but I know you better than that."

I laughed despite my tears.

"Try not to carry that weight. You can't help the circumstances."

I nodded.

"And don't worry. You'll come back to her."

"We'll both come back," I countered, more confidently than I felt.

The following afternoon, I stared at my phone calculating the time difference. *9 a.m. Pacific Time.* There was no time like the present.

I sighed and reached for my phone. I stared at my mother's contact card and hesitated for only a moment before punching the Face-

Time button.

My mom beamed as she answered the phone. "Hi, honey. How's everything going?"

"Good. How are things in the Pacific Northwest?"

"Nice. It's a weirdly dry week for November. You just missed Gram—she went for a walk."

I'd forgotten Gram was visiting her. It was her second trip since I'd left for Paris, and I instantly felt better knowing Gram was with her.

"Why don't you tell me what's wrong, Hadley?" my mom said, her brow creasing.

"Momma," I started. I paused, resting my head in my hands, wondering how to begin. "I'll be gone for a little while, and I won't be able to reach you."

My mother's expression changed slightly, confusion flashing across her features. "What do you mean?"

"Fitz and I have been asked to take care of some business that will have us away for quite some time."

"Just you and Fitz?" she asked warily, her hazel eyes narrowing.

"A few other people are joining us."

"I don't understand. Wherever you're going . . . we can still talk?"

"I don't think so," I said.

"How long will you be gone?"

"I'm not sure. It depends on how quickly we finish."

"Hadley, you've got to give me something here. This sounds ridiculous."

"I know."

"This can't deal with your work," my mom said.

"It deals with another type of work," I said, "but I can't talk about it, Momma."

"Why on earth can you not tell me about this?"

"Because I'm not supposed to tell anyone about this."

"But I'm your mother," she said.

"This is a mission of sorts, one I can't talk about. There would be consequences for both of us."

She stared, searching my face, and a fire rested in her eyes that I well recalled from my teenage years. She was angry, and I knew why. This couldn't make any sense to her, and I wasn't even doing a decent job of explaining the information I was able to share.

"Okay, here's the deal: we've been recruited for an assignment by a branch of government and are under strict orders to keep it confidential. I don't know how long this mission will take, but I'll contact you as soon as we're back. I can't tell you any more than that."

"Is this with the military?"

"You could say that."

"This is still not good enough," she returned, her voice terse.

"You know I've always been different," I said. "I know you realize Fitz and his family are too. We're the same type of different, okay? People like us are called to duty sometimes because of our skill sets."

My mom remained quiet, but I saw the conflict raging through her features. My departure would hurt her, and the thought broke my heart.

"I can't accept that."

"You have to accept it because you don't have another choice. And if you can't accept it, then you won't be able to see much of me in the future. Please understand what a difficult position I'm in."

"I'm sure we can get you out of this. I wish your father—" she broke off, trying to suppress tears.

"If Daddy were here," I said softly, "things wouldn't be any different. He told you a couple of things about a conversation he had with Fitz, didn't he? Right before we lost him."

My mom's eyes widened.

"Look, I don't know what he told you, but . . . Daddy knew everything there is to know about me, and about Fitz. And if he were here, knowing what he did, he'd tell you that I have no choice. I'm doing what I need to do."

"Oh god, Hadley."

"I know, Momma. It's a lot. And Fitz would be in a ton of trouble for sharing what he did. The same would happen to me if I told you everything now."

"Meaning I just have to trust what you're saying and never expect any more explanation," she finished, her expression flat.

"Pretty much. But what we're about to do—it's a good thing, I promise you that. I'm on the right side of things."

"Do you really have to do this?" she asked, echoing the same question she'd posed to me before I left for Paris.

I nodded. "Yeah . . . I do. I wish I could explain this better, but I need you to trust me. Please . . . have faith in me."

"I've always had faith in you, Hadley."

"I love you so much, Momma. And I'm so sorry."

CHAPTER FORTY-FOUR

Fitz had surprised me earlier that morning, sharing we'd dine some-where nice that evening. My mind was weary from the call with my mother and all that lay ahead of us. A night out would do some good—one good night out in our city before our world changed forever.

I felt bold as I dressed for the evening. I donned a burgundy, floor-length dress for the occasion. Though the sleeves sat off the shoulder, my arms were covered in soft fabric, which guarded against the cold, Scottish air. With a plunging neckline and a silhouette that hugged tightly to my torso, I intended to capture Fitz's full attention.

I carefully applied makeup and coiled my hair at the nape of my neck. By the time I shimmied into the living room, I felt better than

I had in days.

Fitz stood by the fire, draped in a tux, complete with a white button-up and black bowtie, a glass of Scotch in hand.

"Holy hell," he mumbled as I walked through the door.

"Okay?"

"You're bonnie," he whispered, his hand sliding around my waist, pulling my body toward his. He kissed my neck, carefully avoiding my freshly painted lips.

After assisting with my coat, Fitz held out his arm and led me into the cold, damp evening streets of Edinburgh. He was tight-lipped about where we'd dine, but as we turned deeper into Old Town, I narrowed down the options. We avoided the steady trickle of water rolling down the street, and I turned my eyes toward the sky, finding that the clouds had cleared, a welcome break from the heavy rain of the day.

Reaching the Royal Mile, Fitz turned toward the esplanade of the castle rather than the many restaurants of Old Town. As we approached the gates, I looked at him curiously. There was a teahouse inside, but the castle was closed for the evening. He smiled, and a rap from his free hand resulted in the large wooden door swinging open.

"James?"

"Good evening, my lady. Sir." He nodded at Fitz, who was strug-gling to keep his composure.

"Right this way."

We followed James to an upper courtyard set with a table draped in white linen. A beautiful array of plants and flowers surrounded the table, and strands of lights spanned the distance of the ancient stone walls. The courtyard was open, exposing us to the cool night air, though roaring chimeneas were placed strategically around the space, all alight in their promise of warmth. The soft illumination of the castle's medieval architecture was a magical backdrop.

James took my coat, replacing it with a soft, fuzzy wrap, and seated us properly before disappearing under a dark archway.

"Why is my boss here?" I whispered.

"He made this evening at the castle possible. And then he asked to help with dinner." Fitz shrugged.

"What in the hell is going on?"

"Patience, Hads. Just enjoy the night," Fitz answered, smiling coyly.

Soft music floated in the breeze as a waiter arrived with Chateau de Ferrand to begin our meal.

"This always reminds me of Paris," I said

The waiter took pride in our dinner, explaining that the chef had selected and prepared the meal as a direct complement to Fitz's wine selection. The meal was, indeed, flawless, but I was distracted by Fitz's mounting nerves all through the main course.

As dinner was cleared from the table, I leaned forward. "Oh, is this all?" I teased.

Fitz reached for my hand, and his brow creased. "Actually, there's something I'd like to talk to you about."

"You know you can tell me anything."

"We've faced some tough moments in the last few months. But the way you stood against Lorenzo . . . you fight so bravely, my wee firecracker."

I laughed softly at his nickname for me.

"I couldn't be prouder of you."

I laid my hand tenderly against his jaw.

"But facing that danger and making the decision to join the fight against Lorenzo has reminded me that life isn't promised to us.

Nothing is certain . . . except for us. You're my anchor, Hadley."

He knelt before me, and I inhaled sharply, anticipating what came next.

"I've loved you since the day I met you. You're my best friend . . . the only one I need by my side. I'll love you long after time itself has fallen away."

I raggedly exhaled, my heart pounding in my chest.

"I don't want to travel into the next world without this ring on your finger. Hadley . . . will you marry me?"

He opened the box, revealing a ring. Platinum metal bands held the infinity diamonds into place and were molded together to form an "X" at the front and again at the back of the ring.

I dropped from my chair and into his arms. With my lungs unable to grant me the air to respond, I pressed my lips against his, and his fingers wound through my hair. I pulled away, laughing nervously and took a napkin from the table to wipe my lipstick from his face.

"I think I was dreaming. Say it again," I said softly.

Fitz grinned. "Marry me, Hadley."

"Nothing would make me happier. Of course, I'll marry you."

His hand stroked my cheek gently before presenting the ring. I extended my left hand, inviting him to slip the beautiful ring onto my finger.

We clung to each other as we rose from the stones. So engrossed in the moment as I was, I didn't notice the figures emerging from the shadows until they were standing beside the table.

"Aye, Fitz!" Henry shouted before pulling me into a warm hug. "Congratulations, Hadley."

Alight with excitement, he then embraced Fitz as the others surrounded us with smiles and laughter. Izzy, Ian, Ann, Henry, Isaac,

Tanner, and even James and Maka. Fitz had invited the crew to join us for drinks and dessert, and it couldn't have been more perfect; they were all present and ready with congratulations.

"Hads! Get into these loving arms," Isaac exclaimed, beaming.

"Isaac! Oh my god!" I laughed, holding him tightly.

"I know, baby girl. Now, let me see those diamonds."

"I have a sister!" Izzy exclaimed.

She wiggled her way into a group hug with Isaac and me, only to be followed by Tanner.

"Hads, I have a wee present for you," Fitz said. "Henry and Isaac have been helping me work on your family lineage."

"Wait, really?"

Fitz nodded. "You're Scots Irish."

I laughed. "How fitting."

"Gram was a Galloway before marrying your grandfather, the bloodline pure on both her mother and father's sides. Your grandfather—now he bore the name Weston, as do you, but upon tracing back, your people are *no* Westons."

"What do you mean?"

"Remember the story of Esther and Hamish's last name?"

"They changed it because your last name was outlawed by the king."

"Aye. Your grandfather was a Munro. Your ancestor changed his surname from Munro after escaping English troops. He was almost captured after surviving the Battle of Culloden. The Jacobite survivors were branded traitors and hunted by the English."

"My god," I gasped.

"Your mother's side is Irish—but it seems they fled to Ireland from a neighboring country. We're working to verify where they fled from, but my money is on Scotland."

"And what about my magical lineage—any leads yet?"

"Not yet," Isaac answered. "But now that we've traced back pretty far, we'll start referencing additional council records to find the witches hiding in your family tree."

My eyes misted.

"You good, Hads?"

"Yeah, I'm good. I just—thank you all so much for looking into this. You have no idea what this means to me."

A few tables were brought in so our friends and family could join us for celebratory champagne, and we fell into the rhythm of laughter and happy conversation.

Ian tapped a spoon against his champagne flute, and he and Ann rose from their seats.

"If we could have everyone's attention for a moment. I promise I willnae bore you for long."

The group laughed.

"But Ann and I want to offer our congratulations to Fitz and Hadley."

He turned to Ann, who began to speak. "I didnae have to meet Hadley to ken she'd one day join our family. Fitz left the lake house one summer afternoon in search of Izzy, and when he returned, he had changed. His entire world shifted in a moment."

I turned to Fitz, and he shrugged shyly, a smile spreading across his lips.

"It's been a long road to get to this night, but I think we all ken it was worth the fight. The world tried to write them off as star-crossed lovers, but even the world couldnae keep them apart."

Ann looked to Ian.

"Ann understood in an instant," Ian said. "But I had seen the consequences of defying council orders firsthand. I worried that these two didnae understand the challenges that lay before them. But they had more love and more courage than I thought possible."

Ian cleared his throat, and Ann slipped her hand into his.

He continued. "You two inspire me. Ultimately, your courage is what led us all here. When we face whatever the coming months bring, it is courage and love that will carry us through it. Thank you for reminding me of that. I'm so proud of you both. Congratulations."

Ian and Ann raised their glasses, and we all followed suit.

After the toast, tears were dried, and second glasses were poured. Sitting atop Edinburgh, one fiancé and eight friends made me feel as though I was sitting on top of the whole world.

After a night of celebration, Fitz and I wanted time to ourselves. The following morning would bring our first meeting with the Scottish National Coven Council, but for tonight—there was only us and our city. I held Fitz closely, and the world spun away.

The swirl of stars from the in-between faded, revealing the softer glow of our own galaxy far above and the expanse of Edinburgh below. Fitz wandered toward the cliff's edge.

He'd brought us to Arthur's Seat.

"I can't believe it's only been a few weeks since I first brought you here," he said.

"A lot has happened . . . And now this could be our last trip up here before we leave for a foreign planet."

I crossed the distance, taking my place next to Fitz. The city lights sparkled endlessly across the horizon.

"I can't even begin to grasp what our future holds."

"Neither can I," he returned. "We found a place to call home together, and now everything is changing." He slipped his hand in mine. "But I know our future is together. As long as that is true, I can face any trial this new world brings."

I rested my head against his.

"We'll come back, Hads. We have to."

"We'll be different."

"Aye."

A fleeting sadness crossed his features before he pulled me close. "You're cold."

"The wind is freezing."

"We can go."

I shook my head, pulling myself free from his grasp. I reached my hand into the empty air, and as I pulled it back, my favorite gray coat materialized, draped across my arm.

Finally, I had mastered concealment.

"You're proficient," Fitz said.

"Once I understood the elements . . ." I shrugged at his compliment, but I was truly proud of my accomplishment.

"How are you feeling after your encounter with Lorenzo?" Fitz asked.

"I'm mostly okay. I handled it better than I thought."

"Aye, you've done well, Hadley. I'm proud of the force you've become."

My heart swelled at his compliment. He'd never know how much that meant to me.

Silence fell as we gazed at the city lights.

"Perhaps this is our last time here for a bit. Perhaps not. But either way, let's have some fun."

"What did you have in mind?"

Fitz broke into a wide grin and walked to the edge of the cliff. He turned to face me and took a step backward. Instead of tumbling off the cliffside, his body floated high above the ground.

I closed my eyes momentarily, though I already knew what I'd find—there was no one nearby. I asked the elements to support me as I stepped off the ground and into the cool night air alongside Fitz. I laughed, albeit a bit nervously, and worked up the courage to look down. The sheer drop was sobering, but I'd come to know the elements well. I reminded myself I had nothing to fear.

"That first night we came here—could you have ever envisioned this?"

"Not in my wildest dreams."

Fitz tugged on my arm, pulling me into his embrace. I ran my fingers the length of his face, before planting my lips firmly against his. He met me in a slow, deliberate kiss as the air cradled us high above our city. When we floated back to the earth, we descended the landmark hand in hand, still hopeful, regardless of the days to come.

EPILOGUE

Lorenzo's Fortress, Opimae
Present Day
Gabriella

Gabriella's heels echoed loudly through the stone hallway. The door hinges of her master's dinner chamber groaned in protest as she turned the large iron ring and pushed the towering wooden door open.

"Gabriella, my darling girl," Lorenzo's thick Italian accent floated on the wintry air. "What news do you have for me?"

She crossed the room quickly, having been the subject of both his impatience and his disapproval of delivering information from across the room. The chill against her bare arms was insufferable. Gabriella couldn't understand why Lorenzo preferred to dine in the cold, damp air of the windowless room.

"*Signore,* they're preparing to cross over." Gabriella winced as her master's burning gaze rested upon her.

"What have I told you about information?"

"That it should always be clear and concise."

"Would you care to try that once more, *darling*?" he questioned, a mocking tone resting on his favorite term of endearment.

Gabriella cleared her throat. "Three members of Earth's witch-kind councils will cross the portal into Opimae. They will bring a team with them."

"That includes Fitz MacGregor, yes?"

"Yes, *Signore*."

Lorenzo turned to his dinner partner, who remained silent. "Alexander, what do you make of this?"

"Things are progressing in accordance with the plan the informant provided."

"We need Fitz to perform his duty."

"And he will."

A soft laugh escaped Lorenzo's lips as he swirled the wine in his glass. Gabriella wasn't supposed to stare at her master, but she couldn't help herself. How could someone be so beautiful . . . and so cruel, she wondered. She'd promised herself she would escape, but something about Lorenzo was magnetic. Once you joined his ranks, it was impossible to leave—and she hated herself for it.

"You Russians are too straightforward. It's always gotten you into trouble. This is tricky, Alexander, and you'd better remember that. These witches are dangerous."

"Of course, sir."

"Gabriella, is the woman with him?"

"Yes, Signore. Had—"

"For God's sake," Lorenzo interrupted, delivering his strike in a a calm, icy tone. "You do not say her name . . . none of you say her name. Not yet."

His eyes blazed as his fist met the table with a startling blow.

Camille glided through the doorway, holding a tray of Lorenzo's favorite cigars. Gabriella wasn't sure how Camille did it, but somehow she always appeared at just the right moment and calmed their master. She lit Lorenzo's cigar of choice, and his eyes cooled as he exhaled more than the smoke. His lips curled around the cigar, and Gabriella followed his every movement, wondering what they—no.

She wouldn't allow her thoughts to travel there, not again. Once the crusaders arrived, she'd be free of Lorenzo's grip—and free of the thoughts in her mind that were no longer her own.

Lorenzo motioned for Gabriella to move closer. He tucked her raven hair behind her ears, his gaze intense. "You know I prefer your hair pulled back." He looked over her appraisingly. "But that dress does make your eyes greener. I like it."

"Thank you, sir. I'm sorry to displease you."

Lorenzo nodded, and she followed his eyes to Camille. Her honey hair was swept on top of her head, a few delicate tendrils escaping along her neck. Camille never displeased the master. Gabriella knew she must learn from Camille if her time in the fortress was to pass without incident. She would fly under the radar as much as possible—it couldn't be much longer.

Gabriella took solace in one belief that she considered absolute truth. Hadley and Fitz would bring one hell of a fight to their army, and she hoped to god that she was standing in the fortress of the losing side.

Forfar, Scotland
1662
Esther

I sprang up in bed, my heart pounding, my breath ragged, and my energy scaring the hell out of Hamish.

"Esther! Is something the matter?"

"Aye," I returned breathlessly. "It's Gabriella. I've connected to her once more."

Hamish's sleep ravaged mind finally understood. "What did ye see?"

"I saw him. The witch who's been watching Fitz and Hadley."

"Breathe," he returned, rubbing my back gently. "What more?"

"The crusaders are preparing to cross over. Oh, Hamish . . . he knows. He's been waiting for them."

GLOSSARY

Aye – yes

Bairn – kid

Bonnie – handsome, pretty, beautiful.

Braw – good looking, beautiful, really nice.

Cannae – can't

Couldnae – couldn't

Didnae – didn't

Dinnae – don't

Hadna – hadn't

Gonnae – will you

Greet – to cry

Ken – to know

Nae – no

No – (in certain contexts) used in place of not

Och Aye – (Old Scots) oh yes

Scran – food

Shouldnae – shouldn't

Tartan – a plaid textile design of Scottish origin, usually patterned to designate a distinctive clan

Wasnae – wasn't

Wee – little

Willnae – won't

Wouldnae – wouldn't

AUTHOR'S NOTE

First things first, I'd like to ask the reader to please excuse the liberties I've taken with this story. As I'm sure many have noted, Hadley and Fitz's reunion takes place atop a historic landmark which is not accessible to the public in 2023. When I first wrote this scene in Summoned in 2015, Notre Dame was precisely the meeting spot I envisioned. After the mighty cathedral caught fire in 2019, public access was restricted, including access to the iconic rooftop, which held sweeping views of the Paris skyline.

Whether or not to keep the same meeting spot came in to question as I dove into this rewrite with my editor. We discussed my options, considered feedback from beta readers, and ultimately, I decided not to alter the location. In the end, it was far too dear for me to let go of, even if it does mean the location is impossible with this new timeline. However, I wanted to bring this story forward, rather than leaving it fully set in the past. Simply put, I could part with the timeline, but I couldn't part with Notre Dame. For this reason, I ask the reader to suspend their disbelief and step into a world where the magnificent landmark never caught fire.

Secondly, I must ask for forgiveness from Scottish readers—and those familiar with Scottish culture—for the choices I've made with regard to my Scottish characters' dialects. Though I desired to incorporate Scottish dialect, I also sought to ensure the book would read easily for those who are not familiar with Scottish speech. In striking this balance, I've included words like "dinnae" and "cannae" in the speech of several of the Scottish characters—Henry and James, for instance. With a character like Fitz, I strayed from that, opting for "clean cut" Scots since he varied his time between Scotland and the States. I've chosen to use the aforementioned Scottish words in his speech typically when he's angry. As a U.S. Southerner who lives in the Pacific Northwest, this is what I've found to be true of my own dialect and accent. When I'm tired, angry, or around my family, my dialect and accent slip back into their old habits. And I've allowed that to guide my choices.

I hoped these choices would create some appropriate distinction between the Scottish characters—taking into account factors like age, region, and whether or not they'd lived outside of Scotland.

For any egregious errors, I ask your forgiveness.

And from the characters' languages to style and beyond, I've asked myself how things might vary in a world where witches exist. In turn, I've asked myself which traditions or manners of speech might be held on to longer than they are with humans, especially with witches living 200+ years.

I have done my best to balance the real world with fantasy, and with these explanations, I hope my audience will indulge my imagination.

ACKNOWLEDGEMENTS

What an unbelievable journey this rewrite has been. Rewriting a book sounds like a relatively simple act. I thought I would make a few changes to improve the original text and move on. I couldn't have been more wrong. And I wouldn't have survived this process without many wonderful people. I extend a warm and hearty thank you to all who made this possible.

First and foremost, to my husband, Trent, for sharing a home with an author who decided to take on the most impractical goal she possibly could. Thank you for your continued support, patience, and good humor, and for stepping into many different roles over the course of the last few months to help make this book a reality and keep our lovely inn running at full speed.

A massive thank you to my editor, Jamie Ryu for seeing the potential in Summoned and convincing me that I could accomplish this goal. Thank you for believing in my world, and even more miraculously, thank you for believing in me. You have pushed me to learn and grow in ways I couldn't have imagined. Thank you for elevating this story and maintaining your professionalism even when this process grew overwhelming . . . and let's be real here; that was for most of it. But look—we did it! There never was, and never will be, a more powerful duo.

To my family and friends for your support and patience through this process. I know I've been far too absent, and I'm grateful y'all understand me. To my parents, my sister, and my Aunt Elaine, I'd like to say an especially strong thank you—for all of it.

To the Miller Tree Inn family: Bella, Julia, Marissa, Triana, and Jalisa. You give Trent and I purpose. Thank you for everything—every bit of it.

Thank you to my wonderful Summoned cast and crew for your support and your belief in me through this process. You have given so much more than you signed on for. An especially strong thank you to:

Samantha Rose Baldwin for your continued partnership with Summoned and your unwavering belief in it. Thank you for believing in me even when I doubt myself and for the countless hats you wear in the Summoned-verse. I'm grateful I get to share Hadley's journey with you.

To Anna McGuinness for stepping into many different roles during this process, for endless encouragement, and for sending me your commentary in all caps while reading *Summoned*.

Monique Messman and Cherish Danae for being the best Summoned Patreon team to ever grace this planet—or the next. And another thank you Cherish Danae for creating incredible original Summoned music to accompany this release.

Britt Byrd, Kathryn Gaddy, Vee Elle, Charlotte Gilgallon and Ashleigh Harvey for being some of my first readers and for offering valuable feedback.

Jon Stubbington for continuing to bring my book cover dreams into reality. I have to say, this is your best yet.

The ARA PR team for your incredibly hard work and for moving mountains. You amaze me every day. Grateful for you.

And finally, to our Summoned Patreon members. Your support, encouragement, and enthusiasm keep me going. You are the real magic.

Flip the page for a
sneak preview of

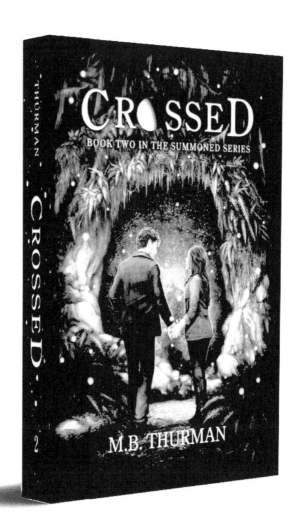

Available now

EXCERPT

The journey from the inn to the trailhead for the High Divide was familiar, a route I'd traveled countless times over the years, and memories from my childhood flooded my mind. My dad and I had hiked the High Divide countless times over the years. It had been almost a year since we lost him, and I couldn't help but to think of him as we neared the turnoff, allowing myself to feel just how much I missed him. Lost in reverie, I was disoriented when the car came to a stop. I buzzed with excitement, though my nerves tingled through me in equal measure. Fitz and I had both tossed and turned most of the night, and my acute desire for sleep only muddled my feelings further.

I looked around the vehicle, realizing I wasn't the only one in somewhat of a trance. Everyone was a bit dazed. I closed my eyes momentarily, taking in the pops of electricity radiating through the car, nervous energy clashing through the air. Fitz squeezed my hand, for his own reassurance as much as mine, and we jumped from the van, our feet crunching against the gravel road. The gate that allowed access to the parking lot was closed, meaning snow had accumulated on the road and hadn't been cleared.

Two large vans parked behind us, carrying the additional time-walkers. Like Fitz and Molly, they harbored the power of transport and would help us reach the portal since we couldn't hike the trail this time of year. The December weather wouldn't go easy on us either. The road was pooled with water, and the rain thumped heavily through the thick tree canopy on either side of us. I pulled my rain jacket tighter, shivering against the frigid air as Fitz opened an umbrella and held it above my head.

Chloe jumped from one of the vans, and her smile brightened as she met our gaze.

"Great to see you again, Hadley," she said in her identifiably Australian accent. Blonde curls tumbled loosely down her back, and her cunning blue eyes were bright, even in the dreary morning.

"We're happy to finally have you with us," I said.

"I had a bit more business to tidy up before I crossed over, but we've got some great council members stepping in to help Solomon and me while we're away," she said while zipping her navy puffer coat all the way to her chin.

Right on cue, Solomon stepped from the van, ending a phone call and reaching for a long overcoat.

"You ready for this?" Chloe asked, nodding toward the forest.

Solomon shrugged. "Who could ever be ready for a journey like this? But I am ready to see this new world."

Fitz and Molly grouped with the rest of the time-walkers as they reviewed a few final details. I wandered to the edge of the road until I felt the buzz of the privacy shield and turned around. Countless witches were scattered down the roadway chatting through our plans and making last minute phone calls. Molly was at the far end of the shield, standing with her eyes closed while being briefed. She had been distant ever since her arrival, and I wondered if she felt left out, having no prior connection to anyone on the team. I made a pact with myself that I'd try to help her integrate into the group as quickly as possible.

Isaac's voice pierced through the chatter. He was talking excitedly with one of the lower council members about elves. I smiled. The information he'd been so captivated by was about to come alive for him.

Mia caught my attention standing across the roadway from me. I'd learned that Mia had spent most of her formative years in Seattle. Had it been anyone else, I would've thought we could connect over growing up in the Pacific Northwest, but Mia and I hadn't found our footing with each other.

Mia was focusing her energy on the falling rain. Every few seconds, she pointed her finger and froze random droplets. They hovered in the air until she flicked her finger, tossing the ice aside. I struggled against a wry smile, thinking of how fitting her cryokinesis power truly was, when Fitz called my name.

It was time to say our goodbyes.

Ann embraced Fitz and then me. "Take care of each other," she whispered as tears rolled down her face.

"We will—and Ian, too."

Fitz hugged his sister for the last time for only God knew how long. Izzy smiled, tears welling in her eyes, before she turned to me.

"Thank you," I paused. "Thank you for everything the past couple years. I wouldn't be where I am without you."

"It's been the greatest honor of my life watching you grow into the witch you are."

"I'll miss you, Iz."

"No more than I'll miss you." She hugged me tightly. "Now, go do what you were born to do. Show him a real fight, love."

James called everyone to order, and we paired off for transport. Fitz wrapped his arms around me. I did the same to him.

"Remember: don't let go of me, and don't lose focus," Fitz reminded me.

I nodded, recalling that if I did either of those things, it could result in me being trapped in the in-between, a possible death sentence.

I looked around one last time at the towering trees, damp ferns, and thick moss. There was something poetic, I thought, about crossing into a new world with Fitz in the very place where our journey had begun—where my magical awakening started. Chloe caught my gaze as she passed Tanner. The two smiled at each other, and something prickled at my witch's eye. Tanner's gaze flickered to mine, but he looked away quickly.

Everyone stepped into position, and Solomon sounded the countdown. The world around me spun away, and it was replaced by a midnight sky and the swirling stars of the in-between. The seemingly endless void held the threads of space and time, allowing time-walkers to navigate through the past and present—to anywhere in our world, and sometimes beyond.

I hadn't traveled through its depths since my last mental transport to Lorenzo's fortress. This journey was much calmer—and brief. But in less than a minute, we stepped from the in-between into a startling scene. Snow swirled viciously, assaulting my face with large flakes. I looked around, but I could discern nothing. The snowfall was so thick it obscured my vision.

"Fitz!" I yelled. "Can you see anything?"

The wind tore at our exposed faces, and we huddled together for warmth.

"Nae!" he shouted back, his accent thickening. "I cannae see a thing!"

"Where should the portal be located from here?"

Fitz closed his eyes, and his face scrunched as he tried to focus on the answer.

"I cannae tell with the weather like this, but I feel an odd energy in that direction." He pointed behind me.

I turned around and focused on locating the energy he'd found through the chaos. Something nudged softly against my face, and I had a feeling Fitz was right.

"Support me for a second?" I asked.

He nodded, understanding.

I focused on the faint energy until my spirit separated from my body, and I followed the path carefully. When I met a privacy shield, I knew I'd met my mark. We were close—maybe twenty yards away. I quickly returned to my body and was greeted by several familiar faces when I opened my eyes.

Fitz pulled me back to my feet as more of our companions materialized through the whiteout conditions.

We began pressing forward along what seemed to be a ridge line, and Tanner warned everyone to be mindful of where they stepped.

My heart fluttered with anxiety. The team was quiet—focused—and their mix of nerves permeated the air. Our progress was slow and timid, but we made some headway as we labored through the blizzard.

Then Isaac's foot pushed through a large snowbank, and he began to slide toward the cliff's edge. Without thinking, I turned and asked the elements to cradle his body, but Fitz was one second ahead of me, so connected to the elements as he was, and he floated Isaac next to us.

"Are you okay?" I shouted above the wind.

Isaac nodded, his breath short. I embraced him and pushed a bit of calming energy into his system. His heart rate eased, and we prepared to move forward.

"We should walk single file," Tanner said.

"Aye, and we need to lead carefully," Fitz added.

"I'll lead," I said. I had spent countless time on the trails, but beyond that, I had a decided advantage over the others.

"Hads, no." Fitz shook his head.

I held his gaze as I called forward my fire magic, and within seconds, my fingertips were covered in flames.

A soft smile rose to Fitz's lips, and he motioned for me to walk ahead of him. I focused on the ground before me and cast bursts of flames into the snow until the rocky terrain was visible. The fresh, falling snow sizzled against the baking rocks, but that wouldn't last. I moved as quickly as possible clearing a path until I met the privacy shield.

"Do we just walk through this?" I shouted back to James.

"Aye!"

I kept my fire burning, unsure of what I'd find on the other side

428

of the shield and stepped through.

Chills crawled the length of my spine, my second sight awakening to the presence of the portal's power, even as I was met by the warmth of flames that I could not claim as my own. I gazed at the snowless scene before me. Three witches sat around a campfire. The scent of coffee, smoke, and damp earth permeated the air, along with the sound of laughter, though it abruptly ceased as they settled their gaze on me. The light within the shield was dim, almost like we had stepped from day into night. Tents were scattered near what appeared to be a rocky cave, and countless books, maps, board games, and laptops were strewn around the fireside.

"Looks like it's time for the big group," a woman at the far side of the fire said.

"Come on in, guys. I know it's bad out there," the man next to her said.

I imagined being a portal guard wasn't all that exciting, especially during the winter months, but it looked like they'd made the best of it.

"Looks like the government set up a permanent shield," I observed.

"Aye," Fitz agreed. "The privacy shield would be permanent, but this protection shield is certainly set up for inclement weather."

James, Chloe, and Solomon met with the crossing guard and secured the last details of our journey. They lined us up to cross— groups of two would step into the portal at a time.

"We're all rooting for you guys," one of the guards said warmly.

Nervous smiles and nods echoed through our warm cocoon.

"If you're ready, so are we. Let's get started," the woman said.

We slowly made our final steps to the entrance of the next world. The naked eye would perceive nothing of importance, only boulders fallen from the mountainside, but the reverberations of energy hummed through the air. The energy grew louder and stronger with each step until it was almost unbearable. One more step would send us into the oblivion of the unknown. My mind's eye scoured the area, granting me as much intelligence as it could possibly gather, and I found where our world opened to the next.

I turned to Fitz. "See you in the next world," I whispered.

"I love you."

I gripped his hand tightly, and together we stepped through the unknown, and into the curious world of Opimae.